PRAISE FOR
THE SIDEWAYS LIFE OF DENNY VOSS

"*The Sideways Life of Denny Voss* will be a modern classic. Kennedy's Denny is not idealized. Instead, he is fully revealed, with a clarity not seen in the pages of a novel since Carson McCullers wrote *The Heart Is a Lonely Hunter*. His story is a meditation on justice, bigotry, gun violence, and equity. Read it, perhaps as I did, all night, in one sitting, then look deep into your own community—and into your own heart."

—Jacquelyn Mitchard, *New York Times* bestselling author of *The Deep End of the Ocean*

"I can't rave enough about this novel. *The Sideways Life of Denny Voss* is simply magical, a heart-wrenching, unconventional tale that moved me from laughter to tears. Denny is a true original, an authentically portrayed protagonist who leaps off the page. His story is irresistible. I want to know him. I want to be his friend. And even though the feel-good ending was perfect, I didn't want his story to end."

—Patricia Wood, PhD in disability studies, author of *Lottery*

"*The Sideways Life of Denny Voss* is a coming-of-age story that ticks all my boxes. Beautifully written, authentic characters that will tug at your heart, and the kind of story that will keep you turning the pages long after lights out. It's the best novel I've read in a very long time. Don't miss this one!"

—Lesley Kagen, *New York Times* bestselling author of *Whistling in the Dark* and *Every Now and Then*

THE SIDEWAYS LIFE OF DENNY VOSS

OTHER TITLES BY HOLLY KENNEDY

The Tin Box

The Penny Tree

The Silver Compass

THE SIDEWAYS LIFE OF DENNY VOSS

a Novel

HOLLY KENNEDY

LAKE UNION
PUBLISHING

This is a work of fiction. Names, characters, organizations, places, events, and incidents are either products of the author's imagination or are used fictitiously. Otherwise, any resemblance to actual persons, living or dead, is purely coincidental.

Published by Lake Union Publishing, Seattle

www.apub.com

ISBN-13: 9781662525926 (paperback)
ISBN-13: 9781662525919 (digital)

Cover design and illustration by Philip Pascuzzo

Printed in the United States of America

This book is dedicated to two rare and remarkable women who continue to inspire me to tell stories that matter. I miss you both beyond words.

Roberta Talmage
1968–2018
Brenna Talmage
1995–2024

In a gentle way, you can shake the world.
—Mahatma Gandhi

Getting Arrested

Eight days after I got myself arrested, Dr. Harland tap-tap-tapped a pencil against his notebook and said, "This isn't working, Denny. We keep going in circles." Then he rubbed his face with his hands (up/down, up/down) and he said, "Let's talk about the day you got arrested. What would you do differently if you could do it all over again?" and I told him I wouldn't *want* to do it all over again, but then he said, "Please try to answer the question anyhow," so after lots of thinking (and some staring out the window) I told him if I had to do it all over again, I'd probably call first.

Dr. Harland frowned. "Who, Denny? Who would you call?"

"The police station?" I was rocking back and forth in my chair. "I'd call and say, 'Hello, my name is Denny Voss and I'll be there at three o'clock with eight guns.'" I leaned forward and whispered, "They know I had eight with me, right?"

Dr. Harland pinched the hump on his nose. "Yes, they know that."

"—and four boxes of bullets," I finished.

"And why would you do that?"

More thinking. More staring out the window.

"So I could get home by four to watch *The Price Is Right*?" But I don't think that was the right answer because Dr. Harland's chin dropped to his chest like a broken hinge, and he breathed in and out real slow.

Dr. Harland is an old guy (lots of wrinkles) and he has a head with no hair on it and skin like a HERSHEY's chocolate bar. The first time I met him I didn't like him because he asked too many hard questions, but I changed my mind when he told me he had a dog. His dog's name is Tank, by the way, which makes no sense at all because it's a teeny-tiny Chihuahua, but each time I bring it up Dr. Harland says, "That's neither here nor there, Denny. Can we *please* move on?" The second time we met, he was wearing a vest and that's when I decided to trust him. You see, when Papa-Jo was still alive he always wore vests, so now whenever I meet someone who's wearing a vest, I know they're a good person—that's just how vest-people are.

Nana-Jo doesn't wear vests but she's a good person too. She's always praying for other people and crossing herself, and saying, *For the love of God, if everyone just followed the rules, we'd be so much better off on this planet.*

And that's what I was doing when I got myself arrested—following the rules, and being a good guy, and doing the right thing. But then everything went wrong (really, really wrong) and before I knew it a police car came skidding to a stop at the bottom of Penguin Hill and the lights were flashing and the siren was on—**WHOOP! WHOOP!**—and I was stumbling all over the place because I'd just crashed my sled full of guns and bullets into an oak tree. My face suddenly felt warm and wet, so I stopped moving and I touched it and thought, *Uh-oh, blood.* Then a gray-haired cop and his lady partner jumped out of the police car and they pointed their guns at me just like you see in those fast-moving TV shows.

When the gray-haired cop saw me, his eyebrows jumped and he said, "Shit, here we go again!" He tilted his head a little. "It's Denny, right?" I nodded. "All right, Denny, can you tell me what's going on here?" and I said, "Sure," but then I started to stutter, which happens whenever someone points a gun at me, or a knife, or a broken beer bottle.

"I . . . I was—was follow . . . following—"

The gray-haired cop frowned. "Who were you following?"

I smacked the side of my head to make the stuttering stop. "The rules—I was follow . . . following . . . the rules."

"You're obviously upset," he said, "but I need you to calm down, okay?" so I took a deep breath and I started over. I talked slow and I didn't stutter, but the gray-haired cop and his lady partner still looked confused (lots of frowning). And yeah, I know there was blood on my hands and face, and the plastic wrap I'd used to wrap all the guns in a bundle had ripped open and now there were guns and bullets everywhere, but it just seemed to me like they weren't *listening*.

"Yes, Denny," the gray-haired cop said slowly. "We . . . hear . . . you. We are *listening*." But then I saw the look he gave his lady partner and that's when I understood—they *heard* me; they just didn't *believe* me.

I'm not stupid.

I know what's what.

The gray-haired cop carefully pushed the guns out of the way with his foot while his lady partner kept hers pointed at me. Her hair was in a ponytail—dark at the roots, blond tips—and she didn't smile or even try to be friendly, which is how I knew she wasn't doing flirting with me. The gray-haired cop said, "Listen, I won't handcuff you from behind this time, but I need you to hold your hands out so I can put them on in the front," so I held my hands out and he snapped the cuffs on my wrists where I could see them, which was way better than last time.

Then he said, "You have the right to remain silent. Anything you say may be used against you in a court of law . . ." and because I'd been arrested before, I already knew that part, so I told myself not to be scared.

I was doing pretty good until the lady cop opened the back door of the police car and told me to get in. Just so you know, I don't like riding in the back seat of a car. When I was a little kid I didn't mind so much, but then I grew bigger and my head started to rub against the roof of Nana-Jo's Subaru and my stomach would slosh back and forth, and I'd projectile vomit, which is when it shoots straight out of you like a rocket.

More stuttering. "No. I—I don't—"

"I'm not telling you again," the lady cop said.

"I—can't . . . can't . . ."

"Get in the car!" she shouted.

A crow (which is a black bird) swooped down from a tree and landed on one of my guns, and he opened his wings wide and flapped them and screeched **CAW! CAW! CAW!** and because I don't like when birds flap their wings like that, everything started to spin and wobble, and I had to take two steps sideways to fix my balance. That's when the lady cop got all amped up and she started yelling and waving her gun around, and my heart started going **BOOM-BOOM-BOOM** so to calm myself down I rocked back and forth a bit, and when that didn't help, I closed my eyes and sang the theme song for *Toy Story*—"You've Got a Friend in Me"—which is what I do whenever a situation goes sideways on me.

"Holy shit, can you believe this guy?!" the lady cop said, and the gray-haired cop laughed and said, "Yeah, he's a funny fucker."

"Well, he's pissing me off!"

And that's when she hit me with her gun.

—*Thwack!*

"Louella!" yelled the gray-haired cop. "What the hell—!"

The side of my head suddenly felt warm and wet, and I reached up and touched it and thought, *Uh-oh, more blood.* Then, just like Nana-Jo taught me, I said, "I am not a threat," but I don't think Louella-the-lady-cop heard me because she went into a ninja crouch, and she twisted at the waist, and she snap-kicked me in my genitals.

—*Wham!*

I dropped to my knees and flopped sideways and did moaning, but Louella-the-lady-cop didn't care. She just kept lunging at me, yelling, "What?!" and "Come on!" and "You want a piece of me, asshole?!" So I did what Nana-Jo always said I should do next. I looked at Louella-the-lady-cop and said, "Violence is not the answer to our problems," and she went very still (like a statue) and she shouted, "Just get in the fucking car!" Then the gray-haired cop told her to "back off!" and "tone it down!" and he helped me up and he brushed off all the snow and he put me in the back seat, and I didn't even try to argue with him because like Nana-Jo sometimes says, *Enough is enough, Denny.*

The police car was warm inside, which was nice because I was cold and wet and my genitals hurt real bad, so I rocked back and forth and did moaning while Louella and the gray-haired cop loaded all my stuff into the trunk, including the guns and the bullets, the plastic wrap, and my smashed-up sled.

Then we drove off, and just so you know, I did not projectile vomit on the way to the police station because Louella-the-lady-cop used *excessive force*; I projectile vomited because I don't like riding in the back seat of a car.

Dr. Harland snapped his fingers—once, twice. "Denny?"

"Yeah?"

"I asked if there's anything you regret?"

There was, but I didn't want to talk about that yet. I was tired and I was done talking, even though Dr. Harland had already explained (three times) that me being 100 percent honest was the only way to unravel this mess.

More quiet.

More tap-tap-tapping.

"Denny, are you all right?"

And I stared out the window and said, "No," because I wasn't all right. I missed Nana-Jo and I missed my dog (George) and I wanted to go home, but Dr. Harland had already explained (three times) that I couldn't because the charges against me were very serious and we had to get this figured out. He carefully set his pencil on the table. "Listen, Denny, I think we should wrap things up for today. Why don't we meet again tomorrow after we've both had some sleep?" and I said, "Hallelujah," because like Nana-Jo always says, it's important to end every conversation on a positive note.

Doing Processing

After I got myself arrested, the gray-haired cop and his lady partner, Louella, drove me to Woodmont County Jail and the gray-haired cop said I had to keep my handcuffs on and he took me down a hallway to a room called the *intake center* and the people who work there do something called *processing*.

It was not a happy place.

A lady with a name badge on her shirt that said **TAHNI** made me sit in a chair while she filled out some forms and she asked a bunch of questions and some of them were easy and some weren't. Like when she said, "How tall are you?" I said, "Six feet, two inches," and when she said, "Weight?" I said, "208 pounds," but then she said, "Sex?" and my face got hot because I didn't want to tell her I hadn't done sex yet, so I just stared at the wall until she finally said, "Whatever," and checked a box with her pencil.

"How old are you?" she asked.

And I said, "Today or seven days from now? Because my birthday is seven days from now and I'll definitely be older then."

"How old are you *today*?"

"I'm twenty-nine."

There was a flowery plant on Tahni's desk with a **Save the Bees** sticker on the pot and I told her I like bees too because they're pollinators (without them, food won't grow) but she didn't say anything back and that's how I knew she didn't want to do visiting with me. Then I saw a poster on the wall that said **IT'S IMPORTANT TO COOPERATE WITH POLICE** BUT **IT'S ALSO IMPORTANT TO KNOW YOUR RIGHTS** and under that it said:

1. YOU HAVE THE RIGHT TO REMAIN SILENT.

2. YOU HAVE THE RIGHT TO BE TOLD WHY YOU WERE ARRESTED.

3. YOU HAVE THE RIGHT TO SPEAK TO A LAWYER.

4. YOU HAVE THE RIGHT TO AN INTERPRETER.

5. YOU HAVE THE RIGHT TO A SPEEDY TRIAL.

I said, "What's a speedy trial?" Tahni looked at the poster and she said, "It means once you've been charged with a crime the government can't drag its feet taking you to trial. They have to do it as quickly as possible to be fair to you."

"Oh," I said. "That's good."

She went back to her paperwork and it got quiet again; then I said, "Why was I arrested?" Tahni picked up a paper and read it with squinty eyes. "For resisting arrest and possession of firearms without a permit."

And I said, "I don't understand."

Tahni lifted one eyebrow. "Did you want an interpreter?"

And I said, "Sure."

"For what language?"

"Ours?"

She tilted her head and I watched her do thinking about me; then her voice got a little mean and she said, "How about enough with the joking around? I've had a shitty day," and I said, "Every day is a gift," because that's what Nana-Jo says when I'm having a bad day, but Tahni just put some papers into her stapler and slammed it down to staple them together—CRUNK! Then she used an old-timey ink pad to take my fingerprints. She also took my booking photo (mug shot) and I had to stand against a wall and hold a sign with **WOODMONT COUNTY JAIL** on it and this number at the bottom—BK1528—and she kept saying "Stop closing your eyes" and "What is the *matter* with you?!"

After that, an officer with a walkie-talkie and a name badge on his shirt that said **CHAUNCE** took me to a small room with a bathroom attached and he unlocked my handcuffs and told me to go in there and take my clothes off. He also gave me an orange jumpsuit to wear with **COUNTY INMATE** printed on the back, and orange rubber shoes that were a bit like the Crocs I wear at home. And when I came out, he took my clothes and he put them in a big see-through plastic bag.

Chaunce told me I was allowed to make one phone call, then he stood beside me while I used the phone on Tahni's desk to call Nana-Jo. But when I called our green wall phone at home it didn't ring; there was just a **BEEP-BEEP-BEEPING** sound. I told Chaunce maybe I called the wrong number and could he help me find Sharon and Bill's number instead because Angus was in Mexico so I couldn't call him. But he told me to ask my lawyer for help because "this shit isn't in my job description."

The next day, they gave me a lawyer (a guy named Ruben) and he took me over to the courthouse and there were other people there who'd also gotten themselves arrested (for vandalism, assault, and shoplifting) but they were ahead of us, so we had to wait our turn. The rest happened fast. We stood up and the judge read the charges against me, and he said, "How do you plead?" then Ruben bumped my arm, and I said, "Not guilty." Ruben told the judge I was a good guy and he asked for something called *bail*, but the judge said because I'd resisted arrest and I'd been arrested before, and I had all those guns with me when I got myself arrested this time, he thinks I could be *a flight risk*. Then he banged his gavel (wooden hammer) on a coaster on his high-up desk and said, "Bail denied."

So yeah, now I'm stuck in jail.

And I still don't know what happened to my clothes.

Being Incarcerated

Being incarcerated (locked up in jail) isn't easy.

My cell is eight feet by ten feet and the walls are made from cement blocks and someone painted them the color of cardboard. Also, my bed is too small and the food is awful (no pizza) and they won't let me watch TV. There's a small window up high with bars on it and a steel door with bars on it that makes lots of noise when it slides open and shut. And there are five cells on my side of the jail and five cells across from me on the other side, and a walkway in between so the guards can check on us every now and then to make sure nobody is trying to escape or commit suicide (kill themselves).

I also keep getting dizzy and when that happens, I have to put my head between my knees and count the tiles on the floor, but sometimes all that counting backfires and then my heart revs up like the motor in Nana-Jo's Subaru when she gets it stuck and has to rock the car back and forth to get it unstuck.

Dr. Harland told me these are *anxiety attacks* and they have *less to do with guilt or innocence than they do with fear*. Today he was wearing a green vest and he said it would be helpful for him and therapeutic (good for me) to write down everything that happened *before* I got myself arrested. Then he gave me this blue notebook to write everything down in. "Take me back to the beginning, Denny," he said. "Tell me how this whole mess got started." And I raised my hand and said, "I don't know how it all got started," and Dr. Harland said, "*Please* stop putting your hand up."

Then he rested his forehead on the table, and he said, "I'll help you figure it out."

And I said, "Are you sure?"

And he said, "That's what I'm here for."

But each time I try to remember *how this whole mess got started*, my mind starts jumping around and I get tired. When I told Dr. Harland that, he said I could take a break, but after my break could I *please* share a few things to help him understand the situation better?

And I said, "What's the situation?"

"This, Denny," Dr. Harland said, waving at the room. "*This* is the situation! What you're doing here, with me, is the situation. Tell me about yourself. Who you are, who your family is, how you got here. All of it."

So, I took a short break.

And now here we go:

My name is Denny Voss and I'm thirty years old and I live in Woodmont, Minnesota. I got myself arrested eight days ago at the bottom of Penguin Hill with a bunch of guns and bullets. Before I left the house, I stood them up so they were leaning against each other, then I went around and around them with a big roll of clingy plastic wrap until they were all stuck together in a bundle. After that, I strapped the bundle to my sled with a bungee cord and I pulled it to the top of Penguin Hill. It was very slippery sledding down the other side, though, and I lost control on some ice and crashed into an oak tree at the bottom. Then the bungee cord broke and my bundle went flying and when it hit the ground, the plastic wrap ripped open and—**BAM!**—there were guns and bullets everywhere!

The police showed up a few minutes later and I got myself arrested, and now I'm in Woodmont County Jail.

So yeah, there's that.

Also, once a year Nana-Jo takes me to see Dr. Baker so he can make sure everything is working the way it should be working, like my ears and my eyes and my brain. He gave Nana-Jo official papers years ago that say I'm *developmentally challenged* (we keep them at home in the basement freezer with our other official papers) and he explained that my brain works differently than the average person in how I learn, communicate, and understand things. But then last year Dr. Baker gave us new official papers that say I'm *neurodiverse*, and when I asked him what that means, he said, "There's no need to worry, Denny. It's just a different way of saying the same thing. You haven't changed, the world has!"

That's when I leaned forward and whispered to him, "Sometimes people call me simpleminded or an idiot or a half-wit," and Dr. Baker frowned and said, "Well, they're wrong, Denny. You have an IQ of 72 and you're fine just the way you are." Then he put my file away and before we left, he told me I have a good heart, which is more than he can say about some people with bigger IQ numbers than mine.

On the drive home that day, Nana-Jo squeezed my hand and said, "Did you hear what he said, Denny? Bigger isn't always better."

Nana-Jo loves me to the moon and back (which is the most you can love anybody) and I know because she tells me all the time and I have a picture of her holding me after I got myself born and in it she's kissing my head and crying happy tears. She always says, *Denny, if people ask why you are the way you are, tell them you were a late-in-life baby and the rest is none of their business.* She also told me my *umbilical cord* (which is like a flexible hose attached to a baby's belly at one end and a mom's belly at the other end) got wrapped around my neck when I was being born and I didn't get enough oxygen.

So yeah, there's that too.

Nana-Jo is my mom but I call her Nana-Jo, same as everybody else. She's also my only parent because Papa-Jo died when I was fourteen. Nana-Jo is old and wrinkled and sometimes when she bends down she has trouble getting up again. She does volunteering at the Take It or

Leave It (a place where people take things they need and leave things behind they don't need) and with Meals on Wheels (a place that takes meals to people who can't cook for themselves) and with the suicide hotline (a place people call when they're extra sad and someone will answer and say, "Please don't jump" or "We are here to help").

I also have a sister named Lydia who lives in New York City (where I've never been) with her husband, Marco (who I've never met), and they don't have kids, but they have a parrot named Rio who swears a lot.

Lydia has an important job taking pictures of naked people for a magazine. She also has a passport, which is sort of like a hall pass that lets her travel all over the world, which is what she has to do to find the best naked people available. Lydia is tall like me and we both have green eyes like Nana-Jo, but she's older than I am and she doesn't come home very often. I keep thinking maybe she'll come back to Woodmont now that I'm incarcerated, but my cousin Angus says I shouldn't hold my breath.

You'd like Angus.

So far, he's my steadiest visitor (once a day, twice on Sundays). Whenever the guard comes and says, "Time's up!" Angus leaves, but he always promises to come back the next day, and he does. You can count on Angus like that—he's a man of his word.

Just so you know, me and Nana-Jo share a side-by-side house with Angus and he was in Mexico on vacation (first one of his freaking life) when I got myself arrested, but as soon as he got home our neighbors told him what happened and he rushed over to the jail to see me. When he got here, he was wearing a T-shirt that said **It Was Me—I Let the Dogs Out**, and he kept pacing back and forth and tugging on his goatee (tiny beard on his chin).

"What the fuck happened, Denny?!"

I shrugged. "Things went sideways."

"It was on the front page of the paper."

"What was?"

"The story! Your picture! How you had an arsenal of guns and ammunition, how you resisted arrest, all of it." Angus's face got red and splotchy.

"Wow, the first time I got arrested it was on page six."

Angus put his hands on top his head. "Man, this is bad. This is so bad."

"The second time it was on page two, though, remember? I have copies of those stories in my scrapbook."

"Nobody cares, Denny."

"Sure they do, Angus. Being on the front page is pretty cool."

Angus took a breath, blew it up at the ceiling. "No, Denny, it's not."

I chewed on my thumbnail. "Angus?"

"What?"

"Can you buy me a copy of the paper for my scrapbook?"

He stared at me without blinking, then he came closer, and he said, "Denny, I need you to focus on what I'm saying here." He unfolded a piece of paper and he held it up, and I squinted and read *SEARCH WARRANT* at the top in big letters. "The police went through the house," he said all angry-like.

"Wow, that's not good."

"No, Einstein, it sure as hell isn't!"

Angus calls me *buddy* when he's in a good mood and *Einstein* when he's mad at me. I talked to Dr. Harland about it and he thinks maybe Angus was upset because when the police went through our house (8B), that would've put them close to Angus's house (8A) and the secret plants he's been growing in his basement. He has fifty of them but he's only allowed to have eight and he's not supposed to be selling dried-out leaves in little plastic bags either. Nana-Jo doesn't know about Angus's secret plants, just me—and now Dr. Harland.

Angus was pacing back and forth. "They spent hours going through 8B, even the root cellar. Sharon saw them leave with Nana-Jo's computer. Damn it, Denny. What were you *thinking*?!" So I closed my eyes and tried to remember, but I couldn't.

Angus is my cousin but he's also my boss at DOT (Department of Transportation). He works full time (five days a week) and I work part time (three days a week). Angus says we're a *mobile response unit* but I say it more plain: we fix broken road signs and we clear blocked culverts and we clean up roadkill (animals who get themselves killed by vehicles). We share the job fifty/fifty: Angus drives the DOT truck and I do the roadkill pickups, which is easy if it's a skunk or a raccoon or a porcupine but much harder if it's a moose or a deer or a cougar because then I have to use the electric lift and none of the plastic bags they give us ever fit.

Angus says DOT is lucky to have me because there's always lots of roadkill on the days I work and none on the days I don't.

Sometimes I get sad when I'm doing roadkill pickups and Angus will say things like *Buck up* or *Don't be a pussy* or *Life is hard all over*. The worst part of our job is when an animal isn't dead yet because then it has to be *put out of its misery* (but I don't like to talk about that) and the best part is when there's no roadkill at all because then we get to drive around eating doughnuts and listening to music.

Angus has a bunch of songs on his phone that he listens to all the time. When he's happy he listens to Bob Marley, and Post Malone, and the Weeknd, and if he gets dumped by a girl he listens to a song called "Insensitive" by Jann Arden over and over again. (I'm not supposed to tell anyone that, though.) My favorite song is "It Wasn't Me" by Shaggy. I know all the words and it's bumpy and bouncy and Angus lets me listen to it over and over, but I'm not allowed to play it at home because Nana-Jo says the lyrics (words that make up the song) are filthy. Whenever I get sad doing roadkill pickups, Angus lip-synchs (pretend sings) Taylor Swift's "Shake It Off" to cheer me up and if our boss, Lonny, calls on the two-way radio and tells us to get our asses back to the shop, Angus tells him we are 1) changing a flat tire, or 2) cleaning out a blocked culvert, or 3) loading a dead moose, which could take a while.

I'm a good liar, but Angus is even better.

Yesterday was my birthday and if you're incarcerated on your birthday, nobody bakes you a cake or sings happy birthday or gives you presents, even though you just turned thirty years old. Nobody worries about being polite in here either. Like the guy in the cell across from me. His name is Dirty Doyle and he has tattoos on his arms and his neck and he keeps his hair tied back with an elastic band. Yesterday, he said he didn't want to hear another word about my birthday or Penguin Hill or my *stupid fucking dog* and if I don't shut my pie hole (mouth) he's going to kick the shit out of me.

When you get yourself arrested, they give you a lawyer for free but not forever (you have to give her back when your case is done). My new lawyer is Bridget Klein (no relation to Calvin-the-underwear-guy). Her hair is the color of honey and she smells like lemons and she makes me feel warm inside. The first time we met, she was wearing a dress that looked like a wet suit and I couldn't figure out how she got into it so I kept staring at her, trying to figure that out. Bridget also wears eyeglasses with blue frames, but they don't work very well because sometimes when we talk about my case she squeezes her eyes shut and keeps them like that for a long time, which isn't a good sign, no matter how you look at it.

Lawyering is new to Bridget. When she told me I'm her first real case, she whispered it like she was embarrassed, so using good manners (looking down and away so I didn't stare at her boobs) I said, "That's okay. Practice makes perfect." I also told her I watch *Judge Judy* on TV all the time so I could help her with her lawyering if she got herself confused, but she said, "That won't be necessary, Denny." So far, the only good thing about being incarcerated is having Bridget Klein be my lawyer because she's thoughtful and smart and kind, and I know this because she hired Dr. Harland to help *unravel this mess* and *prove my innocence*, even though he's old and sometimes he falls asleep when I'm talking.

When we got to this part of what I wrote in my blue notebook, Dr. Harland said, "No one wants to read about stuff like that, Denny.

Instead, why don't we talk about Mr. Tesky now," and I put my head between my knees and said I didn't want to talk about Mr. Tesky. Then he said, "Okay, let's try a different approach. Why don't you make a list of the facts first and we'll work on the details later?"

And I said, "Sounds good."

And now, here I am.

So after lots of thinking and writing and erasing, here are the facts:

- I've been arrested three times.
- The first time was when I kidnapped Tom Hanks.
- The second time was when I got caught helping a guy rob a bank.
- The third time was at the bottom of Penguin Hill with all those guns and bullets.
- The first time I had to do consequences (things a judge makes you do when you mess up real bad) but the second time there were no consequences; the judge just shook his head and said, "I have no words."
- Sometimes I do volunteering (jobs where they don't pay you). I did volunteering at a church until they said *my services were no longer required*. I also did volunteering at the Canine Rescue Shelter until Nana-Jo made me quit after I brought home a blind and deaf Saint Bernard named George. George has been with us five years now. He's old and big (150 pounds) and he sleeps a lot, but he loves us, and we love him right back.
- For as long as I can remember, Nana-Jo has cleaned houses for a living.
- She cleaned for Irene and Henry Tesky for twenty-four years.
- Irene Tesky died last December (cancer).
- One month later, Henry Tesky got married again.
- Then he fired Nana-Jo (too old).

- Nana-Jo couldn't find another job (too old).
- Lots of people died last year from *fatal gunshot wounds*.
- Sometimes I get bored and snoop where I shouldn't snoop.
- Nana-Jo told me to stop snooping (I didn't stop).
- Sometimes I watch too much TV.
- Nana-Jo told me to stop watching TV (I didn't stop).
- I'm not allowed to drive a car because you need an official license and I've failed the official test fourteen times now. Instead, I use a bike with one wheel in the front, two in the back, and a metal basket behind my seat to carry stuff in.
- I was biking down the road one day when Mr. Tesky hit me with his Tesla (fancy car) and tried to kill me.
- Mr. Tesky said it was an accident.
- I think he did it on purpose.
- I never liked Mr. Tesky and he never liked me.
- Ten days ago, Mr. Tesky was found dead in his home from a *fatal gunshot wound*.
- After I got myself arrested at the bottom of Penguin Hill, the police tested all my guns, and they said one of them had been used to murder Mr. Tesky. They also said I had *motive*, *opportunity*, and *no alibi*.
- If I were talking to you in person, I'd whisper this part—I have been charged with Mr. Tesky's murder.

Getting Arraigned

I had to go back to the courthouse today to get myself arraigned again but this time it was a different judge because the other charges were *misdemeanors* (less serious crimes) but murder is a *felony* (super-serious crime). So yeah, new judge, and new lawyer (Bridget) but otherwise same old, same old. Before we went over to the courthouse, though, Bridget came to see me in jail and she kept fiddling with her eyeglasses, and she said, "Listen, Denny, because Henry Tesky was running for mayor, this case is drawing lots of attention."

And I said, "I don't understand."

She chewed on her thumbnail. "Well . . . there are some reporters at the courthouse, so when we get there it might be a little chaotic and you might feel overwhelmed, but it's important that we have a good optic on this so try not to look at anyone and don't answer any questions, okay?" And I wanted to ask her what an *optic* was but Bridget looked a bit sick to her stomach, so I just said, "Okay."

When we got to the courthouse, there were people outside and we had a deputy with us and when we got out of the car, those people ran over with cameras and microphones, shouting, "Mr. Voss, did you kill Henry Tesky?" and "Were you at his home the night of the murder?" The deputy said, "Give us some room," and Bridget took my arm, and I looked up at the clouds while I walked so I wouldn't have to look at anyone.

Angus was waiting for us inside and he also looked a bit sick to his stomach. "How you doing, buddy?" he asked, but I just stared straight ahead because Bridget said not to answer any questions and I was trying to do a good optic. Then Bridget and the deputy took me into the courtroom and Angus followed and he sat on a bench behind us. Bridget took me through a swinging wooden gate and we sat down at a table up front. Then a man in a brown uniform stepped forward and said, "All rise. This court is now in session. The Honorable Judge Milton Saginaw presiding."

Bridget told me to stand up, so I did.

And it got very quiet.

A door at the back of the courtroom opened and Judge Saginaw came in and he was wearing a black robe with long sleeves that looked like Harry Potter's Gryffindor robe only it didn't have a hood and there was no red trim on it. He had a mustache and bushy eyebrows and when he sat down, everyone else was allowed to sit down again too. Then he nodded at Bridget and he said, "Ms. Klein, your motion to relocate this trial to another county on the grounds that Mr. Voss won't be able to get a fair trial here in Woodmont County is denied. I see no evidence to suggest that Mr. Voss has suffered from any more prejudices in this county than he would in any other county in the state of Minnesota."

I bumped Bridget with my elbow. "Tell him I want a speedy trial so I can go home to see George and Nana-Jo."

"Counsel, please control your client," said Judge Saginaw.

"Yes, Your Honor."

Bridget touched my arm. "No more talking, Denny."

Judge Saginaw looked at me. "Dennis Joseph Voss of Woodmont, Minnesota, you are charged with murder in the second degree of one Henry David Tesky, formerly of Woodmont, Minnesota, which carries a maximum penalty of forty years in prison." And after that he did talking about my constitutional rights and my legal rights—blah, blah, blah—then he said, "How do you plead?" and just like Bridget told me, I said, "Not guilty."

That's when the people behind us started doing whispering and chatting, and Judge Saginaw banged his gavel on a coaster on his high-up desk, and he said in a loud voice, "Order in the court." After that, Judge Saginaw said a trial date would be set as soon as possible and we left the courtroom with the deputy, and Angus came up to me and said, "Everything'll be okay, buddy." Then Bridget and the deputy took me outside again and we got in the car and drove back to Woodmont County Jail.

And it was Tuesday.

And if you're incarcerated at Woodmont County Jail on a Tuesday you get a bun and a bowl of chili for dinner, so that's what I had.

The Gun That Killed Mr. Tesky

After breakfast today (lumpy oatmeal) a guard named Grant who works the day shift took me to the special meeting room where I usually meet Dr. Harland but instead Bridget Klein was there, and she was wearing a white button-up shirt and a green sweater.

"Good morning, Denny."

And I said, "Morning," then I said, "Where's Dr. Harland?"

Bridget opened her leather bag. "He'll be here later. There's something I'd like to talk to you about first."

"We're doing a meeting?"

"Yes, we are." Bridget waved at a chair and said, "Take a seat," so I did, and she pulled some papers out of her leather bag.

Bridget asked how I was, and I said, "Fine, thank you," because I was trying to be positive because like Angus always says, *Nobody likes a whiny little bitch* (complainer). Then Bridget asked if I was eating, and I said, "Yup. Grant-the-guard showed me how to sprinkle brown sugar on my oatmeal, which makes it taste one hundred percent better, and now he brings me four packets every morning and I eat everything on my plate."

Bridget blinked a few times. "Right. Well . . . that's good."

Then she folded her hands together on the table and she said, "Denny, I'd like to talk about the guns you had with you when you were arrested, specifically the gun that was used to kill Mr. Tesky." And I looked at her for a long time and I said, "Okay," even though my stomach felt flip-floppy inside. But because Bridget is my lawyer and we're on the same team, I decided I'd talk about the guns I'd bundled up in plastic wrap that day and what I knew about each one, and this is what I told her about them:

1. Remington Model 870 twelve-gauge shotgun (good for sport shooting and hunting; militaries use it all over the world).
2. 30/30 Winchester Model 1894 (popular hunting rifle).
3. .22 Cooey (made in Canada, very old; Papa-Jo's dad gave it to him).
4. Mossberg Model 500 twelve-gauge shotgun (Papa-Jo's favorite gun).
5. .22 Savage Mark II (a bolt-action rifle, good for target shooting).
6. Springfield Model 1903 bolt-action rifle (used in World War II as an infantry rifle and in the Korean War and Vietnam as a sniper rifle).
7. .303 British rifle (made in Britain in 1888; Papa-Jo kept it in a display case until he died, then Nana-Jo threw it in a metal gun box in our root cellar with the other guns).
8. Smith & Wesson .38 Special snub nose (this is a handgun, not a rifle).

Bridget slid a picture across the table of the handgun I'd wrapped in clingy plastic wrap and put in my sled with Papa-Jo's rifles the day I got myself arrested at the bottom of Penguin Hill. It had a wooden handle and the words *Smith & Wesson* on the barrel of the gun. Bridget folded her hands together and said, "Denny, I want you to think about this very carefully. Did you ever see this gun before the day you got arrested?"

I looked out the window and said, "No."

Then I looked at Bridget again and I saw that she had a Band-Aid on her thumb so I asked if she'd cut herself with a knife and she said, "Uh . . . no," then I asked if she got herself a paper cut, because paper cuts bleed a lot, and she closed her eyes and said, "Denny, please stop," and I said to her, "I cut my finger on a tin can once and it bled for an hour—"

"Denny!"

Bridget moved her hand in little circles like she was washing a window. "I *do not* want to talk about this right now. Please, let's move on." She pushed the picture of the gun closer to me. "So . . . the first time you ever saw this gun was when you found it in the root cellar with your Papa-Jo's guns?"

And I said, "Yes."

"Are you telling me the truth?"

And I said, "Yes."

Then she said, "Because you know what, Denny? Lying to your lawyer is never a good idea," and I said, "I'm not lying, Bridget. I'm a good liar, but I'm not lying today. Scout's honor," and I put my right hand in the air with three fingers pointed up just like Angus learned how to do as a Boy Scout before they kicked him out of the club.

Bridget took off her eyeglasses. "Denny, this gun is registered to Irene Tesky."

"I don't know what that means."

"It means Henry Tesky's wife, Irene, owned this gun."

"Irene Tesky died last year."

"Yes, but she owned this gun when she was alive."

And I said, "Huh."

"But even though Irene Tesky owned this gun, you said you found it in your root cellar two days after it was used to kill Mr. Tesky. Don't you think that's strange?" And I looked at the wall and did thinking, and then I said, "Yes, because Papa-Jo died years ago and he didn't like handguns, he only liked rifles, so that is strange."

"Exactly." Bridget frowned. "Do you think maybe Nana-Jo could've borrowed the gun from Irene Tesky?"

And I said, "No way. Nana-Jo hates guns."

"What about Angus?"

"I don't know what you mean."

"He has a key to your house, doesn't he?" Bridget asked.

And I said, "Yes, he does," and I looked out the window again and tried to do remembering if Angus had ever used his key to get inside 8B to go down to the root cellar to look at Papa-Jo's guns, but then all that remembering made me feel dizzy and I had to put my head between my knees and count the tiles on the floor. (Dr. Baker says when I do stuff like this it's called *stimming*, which is when you do something over and over again to calm yourself down when you feel scared inside.)

Bridget got out of her chair and she walked around the table to my side, and she put her hand on my shoulder. "Denny . . . Dr. Harland and Angus and I have talked at length about your situation and Angus has been very helpful, but now I think it's time for you and I to talk about Mr. Tesky. Do you think we can do that?"

And my face got hot and I stared at the floor. "I don't want to talk about Mr. Tesky right now, Bridget."

"I know, but we need to talk about him soon."

"Okay, but not now."

Dr. Harland knocked on the door and Bridget let him in, and he brought me a vanilla sprinkle doughnut, so while they did chatting I ate my doughnut and did humming. (When I'm upset or scared, I do moaning, but when I'm happy, I do humming.) When they were done chatting, Bridget packed up her leather bag and turned to me. "I have one more question, Denny. Has Angus ever asked you to lie for him?" So I closed my eyes and tried to do remembering, then I said, "No. Sometimes he says, 'Don't ever tell anyone about this,' but he's never asked me to lie for him," and Bridget looked at Dr. Harland, and she said, "Thank you, Denny," then she left to go do more lawyering.

Where's Nana-Jo?

I miss Nana-Jo.

She didn't come to the police station after I got myself arrested and she didn't come see me in jail the next day, or the day after that, even though I gave the police a piece of paper I keep in my wallet with her name and number on it. I kept asking them to please call her, and Grant-the-guard kept saying, "They're working on it," but one day went by, and then another day went by, and she still didn't come. Then, on the third day, I remembered that our green wall phone in the kitchen doesn't work anymore (phone company cut us off) and I started to do moaning because that's when I knew the police *couldn't* call Nana-Jo.

That night, Dirty Doyle rolled out of bed in his cell and he said if I didn't shut my fucking pie hole, he'd give me something to moan about. So after that, instead of doing moaning, I rocked back and forth and did thinking because I couldn't sleep because my bed was too hard and my blanket was scratchy and my pillow smelled funny.

By then I was pretty scared.

I still had Nana-Jo in my corner, though, so I wasn't super scared yet. Just so you know, when I get super scared, my throat closes up and I feel like I can't breathe, and then my mind shrinks down to a tiny ball and—**BAM!**—that's it, I don't come back for a while. I didn't get scared like *that* until the first time Angus came to see me in jail after he got home from his Mexico vacation.

Like I said before, first we did talking and Angus did swearing, then he showed me that piece of paper with *SEARCH WARRANT* on it, and a guard came and said, "Time's up!" and he had to leave. Before Angus left, though, I asked him where Nana-Jo was and he looked away, so I asked him again, and that's when he told me she'd had a *stroke* (which is when your brain shorts out like a bad electrical fuse).

My heart started going **BOOM-BOOM-BOOM.**

And I said, "When did that happen?"

Angus put the search warrant paper back in his pocket. "After they arrested you." More pacing. More goatee tugging. "By the way, did you guys know your landline's disconnected?!" He shook his head. "Anyhow . . . they sent two officers to 8B to tell Nana-Jo you'd been arrested and after they explained everything that happened, she passed out and they had to call an ambulance to take her to the hospital."

I stared at Angus for a long time. "Is she home now?"

He did a sigh. "No, she's still in the hospital."

"Can I talk to her on your phone?"

More pacing. "Sorry, buddy. She can't talk right now."

"Why not?"

Angus looked at the ceiling. "Because she has something called aphasia. It happens sometimes when people have strokes. They lose the ability to talk, sometimes for weeks or months, sometimes longer. But listen, buddy, everything's going to be fine—"

"When can she come visit me?"

Angus stuffed his hands in his pockets. "She can't, Denny. Nana-Jo has to stay in the hospital for a while."

I felt dizzy. And sick inside. "Who's taking care of George?"

"Elaine is. She's staying at 8B."

He also told me that the sheriff tried to call Lydia a few times but she's away for work, taking pictures of naked people in a place called Brazil, and she isn't answering her phone, so a judge signed official papers to make Angus be my *temporary legal guardian* (which is a person who takes care of another person, making sure they eat right and get enough sleep and change their underwear). Angus also told me that Uncle Maynard, his dad, keeps calling from Florida to ask how me and Nana-Jo are doing, and he wishes he could be here but because he needs a wheelchair to get around now, he wouldn't be much help . . . and Angus kept talking and talking but his words were loud and echoey so I sat down and I put my head between my knees and I counted the tiles on the floor.

One, two, three . . .

Angus snapped his fingers. "Denny, look at me."

Four, five, six, seven . . .

More snap-snap-snapping. "I'm serious, Denny. Look at me!" so I did, but Angus looked scared too and that made everything worse.

And he kept talking, but I wasn't really hearing his words, then I stood up and I closed my eyes, and I sang the theme song for *Toy Story*—"You've Got a Friend in Me." That's when Dirty Doyle yelled at Angus across the walkway, and he told him if he didn't get me under control all kinds of crap was gonna hit the fan, then Angus yelled back, "Holy shit, dude! Can't you see I'm dealing with a sensitive situation here?!" And they sounded very far away, and then my throat closed up and I felt like I couldn't breathe, so I slid down onto the floor and Angus ran to the guard's desk, yelling, "Hello?! I need some help here!" and my mind shrank down to a tiny ball and then—**BAM!**—that was it, I didn't come back for a while.

When I finally did come back, I was sitting at the table in our special meeting room and the inside of my brain felt bruised (sore) and Dr. Harland was there and so was Angus, and their mouths were moving but I couldn't hear their words, only a buzzing sound like our TV makes when it goes off the air. And my blue notebook was on the table next to a vanilla sprinkle doughnut on a napkin, and six of the candy-colored sprinkles had fallen off the doughnut—two blue, one red, three yellow—so I pressed my finger against them one by one until they stuck to it, then I put them in my mouth and I ate them.

The buzzing sound suddenly stopped.

"How long do these 'going away for a while' episodes last?" Dr. Harland asked.

Angus shrugged. "An hour, sometimes more."

"Does it happen a lot?"

"Not really. Denny's life is one big routine, and routine makes him feel safe, and when he feels safe everything's good."

Dr. Harland frowned. "When was the last time it happened?"

"Last year when he was arrested the first time, then again when he was arrested the second time, and now today. I honestly think finding out Nana-Jo's in the hospital was just too much for him."

"It's a sensory overload issue," Dr. Harland said, sounding doctory. "Denny is disassociating or spontaneously clocking out of a situation emotionally, and when he does that he loses periods of time and memories because he's entered a kind of fugue state. Essentially, it's a coping mechanism, like an escape valve to relieve pressure on his mind."

Angus aimed a finger gun at him. "Bingo! That sounds right. Can I give you some advice, though? Don't push him too hard or he'll shut down on you. I've already told you and Bridget about Henry Tesky's involvement in Denny's life, and eventually I'm sure Denny will tell you more himself, but only when he's ready. Trust me, I know having a conversation with Denny can be like herding cats—"

I did a sigh. "You can't herd cats, Angus. You can herd sheep, but not cats."

Dr. Harland turned to me, then Angus jumped up and said, "Welcome back, buddy. How you feeling?!" and I shrugged because I wasn't sure yet. "Well, you look good! Doesn't he look good, Dr. Harland? His color's way better." Angus pointed at me. "You are a warrior, buddy, a fucking warrior!" and he was acting all weird and showoffy, so I said, "Me and Dr. Harland have work to do, Angus, so I think you should go."

He crossed his arms. "Why? I don't mind sticking around."

"Because we can't do talking when you're doing interrupting."

"I won't interrupt."

But he always interrupts when I do talking and I was tired and didn't want to do arguing, so I said, "If you don't go now, Angus, maybe I'll tell Dr. Harland some of our secrets, like how we did wedding crashing one whole summer just like in that famous movie . . . or how you got drunk last year, put on a T-shirt that said 'I Promise to Be Your Greatest Adventure,' then tried to crash Mr. Tesky's wedding to his new wife, Malinda, but they wouldn't let you in, and you got mad and broke a window with your fist, and then you had to go to the hospital for stitches—"

Angus threw his hands up. "Fine, I'm leaving!"

His face was red and splotchy, and he turned to Dr. Harland and said, "Hand to God, he makes up shit like this all the time. Call me if you have more questions. Like I said, he's pretty predictable when he's not triggered, but if this 'going away for a while' thing happens again, you'll be screwed for a few hours."

Dr. Harland closed his notebook. "Thank you, Angus." Then he said, "I think we've got it from here, though, right, Denny?"

And I did a thumbs-up, which means YES, WE DO, then I folded my arms on the table and I rested my head on them and said, "Time to go, Angus." Then I did another sigh, because Angus likes to think he knows everything about me and how the inside of my brain works, but he's wrong. He doesn't know everything.

Homesick for 8B

Bridget has been working on my case doing all kinds of lawyering and while she does that I've been meeting with Dr. Harland so he can *assess me* (figure out what makes me tick) and help untangle this mess. Each day after breakfast the guard named Grant takes me to a special meeting room where Dr. Harland is waiting for me and it's always the same room with a table and four chairs, and Dr. Harland sits on the left side and I sit on the right side and we do talking, then I go back to my cell and write words in my notebook, and the next day Dr. Harland reads my words and we do more talking.

Here are some of the words I wrote yesterday:

I miss Nana-Jo and George, but I also miss 8B. Just so you know, Turtle Creek runs behind 8B and it's not deep enough to swim in or paddle a canoe down, but on hot days in the summer me and George go down there and I stick my feet in the water and do thinking. Painted turtles live in Turtle Creek (some people call them mud turtles) but I've also seen false map turtles and snapping turtles and once I even saw a Blanding's turtle, which is an endangered species, which means it won't be on our planet much longer because there aren't enough Blanding's turtles left to do sex and make more Blanding's turtles.

After Dr. Harland read my notebook today, he said I'm doing an excellent job, but I shouldn't get *fixated* on the turtles (that's when you get stuck on something and you can't stop thinking or talking about it) because writing about them isn't going to *add anything to the story*, then he asked me to tear out six pages of turtle information I'd written.

So yeah, that sucked.

And while me and Dr. Harland were doing talking, Angus stopped by and they let him into our special meeting room because he's my temporary legal guardian and Dr. Harland said it was okay. He was wearing a T-shirt that said **You Had Me at "We'll Make It Look Like an Accident"** and he paced around the room and listened for a bit, then I said, "Time to go, Angus. We're busy here," so he left.

Dr. Harland went back to reading my notebook. He flipped through the pages, then he rubbed his face with his hands (up/down, up/down) and he said, "Listen Denny, it's interesting that coniferous trees keep their needles year round and deciduous trees change color and lose their leaves in the fall, but none of that is *relevant* here because it has nothing to do with what you were planning to do with those guns when you put them in your sled and rode it down Penguin Hill toward the elementary school."

"I already told you, I was taking them to the police station."

"I know, Denny, but like I said before, nobody knew that."

And I looked out the window and did thinking about that; then I started to feel sick inside, and I thought, *Uh-oh,* because that's when I understood that the cops who arrested me probably thought I was a *violent guy* instead of a *good guy*.

I looked at Dr. Harland and said, "I wasn't going to hurt anyone."

He nodded. "Okay, Denny, but here's the thing. When you write in your notebook, you need to tell your story in the clearest possible way and I realize that'll be challenging because your mind keeps jumping around, but that's why I'm here. To help keep you on track so you can tell your story one step at a time, and we can give Bridget Klein all the relevant facts she needs to get you home."

I said, "Okay, Dr. Harland." And that's when I decided to try harder to do what he asked me to do. So yeah, Woodmont has Turtle Creek but it also has Penguin Hill, which is an important part of my story, and this is everything I know about it.

The town of Woodmont is near the Sawtooth Mountains, which got made from lava that erupted from the earth 1.1 billion years ago. All that lava flew up into the air and landed back on earth and slid all over the place, and when it cooled off it made some hills and small mountains, and we have one of those hill/mountains here in Woodmont, and it's three miles long and three-quarters of a mile wide and snow won't stick to the southeast side at the bottom because of the lava that's mixed in, so in the winter our hill/mountain looks like an emperor penguin lying on his back (white on top, black on the bottom).

Years ago, Woodmont had a contest to name our hill/mountain and the winner was a lady who said it should be called Penguin Hill, then after that the town opened Penguin Hill Estates at the top of our hill/mountain and they built a bunch of McMansions up there (big, fancy houses) and all the bigwigs in Woodmont (people who think they're important) wanted to live up there, including Mr. Tesky.

The town also made Penguin Hill Park up there with a bunch of benches and walking trails. And because there's almost no lava on the northeast side of Penguin Hill and that's the ONLY PART where the snow stays all winter from the top to the bottom, that's where they also made the best tobogganing hill ever, and I go there all the time because it's close to 8B, which is at the bottom of Penguin Hill on Deyton Avenue.

Also, just so you know, at the bottom of Penguin Hill on the opposite side from where I live is a police station and an elementary school, which is where I was going with all those guns and bullets when I got myself arrested—the police station, *not* the elementary school.

I haven't always lived at 8B, though. We used to live on an acreage (piece of land) outside of Woodmont. It had four bedrooms, four bathrooms, and a wraparound porch with a swing that dangled from two chains. We also had chickens and a cow named Lady, and the chickens gave us eggs and Lady gave us milk. We lived there for a long time

(Lydia grew up there too) but then after Papa-Jo died, Nana-Jo had to sell it so she could pay off some bills Papa-Jo forgot to pay. After that, Uncle Maynard (Papa-Jo's brother) sold Nana-Jo 8B, which is half of a side-by-side house he owned in Woodmont, and we've been there ever since. Uncle Maynard is also Angus's dad, and Angus has lived at 8A for as long as I can remember.

8B is 908 square feet, which is a lot smaller than our other house. It has two bedrooms, one bathroom, a sewing room, a kitchen, a living room, and a basement where we store things, but there's just me and Nana-Jo and George, so we don't need lots of room. We also share the backyard with Angus (three-quarter acre) and it has a fence around it and trees and a garden and a firepit for when we have friends over.

Just so you know, today hasn't been a good day because my mind keeps jumping around and I want to lie down for a bit, but I can't because Dr. Harland said we have work to do. But then he sighed, and he said, "Why don't we take a break and you can draw a map of where you live so it's easier for me to visualize things?" (picture them in his mind).

And I said, "I can't. I'm bad at drawing."

Then Dr. Harland said, "Let me see what I can do," and he found a woman named Charla who does drawing for her work and she came to our meeting room and while Dr. Harland did chatting with Bridget Klein on his phone, I told Charla all about where I live and she drew a map for me. Charla had a diamond tattoo on her pinkie finger and the word **LOVE** on her middle finger and a hummingbird on her arm, and I asked if it hurt to have a needle go in and out of her body over and over again to make a tattoo.

Charla shrugged. "Not really."

And I said, "Did you throw up?"

She laughed. "No!"

"Was your tattoo person a guy or a girl?"

"A guy," Charla said.

"Did he do flirting with you?"

She frowned. "Um . . . no. Why would he?"

And I said, "Because when a girl is pretty like you are, guys like to do flirting to show you they think you've got it all going on."

Charla tilted her head. "Are you serious right now?"

And I said, "Serious as cement," because I heard Angus say that once and it sounded cool. I also told Charla I'm getting a tattoo when I get out of jail because that's what ex-convicts do, and she said, "What kind?" and I said, "Maybe a unicorn?" and she said, "Dog paws are popular right now. You got a dog?" That's when I decided to get a tattoo of George's paw on my arm. So yeah, me and Charla did visiting, then she finished doing drawing, and now there's a map of where I live to help Dr. Harland *visualize things* while I tell my story.

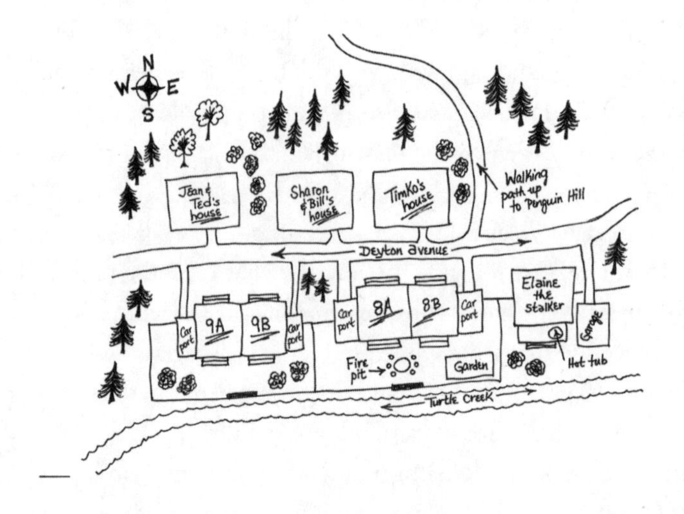

So yeah, me and Nana-Jo live at 8B at the bottom of Penguin Hill on the southeast side, and the Teskys used to live in a McMansion (big fancy house) at the top of Penguin Hill on the northwest side, and me and Nana-Jo are still alive and kicking, but Irene Tesky died last year (cancer) and Henry Tesky died two weeks ago (fatal gunshot wound) and there's nothing anyone can do about any of that.

How This Mess Got Started

Dr. Harland brought doughnuts again today and while I ate mine, he opened his notebook and tap-tap-tapped a pencil against it. "All right, Denny," he said. "Tell me all about kidnapping Tom Hanks and how you got arrested for that."

So that's what I did.

I told him how Tom Hanks the goose is nothing like Tom Hanks the movie star. He's an angry Canada goose with a brown body, a white belly, a black neck and head, and a white chin strap. He's also mean and he can't fly anymore because he broke one of his wings, which is how he got himself stuck in Woodmont two years ago and why Mrs. Timko, our neighbor across the street, adopted him as her pet. I told him how Tom Hanks chased me down the sidewalk one day, hissing and spitting, and when I zigged and zagged (tried to lose him) one of my Crocs fell off and I tripped and fell and Tom Hanks opened his wings wide and he flapped them, then he jumped on me and he bit me over and over and over again.

—Pinch! Pinch! Pinch!

That's when Angus ran outside and chased Tom Hanks away. "Holy shit, Denny! Are you all right?" Angus was barefoot and he was wearing boxer shorts and a T-shirt that said **SHITSHOW SUPERVISOR**. After he helped me up, he bent over and put his hands on his knees and he laughed and laughed. He wanted me to walk past Tom Hanks's yard again only this time he told me he'd use his cell phone to make a video of me getting beat up, then we'd post it on the internet (World Wide Web) on something called TikTok and if it went viral (which is when LOTS of people look at it) I'd be famous.

I had cuts and bruises on my arms and face, and I told Angus I didn't want to be famous; I just wanted Tom Hanks to stop being an asshole.

Angus filmed me saying that with his phone, then he laughed even harder. "I swear, Denny, if I followed you around and filmed you for a week, we'd get a dozen offers for a reality show." Sometimes Angus likes to kid around (do jokes) so I said, "For real?" and he said, "Scout's honor," and he put his right hand in the air with three fingers pointed up.

"Would it be like *Keeping Up with the Kardashians*?" I liked the idea of being rich and living in a mansion.

Angus laughed. "Probably more like *Honey Boo Boo*."

"Nana-Jo didn't like that show."

"I know."

"She said it was tacky."

"Sure, but Nana-Jo isn't our demographic, is she, buddy?"

"What's a demographic?"

Angus closed his eyes. "Never mind."

He picked up my Croc and handed it to me. "Think about it, buddy, how cool would it be to have your own TV show? I could be your agent. Can't you picture me in a producer's office, pitching the idea? *The Adventures of Denny Voss.* Hell, we'd make some serious coin. I could get a new truck and you could move to Key Largo and get yourself a beach house." Angus's dad, Uncle Maynard, lives in Key Largo (island in Florida) and Angus knew how much I liked the ocean and beach houses, and he was always looking for *a million-dollar idea* but sometimes when he got excited like this he talked too fast and it confused me.

I put my Croc back on. "I don't want to move to Key Largo."

"Why not?"

"I have a good life here."

"I hate to rain on your parade, buddy, but you don't."

"Yes, I do."

"No, you don't. You live with Nana-Jo, you have a part-time job picking up roadkill, you just got attacked by a goose for—what?—the third time this month, and you spend all your spare time walking a blind and deaf dog."

"Leave George out of this!"

"—and when you're not walking George, you're flaked out at my place like a couch potato, watching TV."

Sometimes Angus is mean. I'd helped Nana-Jo dig potatoes in the garden and they were dirty and lumpy and boring, and I wasn't any of those things. I did watch lots of TV at Angus's house, though, because our TV was old (made from tubes) and me and Nana-Jo only got four channels but Angus had a sixty-five-inch flat-screen TV (no tubes) and every channel on the planet. He also let me save shows on his PVR, which is a black box, so I could watch them over and over again. Me and Nana-Jo don't have a PVR so when we watch *Schitt's Creek* (best show EVER) we can't save the episodes and that makes me sad.

Angus's favorite shows are *Ozark*, any James Bond movie, and all the Bourne movies, and mine are *The Price Is Right*, *Schitt's Creek*, and fast-moving shows like the Bourne movies. The good thing is that Angus's PVR has lots of room on it, which is nice because we both like to save lots of shows.

"Angus?"

"Yeah?"

"I'm not a couch potato."

"I only want what's best for you, buddy."

Angus says that all the time. He also says, *The world is your oyster!* or *Shoot for the stars, Denny!* and sometimes I get mad and tell him to get his own oyster or shoot for his own stupid stars. Angus has been working on his stars, though. I've seen it with my own eyes. Like how he's been drying out the plants in his basement and selling them in plastic bags to make extra money for his vacation, and how he's been doing sit-ups to tighten his belly, and how he isn't drinking as much as he used to.

Angus drank A LOT after Mr. Tesky fired him from his job at Norida, which is a yogurt-making factory that makes low-fat yogurt, Greek yogurt, probiotic yogurt, drinkable yogurt, and oat-based yogurt. Norida is also one of the *top-selling yogurt brands* in North America, which means lots of people eat their yogurt.

A man named Roger Marsh opened Norida after his wife died and at first it was a small company, but then it grew and grew until finally Mr. Marsh had to build a yogurt-making factory here in Woodmont so Norida could make more yogurt for all the people who kept eating it. And Roger Marsh had two daughters—Irene and Toni—and Toni got herself married and moved to Canada, but Irene stayed in Woodmont to help her dad run Norida because she was *good with numbers* (knew how to work a calculator).

Nana-Jo told me all this. She also told me how Henry Tesky got himself hired at Norida in *quality control* (a department that makes sure they make good yogurt instead of shitty yogurt) and how he did flirting with Irene. Then, six months later, he asked Irene to marry him, and she said yes, even though her sister, Toni, said, "No, Irene, don't do it!" (Toni did *not* like Henry Tesky.) Four years later, Roger Marsh, who was old by then, died from a heart attack, and Henry Tesky moved into Roger's office and took over running the business.

Angus used to work for Norida as head of security (important job), then one day he got himself fired for being late, but Angus told me it wasn't because he was late, it was because when he did his security rounds one night he'd walked into an office and caught Henry Tesky and his new secretary, Malinda, doing sex on a desk. (Malinda is Mr. Tesky's widow now that he's dead, but back then she wasn't even his second wife yet.) Angus thinks he got fired because Mr. Tesky didn't want him around as a reminder that he got himself caught *doing an affair* (affairs are when someone cheats on their husband/wife by doing sex on a desk with another person). So yeah, Angus got himself fired, and for a while he couldn't find another job and he drank A LOT, but Nana-Jo says he's much better now, mentally and emotionally.

Anyhow, sometimes Angus made me mad, but maybe what he said about me not having a good life was a little bit right? Maybe my life in Woodmont isn't that great because my job at DOT makes me sad, and Tom Hanks is an asshole, and I've never seen the ocean or a real beach house, just the pictures Uncle Maynard mails me that I keep on my bulletin board.

"Hey, Angus?" I said.

"Yeah?"

"If I moved to Florida, do you think I could get a job driving a Frito-Lay truck?"

Angus took a breath, blew it out. "Really? Again with this shit, Denny?! First of all, find a better dream, buddy. Aim higher. And second, I have told you a dozen times you need a license to drive a Frito-Lay truck, doesn't matter if you live in Minnesota or Florida or Timbuk-fucking-tu!"

"Are you sure?"

"I am."

When I got home from 8A, Nana-Jo was back from her doctor appointment, sitting at the kitchen table, staring out the window. She looked tired (dark circles under her eyes) and she blew her nose and asked me to take George outside so he could do his business. George was shuffling around the kitchen like a giant Roomba (robot vacuum), bumping into walls, then backing up and going in a new direction.

I showed Nana-Jo my arms and face. "Tom Hanks beat me up again."

"That's too bad." She pointed to George. "Better take him out now, Denny, before he pees in the house."

I opened the fridge freezer, got an ice cube, and held it against my face. "Could you ask the Timkos to lock Tom Hanks in their backyard?"

Nana-Jo was digging through her purse. "I've got bigger fish to fry right now, Denny. You'll have to do it yourself." *Having bigger fish to fry* meant she had more important stuff to do now that she didn't have a job—like figuring out how to pay the bills or how to pay for the broken-down knee operation she needed REAL BAD because Medicaid (government program) won't pay for it yet even though her knee is sore and swollen, and the pills they gave her aren't working and neither are the exercises or the *cortisone injections* (needles they stuck into her knee to stop the pain).

"Can you go with me, Nana-Jo?"

"No, Denny. You need to do it yourself."

"I tried that a few weeks ago, remember? Tom Hanks chased me down the block and I rang their doorbell and Mrs. Timko answered, but she said her hearing aid wasn't working so 'come back another time,' so I rang the doorbell an hour later but no one answered, then I rang it again and again and finally Mr. Timko answered and he was mean to me."

"Were you being annoying?"

"No, I wasn't."

"Because sometimes you can be." Nana-Jo rubbed her sore knee.

"I wasn't. When Mr. Timko opened the door, he had his barbecue apron on and he was holding a bloody steak and a knife, and I said hello and when I told him what Tom Hanks did to me, he started doing Hungarian—"

"*Speaking* Hungarian."

"—and he waved his knife around and I got scared. Then I started stuttering because it was a really big knife, and then Mr. Timko pointed it at me, and he said, 'Get off my fucking porch,' so I did."

Nana-Jo snapped George's leash onto his collar and handed it to me. "Well, that's unfortunate," she said. "I'll talk to Olga about it the next time I see her. In the meantime, if you have a problem with Tom Hanks, you need to deal with it yourself, Denny. I can't take care of everything for you."

And I said, "But you always take care of everything for me."

"Not anymore."

"Why not?"

Nana-Jo sighed. "Because I'm getting old, Denny, and I won't be here forever to help you with things like this. It's time you started thinking for yourself. What are you going to do when I'm gone? What's going to happen then?" So I took George outside to go pee and he walked into a tree—**SMACK!**—because I forgot to steer him around it. Then I knelt down and hugged him and said, *Sorry, sorry, sorry* because I was, and I also didn't know what was going to happen when Nana-Jo wasn't here anymore, and that made my stomach hurt worse than the cuts and bruises from Tom Hanks beating me up.

Making a Plan

Dr. Harland tap-tap-tapped a pencil against his notebook. "Denny, has Nana-Jo always helped you with your problems?" and I said, "Yes. My whole wide life, whenever I had a problem to fix my brain would start jumping around and then I'd lay down for a bit to rest, and Nana-Jo would help me figure things out. But she wouldn't help me with Tom Hanks. She just kept saying, 'You can do this, Denny. Think it through. Take it one step at a time and make yourself a plan.' So that's what I did."

I told Dr. Harland all about my plan.

How the next day after Nana-Jo left to buy groceries, I fed George breakfast, then I went into the living room and I sat at the desk in the corner by the window and I turned on Nana-Jo's computer and I asked Google to tell me everything about Canada geese. (Angus showed me how to do Google—it knows *everything*.)

And I learned a lot. Like how Canada geese like to hang out in gangs and how they have very long memories and how they don't like to be touched, which was probably why Tom Hanks didn't like me because the first time I saw him I tried to hug him and he got mad, and the same thing happened the second time I saw him, and the third time. I also learned that Canada geese can live more than twenty years and they like to fly in a V when they are traveling with their gangs because it's efficient (saves energy).

And when Canada geese are two years old, they find one mate they like A LOT and they stay with that mate for the rest of their lives. It's like a rule they all follow—one goose partner forever, no cheating or changing partners like some humans do when their partners get old and wrinkled and they want a new one who's younger and not wrinkled.

This is everything I know about the Timkos:

They live across the street and they have a white Lada (Russian car as old as I am) and sometimes they speak English and sometimes they don't. Mrs. Timko limps when she walks and sometimes her lipstick gets smeared on her teeth. Mr. Timko uses suspenders to hold his pants up and he also drinks a special kind of vodka that comes from a place called the *old country* and if he likes you, he'll share his vodka (sometimes he shares it with Angus) and if he doesn't like you, he'll tell you to *get off his fucking porch* (he's told me that three times this year).

Angus was at work but I had a key to his house so I went next door to borrow his binoculars and I sat on the front steps and watched Tom Hanks all week when I wasn't working at DOT, and when Nana-Jo asked why I was sitting out there so much, I told her I was doing research, which is a special kind of investigating to find facts.

I wrote everything down, like how Mr. Timko didn't seem to like Tom Hanks because every morning when he left to play cards at the Legion, Tom Hanks would run at him honking, and Mr. Timko would say, "Come closer you little shit and I'll give you something to honk about!" or "You're about as useful as a screen door on a submarine, aren't you?"

Mrs. Timko fed Tom Hanks oats every morning and she gave him birdseed every afternoon. She'd limp outside and set a plate on the grass and she always put it in the same spot and when she set it down, she'd make funny noises with her mouth—**HRONK! HRONK!**—and no matter where Tom Hanks was, he'd come running.

Here are some other things I learned:

Tom Hanks was a goose, but he waddled like a duck and he had webbed feet (good for swimming) and he could open his right wing very wide, but because he broke his left wing two years ago, he could only open it partway wide. After watching him for a week and writing everything down and *thinking things through*, I decided Tom Hanks was probably mean and angry because he got himself stuck in Woodmont and he couldn't fly back to Canada where his special mate lived, and his special mate was probably floating around on a lake up there all by herself, wondering where Tom Hanks was.

And that made me sad.

Then I thought to myself, *Maybe Tom Hanks* isn't *an asshole. Maybe he's just stuck here in Minnesota and more than anything in the world all he wants to do is go home to Canada so he can be with his special mate, and it seems like maybe he's been trying to tell everyone that, but nobody's been* listening.

And that's when I decided to kidnap Tom Hanks.

Kidnapping Tom Hanks

Dr. Harland said, "You're doing a good job, Denny," and I said, "So are you."

Then we took a break and Grant-the-guard came to take me to the bathroom and he waited outside until I was done, but Dr. Harland used a different bathroom and nobody waited outside for him because he's not incarcerated and he has a badge that says **AUTHORIZED VISITOR**, which means no one cares if he tries to bust out of here and run away as long as he doesn't try to take me with him.

After our break, I went back to telling Dr. Harland how I kidnapped Tom Hanks. "Just so you know," I said, "Canada's ten miles north of Woodmont, and I couldn't ask someone to drive me because Nana-Jo said I needed to 'deal with the Tom Hanks problem by myself.' So, I made a list of what I had to do to make sure it would be a successful (good) kidnapping, and this was what I put on my list . . ."

1. Catch Tom Hanks.
2. Stuff him in a pillowcase.
3. Put him in my bike basket.
4. Ride my bike to the Canadian border.
5. Throw Tom Hanks over the fence.
6. Bike home.

I'd been to Canada's border twice before when me and Angus were driving around looking for roadkill for DOT.

The first time, he showed me the *official border crossing* (two buildings with blinking lights and lots of signs) where you have to show your passport before they'll let you in to buy maple syrup or watch a hockey game or go shopping. The second time, we took a gravel road north until we saw a sign that said **No Trespassing** and we turned down a bumpy road (lots of potholes) that followed the edge of a farmer's field, and that also brought us to the Canadian border, only there were no buildings or lights or signs to tell us where we were. Angus just knew—he's smart like that.

Earlier that morning, we'd found a half-dead bobcat and had to use the DOT gun to put him out of his misery, then I got sad and Angus played Pharrell Williams's "Happy" song to cheer me up but it didn't work, so he turned up the volume on his phone and got out of the truck. Then he stood on the side of the road and he lip-synched all the words to Taylor Swift's "Shake It Off" and he used a water bottle for a microphone, and he made all the right faces, and he did all the moves Taylor does in her music video—circle, circle, BUMP! circle, circle, BUMP!—but none of that made the sad go away either.

Angus knows I've always wanted to go to Canada for real, though, so that day he took me across the border to cheer me up. He was wearing a T-shirt under his jacket that said **Not a Prince, Not Charming**, and he looked over one shoulder real quick-like, then he looked over his other shoulder, and he grabbed my arm and said, "Listen, buddy, there's still time for you to back out of this, but you need to decide right now because if we get caught going over that fence, we'll be in a shit ton of trouble!"

And I could feel my mouth making a smile because I could tell he was pretending to be Matt Damon in one of those fast-moving Jason Bourne movies we watch all the time, so I said, "Do you think someone's watching us, Jason?" Angus looked up through the windshield and he said, "There's *always* someone watching us!" then I said in a whisper, "Angus, are we really going to climb over that fence?" and he said, "Fuck yeah, we are!"

So that's what we did.

We got out of the DOT truck and we climbed over the fence, and Angus cut his hand on the barbed wire and he kicked a fence post and said, "Fuck me!" then I gave him a rag to wrap around his hand. And we sat down in Canada and ate our lunch (tuna sandwiches) and I had an apple juice squeeze box and a can of Coke in my lunch kit, so when Angus stretched out on the grass, I asked if he wanted something to drink, and he said, "Sure," and I said, "What would you like?" and he said, "A martini, please. Shaken, not stirred," just like James Bond does, and that made me laugh.

By then, I wasn't sad anymore.

Angus showed me how to use my jacket like a pillow and we fell asleep in the grass, which is probably why we didn't hear Lonny yelling at us on the two-way radio. And when we woke up, there were ants crawling all over Angus and he jumped up and ran in circles, slapping at them, and I laughed and laughed until he said, "Not fucking funny, Einstein!" Then we jumped over the fence and we hurried back to the DOT shop and there was Lonny, pacing around outside, waiting for us.

Angus parked the DOT truck and said, "I've got this, Denny."

He hopped out, holding his hand, which was still wrapped in a bloody rag, and he told Lonny the dead bobcat in the back of the truck bit him before we could shoot it, and Lonny's eyes got big and he forgot to be mad. Instead, he told Angus to get his ass over to the hospital for a tetanus shot so we jumped in Angus's truck and *got the hell out of Dodge* (drove away fast) and we didn't stop until we got to Pizza Planet, where we ordered take-out pepperoni pizza for dinner, same as we do every Friday after work.

So yeah, it wasn't a good day at first but then it was because I went to a foreign country, even though I didn't get to buy maple syrup or watch a hockey game or do any shopping. "We can do that next time," Angus said, and I asked when next time would be, and he shrugged, so I asked again, and when he didn't answer me I asked again and again . . . and that's when Angus hit the brakes and the truck skidded sideways and the pizza box fell onto the floor. "You just don't know when to stop, do you?!" he yelled.

Then it wasn't a good day again for a while.

Just so you know, I have an excellent memory, which means I remember LOTS of things, like what people were wearing when they did something, and exactly how they did something, and what we talked about while they were doing something, so after I kidnapped Tom Hanks, I knew I would be able to find that farmer's fence by the Canadian border, because I could remember every road and every turn Angus had taken to get us there.

Dr. Baker told Nana-Jo I have the closest thing he's ever seen to something called an *eidetic memory*, which is when a person's mind can go back in time, like pressing rewind in a movie, and remember all kinds of things.

For example, I remember what I was wearing when Billy Kopp beat me up in fifth grade (blue shirt, black buttons) and how the principal called Nana-Jo and she came to get me, and how, when she got there, she still had foam curlers in her hair (pink) and when she walked into Mr. Berman's office and saw me (black eye, bleeding lip), she said, "For Christ's sake, what kind of circus are you running here?!"

On our way home that day, Nana-Jo went through the Doughnut Hole's drive-through and bought doughnuts (vanilla sprinkle for me, old fashioned for her) then she parked the Subaru and her hands were shaking as she pulled out her curlers one by one. When she was done, she said, "You're worth ten of those other kids, Denny, and don't you ever forget it!"

And I didn't.

I also remember what the weather was like the day Papa-Jo died (foggy in the morning, cloudy all afternoon) and how, before he left that morning, I told him he looked tired and he said, "Ack, I'm fine!" But he'd been sick all week and he'd missed work the day before and

Nana-Jo was so mad at him for going hunting that she didn't even get out of bed to say goodbye. Papa-Jo pulled a can of Folgers out of the cupboard so he could make a thermos of coffee and while the machine coughed and sputtered, spitting out the coffee, Papa-Jo coughed and sputtered, spitting gunk into his hankie from being sick.

And it was garbage day so Papa-Jo dragged our garbage can to the end of the driveway then he came back inside to get his orange safety vest and his favorite winter hat (red-and-black plaid with ear flaps, same as mine). And his hunting buddy, Harvey, was late picking him up so Papa-Jo showed me his gun while he waited—M1903 Springfield bolt-action rifle—and he kept coughing and coughing.

And when Harvey's pickup truck finally pulled in the driveway, Papa-Jo did what he always did when he left to go somewhere. He pointed at me and said, "What are you, Denny Voss?" and I said, "One of the best things that ever happened to you," and he said, "You got it, cowboy!" Then he left and when Harvey backed down the driveway, he hit the garbage can and knocked it over and Papa-Jo had to get out and stand it up again. Then they drove away and I never saw Papa-Jo again because he died later that day in the woods at 4:48 p.m. before the ambulance people could get there to save his life.

I also remember how, five years ago, after we got George, Lydia came home for a visit and she sat down on the couch and George put his head in her lap and drooled on her jeans and she pushed him away and said, "You stupid fucking dog!" and I got mad and told her *she* was stupid, then Lydia slapped me—smack!—and Nana-Jo told her if she wanted to act like that, she could damned well leave.

So, she did.

Lydia hasn't been back to Woodmont since then and because she isn't talking to us I don't think she knows that Mr. Tesky fired Nana-Jo, or that Tom Hanks keeps beating me up, or that Nana-Jo needs an operation on her broken-down knee.

So, yeah, I have an excellent memory and there's always lots of stuff like that floating around inside my brain. Last month, I asked Dr. Baker if that's why sometimes my mind starts jumping around and I get tired and want to lie down, but he just shrugged and said, "Could be. What can I say, Denny? You're an enigma!" And on the drive home, Nana-Jo explained to me that *enigma* isn't a bad word; it just means that I'm a mystery, which is good because mysteries are challenging and fun, and so am I.

If you ask Google how to catch a Canada goose it doesn't have any good answers, but I did find a guy named Larry who put a video on YouTube of an angry goose that wouldn't leave his yard. In that video Larry crushed up sleeping pills and put them in oats for the goose and after the goose ate the oats, he got sleepy, then Larry put him in a burlap sack and held him in his lap while his wife, Jeannie, drove to a lake, where they let him go. And Larry said if you ever want to kidnap a Canada goose use a burlap sack because they're made of something called *jute* so when you put your goose inside, he'll be able to breathe, and he won't die while you're transporting him (moving him) off your property.

So instead of using a pillowcase for kidnapping Tom Hanks, I went down to the root cellar and found an empty burlap sack and put it in my knapsack.

After Nana-Jo went to bed, I opened the medicine cabinet in our bathroom to get sleeping pills, but we didn't have any, so I wrote down what we did have in there: Advil, Pepto Bismol, Metamucil, aspirin, Visine, Bengay, Neosporin, TUMS, and Benadryl. Then I went into the living room, and I sat at the desk in the corner by the window, and I turned on Nana-Jo's computer and asked Google to tell me everything about those medicines, but Google got confused, so then I had to ask about them one by one and that took a while.

Thirty-two minutes later, Google finally told me that drowsiness (getting sleepy) was the *main side effect* of Benadryl, which people take when they get hives (itchy red bumps) so I took the Benadryl bottle and put it in my knapsack with a granola bar, a can of apple juice, and a roll of duct tape. And I don't work on Wednesdays, so I decided

Wednesday was a good day to do a kidnapping. Nana-Jo also had an appointment for her knee on Wednesday morning, so after she left I put on my shoes and my bike helmet, and I sat on the front steps with Angus's binoculars and a paper plate and a box of oatmeal. I waited for Mr. Timko to drive away in his Lada to play cards at the Legion (which he did), then I waited for Mrs. Timko to limp down the sidewalk with her cane to do volunteering at the Take It or Leave It (which she did).

I went inside and got Nana-Jo's kitchen timer, which looks like a green apple only it's plastic, and I crossed the street and crawled along the grass beside the Timkos' hedge (called a *Caragana*) to the spot where Mrs. Timko always feeds Tom Hanks. I dumped oatmeal on the plate and poured half a bottle of Benadryl on top, which is kind of like syrup, then I made the same noises Mrs. Timko did when she fed Tom Hanks—**HRONK! HRONK!**—and I got the hell out of Dodge. A few seconds later, Tom Hanks came waddling around the corner of the house. He went over to the plate and ate the oatmeal, and when he was done he waddled back around the corner of the house. That's when I set Nana-Jo's apple timer for thirty minutes because Google said that's how long it would take for Benadryl to start working, and I went home and got my bike, and when the timer bell rang I grabbed my burlap sack and went around the corner of the Timkos' house where Tom Hanks had disappeared.

And there he was, floating in a plastic swimming pool filled with water and his head kept drooping on his neck (*droop, droop*) then snapping back up again. I snuck up behind him and threw the burlap sack over his head and he honked and hissed, but he wasn't as mad as I thought he'd be. I carried him to my bike and put him in my bike basket, and I snapped the lid shut to make sure he couldn't get out, then I got on and started pedaling.

It took two hours and eight minutes to get to the border. And I went past six farmhouses and along the way I saw one rubber boot on the side of the highway and a baseball cap and a cracked key chain that said **MINNESOTA: THE LAND OF LONG GOODBYES**. I also waved at a farmer who was driving a tractor in a field near that **No Trespassing** sign and he squinted at me but he didn't wave back. And I knew I was in exactly the right spot when I got there because after me and Angus ate our lunch that day in Canada, he'd scrunched up his Coke can and threw it on the ground and it was still there in the same spot because we forgot to pick it up.

Tom Hanks was limp (not moving) when I lifted him out of my bike basket, which made it easier to get him out of the sack and carry him over to the fence. I set him down and climbed over the fence, then I got down on my knees and I grabbed him by his webbed feet and tugged him *under* the fence into Canada.

Then—whew!—Tom Hanks was finally home.

And I jumped back from him real quick-like in case he woke up in a bad mood, but Tom Hanks was still limp, so I decided to sit down and wait for him to finish sleeping. But the sun was hot and I was tired from biking and pretty soon my head started to droop, so I rolled up my jacket and used it like a pillow.

Welcome to Canada

Dr. Harland doesn't fall asleep anymore when I do talking. Sometimes his eyebrows jump and once he spit his tea out before he could swallow it, but he doesn't fall asleep anymore, so that's good. After I told him how I tugged Tom Hanks under that fence into Canada, Grant-the-guard opened the door to our meeting room and said, "Time's up," but Dr. Harland told him we needed a few more minutes, so Grant left again.

Then Dr. Harland asked me to tell him the rest of the story.

So I did.

Tom Hanks was gone when I woke up. I was looking for him when a Chevrolet Silverado with orange lights flashing on top and **BORDER PATROL** written on the side came down the dirt road and two men got out and they were wearing green uniforms and bulletproof vests, and they had walkie-talkies and guns. And they pointed their guns at me just like in one of those fast-moving TV shows and my heart started going BOOM-BOOM-BOOM so I put my hands in the air and said, "I am not a threat."

"Get on the ground!" one of them yelled.

So I did.

Then he said, "Put your hands where I can see them."

So I did.

And my heart was still going BOOM-BOOM-BOOM and the grass was poking into my face and I saw a ladybug crawling on the ground and I watched it crawl up and over a rock and keep right on going. Then one of the officer's boots came closer on the USA side of the fence and they were black leather boots and the left one had a big scratch on the toe.

"What's your name?" he asked.

And I said, "I am not a threat."

"I'll determine that, thank you. Just answer the question. What's your name?"

"My name is Denny Voss."

"When were you born?"

"I was born January twelfth, 1995, in Duluth, Minnesota, and it snowed all day until I got myself born at 2:42 p.m., then the sun came out and it stayed out for the rest of the day, which is a good sign, no matter how you look at it."

And he said, "Are you being smart with me?"

And I said, "No."

That's when a Ford F-250 came toward me through the grass in Canada with orange lights flashing on top and **CBSA** written on the side, and a man and a woman got out and they were wearing dark-blue uniforms and bulletproof vests, and they also had walkie-talkies and guns. And my heart was still going BOOM-BOOM-BOOM when they walked over to me, and the officer from Canada nodded at the Border Patrol officers in the USA, then he looked down at me and said, "I need to see your driver's license."

But I didn't have one of those so I held myself very still and I watched the ladybug crawl away from me in the grass and I didn't say anything.

"Do you speak English?" he asked.

And I said, "All the time."

He squatted beside me. "Are you trying to be funny?"

I thought about that, and I said, "No, I'm not a funny guy. Angus is funny. He does jokes, but I don't do jokes."

The man frowned. "Who's Angus?"

And I said, "We work together."

He stood up and looked around. "Is he here with you?"

And I said, "Not today."

"So, you're here alone?"

"No, I'm here with Tom Hanks."

He put his hands on his hips. "All right, enough with the comedy act. Stand up and put your hands behind your head." So I did, then he said, "Don't move," so I didn't, and while the officers in the USA watched, he checked my pockets while his lady partner from Canada pointed her gun at me.

And I said, "I don't have any drugs."

And he said, "We'll see about that."

This is what he found in my pockets: a red whistle for emergencies, an elastic band (yellow), two quarters, and my house key on the key chain Angus gave me that says **One of a Kind**. When he was done, the Canada officer looked at the USA officers and he said, "There's no ID on him," then he pointed to my bike on the other side of the fence where my knapsack was hanging on the handle. "Can you check that for me?"

One of the USA officers walked over to my knapsack, and he said to me, "We're going to search your bag."

And I said, "That's okay."

And he said, "I'm not asking your permission."

And I said, "That's okay."

The woman officer came closer. "Why did you enter Canada here?" she asked, then her partner said, "Do you have any weapons?" and, "Where do you live?" And my mind started jumping around and I didn't know where Tom Hanks was, and I didn't even care anymore—I just wanted to go home. That's when I started to feel dizzy and my arms were tired from holding my hands behind my head, and my heart was going **boom-boom-boom** so to calm myself down I closed my eyes and sang the theme song for *Toy Story*—"You've Got a Friend in Me."

I heard someone say, "I need this shit like a hole in the head."

Then someone else shouted, "Stop singing!"

So I did.

When I opened my eyes, one of the officers in the USA had my knapsack. "Do you have any alcohol, tobacco, or drugs in here?" he asked, and I said, "Yes, I have a drug that makes you feel better when you're itchy."

They all stared at me, but no one said anything. The USA officer looked inside my knapsack and he found apple juice, Benadryl, duct tape, and a hoodie Angus bought me with these words on the front: **An Apple a Day Will Keep Anyone Away If You Throw It Hard Enough.** Then he opened zippers to the smaller areas and he found my Toronto Raptors Velcro wallet, and inside was my library card, my DOT badge for work, and a piece of paper Nana-Jo put in there with her name and phone number for emergencies.

By then I was thirsty and I wanted to go home.

The CBSA woman officer from Canada came closer. "What's your name?" she asked, and I said, "Denny," then she said, "Are you seeking asylum, Denny?" and I didn't know what that meant, but she was talking to me real nice-like and I thought maybe she was doing flirting with me, so I looked away because I didn't want to accidentally stare at her boobs.

"Denny, why did you cross the border here?" she asked.

"I'm looking for Tom Hanks."

She frowned. "Tom Hanks doesn't live in Canada."

And I said, "He does now."

One of the USA officers said, "Technically, he's in your jurisdiction," and the CBSA woman put her hand up and said, "Could you please give us a minute?" Then she turned to her partner, and she whispered, "Did Tom Hanks move to Canada?" and he shrugged and said, "Damned if I know."

And I wanted to explain but I felt like I couldn't breathe because the CBSA man officer still had his gun pointed at me, and I could see right into the barrel where the bullets come from, then I started to stutter, which also happened when Mr. Timko pointed a knife at me that time when I knocked on his door and he was holding a bloody steak.

"I . . . I drug—drugged Tom Hanks—"

The CBSA woman officer turned back to me. "What did you say?"

And I wanted her to know I was a good guy, doing a good thing by bringing Tom Hanks to Canada to see his special mate, so I kept talking. "I drag—drag—dragged him out of his swim—swimming pool . . ."

One of the USA officers said, "He's obviously on something," and the CBSA woman put her hand up again and said, "Could you *please* give us a minute here?"

"Then I . . . I kid—kid—kidnapped him . . ."

"You kidnapped Tom Hanks?" she said.

And I said, "Yes."

Her eyes got big. "Did you hurt him, Denny? Did you hurt Tom Hanks?"

I shrugged. "He would—wouldn't wake up."

A bunch of quiet followed.

The CBSA male officer pushed a button on his walkie-talkie and he talked into it and said, "We've got a situation here. We're going to need RCMP backup . . ." Then he pulled out his handcuffs and he came toward me, and everything started to spin and wobble, and I smacked the side of my head to make the stuttering stop, then I took a deep breath and did some moaning because it felt like nobody was *listening*, and that's when the CBSA male officer pulled out his Taser and zapped me.

—Zap, Zap, Zappppp!

My mouth opened and I could feel my teeth click-clack-clicking and then my legs stopped working and I dropped to the ground, and it felt like I was bouncing around on the grass, and the officer who tased me put his knee on my back and he pulled my arms together behind me and he snapped the handcuffs on.

And it hurt.

A lot.

And that's when I peed myself.

The officer grabbed my arm and helped me up, but my legs were all noodly and I could feel the warm wet spreading down my pants. Then he quickly let go and stepped back, and he said, "I don't get paid enough for this," and one of the USA officers said, "Yup, he is definitely in your jurisdiction."

The CBSA man officer looked at the sky.

"You got something for him to sit on?" the USA officer asked and the CBSA man officer sighed and said, "Yeah, we've got a tarp we can throw in the back seat." Then I saw the CBSA woman officer look at my pants and she made a scrunched-up face, and that's when I knew she wasn't doing flirting with me.

I felt sick inside, and dizzy, and my heart was still going **BOOM-BOOM-BOOM**, then my throat closed up and I felt like I couldn't breathe, and I felt my mind shrink down to a tiny ball, and—**BAM!**—that was it, I went away for a while and I didn't come back until the door to the room they put me in in Canada opened and Nana-Jo came inside with my knapsack and a bottle of water and some clean clothes for me to change into.

And I said to her, "I tried to fix the Tom Hanks problem by myself."

And she said, "Yes, I heard."

Nana-Jo doesn't like talking about my trip to Canada and she doesn't think I should talk about it either, but now that I'm incarcerated for murder, Dr. Harland thinks the first time I got myself arrested is *how this whole mess got started*. And he said, "Because that's when you truly started thinking for yourself, Denny. It's also the first time you didn't have a gatekeeper to make sure your life didn't go off the rails."

I can also tell you this: RCMP officers (Royal Canadian Mounted Police) don't wear red jackets and funny hats and they stopped riding horses back in 1936. They drive cars now just like police officers do in the USA. Also, CBSA officers are called Canada Border Services Agents and they're really nice people—except when they have to tase you because that's their job—and if you're hungry or thirsty they'll give you something to eat and drink, but they don't have maple syrup in their offices at the border, and they don't have ice rinks there, and there are no shopping malls nearby either.

Newspaper Story #1

I asked Angus to bring my scrapbook to the jail so I could show Dr. Harland the newspaper story about the first time I got myself arrested, then after I showed Dr. Harland, Angus took it home again because I'm not allowed to keep things like that in my jail cell.

Man from Woodmont Arrested at Canadian Border for Mischief
by Rhonda Wood

Denny Voss, 29, of Woodmont, Minn., was detained on Wednesday at the Canadian border by CBSA agents and arrested by the RCMP following an incident that occurred after Mr. Voss illegally crossed the border into Canada.

Border Services and the CBSA responded to a call reporting a man who had jumped a farmer's fence into Canada with a goose. It has been reported that Mr. Voss was allegedly trying to release the goose, a pet named Tom Hanks, back into Canada, where he felt it belonged because he believed the goose was sad and depressed living in the U.S.

CBSA detained Mr. Voss using a Taser, and the RCMP arrested him without incident. Tom Hanks the pet goose has yet to be found.

Doing Consequences

A few days after I kidnapped Tom Hanks and me and Nana-Jo got ourselves out of Canada, the Woodmont police came to our house, but it wasn't like in one of those fast-moving TV shows because they didn't have their guns out. Nana-Jo showed them my official papers that say I'm *developmentally challenged*, then the next day we went to the courthouse to talk to a lady judge and she said the Timkos gave her a video from their security camera that showed me kidnapping Tom Hanks from their yard. And I said, "Wow, I didn't know they had a security camera," and she said, "Clearly not." Then she leaned forward, and said, "What do you have to say for yourself, Mr. Voss?"

"Sorry?"

"Sorry isn't good enough. There needs to be some kind of reparation."

"What's that?"

"Consequences for what you did wrong."

Then Nana-Jo did talking with the judge and she asked if I could do community service (jobs you don't get paid for) to make up for what I did and the judge said that'd be acceptable, but she also wanted me to apologize to the Timkos, so the next day me and Nana-Jo knocked on their door and Mrs. Timko answered, and I said, "I'm sorry for kidnapping Tom Hanks," and she burst out crying.

Then she said, "Did he suffer?"

And I said, "Who?"

"Tom Hanks. You killed him, didn't you?"

"No, I took him to Canada so he could be with his special mate."

Nana-Jo bumped me with her elbow, then I coughed and said, "Um . . . I watched him waddle away and he looked very happy," which was a lie, but Nana-Jo was 99 percent sure that's what happened and she said the kindest thing to do would be to tell Mrs. Timko that, so that's what I did, and because I'm a good liar Mrs. Timko believed me.

Before we left, I also gave her a birdhouse I built to show her I was sorry. I'd painted it yellow and it had a perch for a bird to rest on and a hole for it to go inside and make a nest. Mrs. Timko looked surprised, then she blew her nose and said she wanted to be alone, so we left. A few days later I saw her hang it from a tree in her yard, then two swallows moved in and Mrs. Timko started sitting on her porch to watch them while she drank her morning coffee, and I know all that because sometimes I'd sit on our steps and watch her to see if she was done being sad and moving on to being happy again.

I also did something Nana-Jo calls *killing them with kindness*, which goes like this: Every time I saw the Timkos I waved, even though they never waved back and Mr. Timko usually gave me the middle finger, but then one day Mrs. Timko finally did a small wave back, and I told Nana-Jo and she said that was good, because now we were *on the road to healing*, which is a good road to be on.

So instead of going to prison for kidnapping Tom Hanks, I had to do one hundred hours of consequences and when I finished Nana-Jo had to sign an official form saying I'd done those hours (no lying), then we had to give that form to the judge. And for my consequences the judge said I could 1) pick up garbage around town, 2) volunteer at the library, and/or 3) mow lawns, and I said to Nana-Jo, "It's going to take me a long time to finish a hundred hours," but she said that was okay because when I was done I would have learned a valuable lesson (which means I'll never want to do another kidnapping).

One week later, I was busy picking up garbage in downtown Woodmont and I was wearing an orange vest for safety and the *Top*

Gun aviator sunglasses Angus helped me buy from the internet (same ones Maverick wears). A woman came out of the old laundromat, which had been closed for a long time but now it had a new sign with soap bubbles on it that said **The Laundry Basket**.

"Thanks for doing this," she said to me.

"You're welcome."

I threw an empty soda can into my garbage bag, then I looked up at her and did a freeze, the kind where you go very still and your eyes look left and then right before you decide which way to run, because I'd met her before, only this time she was smiling instead of throwing a water bottle at me.

She used to drive the Frito-Lay truck that came to Woodmont on Tuesdays and Fridays to deliver snacks to Walmart and Lucky Dollar Foods. I'd seen her driving the truck, but I'd never seen her up close, then one day I was in line to buy milk at Lucky Dollar Foods and the store was playing music, and the till was beep-beep-beeping . . . and she walked in with her clipboard and all the loud went quiet.

I set my milk on the counter.

And I stared and stared.

She had freckles and wild kinky hair and eyes the color of coffee beans. She also had a tiny silver ring in the left nostril of her nose and she was wearing a red shirt with **Frito-Lay** on the pocket and that's how I knew she was a Frito-Lay delivery specialist. The store manager was an old guy and he walked up to her and they did talking, then he said something that made her laugh, and she went to the back of the store to use the bathroom, and I bought my milk and went outside and put it in my bike basket.

And I got on my bike and then I got off again because I couldn't remember what I was supposed to do next.

The Frito-Lay truck was parked out front and painted on one side was Chester Cheetah and a huge bag of Cheetos, and on the driver's door it said **Frito-Lay: Good Fun!** and there were eight crates stacked on a dolly next to the truck and each crate was filled with bags of

Doritos and Cheetos and Lay's potato chips, and that's when I decided to do a good deed, which is also called being kind.

So, I wheeled that dolly into Lucky Dollar Foods and I started putting those snack bags on the shelves in the snack aisle and I made sure they were neat and tidy and that the front of each bag was facing forward with no wrinkles on it.

Then the Frito-Lay girl came around the corner. "Um . . . excuse me? What do you think you're doing?"

And I said, "I'm doing a good deed."

"Please don't. It's against company policy for someone else to do my job," and she seemed a bit grumpy, so I said, "Okay, just a second," and I kept working because I wasn't finished putting all the snack bags on the shelves.

"Please stop," she said.

"Just a sec." I tried to work faster.

She put her hands on her hips. "I'm calling the manager!"

"Just a sec."

And she said, "I'm sick of secs!" which sounded like *I'm sick of sex* and if Angus was there I knew he'd snort-laugh and that made me smile, and that's when she got angry. "All right, that's enough! What's your name?" And I could tell she was mad and if she gave the manager my name he'd call Nana-Jo and I'd get in trouble, and this was a few months before I got my job at DOT, when Nana-Jo used to say I had *too much time on my hands*.

The Frito-Lay girl came closer. "I said what's your name?"

I put the last bag of Doritos on the shelf, made sure the front was facing forward, and smoothed out the wrinkles, then—**BAM!**—I turned and ran down the aisle and around the corner and the Frito-Lay girl chased me, shouting, "Get back here!" and that's when she threw a water bottle at me and it hit me in the leg, but I didn't stop—I ran like the wind and I jumped on my bike and *I got the hell out of Dodge*.

That was three years ago. Since then, I've seen her around Woodmont a few times. One time at Walmart, another time at Dr.

Baker's office when I walked in and she was talking to the receptionist so I turned around and left, and also last year at the bingo hall, when I saw her sitting with an older lady at the front of the room. And now here she was again, only now she wasn't wearing a red shirt with **Frito-Lay** on the pocket; she was wearing an apron with **The Laundry Basket** written on it.

"Do you have a ladder?" she asked.

I blinked at her behind my sunglasses. "Um, not here? I have one at home, though." Then my insides went all noodly because of her freckles and all that wild kinky hair, which was longer than it used to be.

She turned and waved at the building. "Listen, would you be interested in cleaning my windows? We're having our grand opening this weekend and I need them cleaned before then. I'd be happy to pay you."

I did a swallow and said, "Maybe I can do them for free as part of my consequences?" and then she looked confused, so I said, "The judge told me I have to do a hundred hours of community service."

"Oh, I see," she said. "Why? What'd you do?"

"I kidnapped Tom Hanks."

"The movie star?!"

"No, a goose."

She frowned again, so I said, "They have the same name."

"Right," she said. "Well, let me know about the windows. Like I said, I'm happy to pay you but I need them cleaned in the next few days. I'm Nori, by the way." She stuck her hand out and I gave it a shake.

"I'm Denny."

"Nice to meet you, Denny." Then she tilted her head and looked at me very closely. "Have we met before?"

I thought about doing a lie—Angus says the secret of a good lie is to keep it simple and never overexplain—but then I looked at Nori and my insides tipped over and I was 100 percent honest instead. "Sort of? You threw a water bottle at me a few years ago when I was doing a good deed with your Frito-Lay snack bags, but you didn't tell me your name then, so I guess maybe we haven't met before?"

"Wait. What?!" Nori's eyes got big. Then she pointed at me. "Oh my God, yes, I remember now! That was really . . . strange."

And I stared past her and waited for my 100 percent honesty to *bite me in the ass* (which is when you realize you probably should have lied instead). Then I coughed and said, "Maybe it was strange, but you were a Frito-Lay delivery specialist, which is my dream job, and when I saw someone else doing my actual dream job and she was above-average pretty instead of ho-hum ordinary, I messed up and did the wrong thing."

Nori opened her mouth, then closed it again, and tucked a piece of wild kinky hair behind her ear. To me, she suddenly looked tired. And I watched her do thinking and I thought maybe she was going to say, *You're ridiculous,* or *That's absurd,* so I waited and waited for those words, but instead she did a sigh.

"Why don't we start fresh? I'm Nori. It's nice to meet you, Denny."

And I said, "Same."

That's when a little boy came outside wearing a bathing suit with socks and sandals and Nori said, "This is my son, Theo."

And he stood a bit behind her, watching us, and his left shoulder kept jumping up and down and he was making weird faces (blink/twitch/blink). I watched him for a bit, then I said to Nori, real quiet-like, "Is he all right?" and she said, "He's fine. Theo has Tourette's syndrome. It's a disorder that causes tics." She pulled him closer and messed up his hair. "They usually only show up when he's stressed."

I thought about that. "Does he take medication?"

Nori shook her head. "He does not."

"Me either."

I looked at Theo. "I've got stuff wrong with me too. I didn't get enough oxygen when I was being born and Nana-Jo always says, 'There are no pills to fix what you've got, Denny, so deal with it.' So, that's what I do—I deal with it."

"Who's Nana-Jo?" Theo asked.

"She's my mom. She knows everything worth knowing. She's also one of the best human beings on this planet."

"Sounds like my mom," Theo said—blink/twitch/blink.

I asked him if he ever got bullied and he said, "Sometimes," and I said, "Same." Then I said, "George has stuff wrong with him too," and Theo asked who George was and I told him he's my dog. "He's blind and deaf but there are no pills to fix what he's got either. George just deals with it, same as you and me."

Theo nodded. "I don't take pills, but I take vitamins."

And I said, "Me too."

Theo leaned against his mom. "Mine are chewable."

"You're lucky. Nana-Jo says chewables are too expensive, so I take no-name caplets instead. I used to take iron caplets because my iron was *ridiculously low* but then it jumped up again, so Dr. Baker said I don't have to take them anymore." After that it got quiet again and Theo looked a bit pale to me, so I said to him, "How's *your* iron?"

Nori said, "It's fine, Denny. He eats lots of spinach."

Then I ran out of things to say and I got nervous inside because I don't have many friends and I know if you want to make friends you need to do visiting and ask people about themselves so I said to Nori, "I like your apron," and, "Why is Theo wearing socks with his sandals?" and, "How old is he?" and, "Does he go to school yet?"

Nori blinked at me. "Um . . . I like this apron too? And I guess maybe he wears socks with his sandals because his feet are cold? Theo's six and a half. He starts first grade this fall."

I looked at Theo. "You'll like first grade because Tuesday is Hot Dog Day and Wednesday is Pizza Day and you make Play-Doh on Thursdays, and when you graduate you wear a purple hat with a tassel and everyone sings the graduation song, which uses up all the letters in *first grade*, and it starts with '*F* is for *friendly*, because that's what we are!' and it ends with '*E* is for *excited.* Second grade, here we come!'"

Theo's eyes got big, but he wasn't blinking and twitching as much and his left shoulder wasn't jumping up and down anymore.

Nori wiped her hands on her apron. "We moved here last month. Theo starts swim lessons today and he's nervous about it."

I said to Theo, "I used to get stressed about swim lessons too. Me and Nana-Jo took a parent-and-tot class when I was four and I had to wear water wings, and I learned how to bob and splash in the pool. Then I became a Jellyfish when I was five—no parents allowed—and we wore life jackets and I learned how to get in and out of the pool safely, and how to put my face in the water. After that I became a Tadpole and when you're a Tadpole you learn how to float and kick with your feet. I kept sinking, though, so I stayed being a Tadpole for a few years, then I became a Minnow and that's when I learned how to swim on my stomach."

"Was it hard?" Theo asked.

"Yeah, but it was also fun. And after I graduated from being a Minnow, I became a Guppy and that's when you learn how to tread water," and Theo said, "What comes after a Guppy?" and I said, "You become a Dolphin," then he said, "What do you learn when you're a Dolphin?" and I shrugged and said, "I don't know. I'm still a Guppy."

Theo stepped out from behind his mom. "I was a Tadpole when we lived in Moorhead but now I'm a Minnow."

And I said, "That's cool." Then it got quiet again and nobody was talking so I turned to Nori and said, "I'll go ask Nana-Jo if I can clean your windows with my ladder," and I walked over to my bike and got on it and I left for home, and when I looked back Nori was shaking her head and Theo was smiling.

And I waved at them.

And they waved back.

And that's how I made two new friends doing visiting after I did consequences the judge made me do because I did a kidnapping.

Sparkle and Shine

I asked Nana-Jo if I could wash windows at the Laundry Basket for free as part of my consequences and she said yes, then she asked Angus if he could drop the ladder off for me because it wouldn't fit in her car, and he was grumpy because it wasn't on his way to work but he said he'd do it anyhow. So, I got up at 6:30 a.m. the next day and I put a bucket in my bike basket and inside the bucket I put a sponge and vinegar and Dawn dish soap and tea towels. Then I biked to the Laundry Basket and sat outside on a bench and waited for Angus to drop off the ladder. He finally got there at 8:38 a.m. and he was wearing a T-shirt that said **I'M AWAKE BUT THAT DOESN'T MEAN I'M READY TO DO STUFF.**

Angus unloaded the ladder. "I'll pick it up on my way home," he said, and I said, "Thanks," then he left, and Nori came outside and she was wearing an apron with **THE LAUNDRY BASKET** written on it, and she had rubber gloves on.

"I'm allowed to clean your windows for free," I said, and she said, "Thanks, Denny." Then I held up my bucket and said, "I brought vinegar," and she frowned, so I said, "Vinegar is the secret ingredient for cleaning windows."

And she said, "Well, you're the expert."

And I said, "No, that's Nana-Jo."

I told Nori if she wanted her windows to SPARKLE AND SHINE she had to mix one cup of vinegar with two drops of Dawn dish soap and one gallon of warm water, then start washing at the TOP of the window and work your way down to the BOTTOM using lots of elbow grease (hard rubbing), then dry the window starting at the TOP and work your way to the BOTTOM using the same tea towels Nana-Jo uses (cotton waffle weave, which won't leave bits of fluff behind). I told her this would make her windows SPARKLE AND SHINE because Nana-Jo said so and she's a cleaning expert and you should always listen to experts.

Theo was standing at the window inside the Laundry Basket but he didn't have a shirt on, so I waved at him and said to Nori, "Are his clothes in a washing machine?"

"No, he just woke up. We live upstairs. Anyhow, I really appreciate you doing this, Denny. Thanks." Then Nori went back inside and I washed her windows using lots of elbow grease and it took one hour and four minutes to do the job. When I finished, Nori came outside and tried to pay me but I told her I couldn't take her money because cleaning her windows was part of my consequences now, and she said, "Are you sure?" and I said, "Yup," then I asked her how Theo's swim lesson went and she made a scrunched-up face.

"Not good. He didn't get in the pool. His tics were real bad and the other kids kept staring at him, so he watched but he wouldn't get in."

"That's too bad."

"Yeah, it is." Nori did a sigh. "Anyhow, I'm sure things will get better when he starts school. Theo's a smart kid, way smarter than I was at his age." She did a smile. "Sometimes he leaves notes on my pillow. It's a thing for Theo, a way for him to tell me what's on his mind." She pulled a piece of paper out of her apron and showed it to me.

"He left this one last night after his swim class."

I think people don't sometimes play with me because of my Torrets.

I read it and it felt like someone had punched me in the stomach. "That makes me sad," I said, and Nori chewed on her thumbnail. "Me too. He'll make friends when school starts, though. He'll be fine." But her voice sounded funny to me and it seemed like maybe she needed a hug, but I know you aren't supposed to hug someone if you aren't friends and you don't know them real well, so I didn't.

"Nori?"

"Yeah?"

"I can be Theo's friend."

She did another sigh. "Thanks, Denny. I meant kids his own age, though."

I nodded. "Yeah, but there are no rules about friends. Like, I'm pretty sure you can have as many as you want? Young or old, tall or short, fat or skinny—you just have to be careful to pick good ones, which are people who have the same kind of heart you do. That's the most important thing. At least, that's what Nana-Jo says."

Nori put her fingers over her mouth. I could tell she was doing thinking about me, so I looked away and said, "I'd be a good friend to Theo."

"Yes, Denny. I'm sure you would."

Theo came outside and he was wearing pants and a T-shirt that said **Cool Kid** and socks with sandals. "Hello," he said—blink/twitch.

"Hi, Theo." Then he stood next to his mom and asked me if he could meet George sometime—blink/twitch/blink—and I looked at Nori, and she shrugged and said, "Sure. I'd like to meet him too." And that's when I thought about how Theo *didn't* get in the swimming pool with the other kids and how he'd left that note on his mom's pillow, and I had what Nana-Jo calls a *realization* (which is when you understand what's what and you think you might know how to fix something that isn't working).

"Hey, Theo?" I said. "Why don't I bring George to the swimming pool and we'll watch your next swim lesson?" Theo's eyes got big—blink/twitch/blink—then he said, "Are dogs allowed in the building?" and I said, "Not regular dogs, but therapy dogs are."

"What's a therapy dog?"

"They're super-gentle dogs that make you feel better when you're scared or anxious or stressed out about stuff."

"George is a therapy dog?"—blink/twitch/blink.

And I said, "Yup," which was only partway true because George doesn't actually have *official papers* that say he's a therapy dog, but after I adopted him Angus got him a harness from the internet with **Therapy Dog** embroidered on it in big red letters and now we can take him with us almost anywhere.

Nori did a smile. "Theo's next lesson is at four o'clock on Friday."

And I said, "All right, I'll come watch you, Theo, and I'll bring George but I won't bring my bullhorn because they aren't allowed in the building anymore, ever since Angus got himself thrown out after he went berserk using it to cheer for a woman he liked who was doing synchronized swim lessons."

"Who's Angus?"—blink/twitch/blink.

"He's my cousin."

"What's *berserk* mean?"

I thought about that, and then I said, "It's when you use too much face paint and too much enthusiasm with a bullhorn to cheer for people who are taking swim lessons," then I said, "So yeah, me and George will be there Friday, but no bullhorn."

—

On Friday I took George to the swimming pool and we walked into the building past a sign that said **No Dogs Allowed** and I sat at the end of the bleachers at the bottom and George lay down at my feet. A few minutes later, a security guard came over and asked us to leave, and I pointed to George's harness and told him he was a therapy dog. Then he held out his hand and asked to see George's papers, and I said they were at home in our basement freezer with all our other official papers, and he stared at me for a bit, doing thinking, then he pointed at George and he said, "If he barks once, he's out of here!"

But he didn't.

Because George almost never barks.

So yeah, for the next four months, before I got myself arrested in January with all those guns, me and George went to all of Theo's swim lessons and the security guard never asked to see George's papers again. And it was the best four months EVER because I was helping Theo find his courage and me and George were busy, which was nice.

That first time, Nori sat beside us and when Theo came out of the dressing room in his swimsuit he was twitching and blinking but then he saw us, and he got in the water with the other kids. He hung on to the side of the pool for most of the class—blink/twitch/blink—then near the end he finally let go and did what everyone else was doing. And he did the same thing at his next lesson, but after that it got better and soon he was hardly blinking and twitching at all and he wasn't hanging on to the side of the swimming pool anymore either.

While Theo did all those swim lessons, me and Nori watched him and did visiting and pretty soon I forgot about her freckles and all that wild kinky hair, and that's when I knew we were becoming *actual friends*—like me and Angus, only when I told Nori about a bad day at work she didn't lip-synch Taylor Swift's song "Shake It Off" to cheer me up, she just nodded and said, "That sounds rough," and when I told her what happened at the border after I kidnapped Tom Hanks, she laughed and laughed, and said, "I can't believe they tased you!"

Nori has THE BEST laugh.

And she told me some of her own stories too.

She said Theo's dad *wasn't in the picture*, that he'd taken off a week before Theo was born and she hadn't seen him since. She had Theo when she was twenty-one and they lived in Chicago for a few years, then she got her job with Frito-Lay and they moved to Moorhead and she put him in day care when she did her deliveries. She said it was sometimes lonely being a single parent but she loved her beautiful twitchy boy more than anything in the world. She also showed me a picture of

Theo when he was a baby (bald, chubby, no teeth) and another one of him on his third birthday (kinky hair, less chubby, little teeth).

Then one week before Theo took his Minnow swim test, he lost a tooth, and a few days later Nori showed me a note she found under his pillow. "I forgot to leave money for him three nights in a row, so he left this," she said, laughing.

<u>tooth fairy</u>

please don't rip me off. leave money for my tooth
I worked hard to pull it out

After I read that I felt sad for Theo, and I said, "It's hard to pull out a wobbly tooth all by yourself, Nori," and she said, "I know, Denny, it's just that when I read this, I saw a tiny flash of the kid Theo was *before* we moved here and I wanted to show you, that's all." And I stared at her and said, "So are you going to leave money for him?" and Nori said, "Yes, I'll leave it under his pillow tonight." Then I asked if she needed to borrow some money, because that's what friends do for each other, and Nori said, "No, Denny. I'm fine. I've got this." And she did—after Theo's next swim lesson, he opened his Velcro wallet and he showed me a brand-new five-dollar bill the tooth fairy had left for him.

So yeah, everything got itself worked out.

Me and George were at the swimming pool with Nori when Theo passed his Minnow test and became a Guppy, and he ran over and hugged George. Then we walked to the Doughnut Hole and got doughnuts to celebrate (vanilla sprinkle for me, long johns for Nori, Theo, and George) and it was an EXCELLENT DAY because Theo wasn't blinking or twitching, he was just happy, the way six-year-old kids should be.

When me and George said goodbye that day, Theo said, "Thanks for coming to my lessons, Denny. You and George are my lucky charms."

And I said, "No problem."

One month later, Theo started taking Guppy swim lessons on Thursdays after school and, same as before, me and George went to watch him. So yeah, that's how me and Nori and Theo became actual friends. We spent time together and they both fell in love with George, same as everybody else. Theo had lessons every week until Christmas and after that the swimming pool closed itself down for what's called a winter break and Theo's final Guppy test got put on the schedule for the end of January.

Then everything went sideways when I got myself arrested at the bottom of Penguin Hill with all those guns and bullets.

Doing Training at Home

Same as always, Dr. Harland was waiting in our special meeting room this morning and we ate our doughnuts and talked about the weather (very cold) and the snow (lots of it), then he said, “Did you want something to drink, Denny?” and I said, “No, thank you.” Then he did a stretch with his arms, and said, “Would you like to chat a bit more before we get to work?” and I said, “Yes, please,” because when we do chatting Dr. Harland doesn’t write in his notebook and he doesn’t ask questions about Mr. Tesky.

So yeah, no pressure.

Also, when we do chatting *before* we do work we both get to ask questions and today it was my turn to ask first because he asked first last time, and I had my question ready. “Where did you get your training from?” I asked, and he said, “The University of Pennsylvania,” and I said, “Is that far away from here?” and he said, “It’d take twenty-four hours to get there if you drove, so yes, it is quite far from here.”

And I said, “I got most of my training at home.”

Dr. Harland lifted his eyebrows. “Really? I’d love to hear more about that.”

So I told him more.

I told him how I went to school with all the other kids in Woodmont when I was little, but then Nana-Jo pulled me out when I was twelve and we did the rest of my training at home. And I was waiting for her in the principal’s office when she picked me up that last day because Joey Gobel dumped paint on my head in art class (inky black) and when Nana-Jo walked in and saw me her face got red, and she said, "Enough is enough."

The principal, Mr. Berman, was fixing his comb-over with his fingers (which is hair that's used to cover a bald patch) and he said, "Joanne, can we talk about this?" and Nana-Jo said, "No, we cannot." Then she helped me clean out my locker and we were putting everything in a plastic bin when two boys walked by and one was Billy Kopp, and he said, "Look, it's the half-wit." And I whispered to Nana-Jo, "He's the one who beat me up in fifth grade," and she said, "Really?" then she reached out and tapped Billy on the arm.

Billy turned. "What?"

Nana-Jo poked him in the chest—once, twice. "Do better!" she said. "Try acting like a decent human being. It's not that hard." That's when Mr. Berman came around the corner and me and Nana-Jo walked past him, and when he said, "Joanne, please . . . ," she just kept walking and I followed her with my plastic bin.

I've always loved Nana-Jo, but that day I loved her extra.

When Papa-Jo came home from his work at Voss Welding that night, Nana-Jo told him what happened and he came upstairs to my room and asked if I was all right, and I said, "Yup," and he said, "Are you sure?" and I said, "You got it, cowboy," because I didn't want him to do worrying about me.

Nana-Jo was an excellent teacher. After she pulled me out of school, she taught me all about right and wrong and how to have good manners, like not talking when my mouth is full (rude) and not interrupting when other people are talking (rude) and to never scratch my genitals in public (very rude). She taught me not to stand too close to people (freaks them out) and not to hug someone unless they asked to be hugged (you might get punched) and to never ever stare at a woman's boobs. She also taught me how much things cost at the grocery store and as part of my training we watched *The Price Is Right* on TV every day at 4:00 p.m. (still do). She taught me how to make a budget, how to pay bills, and how to put money in my bank account to *save for a rainy day*. She showed me how to grow a garden (which we do every year) and how to wash clothes (which we do every Sunday) and how to cut the grass with a push mower (which I do every week in the summer). And she also took me to the library every Tuesday so we could do reading together and I got real good at it.

She also said I shouldn't drink alcohol or do drugs (which I don't).

But some of her training didn't work.

Nana-Jo said I should always follow the rules, but sometimes I don't. Also, when I get angry she said I should count to ten to calm myself down (never works) and if a situation goes sideways on me, I should take deep breaths to keep myself calm (never works). Then one day at the firepit I told Angus those things weren't working for me and he took a drink of beer and said, "Well . . . instead of counting to ten or taking deep breaths, maybe try singing the theme song for *Toy Story*—'You've Got a Friend in Me.'"

"Do you think that'll work?"

He laughed and said, "Can't fucking hurt, buddy!"

So the next time things went sideways, I sang the theme song for *Toy Story* and everyone around me got very quiet, very fast, and my heart stopped going **BOOM-BOOM-BOOM** . . . so now that's what I do whenever things go sideways.

Papa-Jo did some of my training at home too. Before he died, he taught me how to clean the gutters (which I do every October) and how to change the furnace filter (which I do every four months). He also taught me how to do target shooting with tin cans and grapefruits. Then after he died, Nana-Jo found out his business had too many employees and not enough customers, and he also didn't have life insurance (official papers your family can cash in for money after you die) so she had to shut down Voss Welding.

There were lots of people at his funeral and a whole bunch of flowers and Uncle Maynard and Aunt Ruby organized everything because Nana-Jo wouldn't get out of bed. There was a big photo of Papa-Jo at the front of the church on a stand and at the bottom it said: *Joseph Voss, loving son, brother, husband, and father.* It was my favorite photo of Papa-Jo because he was laughing and behind him in the sky was a rainbow and he had his head tilted back and it looked like the rainbow was coming out of his mouth. Me and Nana-Jo sat up front with Lydia and Angus and Uncle Maynard and Aunt Ruby, and the minister read from the Bible and people were crying, and Nana-Jo kept squeezing my hand, and then the minister said Papa-Jo was a good man who never should've died so young.

Dr. Harland tap-tap-tapped his pencil against the table. "Denny, let's back up a bit. You said Papa-Jo taught you how to do target shooting?"

"Uh-huh."

He did a frown. "How old were you then?"

"First I was twelve, then I was thirteen, and then fourteen."

Dr. Harland asked how often Papa-Jo took me target shooting, and I said, "Only when Nana-Jo was at work. He'd put grapefruits on fence posts and get me to shoot them, but sometimes he'd use oranges or tin cans because they were harder to hit."

"Were you good at it?"

And I said, "I was excellent at it."

Dr. Harland nodded. "Denny, did Papa-Jo ever tell you why he thought you needed to know how to use a gun?" and I said, "So I could protect myself," and he lifted one eyebrow, and said, "From who?" and I did thinking about that, and I said, "I guess from anyone who might try to hurt me?" Then Dr. Harland wrote some words in his notebook, and he said, "And what kind of gun did you use for target shooting?"

"I used a .22 Savage Mark II rifle. It was the only gun Papa-Jo ever let me shoot. I shot it lots of times until Nana-Jo found out what we were doing, then she said I wasn't allowed to do target shooting any-more and she made Papa-Jo promise to never take me again."

Dr. Harland sat back in his chair. "Why do you think she did that?"

I looked out the window again, and said, real quiet-like, "Because Nana-Jo thinks guns are dangerous." Then he set his pencil down and he said, "And what about you, Denny? Do you think guns are dangerous?" and I looked at all the snow in the parking lot and I felt myself going **DOWN-DOWN-DOWN.**

And I said, "I do now."

Losing Papa-Jo

I asked Angus to bring my scrapbook back to the jail so I could show Dr. Harland more of the memories I keep for myself and when he got here he was wearing a T-shirt that said **ADULTING IS BULLSHIT**. And my scrapbook is green and it has one hundred pages inside and taped to those pages are memories and some are happy (they're at the front) and some are sad (they're at the back) but Nana-Jo told me happy *and* sad things happen to everyone when they're doing life and it's important to remember both.

One memory taped inside my scrapbook was a photograph of me holding the first paycheck I ever got from my job at DOT ($168) and I also had a photo of George's official adoption papers (we keep the real ones in our basement freezer). I was showing those memories to Dr. Harland when Grant knocked on the door and said our time was up, so I told Dr. Harland to take my scrapbook home with him because I'm not allowed to keep it in my cell, and before he left he asked if he could look through it on his own, and I said, "Sure," because we're on the same team, so I thought, *Why not?*

That was yesterday and today Dr. Harland was quiet while he drank his tea, then he pushed my scrapbook across the table and flipped it open to the last page. "I know this might be hard for you, Denny, but I'd like to talk about Papa-Jo if that's okay."

And my stomach got all flip-floppy because his voice sounded different. "Why do you want to talk about Papa-Jo?"

Dr. Harland said, "Because he was an important part of your life and if we want to untangle this mess and get to the truth, we need to talk about some difficult topics, and Papa-Jo is obviously one of them."

So I rocked back and forth and did thinking, and my heart started to go **BOOM-BOOM-BOOM**, then I got up and went to the window to look outside. And Dr. Harland drank his tea and watched me while I did remembering about how Papa-Jo built me a swing for my tenth birthday and how we used to go ice fishing every winter and how, the day he died, we were going to have baked potatoes and rib eye steaks for dinner (his favorite) and then we were going to watch our VHS tape of the 2009 NBA championship game with the Los Angeles Lakers even though we'd already watched it twice since they'd won.

And I thought about how I always felt safe and happy when Papa-Jo was alive, and how for a long time after he died, I didn't.

Dr. Harland tilted his head. "Are you all right, Denny?"

And I said, "No."

I walked back to the table and pulled my big green scrapbook closer. "At Papa-Jo's funeral I remember people hugging Nana-Jo and they said his death was 'a tragedy' and 'such a waste.' She didn't tell me how he died until *after* the funeral, though, then I remember doing shouting and I was **VERY ANGRY** and Uncle Maynard had to hold my arms and Angus was there too, and he kept saying, 'Calm down, buddy! Calm down.' And you know what, Dr. Harland? It was a terrible, horrible, awful day, so now, whenever people ask me about Papa-Jo, I tell them he died because his heart stopped working . . . but that's a lie, because that's not what really happened."

"I know, Denny," said Dr. Harland.

"He died because someone shot him in the back."

Dr. Harland nodded. "I know."

Taped on the last page of my scrapbook was a newspaper story that had turned yellow because it was so old, and I made myself read it even though I felt sick inside, and my heart was going **BOOM-BOOM-BOOM**.

Woodmont Man Shot and Killed in Hunting Accident

by Rhonda Wood, October 24, 2009

A day of hunting ended in tragedy Saturday when emergency crews were called to a rural area south of Woodmont. According to EMS, paramedics had to hike a mile through thick trees to find the patient.

A preliminary investigation has determined that a 62-year-old man was hunting with a friend when he was accidentally shot by a third hunter. Paramedics were unable to revive the man, who has been identified as Joseph Voss of Woodmont. He was treated at the scene and pronounced dead.

Police have confirmed that a 73-year-old man shot at what he thought was a deer and accidentally caused the fatal injury. He's currently facing a charge of careless use of a firearm in relation to the incident.

"Would you like some water?" Dr. Harland asked.

And I said, "Yes, please."

Then he got up and left the room.

And it felt like someone was running around inside my head with spiky shoes on because even though Papa-Jo died years ago, I still didn't like to think about it. The last time I read that newspaper story, I got so upset that I went away for a while, and then I heard Nana-Jo's voice and suddenly she was there beside me, smelling like Lemon Pledge, and she closed my scrapbook and said, "No, Denny. We're not doing this again. Not now."

And I said, "Okay, Nana-Jo."

Then she put an arm around my waist and she helped me climb into bed, and even though we'd just adopted George, he got up there with me and he put his head on my chest because that's just how George is.

So yeah, I don't like thinking about how Papa-Jo died.

And I don't like talking about it either.

Because after his funeral, no matter how much we missed him, or how bad it hurt that he wasn't there with us, me and Nana-Jo had to do life without him, just like we have every day since he died from that fatal gunshot wound.

Elaine-the-Stalker

Elaine-the-stalker came to visit me today and she held her phone up and showed me a picture of George asleep on my bed, and one of him asleep on the sofa, and another one of him asleep next to Nana-Jo's armchair (he sleeps a lot). Then she showed me a video of George walking up Penguin Hill and it felt like someone punched me in the stomach.

"Do you think he misses me, Elaine?"

"He misses you a lot."

And I said, "Same."

Elaine lives next door to me and Nana-Jo, and her last name is Moretti, and her family comes from a country called Italy, which is shaped like a boot. She has long curly brown hair and she's lived in Woodmont her whole life, and she's thirty-eight, which is the same age as Angus. She also used to be chubby until she lost weight, and she used to have crooked teeth until a dentist fixed them so they aren't crooked anymore.

Elaine's house has a wraparound deck with a roof over it and a hot tub that fits eight people and it used to be a side-by-side house like ours (7A and 7B) until a man who was renting 7A used a backhoe to put a fence in and he hit a gas line without knowing it, then went for lunch and the gas leaked into 7A and 7B and—**BOOM!**—the whole house blew up just like in one of those fast-moving TV shows.

It happened when everyone was at work, though, and I was at a dentist appointment with Nana-Jo, so nobody got themselves killed and none of the other houses on our street blew up. A few months later the insurance company told Elaine's dad, who owned 7A and 7B, that they'd rebuild his side-by-side house for him, but instead he had them build one house in the same spot and he gave it to Elaine, then he died a year later (heart attack). And because he left Elaine some money, she doesn't have to work, but she does because she's a *physiotherapist* and she likes her job doing massages and exercises to help people when they have trouble walking, or sitting on a toilet, or getting out of a chair *due to muscle weakness or joint trouble.*

And even though Elaine is Angus's stalker (which is a person who won't stop phoning or texting and sometimes peeks through his windows) me and Nana-Jo like her. Elaine joins us at the firepit in our backyard all the time, and when I bring out my karaoke machine, she's always the first person to get up and sing—her favorite song is "Don't You Want Me" by a band called the Human League.

Angus says he doesn't like Elaine, but I don't believe him.

Just so you know, here's what's called a family secret, because everyone in the family *knows* about it, but no one *talks* about it:

Angus and Elaine went to high school together, but Angus wasn't interested in Elaine. He liked her younger cousin, Malinda, who eventually got herself married to Mr. Tesky one month after his first wife, Irene Tesky, died from cancer.

Anyhow, twenty years ago, Angus asked Malinda if she'd be his date for his high school graduation and she said no, so he took Elaine instead. Then, after the graduation ceremony was over, Angus and Elaine *went on a tear* for a few days (partied their asses off in a crazy reckless way) and they ended up getting married at a place called the Chapel of Love. Angus filed for *an annulment* three days later (which is when *His Holiness* says a marriage that happened isn't legal) because he said he wasn't *right in the head* when he did his wedding vows. So yeah, Angus and Elaine got married twenty years ago, then they got unmarried, and now Elaine lives next door by herself, and Angus still has a crush on Elaine's cousin, Malinda (but I'm not supposed to talk about that).

A few months ago, Angus came over for dinner and he was complaining about Elaine. "Have you guys noticed who she sits next to when she comes to the firepit? Me! Every. Single. Time." Then he said, "Yesterday, she came by to drop off a piece of mail addressed to me that *accidentally* got delivered to her."

Nana-Jo smiled. "Aren't you overreacting?"

Angus pointed his fork at her. "You don't know the half of it. I made the mistake of giving her my cell number for that neighborhood watch group they put together and now she's constantly texting and sending emails."

"About the neighborhood watch?" Nana-Jo asked.

"That"—he pointed his fork at her again—"and other, more personal, things. Like last week she sent me an email asking if I was *handy* with furnaces and if I had any *tools* I could lend her, something *with a good grip*."

"Was she doing flirting with you?" I asked.

Angus threw his hands up. "Ab-so-fucking-lutely!"

Nana-Jo shook her head. "Her furnace has been acting up. She's mentioned it a few times, Angus. Did you take a look at it?"

"No, I told her to call a furnace repair company." He twisted spaghetti around his fork in an angry way. "Yesterday, I caught her looking in my kitchen window!"

Nana-Jo laughed. "She was just trying to drop off an apple crisp she baked for you. That's what neighbors do, Angus. You don't lose your mind when I come over to drop off fresh cinnamon buns."

"That's different. You're my aunt."

"Are you maybe giving her mixed signals?" Nana-Jo said.

Angus squinted at the ceiling. "How? By dating other women?! Two weeks ago, I brought a girl home and she stayed the night, and when I got up the next morning Elaine had keyed my truck." (Keying a truck is when you use the pointy end of a key to scratch **Fuck You Angus** into the paint on the door of your truck.)

Nana-Jo sighed. "I'm sorry, but I highly doubt Elaine keyed your truck. Let's face it, Angus, there's always some strange girl leaving 8A, doing the walk of shame. Maybe you upset one of them."

The next day at work, Angus told me that *doing the walk of shame* means when two people do sex and then one of them sneaks out to go home the next morning wearing the same clothes they had on the night before. And I said, "Is that like the time I came over to your house to borrow milk one morning and Elaine was there, and she was wearing your T-shirt and her underpants, but nothing else, then she got herself dressed, and when she left, she was wearing the same clothes she had on at the firepit the night before?"

Angus pulled his gloves off. "What happens between me and Elaine is none of your business, Denny! Matter of fact, I've had it up to here with you lately." He tapped his forehead like he was doing a salute. "Sure, we're related, and we work together, and we share the same yard, but that doesn't mean you get to needle me about how I'm living my life." Then he climbed into the truck and slammed the driver's door.

And we'd just finished installing a stop sign, so I loaded my shovel and the orange safety cones into the back of the truck, then I used a broom to brush the gravel away from around the bottom of the signpost to make it neat and tidy, and while I did that, I tried to figure out why Angus was so mad at me, because I never carried needles around and I'd never poke him with one either—not ever.

I got in the truck and carefully closed the door. "Hey, Angus?"

He started the truck. "What?"

"Thanks for explaining what 'the walk of shame' means," and he nodded, and said, "You're welcome." Then I said, "You're always teaching me important stuff and I want you to know I appreciate it." He nodded again, then I said, "Can I ask another question, though? What's it called when a woman like Malinda Tesky picks you up from a DOT jobsite during the day in her fancy sports car—you know, like she did last week?—and you get in with your knapsack, then you guys drive off, and when she brings you back twenty minutes later, you get in the DOT truck and stare straight ahead like nothing weird or unusual happened even though that was very weird and unusual?"

Angus turned and looked at me for a long time without blinking. "Did you tell anyone else about that, Denny?"

And I said, "No, I've never told anyone about it. I promised I wouldn't, remember? But I don't remember you saying I couldn't ask *you* questions about it." Then he flexed his hands on the steering wheel a few times, and he said, "Well, you can't. No more questions about Malinda Tesky *or* Elaine, all right?"

And I said, "Okay, Angus, I won't ask any more questions about them."

"Damn straight you won't, Einstein."

You Have a Visitor

Grant-the-guard came to my cell this morning and he said, "Denny, you have a visitor," and I said, "Is it Bridget or Dr. Harland?" and he said, "It's someone named Nori."

Nori brought me a loaf of banana bread she baked and Grant had to inspect it to make sure there were no sharp objects hidden inside to help me hurt myself or break out of jail (it's a government rule, he has to do it). And when that was done, he brought Nori to my cell, and her face looked worried.

"Hi, Denny. I decided to come because I want you to know I'm here for you."

"Thank you."

I looked past her and did thinking about how Theo high-fived me when he passed his Minnow test and how he doesn't blink or twitch when he's around me and George anymore. "Does Theo know I'm in jail?" I asked. "Did you tell him how I crashed my sled full of guns and bullets into an oak tree and how they think I killed Mr. Tesky? Because that's private, Nori, and I don't want Theo to know any of that because I'm his friend and good friends shouldn't get themselves arrested like that."

Nori stuffed her hands in her pockets. "No, Denny, he doesn't know any of that. Theo's too young for me to share that kind of stuff. I just—I told him there was a 'misunderstanding' and that you had to get it sorted out before you can come home. I decided that's all he needs to know for now."

And I said, "Thank you."

"Anyhow . . ." She waved at the banana bread. "Try some and tell me what you think."

So I did and it was terrible, but I ate it anyhow and while I did, Nori told me how business was going at the Laundry Basket (good) and how Theo was doing in first grade (better every day) and I told her I missed George and Nana-Jo but I was happy that Bridget Klein was my lawyer because she's smart and she's working hard to get me home soon. Then I asked how Theo was doing with his swim lessons.

"Not great." Nori made a face. "He failed his Guppy test and he said he doesn't want to take any more lessons."

"Don't let him quit!"

"Why not?" Nori crossed her arms. "People quit things all the time. They quit on themselves and they quit on each other. That's just life, Denny. Anyhow, it's not like he signed up and now he wants to quit halfway through. He just doesn't want to do it over again and I'm not going to make him."

I frowned and did thinking, then I called for Grant and I asked if he could get me a pencil and some paper and he did an eye roll but he got me what I needed. And I carefully wrote a note for Theo, then I gave it to Nori and I asked if she could give it to him for me, and she read the note and said, "You can't say stuff like this to a little kid, Denny."

"Why not?"

The note said, *Buck up* and *Don't be a pussy* and *Life is hard all over* and I told her Angus said those things to me all the time and Nori said, "Yeah, but you're not six years old, are you?" and I shrugged and said, "Not anymore, but Angus used to say those things to me when I was six years old too."

"Seriously? And how old was he then?"

"He was fourteen."

Nori rolled her eyes. "I'm not giving him that note, Denny."

And I said, "Okay" and "I'm sorry," then I took another piece of paper and I wrote another note and I gave it to her through the bars. "Can I say this?" I asked, and Nori read it and said, "Sure, I can give him this."

Then she told me to *hang in there.*

And she left.

A few minutes later, Dirty Doyle threw his breakfast against the wall (oatmeal) and they moved him to a new cell so they could clean up the mess, and when I got back from my meeting with Dr. Harland a lady named Kris was in the cell across from me and she was very talk-talk-talky. She said she got herself arrested because she knocked her husband out with a fry pan and I thought she was doing a joke, but she wasn't.

Kris told me she's been married for thirty years and she used to be *dewy eyed* (innocent and trusting) but now she's going through something called *the change* and her husband thinks she's *batshit crazy* (losing her mind) but she's just tired of living with a bossy guy. She said they went to church every Sunday "rain or freaking shine" and they have pork tenderloin every Wednesday "rain or freaking shine" and every year her husband signs her up for a course at their church called "How to Obey Your Husband and Be a Better Wife," but this year she refused to go, so he called her a nasty name, and she hit him with a fry pan.

I asked how many times her husband made her take that course and Kris shrugged and said, "I've lost count," and that made me sad because I've taken my driver's license test fourteen times now and I can't pass it either. So yeah, Kris was very talky, but I guess the judge didn't think she was a *flight risk* because he let her do bail and her daughter came and picked her up—and now Dirty Doyle's cell is empty again.

Grant came down the walkway to my cell and he said, "You have a visitor," and I said, "Is it Bridget or Dr. Harland?" and he said, "It's Angus."

After I got myself arrested, Angus was SUPER stressed, but eventually he relaxed and now when he comes to visit if I complain about how tough jail is, he says "cowboy up" (quit your whining) or "lean into it" (which means embrace a negative experience to make it a positive experience) and because he's an ex-convict, I listen to him. Angus got caught fishing without a license five years in a row and they gave him tickets but he never paid them, then last year he didn't show up for a court hearing so a judge *issued a bench warrant* (sent the law after Angus's ass) and he had to pay all his fines and they put him in jail for six days.

Angus came down the walkway to my cell. "How you doing, buddy?" he asked, and I said, "I'm okay." Then he said, "Lydia's outside." He tugged on his goatee. "She got here last night. She wants to see you for a few minutes." And I stared at him without blinking, then I shook my head and said, "No way, José."

Angus chewed on his thumbnail. "Come on, Denny, don't be like that. She's here to check on Nana-Jo and see how you're holding up."

"Tell her I'm holding up fine."

"Can you just talk to her for a few minutes?"

"No," I said. "I don't want to see Lydia." And I climbed onto my too-small bed and I pulled my scratchy blanket over me and I hummed "It Wasn't Me" by Shaggy until Angus finally said, "You're a stubborn ass," and left.

Angus can get mad all he wants, though, because I know he doesn't like Lydia that much either. He always says she either doesn't try at all or she tries too hard, and today, because she had him bring her to the jail to see me, she's obviously trying too hard. Angus also says Lydia's conceited (always looking at herself in the mirror) and that instead of dressing like the forty-eight-year-old grown-ass woman she is, she dresses like she's in her twenties.

After she slapped me that time when George drooled on her pants, Lydia didn't call or come visit us for years, which really upset Nana-Jo, then *out of the blue* she called one night to tell Nana-Jo about a photography award she'd won. I remember that night real well because the next day a leaky water pipe Angus had fixed for us snapped off and our basement flooded, and I went down there to clean up the mess and while I was down there cleaning up I did snooping even though I knew I shouldn't.

And that's when everything went sideways.

And it was all Lydia's fault.

So instead of doing a visit with Lydia at the jail, I did thinking about Nori and Theo and George (who I missed) and Nana-Jo (who was still in the hospital) and I also did thinking about the mess I was in, and that's when I figured out that maybe I wouldn't have gotten myself arrested for murdering Mr. Tesky if I'd just thrown that stupid handgun away instead of putting it in my sled with all of Papa-Jo's rifles and bullets.

Saving George

Dr. Harland was late this morning so Grant-the-corrections-officer (he told me nobody calls them *guards* anymore) stayed with me in the meeting room and we played tic-tac-toe while we waited (Grant won four times, I lost four times), then Dr. Harland came in with our doughnuts and Grant left. And I was eating mine, doing humming, when Dr. Harland said, "Denny, can I ask you a question off the record?" and I said, "What's that mean?" and he said, "It means we'd just be visiting. It's not an official question."

And I said, "Sure."

Dr. Harland lifted his hands. "I know you aren't ready to talk about Mr. Tesky yet and I respect that and I respect your boundaries." He leaned forward. "I am curious about something, though. What was he like?"

I wiped my hands on a napkin. "You never met him?"

"No. I saw his campaign posters, but I never met him."

So I looked out the window and I thought about it, and because Dr. Harland wore vests like Papa-Jo used to, and he brought me a vanilla sprinkle doughnut every day, and we were almost friends, I said, "Mr. Tesky wasn't a good guy. He was a liar and a cheater and he was someone who likes to fire people." Then I took a deep breath because I'd never told anyone this part before: "He also tried to kill George."

Dr. Harland spit out his apple fritter. "He tried to kill *your dog*?!"

He picked up the apple fritter chunks with a napkin and threw them in the garbage, and I told him how Mr. Tesky trying to kill George was upsetting to think about because a world without George in it would be a very sad world.

Dr. Harland said, "When did this happen?"

So I told him everything.

I told him how I used to do volunteering at Woodmont's Canine Rescue Shelter and how, even now, when I biked past the building, I still waved at it because it's a good building and the people who work there are good people, and that's where I met George.

The first time I saw George he had an *inflatable dog collar* around his neck so he wouldn't lick his stitches (like those neck pillows I've seen people use on airplanes on TV). My boss, Marilyn, said someone left him tied to the flagpole out front during a snowstorm and when she got there in the morning George was covered in snow. A veterinarian operated on his ears to help him hear again but it didn't work (George stayed deaf) and he was already blind in one eye, but then they had to remove his other eye because it had cancer growing on it (they sewed it shut when they were done) and after that they neutered him (cut off his balls) so he couldn't make Saint Bernard puppies anymore.

And lots of people came to see George and they'd take him for walks and hug him and say, "Aren't you handsome!" but nobody wanted to adopt him. "He's such a sweet boy," Marilyn said one day. "But he'll be a lot of work for whoever adopts him."

And I said, "Is it hard work?"

Marilyn frowned. "Well, he's never been in a house and he's never climbed stairs, so there'd be lots of adjustments for him to make." She said George came from a *backyard breeder* (an unethical person who doesn't care if they breed unhealthy dogs) and that lady kept him in a cage outside for years, and she didn't feed him every day, and she didn't take him to a vet. All she cared about was the money she could get from selling the puppies George made for her. Then, when George's health got bad, she dumped him at the Canine Rescue Shelter.

I asked if that's why George had lots of stuff wrong with him, and Marilyn said, "That's part of the reason, yes," and I thought about that, and I said, "I have stuff wrong with me too," and that's when Marilyn laughed, and she said, "Oh, Denny, you're fine just the way you are," and I said, "So is George."

My volunteering job was to clean all the cages and I watched George and he didn't bark or whine, and he didn't know what to do with balls or toys or stuffed animals because he'd never had them before. Visitors came and went, and George was quiet and gentle, but mostly he leaned against the wall in his cage trembling (shaking/shivering) and I learned that when he was scared, he trembled. Then one day I opened his cage, and I sat down next to him on the floor and I told him everything would be okay, even though I wasn't sure it would be, because that's what Nana-Jo always said to me when I was scared. And I kept doing that, and a week later George lay down beside me, and he put his head in my lap, and he stopped trembling.

Woodmont's Canine Rescue Shelter has a board of directors (which are people who sit at a table four times a year doing talking about *how to keep the lights on*) and Marilyn was one of them and so was Mr. Tesky and so was a lady named Hilma. Marilyn told me Irene Tesky used to be on the board of directors too and she always gave the shelter money to keep it running, but Mr. Tesky hated giving them money.

I was doing volunteering at the shelter one day when Mr. Tesky came in. He walked right past me like he didn't know who I was to go do a board meeting with Marilyn and Hilma in Marilyn's office, then he left an hour later, and so did Hilma, and when Marilyn came out her eyes were red, and she taped a paper to the wall that said this:

> NOTICE TO ALL STAFF AND VISITORS
> On many occasions in the past, Woodmont's Canine Rescue Shelter has reached its capacity for care based on, but not limited to, these parameters (number of cages, staff shortages, monthly costs, length of stay).

> Please note that as a privately funded organization, effective immediately we will shift our focus by implementing the following criteria for future surrenders:
>
> 1. Senior dogs (over 6 years old) will no longer be taken in.
>
> 2. Dogs with special needs will no longer be taken in.
>
> 3. Dogs will be housed for no more than 90 days.
>
> 4. If a dog hasn't found a home within 90 days, it will be euthanized.
>
> 5. Given these new parameters, and that we currently have limited space for new intakes, the following dogs will be euthanized this Friday:
>
> Cage #10: Beagle named Marley (12 years)
>
> Cage #12: Golden retriever named Quaker (8 years)
>
> Cage #18: Saint Bernard named George (6 years, special needs)

I asked Marilyn what *euthanized* meant, and she said, "It means we have to put these dogs to sleep, Denny," and I said, "You mean kill them?" and she nodded. "Hilma and I voted against it, but as our primary benefactor Henry Tesky overruled us. We either adopt a ninety-day kill shelter business model or he'll shut us down."

Then Marilyn went back to her office and she shut the door, and I stared at those words on the wall and I rocked back and forth and did moaning.

Adopting a dog is a big deal and that day I adopted George. I signed my name on the official papers and Marilyn *waived the adoption fee* (which means she didn't charge me anything to adopt him) then I lifted my hand like they do on TV when someone takes an oath, and I said, "I promise to love George and take care of him for the rest of his life," and Marilyn said, "I know you will, Denny."

I left my bike locked to the flagpole that day and me and George walked home, which took an hour and six minutes because he's blind and deaf, so I had to use the leash to steer him down the sidewalk and across intersections and around those cement planters with flowers in them that the town puts out every spring to make Woodmont a cheerier place to live. And I could tell George was VERY SMART because after a while if I moved the leash a bit to the right, he'd go right, and if I moved it a bit to the left, he'd go left, and even though he couldn't hear me, I kept telling him he was a good boy because I was sure he could feel good vibes.

When I finally got home, Nana-Jo was waiting for me on the front steps and Angus came outside too and he was wearing a T-shirt that said **JUST BECAUSE I CAN'T SING DOESN'T MEAN I WON'T SING**, and he did a smirk and said, "All right, I'll bite. What's going on, buddy?" And I waved my hand like a magician does and I said, "This is George. He's blind and deaf and Mr. Tesky wanted to kill him, so I adopted him and saved his life."

Nana-Jo said, "Dear God."

Angus put his hands on his knees, and he laughed and laughed.

That first night was hard, though, because me and Angus had to lift/carry George up the front steps into the house, and Angus wouldn't stop laughing, and George's legs were stiff like how a cow's legs go stiff after it dies (I had to winch one into the DOT truck once after he got himself killed by a Honda Civic). And when we finally got George inside, he started scratching and digging at the floor like he was trying to make himself a bed from dirt that wasn't there, then he went from room to room like a giant Roomba, bumping into the TV and the fridge and the stove over and over again.

He knocked over Nana-Jo's magazine stand and a lamp and the next day I called Marilyn at the shelter and she told me George was *mapping*, which blind dogs do to *make a mental road map of their surroundings* and that we shouldn't rearrange furniture because that would just confuse him.

"Is there anything else we shouldn't do?" I asked.

Marilyn said, "Stick to a routine. Keep his food and water bowls in the same spot so he learns where they are." Then Nana-Jo took the phone and she said, "I don't think this is going to work, Marilyn. I told Denny we'll give it a shot, but don't be surprised if we bring George back," and Marilyn said, "All right. I understand, Joanne," and she promised to call every few days to see how we were doing.

And she did.

She called us a lot.

And she even stopped by to check on us a few times.

So yeah, one week went by and then a few more went by, and then George finally stopped mapping and bumping into things, and he also stopped trembling. We stuck to a routine, and we kept his bowls in the same spot in the kitchen, and each night after dinner George started flipping over with his feet in the air while we watched TV, and Nana-Jo would reach down and rub his belly, and his tail would go **THUMP-THUMP-THUMP**. Before that, I'd never seen George wag his tail, not once.

Then one night after dinner (roast beef), me and Nana-Jo were watching *Schitt's Creek* and the phone rang. Nana-Jo answered it and said, "Hello?" and she listened to the person on the other end for a bit, then she looked at me and did a sigh, and she said, "George isn't going anywhere, Marilyn. He's family now."

And that was that—George was ours forever.

So yeah, Mr. Tesky tried to kill George.

And I saved him.

What's a Gift Horse?

This morning me and Grant waited for Dr. Harland in our special meeting room and we played tic-tac-toe again (Grant won twice, I lost twice), then Dr. Harland came with my vanilla sprinkle doughnut and Grant left. And I ate my doughnut while Dr. Harland hung up his jacket and drank his tea, then he said, "I was going over your list of facts, Denny, and you said"—he opened my blue notebook, flipped to a page near the front, and squinted at my words—"'Lots of people died last year from fatal gunshot wounds.' Can we talk about that?"

And I said, "Sure."

"Why did you put that on your list?" he asked.

"Because it's true?"

"All right, but what was the *point* of putting it on your list?"

So I looked out the window and did thinking about that, and then I said, "I put it on my list because last year when I was doing something I wasn't supposed to be doing, I learned that lots of people were dying from *fatal gunshot wounds* and if Nana-Jo knew what I was doing, she would have been mad at me, but I kept doing it anyhow . . . and first there was one shooting, and then there was another shooting, and another one . . . and it kept happening over and over again, and I just could not stop thinking about all those shootings."

Dr. Harland rested his forehead on the table. "Denny, can you take me back to the beginning? When was the first time you did this *thing* you weren't supposed to be doing where you learned about all these people who died from fatal gunshot wounds?" So I did thinking again until I was 100 percent sure I had it right, and then I said, "The first time it happened was the day Nana-Jo *didn't* look a gift horse in the mouth."

More quiet.

More tap-tap-tapping.

Then Dr. Harland did a sigh. "All right. Start there. Tell me all about that."

So I told him how I was cutting George's toenails, like I do every six weeks, when the doorbell rang and I opened the door and there was a woman wearing brown shorts and a brown shirt with a badge on her pocket that said **UPS**, and there was a delivery truck parked out front that said **UPS Worldwide Services**. And I could tell she wasn't doing flirting with me because she said, "I have a delivery for Joanne Voss," which is Nana-Jo's official name.

And I said, "Nana-Jo isn't home."

The woman frowned. "Does Joanne Voss live here?"

I nodded. "She does."

"Great. I need someone to sign for this." She showed me an envelope with UPS on it and the words *Express Envelope*.

And I said, "Can I sign?"

"Sure."

She gave me a black pen with no ink in it and she watched me for a bit, then she grabbed my hand and said, "Please stop shaking it like that," and she pointed and said, "Just sign here," and I carefully printed my name on the teeny-tiny glass window of her mini-computer, and it worked, then I said, "Best wishes, warmest regards," just like David and Stevie do on *Schitt's Creek*, and I shut the door.

When Nana-Jo got home an hour later, she opened that UPS Express envelope and she took out some official-looking papers and she read them. Then she plopped down in a kitchen chair and put her hand over her mouth.

"What's wrong, Nana-Jo?"

She waved the papers at me. "Well, it looks like I have a guardian angel, because yesterday someone"—she squinted at the papers and read out loud—"an 'anonymous benefactor,' prepaid for my knee operation. All of it, every last penny!"

And I said, "Who?"

"I don't know. Being anonymous means that you don't give your name."

I knew Nana-Jo had been worried about how she was going to pay for the broken-down knee operation she needed so badly, which cost $22,748, which I know because I snooped where I shouldn't snoop and saw what's called a *medical estimate* from the Woodmont Hip and Knee Clinic, and when I saw that I felt sick inside because that's a lot of money.

Nana-Jo slid those official papers back into the UPS Express envelope, then George came into the kitchen and found her, and she leaned down and kissed him on the nose, and he put his head in her lap and stood there for a while.

A few minutes later, Angus showed up with his toolbox to fix a leaky water pipe in our basement that Nana-Jo had told him about. "Don't hire a plumber," he'd said. "They're way too expensive. I can fix it for you."

He was wearing a T-shirt that said **Woke Up Sexy as Hell . . . Again**, and he went downstairs to fix the leaky pipe and we could hear him swearing a lot down there. An hour later, Angus came upstairs and Nana-Jo told him that *an anonymous benefactor* had paid for her broken-down knee operation.

He wiped his forehead. "Are you serious? Who would do that?"

Nana-Jo shrugged. "I don't know. I've cleaned for lots of people over the years and some of them are well off, but I can't imagine anyone putting out that much money. I also haven't told many people how bad my knee is, so I honestly don't know."

Angus frowned. "I'd be skeptical if I were you."

Nana-Jo picked up the envelope. "Skeptical of what? I have a legal document from a law firm and a prepaid receipt that says the full cost of my operation has been taken care of. This is good news, Angus."

I stopped brushing George. "So you don't care who paid for your broken-down knee operation, Nana-Jo?" and she said, "I do, Denny, but this person wants to remain anonymous and you should never look a gift horse in the mouth," then I told her I didn't know what a gift horse was, and she said, "It means 'don't be ungrateful when you receive a gift, even if you don't know who gave you the gift.'" It also means Nana-Jo won't have to worry about paying for her broken-down knee operation anymore—I figured that part out by myself.

Then it was time for me to do my consequences by picking up garbage that hadn't made it into the trash bins on Penguin Hill and because I needed proof that I was doing consequences, Angus took a picture of me waving as I left 8B with an empty garbage bag, and then I had him take a picture of me waving when I got back an hour later with a full garbage bag.

When I got back, there was a note on the table from Nana-Jo saying she'd gone to bingo and even though I'm not allowed to watch TV by myself, I turned it on and there was a news story about a shooting in Akron, Ohio. The reporter said the shooter was a man who got himself fired from his job and he wanted revenge, so he took a gun and went back to where he used to work and he killed eight people—five men, three women.

And I knew I should turn the TV off.

But I didn't turn it off.

I stared at the yellow tape that said **CRIME SCENE DO NOT CROSS**, and at a bunch of people who were doing hugging and crying, and there were ambulances and they were loading people into them, and I felt dizzy and sick inside, and my heart was going **BOOM-BOOM-BOOM** so I rocked back and forth and did moaning. Then I turned the TV off and I went to my room and lay down for a while.

Dr. Harland held up his hand for me to stop. "Wait a second, Denny. Did you just say you weren't allowed to watch TV by yourself?"

And I said, "Yes, I did."

"Why not?"

So I closed my eyes and tried to do remembering about what Nana-Jo had said when she made that a rule. "Nana-Jo told me I'm not allowed to watch TV by myself because I'm too *suggestible*, I take things too *literally*, and I *fixate on the wrong stuff*, and the world has enough *unbearable heaviness* to it without adding the *daily anguish* of having me watch something that can't be unwatched, and that watching too much TV could send me *down the wrong path and into an emotional tailspin*."

Dr. Harland carefully set his pencil down on the table. "Do you know what any of that means, Denny?" he asked, and I nodded and said, "Yeah, it means I'm not allowed to watch TV by myself."

"But you still did?" he said.

I looked out the window. "Yes, I watched lots of TV last year when I was by myself," then Dr. Harland asked me if doing that had maybe sent me down *the wrong path*, and I thought about that for a bit, then I said, "I guess so because I went and got myself charged with Mr. Tesky's murder, right?"

Broken-Down Knee Operation

Dr. Harland said, "Denny, let's talk more about how you said, 'Lots of people died last year from fatal gunshot wounds.' So, you were watching TV by yourself when you saw a news story about a shooting, right?" and I said, "Uh-huh," then he said, "And after that you kept watching TV by yourself, even though Nana-Jo told you not to?"

"Yes."

"Why'd you do that?"

"Because I wanted to know what was happening in the world, even if it wasn't good news. And I kept doing it and I kept seeing stories about shootings where people died, and those stories piled up in my head and I thought about them a lot."

Dr. Harland nodded. "Tell me about the second shooting."

"Okay," I said. "But first I have to tell you about Nana-Jo's broken-down knee operation so you know where I was when I heard about the second shooting," and he closed his eyes and said, "Fine. Tell me about Nana-Jo's knee operation."

So I did.

And I told him everything. Like how a broken-down knee operation is a big deal no matter what anyone says and how Nana-Jo let me go with her to her last appointment at the Woodmont Hip and Knee Clinic because I wanted to ask Dr. Jill Hammond, who is an *orthopedic surgeon*, how long the operation would take, and what happens during these operations, and how many of them has she done before.

Nana-Jo did a chat with her first, then Dr. Jill Hammond called me into her office and this is what she said: "The operation usually takes one to two hours. First, I'll cut into the knee and remove the broken part of the knee joint, then I'll attach a prosthesis, which is an artificial knee that's made from metal and plastic, and a plastic spacer will go between those pieces to help the new joint move smoothly. I do approximately fifty knee replacements a year and I've been doing them for a long time."

And I said, "How long?"

Dr. Jill Hammond said, "Eighteen years."

And I said, "That's good."

She smiled. "Nana-Jo will be fine, Denny."

And I said, "We'll see about that," and I stared straight at her and I didn't smile back because I wanted her to know I was watching her so she'd be on her best behavior when she was doing Nana-Jo's operation.

On our way home, Nana-Jo squeezed my hand. "Don't worry, Denny. Knee replacement surgery is very common these days."

And I said, "Uh-huh," but my stomach hurt inside and I wasn't hungry at dinner and I had trouble sleeping that night because I kept thinking about Papa-Jo and how, when he left the house that morning years ago his toothbrush was still on the counter in the bathroom, and his slippers were beside his chair in the living room, and he'd left a note on the last piece of apple pie in the fridge that said *Papa-Jo's. Don't touch*, but then he never came home again, and sometimes, when you're doing life, things can go sideways and there's NOTHING anyone can do about it—not a thing.

When I got up the next morning, my stomach was splish-splashing all over and I ate some Cheerios and then vomited them up into the toilet, but I didn't tell Nana-Jo because I didn't want her to do worrying about me.

I brushed my teeth and fed George and took him for a walk, then Angus came over and he was wearing a T-shirt that said **Never Dreamed I'd Be Cool, but Here I Am Killing It** and he helped me lift George into the back of Nana-Jo's Subaru (there wasn't enough room in his truck for all of us). And even though I don't like riding in the back seat, the hospital wasn't far away, so I got in the back and I let Nana-Jo sit in the front, and while Angus drove to the hospital, I rocked back and forth.

"You okay back there, buddy?" Angus asked.

And I was looking out the window and I gave him a thumbs-up, which is the same thing as saying, *Yeah, I'm fine.*

Nana-Jo's operation was scheduled for 8:45 a.m. and we got there early, and Angus went inside and checked her in, then he left for work and me and George waited outside on the grass like I told Nana-Jo we would. After a while, I got bored so I walked George around the hospital three times and I peeked in a few windows to see if I could see Nana-Jo, but I couldn't find her. That's when a security guard came outside to do talking with me and he was wearing a blue uniform with silver buttons, but he didn't point a gun at me, so I wasn't scared and I didn't stutter. And when he said, "What do you think you're doing?" I said to him, "I am not a threat," then I rocked back and forth and I told him that me and George were waiting for Dr. Jill Hammond to finish Nana-Jo's broken-down knee operation.

The security guard pointed at me. "Don't move," he said, then he stepped away and he did talking into his walkie-talkie while me and George stood very still.

Six minutes later, the security guard pointed to a bench, and he told me to wait over there and not to peek in any more windows because I was freaking everyone out.

So that's what I did.

Me and George waited and waited.

Then at 10:48 a.m., Dr. Jill Hammond opened a door that said **Emergency Exit** and she smiled and gave me a thumbs-up, and I shouted, "How's Nana-Jo?" and she shouted back, "She's fine, Denny. Everything's fine."

And I shouted, "Thank you!"

Then I knelt down in the grass and I buried my face in George's fur, and I said, *Thank you, thank you, thank you,* and a few minutes later me and George walked home and on the way we stopped at the Doughnut

Hole and we stood behind two cars in the drive-through lane, and we walked up to the window and I bought doughnuts to celebrate (vanilla sprinkle for me, long john for George) and it ended up being a VERY GOOD DAY because Nana-Jo's broken-down knee operation didn't go sideways and she didn't die.

At home, I made myself a cheese sandwich and I turned on the TV and then suddenly it wasn't a good day anymore because one of our channels had a **Breaking News** story about a *mass shooting* and this is what the lady reporter said:

"Twelve people were killed and two injured today when a shooter opened fire at a church outside of Little Rock, Arkansas. The sheriff's department has identified the suspect as Viktor Binney, fifty-seven. Authorities have confirmed that Binney drove to the church, entered through a side door, and fired on a group of congregants who'd gathered to prepare for an annual luncheon. An off-duty police officer, Kyle Barr, has been credited with saving lives when he tackled Binney and disarmed him. 'Mr. Barr is a hero,' said the local sheriff. 'There is no doubt in my mind that there would've been more victims without his quick thinking.' Binney has been booked on twelve felony counts of murder and two felony counts of attempted murder."

I stared at the big metal cross on the roof of the church.

And I did rocking back and forth.

And moaning.

There were stained glass windows above the church's front door and a sign on the grass out front that said **Central Baptist Church** and below that it said: **Honk If You Love Jesus, Text While Driving If You Want to Meet Him**. And there was a Nalgene water bottle on the grass next to a straw hat and police cars parked out front with their lights flashing. There were also ambulances and lots of people doing hugging, and some of them were crying very hard, and I felt myself going **down-down-down**, so I turned the TV off and I went and found George and I hugged him real tight, and when that didn't help, I put my head between my knees and I counted the tiles on the floor.

Would You Like to Buy a Rug?

I told Dr. Harland that Nana-Jo had to stay in the hospital overnight after her broken-down knee operation, then Angus brought her home the next day and me and George were waiting outside with a helium balloon I bought that said *Get Well Soon*. And she was groggy from the drugs they gave her to *manage the pain and swelling* so we got some pillows and we set her up on the couch with the TV remote and a blanket, and George kept trying to climb up there with her so I took him outside so Nana-Jo could rest. And while she was resting, I helped our neighbor Sharon's husband, Bill, rototill our garden with his rototiller, which is a machine like a lawn mower that uses sharp blades to break up the soil so it's easier to plant seeds.

Nana-Jo slept a lot that day.

And I was nervous because I was in charge for the first time ever and Nana-Jo needed me to take care of her and it was usually the other way around. So I kept checking on her and each time I did, she was doing snoring, and when she finally woke up at lunchtime I made her some toast with peanut butter and jam and she took more pills, then she fell asleep again, and I went back outside to help Bill finish rototilling.

At 2:00 p.m. I went inside to check on her and—WHOA!—a man with a droopy mustache was standing in our living room, and he had some rolled-up rugs on the floor beside him, and he was holding one up to show Nana-Jo, and it had a bunch of horses on it. I looked out the window and there was a van parked out front with **Rory's Roadside Rugs** written on it, and I said to the man, "Who are you?"

And he said, "I'm Rory!"

Nana-Jo's hair was sticking up and she had drool on her chin, and she was blinking at Rory extra slow-like, the same way Angus does when he drinks too much. Rory pointed to the front door. "I rang the bell, but no one answered, so I stick my head inside and I see nice lady resting on the couch, and I asked if she wants to buy a rug."

"What did she say?"

Rory smiled. "She say, 'Show me your rugs!'"

So, I helped Nana-Jo sit up on the couch and I wiped her mouth with a tissue the way she used to when I was little and got myself sick with a cold or flu. And I said, "Would you like to buy a rug, Nana-Jo?" and she said something mumbly back that I couldn't understand, then Rory told us his rugs were $80 to $100 and he held them up to show us and there was one with giraffes on it, and one with kittens, and another one with Harley-Davidson motorcycles. Then he held up a rug with Elvis Presley on it and it was pink like Nana-Jo's foam curlers and Elvis was wearing a pink jacket and he was dancing with a pink microphone, and that's when Nana-Jo started to laugh and she would not stop laughing.

"Do you like that one, Nana-Jo?" I asked.

And she laughed even harder.

She laughed so hard that tears leaked down her cheeks and because that rug seemed to make her happy, Rory said he'd do us a deal, which he never does, because this was a special rug that usually sold for $400 but he'd sell it to us for $300 and that was a lot of money but if Nana-Jo wanted it then I wanted to buy it for her. So, I went to my room and I got $300 cash out of my Heinz Tomato Soup can safe with the fake bottom and I paid Rory; then he helped me move the coffee table and we rolled out the Elvis rug and it covered most of our living room floor, which was made of hardwood. Then Rory got himself in a hurry taking the other rugs out to his van and he thanked us for our business, and

Nana-Jo saluted him like he was in the army, then she started laughing again when Rory drove away very fast.

Angus came over after work to check on us. We were in the living room with Elaine-the-stalker, eating chicken potpie on Nana-Jo's collapsible TV tray tables (blue with yellow flowers) and Angus was wearing a T-shirt that said **Making Ordinary Extraordinary Since 1987** and he frowned when he saw the new Elvis rug, and then Elaine said, "Denny bought it for Nana-Jo," and Angus closed his eyes, and said, "Of course he did."

—

Dr. Harland looked at his watch. "Look, I'm glad you got Nana-Jo a rug, Denny, but we need to move things along here. Can you tell me about the next shooting?"

And I said, "Yes, I can."

So I told him how, the next day, I went to work and me and Angus had to unblock two culverts and when we got back to the shop, his truck wouldn't start so I called Elaine-the-stalker and asked if she could give us a ride home, and when Elaine pulled into the parking lot, Angus got in the back and I got in the front. Elaine told me Nana-Jo had had a good day, but she was asleep now, so I should be quiet when I got home.

I asked her if she wanted to come over for dinner, but she said she couldn't because she had a date, then Angus got grumpy and he didn't even say goodbye when he got out of Elaine's car. And Nana-Jo was doing snoring in her bedroom so I closed her door and turned the TV on, and I checked all four channels and that's when I saw another story about a shooting, and the reporter was a bald guy with a big belly and this is what he said:

"Four people are dead in Flint, Michigan, in an apparent murder-suicide. A preliminary investigation shows that Edward McMillan, forty-two, shot his six-year-old son, four-year-old daughter, and his ex-wife, Amy McMillan, thirty-eight, before turning the gun on himself after a dispute over custody. Officers were called after neighbors heard the couple arguing outside on the driveway; then, minutes later, gunshots were heard coming from inside Amy McMillan's home. When police were finally able to gain access to the house, all four individuals were discovered dead from gunshot wounds."

I stared at Amy McMillan's house.

And I did moaning.

Her porch had two chairs on it and there were saggy *Happy Birthday* balloons tied to the front door, and a skateboard leaning against the wall, and a sign by the door that said **Bless This Home and All Who Enter**. And my heart was going **boom-boom-boom** and the reporter said, "According to the Centers for Disease Control and Prevention data, one hundred people, on average, are killed by firearms in the US every day . . ." And I stared at those balloons and I felt myself going **down-down-down** so I turned the TV off, then George came and found me, and he put his head in my lap, and we sat there until it got dark outside.

Lydia Wins an Award

After Dr. Harland read my notebook this morning, he wanted to do talking about Lydia and when I told him I didn't want to, he stared at me for a long time without blinking, then he got up and put his parka on, and he wrapped his scarf around his neck. "It's been nice working with you, Denny. I wish you the best of luck."

And I said, "Where are you going?"

Dr. Harland did a sigh. "I don't know, but I do know I have no patience for *this* anymore!" He waved at the room.

And my heart started going **BOOM-BOOM-BOOM**. "It's been a hard year, Dr. Harland, and this is a very hard case."

He shook his head. "No, it's not. You just need to tell me everything that happened. That's all I need from you, Denny. There's no magic to this. Every day, I meet you halfway and I handle you with kid gloves and yet it's still a fight to get you to open up and talk to me."

Everything was going sideways and I liked Dr. Harland, and I knew he was on my side and that he'd never slap me or try to run me down with his car, and there was no reason *not* to do talking with him, even though sometimes I got myself nervous and afraid because I didn't want anyone, not even Dr. Harland, to know the whole wide truth about Mr. Tesky.

That's when he turned to leave.

He opened the door to our meeting room—

And I shouted, "Please don't go! I'll talk to you about Lydia. I'll tell you anything you want to know about her." Dr. Harland thought about that, then he took his parka off and he stayed, and I told him everything about Lydia.

I told him how Nana-Jo was asleep one night when Lydia called and I answered the phone and said, "Hello, this is Denny Voss," and it was weird to hear Lydia's voice because I hadn't talked to her in a long time. I told her Nana-Jo was asleep, then I wrapped the phone cord around my hand and told her Nana-Jo didn't have a job anymore because Mr. Tesky fired her and that she'd just had a broken-down knee operation.

Lydia said, "I know. Angus told me."

I kept talking. "Me and Angus took her to the hospital and I waited outside until the operation was over, then Dr. Jill Hammond gave me a thumbs-up and she told me Nana-Jo was fine, and Angus brought her home and now Nana-Jo's doing a lot of drugs, but don't worry, they're not *illegal drugs* she got from someone in an alley, they're pills she's allowed to take to *manage the pain*, and I've been taking good care of her, and I bought her a pink Elvis rug for the living room that's very soft on her feet, but now she has to use crutches and a walker and her leg is all bruised and swollen—"

"Fuck me," Lydia said.

"Huh?"

"Land your plane, Denny!"

And I said, "I don't have a plane," then Lydia said, "*Please* get to the point. You're making me crazy!" and I said, "I'm not trying to make you crazy, Lydia. I just have lots of important things to tell you about Nana-Jo because you never call anymore since that time you slapped me." Lydia went very quiet and I unwrapped the phone cord because my hand was starting to turn blue.

"Hello? This is Denny. Are you still there?"

"Tell Mom I'll call back later."

"Okay. Thank you for calling."

Then I hung up.

I know Lydia doesn't like me very much—I'm not stupid. I know what's what.

Because I was a late-in-life baby, Lydia grew up with Nana-Jo and Papa-Jo before I got myself born, then she moved to New York and that's why we're not close, but Angus said it wouldn't matter anyhow because *Lydia's all about Lydia*, which means she has to work hard at being thoughtful and kind because those things don't *come to her naturally* (which means she wasn't born that way).

One time, when we were still living in our old house, Lydia came home for Christmas and I asked if she wanted to go sledding with me, and she said, "Are you out of your tiny little mind?" and Papa-Jo got mad at her. She also came home one summer and her and Nana-Jo were arguing outside on the porch. Nana-Jo was trying to get Lydia to move home instead of *starving in New York*, and Lydia said, "I'd rather starve in New York than live here in Bumfuck, Minnesota!" and I opened the screen door and said, real quiet-like, "It's Woodmont, not Bumfuck," and she said, "Jesus, is he serious?!"

Lydia also came home for Thanksgiving once and Nana-Jo asked her to drive me to the grocery store. I had a grocery list and when we got there I asked the manager some questions about their tinfoil and then when we got home I told Nana-Jo that the manager said I had a high IQ, and Lydia said, "No, he said you have a high AQ, which means *annoying quotient*, and that just means you're annoying, Denny."

Whenever Lydia used to come home, she'd watch NBA basketball games on TV and Papa-Jo would have a beer and they'd both yell at the referees and Lydia would high-five Nana-Jo when her favorite player made a basket, and I'd watch the game and try VERY HARD not to ask questions because whenever I did Lydia would say, "Isn't there something else you can go do, Denny?" I'm not good at sports (too clumsy) but Lydia was a basketball star when she was growing up and her trophies and awards covered one whole wall; then Papa-Jo died and Nana-Jo had to sell the house, so Lydia boxed them up and now they're locked in a trunk in our basement marked **Lydia's Keepsakes**.

Me and Nana-Jo still watch NBA games. Her favorite team is the Milwaukee Bucks and mine is the Toronto Raptors, and whenever our teams play each other Nana-Jo wears her Bucks jersey and I wear my Raptors jersey, and we order pepperoni pizza, and I yell at the referees and we high-five when our favorite players make a basket, and I don't ask questions during the games because now I know every basketball rule on the planet.

One night after Nana-Jo's knee surgery the phone rang when we were watching a Bucks/Raptors game and I answered it and listened for a few seconds, then I said, "Thank you for calling. Please call back another time," and I hung up.

Nana-Jo laughed. "Who was that?"

And I said, "Lydia."

Her eyes got big. "Why'd you tell her to call back?!"

I pointed at the TV. "Because we're watching the game."

The phone rang again and Nana-Jo fumbled for her walker, and she tried to stand up and I tried to help her, then she said, "Damn it, the cord's long enough to reach, Denny. Stretch it out and bring me the phone!"

So I did.

And it was Lydia and her and Nana-Jo talked so long that Nana-Jo missed the end of the game. Nana-Jo was saying things like, "That sounds wonderful. I'm proud of you. What kind of award is it?" She sighed and said, "Well, marriage isn't easy, I can tell you that much. I'm sure he'll come back when he calms down," and, "Yes, the surgery went well. Denny's been taking care of me." She listened to Lydia some more and she said, "I agree, therapy is probably the best way to work through that. I'm glad you're talking to someone," then Nana-Jo turned to me and said, "Lydia wants to talk to you."

And I said, "Me?"

Nana-Jo nodded, so I took the phone and I wrapped the cord around my hand, and I said, "Hello. This is Denny. How's the weather in New York City?" and Lydia said, "What?!" then she said, "Listen,

Denny, I owe you an apology. I'm sorry I slapped you that time. I was out of line." And my face got hot and I looked down at George, and I poked him with my foot and his tail thumped twice.

"Denny? Are you still there?"

And I said, "I have to go now. George needs to go outside for a pee," which was a lie, but I didn't want to do this kind of visiting anymore.

"You better go then. But listen, Denny? I'm going to mail a package for George. I got him a toy to play with, it's some kind of wiggly-wobbly ball—"

"George doesn't play with toys. He's blind."

"Right." Then lots of quiet. "Well, um . . . could you maybe tell him I'm sorry I was mean to him that time?"

"George is deaf, Lydia. He can't hear me."

More quiet.

I scratched my ear and said, "Thank you for calling," then I hung up and I got a Mello Yello from the fridge, and I twisted the cap off and took a drink.

Nana-Jo turned to me. "Did Lydia tell you about the award she won?"

"No, was it for one of her naked people pictures?"

"It was for a photo of a homeless woman sleeping under a bridge."

And I said, "Did she have clothes on?"

Nana-Jo said, "Yes, she did. Anyhow, this award is something called an IPA, which is an International Photography Award. Lydia said it's a big deal. She's going to mail us a copy of the photo so we can see it."

"Okay, I'll check the mailbox tomorrow."

Nana-Jo laughed. "It won't be here that soon, Denny."

I picked up the remote and turned the TV off, then I took another drink of Mello Yello and I said, "The Bucks beat the Raptors by one point, Nana-Jo. The Greek Freak did a buzzer beater and you missed it."

"There'll be other games, Denny."

And I said, "Uh-huh."

"She called to apologize and that's an important step, Denny. Lydia's going through a tough time and you need to forgive her for what she did. We all make mistakes." Nana-Jo sighed. "This is family, Denny. Life is too short to hold grudges."

"Okay, Nana-Jo."

Then I did the same thing I do every night. I took out a bag of Cheetos and I waved one in front of George's nose and—**BAM!**—he woke up and ate it SUPER FAST, then I curled my hand around another one and moved it in front of his face and—**BAM!**—George lunged like a snapping turtle, but I yanked my hand away just in time. He got up then, and I slowly backed away, and he followed me outside for his nighttime pee, sniff-sniff-sniffing the air while he tried to find that Cheeto. And when he was finished doing his pee, I gave him the second Cheeto. So yeah, George is blind and deaf and stubborn, and if he doesn't want to get up you can't make him get up, but he'll do anything for a Cheeto.

Doing a Video Visit

After breakfast today, Grant-the-corrections-officer took me to a room for what's called a *video visitation*, which is when someone wants to do visiting with you, but they can't get themselves to the jail, so they show up on a computer screen instead. It was a room with no windows and it had a table with a computer on it and one chair, and Grant had me sit in the chair while he did some clickety-clicking with the mouse to bring the computer to life.

And I said, "I've never done a video visit before."

More clickety-clicking. "Well, then I guess after today you'll be a modern-day renaissance man, won't you?"

I shook my head. "Nope. I'll just be Denny. Doesn't matter what happens today or tomorrow, I'll always be Denny."

Grant typed in a code, nodded at the screen. "All right, you're good to go."

It was a big screen, like a TV, but there was nobody on it to do visiting with—just me in my orange jumpsuit. So I waved at me, and I leaned a bit to the right, then I leaned a bit to the left, and I said, "Grant, am I doing visiting with myself?" and he laughed and said, "No, Denny, she just hasn't signed in yet. Give her a few minutes," so I did some staring at my face, and then I frowned and said, "I need a haircut," and I leaned forward and smoothed down some hair that was sticking up, then I got sad because Nana-Jo always cuts my hair, but she couldn't cut it now because she was in the hospital.

There was a clock on the wall, and it was noisy—

TICK TOCK! TICK TOCK!

—and Grant was sitting on a stool by the door, looking at his phone, and me doing waiting was boring, so I looked at the computer screen and I put air into my cheeks and puffed them out like one of those pufferfish in the ocean, then I sucked all the air out of my cheeks until they caved in. I tilted my head down, then I slowly tilted it all the way back, and I pointed at the screen. "Look, Grant, I can see my nose hairs!" and he laughed and said, "Dude, you're the best thing that's happened around here in a long time."

The computer screen flish-flashed and suddenly my face shrank down into a tiny box, and the rest of the screen got itself filled up with a room that had a fancy fireplace and a coatrack in one corner, and there was a lady sitting there with silver hair and she looked tired (dark circles under her eyes).

She lifted one hand. "Hi, Denny. It's me, Toni Hale."

I did a wave. "Hi, Mrs. Hale."

Toni Hale is Irene Tesky's sister. She used to live in Woodmont until she got herself married and then she moved to Canada with her husband. She came back often, though, to do visiting with Irene, and whenever she was here, they'd both take Nana-Jo for lunch. I met Mrs. Hale when I was a little kid, after Irene hired Nana-Jo to do full-time housecleaning. I was with Nana-Jo when her Subaru broke down at the Teskys' house one time (dead battery), and Mrs. Hale was there, and she offered to drive us home, and on the way she also drove us to the grocery store to get milk and eggs.

So yeah, Mrs. Hale was a nice lady just like her sister, Irene.

She also did *not* like Mr. Tesky—same as me.

Me and Nana-Jo saw her at Irene Tesky's funeral last year (sad day, lots of people wearing black clothes) and she cried but she was also very talk-talk-talky. Mrs. Hale told Nana-Jo she'd had it with Henry Tesky running their family business. "If that man wants a fight, he's about to get one. I'll spend every penny I have to get him ousted from Norida."

Nana-Jo gave her a hug and when Mrs. Hale pulled away, she said, "Do you know he wouldn't let me stay at the house when I got here? Five empty guest rooms and that snake booked me into a Motel 6. He had his secretary drop off four boxes of Irene's things. Can you believe it? Henry didn't have a dime when he married Irene and now he's living in her house and has, quote unquote, a 'secretary' who drives a Porsche."

Nana-Jo said, "I'm sorry, Toni."

Mrs. Hale kept talking. "Irene thought he was cheating on her. They had a prenup, of course, and she knew she'd have to honor that, but she told me she was rewriting her will to make sure he wouldn't get anything else. I brought it up with Henry yesterday and he said he had no idea what I was talking about, that they'd had their wills done years ago, together, and their lawyer had both of them."

Nana-Jo shook her head. "I wish there was something Denny and I could do to help," and Toni said, "I appreciate that, Joanne. You're a gem. I've got this, though. You'll see." She went back to Canada the next day, then later she called Nana-Jo *furious* (very angry) when she found out that Mr. Tesky had fired her from her housecleaning job.

A black cat jumped up next to Toni on the computer screen and it looked like a very friendly cat because it was rubbing up against her and purring. "Are you in Canada right now, Mrs. Hale?" I asked. "Is that why we're doing video chatting?" and she said, "Yes, Denny, I am. I heard about Nana-Jo's stroke and then how those fools charged you with Henry's murder—" She looked away for a second, took a breath, blew it out.

And I said, "It's okay, Mrs. Hale."

She shook her head. "No, Denny, it's not. This is a mess. I just don't know how you got wrapped up in it." She put her elbows on the table. "I was in Woodmont the day Henry died. I had some unfinished business to deal with. It was a quick trip—two days, in and out. I just wish I'd reached out to you guys when I was there. Anyhow, I'm sorry you're going through this. I'm barely sleeping thinking about you in that jail cell."

"Don't worry, Mrs. Hale. Angus brought me a pillow from home yesterday and Dirty Doyle finally stopped threatening to kill me."

Her eyes got big. "Someone threatened to *kill you*?!"

I scratched my neck. "Yeah, but only when he could see me or hear me. They moved him to Cell #10 so now we almost never see each other. And when we go outside to do exercising, which is one hundred jumping jacks for me because I don't like to run laps, they tell him to stay away from me, and he does."

I shrugged. "So yeah—so far, so good."

Toni put her hand over her mouth. "Dear God."

Her black cat flopped down in front of her, doing purring, then he rolled onto his back. And I watched him, and I could feel my mind doing remembering, then I said, "You know what, Mrs. Hale? Your sister, Irene, had a black cat just like yours. His name was Norman and he had a white star on his chest just like your cat does."

Mrs. Hale was rubbing ChapStick on her lips. When she finished, she put the tube in her pocket and rubbed the cat's belly. "Actually, Denny, this is Norman. He's sixteen now but still full of life. When Irene died, Henry refused to give him to me. So, like I said, I had some unfinished business to deal with when I came to Woodmont, and Norman was on that list."

And I said, "Well, I'm glad he gave him to you, Mrs. Hale. I never liked Mr. Tesky but that was a good thing to do."

She lifted one eyebrow. "Trust me, Denny. I didn't give him a choice."

Nana-Jo used to say Irene Tesky was a *fragile, sensitive lady* and Mr. Tesky liked bossing her around, but he seemed scared of Toni Hale whenever she came to visit, probably because Toni was a *tough cookie* who wouldn't put up with BS (bullshit) from anyone. Mrs. Hale rubbed Norman's ears and she told me she'd try to set up another video visit in a week or so. She also asked who my lawyer was and she wrote down Bridget's name, then we both did a wave, and Grant used the mouse to click on a red phone button on the screen and—**POOF!**—Toni Hale was gone.

Big Fat Secret

Nori came by the jail today to drop off a note from Theo and she also brought gingersnap cookies that were so hard I couldn't bite into them. ("Not one of my better batches," she said, looking at the floor.) She also told me Theo had taped my note to his bedroom wall and I said that's good, because now every morning when he wakes up he'll read my words and get himself determined to become a Dolphin. This is what my note said:

Theo, I know your tics get bad when you're scared but don't give up on becoming a Dolphin. P.S. When I'm scared, I sing the theme song for Toy Story. It really helps!

Nori said Theo's been singing that song over and over and it's making her crazy, then she left to go to work and I read Theo's note, and this is what it said:

Okay, Denny, I won't give up on becoming a Dolphin.
P.S. I like the Toy Story song a lot.

So yeah, it was a good morning, then Dr. Harland came and he stayed longer than usual so I could finish telling him my story about Lydia.

I told him how the leaky water pipe Angus fixed for Nana-Jo broke off and then I started talking faster and faster because I wanted to get all the words out, and Dr. Harland said, "Whoa! Slow down, Denny." So I did. Then I looked out the window and I saw a man driving a snow-blowing machine with a brush on the front to clean the sidewalks, and snow was flying everywhere, and I said to Dr. Harland, "Nana-Jo should've hired a real plumber."

Dr. Harland tap-tap-tapped his pencil against his notebook. "Okay, Denny. Take me back to the beginning and tell me all about it."

So I did.

I told him how the leaky water pipe Angus tried to fix broke at the end of September and flooded our basement and Angus's basement, and we didn't even know we had a problem until Nana-Jo sent me downstairs to get bread from the basement freezer, and that's when I went down there and stepped into a foot of water and thought, *Uh-oh.*

And Nana-Jo said she didn't want me to get electrocuted (killed by electric shock) walking around in the water, so she made me put on rubber boots, then she yelled from the top of the stairs to tell me what to do next and I found out our floor drain (which every basement has) was covered up by a Rubbermaid container filled with photo albums. And I had to move it out of the way to open the drain up and because we don't have a sump pump and neither does Angus (which is a pump that sits in a hole in your basement floor and sucks water out of your house) it was a mess down there. I yelled upstairs and asked Nana-Jo what I should do next and she told me to turn the main water valve off.

So I did.

Nana-Jo called a plumber, then she asked me to set up the folding tables we keep downstairs and to get everything up off the floor and onto those tables.

So that's what I did.

One good thing was that our basement floor is concrete, so no rugs, and another good thing was that Nana-Jo likes to store everything in Rubbermaid containers, and we had lots of those downstairs. There was also a folding cot leaning against the wall but the frame was metal and the mattress wasn't touching the water, so I just dried off the frame so it wouldn't rust. And there were four cardboard boxes of books that got ruined, and a beach umbrella (not ruined) and Papa-Jo's tool kit, and the basement freezer, but the motor was up high, so I went to the bottom of the stairs and told Nana-Jo the freezer looked okay, and she said, "Good. Unplug it for a few hours until we can get the water mopped up."

So I did.

Then I opened the basement freezer to get a loaf of bread and I saw the portable safe where we keep all our official papers, and it had a key sticking out of the lock. I opened it and did snooping and on top was the letter someone had sent to Nana-Jo saying her broken-down knee operation had been paid for, and Nana-Jo's passport, and papers with our address on them and the word *Mortgage* at the top. And most of the other stuff in there was boring, so I closed the safe and put it back in the freezer.

I squished everything I could onto the tables like two lamps and folding camp chairs and dishes and a tarp, a box fan, a space heater, and Christmas decorations. A box of magazines got wet so I had to throw them out, and Nana-Jo had a cedar chest filled with quilts and they were wet so I put them in a Rubbermaid bin and took it upstairs. Her eyes got big when I showed her, and she said, "Put them in the Subaru, Denny. I'll take them to the Laundry Basket and wash and dry them in the big machines."

So that's what I did.

Nana-Jo grabbed her keys and her cane, and she left.

And I knew Nori had wheely carts at the Laundry Basket so Nana-Jo wouldn't have to carry the quilts inside by herself. Most of the water in the basement was gone by then so I started to mop up what was left and that's when I saw the blue metal trunk marked **Lydia's Keepsakes** under the stairs, and I grabbed the handle and dragged it out of there.

It was heavy and it had a padlock on it so I got Angus's bolt cutter from the shed and I cut the lock off so I could try to save whatever was inside.

And there were all kinds of keepsakes in Lydia's trunk like basketball trophies and medals and a Polaroid camera and a shoebox of Polaroid pictures, but none of that got wet because it was on top. I put everything in a Rubbermaid bin including Lydia's photography books, and a diary with a teeny-tiny lock on it, and a sweater with **Woodmont High** embroidered on it, and a sweatshirt with **Regional Champs** on the front. At the bottom of the trunk, I found a newspaper from the day Lydia was born and it was old and yellow, and it was wet too. And I knew her keepsakes were private and I knew she wouldn't want me touching them, but I had to go through everything to save what was dry, which isn't called *snooping* because that's called *fixing a problem.*

And I was getting bored and Nana-Jo wasn't home, so I sat down on the stairs and opened another shoebox from Lydia's trunk and that's when I decided to go from *fixing a problem* to *doing snooping* for five minutes, then I'd stop.

Inside that shoebox were newspaper articles about basketball tournaments and Lydia's report cards from high school. She got 92 percent in twelfth grade art class and 96 percent in physical education and 59 percent in English, but only 50 percent in math, so yeah, not good with numbers, and that made me laugh, because Lydia thinks she's so smart.

There were other papers in there too, and one was from Saint Augustine Hospital in Duluth, which was weird, and there was a tiny plastic bracelet with numbers on it and VOSS, INF MALE typed next to them.

Then I found a card with balloons on it that said *NURSERY PASS* and *VOSS, INF MALE*, and it said *BIRTH WEIGHT: 7 lbs., 2 ounces,* and *LENGTH: 22.4 inches*. There was also a tiny piece of newspaper with *BIRTH ANNOUNCEMENT* at the top, and it said: *Dennis Joseph Voss was born into this world on January 12, 1995. The entire Voss family would like to thank everyone at Saint Augustine Hospital in Duluth, Minnesota, for their care and attention.* And that's when I started to get mad inside because why did Lydia have *my* official papers in *her* trunk of keepsakes?! And there was another envelope in Lydia's shoebox so I opened it too and inside was an official-looking paper with *REGISTRATION OF BIRTH* at the top and then it said this underneath:

Child's Name: DENNIS JOSEPH VOSS
Date of Birth: JANUARY 12, 1995
Child's Birthplace: DULUTH, MINNESOTA
Mother's Name: LYDIA MARIE VOSS
Mother's Birthplace: WOODMONT, MINNESOTA
Father's Name: UNKNOWN
Father's Birthplace: UNKNOWN

Inside that same envelope was a Polaroid picture of Lydia when she was a lot younger and her blouse was sticking out in the front and she looked VERY FAT and I'd never seen Lydia fat before, so I stared and stared.

I thought about everything I'd found in her trunk of keepsakes, then I stared at that picture of Lydia again and my head was spinning round and round, and my heart started going **BOOM-BOOM-BOOM**, so to calm myself down I closed my eyes and sang the theme song for *Toy Story*—"You've Got a Friend in Me." And when I was done, I was still holding the picture of Lydia when she was fat.

I looked at it for a long time.

And I thought maybe Lydia looked a bit scared in that picture, but I didn't care because she was also a traitor and a liar.

I felt dizzy, so I rocked back and forth and did moaning, and then my throat closed up, and I felt like I couldn't breathe, and my mind shrank down to a tiny ball and—**BAM!**—that was it, I didn't come back for a while. When I finally did come back, I was curled up on the wet cement floor in our basement holding that official-looking paper and the picture of Lydia when she was young and fat, and I heard Nana-Jo calling out for me, but I didn't answer because no matter what she said I knew my whole wide world was never going to be the same.

Argument with Nana-Jo

Nana-Jo came to the top of the stairs with her cane and she shouted, "Denny, is everything all right?" She sounded worried, so I went upstairs and I gave her the official papers and the picture of Lydia when she was young and fat, and Nana-Jo's eyes got big and she said, "Oh, Jesus," and she sat down at the kitchen table.

And I rocked back and forth, and said, "You aren't my mom," and Nana-Jo said, "Yes, I am. I didn't give birth to you, Denny, but I was the first person to hold you after you were born and from that moment on, I was your mom and Papa-Jo was your dad. We adopted you and we never looked back."

And I said, "Does Angus know the truth?"

Nana-Jo nodded. "He does."

"And Papa-Jo?"

"He knew everything."

And that made me ANGRY and I said some lousy terrible things to Nana-Jo, then I picked up her favorite vase (yellow glass, brown spots) and I threw it against the wall and it broke into a million pieces. Then I put my boots on and my parka, and I went over to 8A to yell at Angus because he was a traitor too, but Angus wasn't home, so I sat down and put my head between my knees and I counted the tiles on his kitchen floor, but that didn't help either, because my heart kept revving up like the motor in Nana-Jo's Subaru when she gets it stuck and has to rock it back and forth to get it unstuck.

I turned on Angus's TV to watch a fast-moving TV show, but I couldn't find one and I fell asleep on his couch and when I woke up it was 10:38 p.m. and Angus was sitting in his La-Z-Boy recliner chair and he was wearing a T-shirt that said **I Don't Know How to Act My Age. I've Never Been This Old Before.**

I sat up and said, "You're a traitor, Angus."

And he said, "Yeah, I heard all about it."

"Did Nana-Jo call you?"

"She did." He pointed the top of his Bud Light beer bottle at me. "And just for the record, I don't like Lydia any more than you do, okay? She was always a pain in the ass, even as a teenager."

And I said, "Lydia's my real mom."

"Who cares?" Angus said. "You're here, you have a good life, and Nana-Jo's always taken excellent care of you. By the way, I've got better things to do than listen to you whine about something that just doesn't matter in the grand scheme of things, so don't even get started on the whole 'woe is me' bullshit."

I slapped the couch. "But I'm mad, Angus!"

He nodded. "Yeah, well . . . I can't blame you for that. I'd be pretty pissed off if I found out Lydia was my mom. How about this, though? Give yourself a few days to be mad, then move on, because you don't want to put a lot of energy into this, buddy. It's just not worth it. What matters most here is *you* and how *you* feel about *your life*, not Lydia and what she did or didn't do when she was a fucked-up eighteen-year-old."

"Why didn't you tell me, Angus?"

He shrugged. "It wasn't my business. And anyhow, who your biological mother is has nothing to do with how I feel about you."

I looked out the window. "I'm still mad at you, Angus."

He set his beer down. "I know, but right now you're mad at everybody and you're not thinking straight. You'll stop being mad at me when you realize, once again, how much joy I bring to your life. I mean . . . Who else dances on the side of a fucking highway singing 'Shake

It Off' when you're in a funk? Can you think of *anyone* other than me who'd be willing to do that? I think not!"

I stared at him, doing thinking about that, then he said, "Thank God for me, right?" and I said, "Yeah, Angus, thank God for you."

He leaned forward in his chair. "Denny, think about this. Your life tomorrow won't be any different than it was today *before* you learned this stuff about Lydia. On top of that, let's do a little experiment. Tell me three things—no, four things—about Lydia that anyone who knows her would say are true."

And I said, "I don't know what you mean."

"I'll go first. Lydia is selfish. Do you agree with that?"

I nodded. "Yes."

"Good. Now tell me something else about her that's true," Angus said.

"Lydia's a shithead."

Angus laughed. "Be more specific."

"She's not very thoughtful?"

"Keep going. Good or bad, throw it at me!"

"Lydia's an excellent photographer."

Angus nodded. "One more. Anything else you can think of."

And I said, "She wears too much makeup, she's messy, she can't cook—"

"Whoa, pump the brakes! That's good. You've given me lots to work with. Now I'm going to ask you some questions and I want you to be one hundred percent honest when you answer them, okay?" and I said, "Okay," then Angus said, "Are you selfish, Denny Voss?" and I said, "No," and he said, "Are you thoughtful?" and I said, "I am," then Angus said, "I don't even have to ask the next question, because you *suck* at taking pictures, always have. You cut people's heads off or the shot's so blurry you can't tell who's in the picture, right?" and I said, "Yeah, that's right. I suck at taking pictures," then Angus said, "And you don't wear makeup, at least not that I know of. You're a tidy freak at your house and mine, and you're a much better cook than I am. Would you agree?"

I nodded. "Yeah, I agree."

Angus smiled. "See, buddy? Lydia gave birth to you but you are *nothing* like her, which means you obviously inherited more of Nana-Jo's traits than Lydia's, which only seems fair since she was the one who raised you."

And I said, real quiet-like, "I'm nothing like Lydia."

Angus took a drink of beer. "Damn straight you aren't. Lydia was a basketball star and you are, hands down, the most unathletic person I've ever met. She sleeps until noon and you're up at six a.m. every day. She's not a dog lover and you love dogs. I could go all day here, but you get the point I'm trying to make, don't you?"

I nodded. "Yeah, I do."

Then Angus gave me a high five and he told me to *get my ass home to bed*, so I went back to 8B because I didn't want George to worry about where I was. And when I got home the glass from the broken vase was cleaned up and Nana-Jo's bedroom door was closed and George was asleep on my bed, so I crawled under the covers, and George woke up and put his head on my chest, same as always.

And I thought about what Angus had said.

And I decided he was right.

It wasn't his responsibility to tell me the truth about Lydia, plus he is the ONLY PERSON who's ever danced on the side of a highway singing "Shake It Off" to cheer me up. But I wasn't 100 percent un-mad yet, because Nana-Jo and Lydia were liars and traitors (people who betray you) and I wanted to show them I didn't need them anymore. I could take care of myself. I could make my own decisions and I didn't need a mother or a grandmother or a legal guardian. I had my job, I knew what was right and what was wrong, and Nana-Jo and Lydia not telling me the truth was VERY VERY WRONG.

Nobody's Talking to Anybody

I looked at Dr. Harland and said, "So yeah, Lydia's my real mom," and he carefully set his pencil down, and he said, "That would've been a difficult fact for you to stumble across," and I looked at him and said, "I didn't stumble, I found out by doing snooping," and he said, "I know, Denny." Then he said, "What happened next?"

So, I told him.

The next day, Nana-Jo called Lydia to tell her about our flooded basement and how I had snooped through her trunk of keepsakes—and what I found—and because my bedroom door wasn't closed all the way, I heard Nana-Jo say, "Of course he's upset!" and "What do I *think*? I think we should've told him the truth years ago." Then she said, "No, Lydia, I'm not willing to listen to that kind of garbage. I'm hanging up," and she did.

After that Nana-Jo wasn't speaking to Lydia and I wasn't speaking to either of them. Every night before bed, I'd listen to the messages Lydia left on our answering machine and she would say things like, "Mom, *please* talk to me," and "Denny, I'm so sorry about this," and "I love you guys. Please don't freeze me out!" (which is when you stop talking to someone and pretend they don't exist) and when I was done listening to all of Lydia's messages I'd press Delete and erase them, and then she'd leave new ones the next day.

Dr. Harland wrote something in his notebook. "How were you feeling at that point, Denny?" he asked, and I told him I mostly felt quiet inside (and sad) and then a few days went by and I felt quiet inside (and mad) but I didn't feel like talking to anyone, so when I wasn't working at DOT, I did my consequences for the judge, then I took George for lots of long walks and that made him happy, which was good because at least someone was happy.

So yeah, me and George did lots of walking.

We walked and walked. One night we went across town to the bridge that splits Woodmont in half and I looked down at the Lester River; then we kept walking until we reached the Norida yogurt plant, which was busy making yogurt, and Mr. Tesky's yellow helicopter was parked out front on a cement pad. Another night, me and George walked all the way to Bob's Gun Emporium, where Papa-Jo used to buy bullets and cleaning supplies for his rifles, and I looked in the window (it had iron bars on it), then I opened my knapsack and I found some paper and I wrote a note that said: *Bob, please stop selling guns, too many people are dying*, and I duct-taped it to the front door.

One night after dinner, it was raining and I put on my coat and my boots and Nana-Jo said, "Denny, please don't go out in this," then I put on my red-and-black plaid hat with the fuzzy ear flaps and I clipped George into his leash, and we walked all the way to Walmart, which is a long way to walk even when it's not raining.

When we got there, I took George inside to buy him a rawhide chew bone and, same as always, no one said anything because he was wearing his **Therapy Dog** harness. And on our way to Pet Supplies, we walked past some blow-up snow tubes and plastic saucers and a sign that said **Stock Up for Winter Early!** and that's when I saw a bunch of snow sleds with **White Lightning** written on the side and there was a shiny poster tacked to the wall behind them that said:

White Lightning Xtreme Snow Sled

58 inches long

Classic toboggan shape

Cutout handles for secure grip

Shell made from recycled dumpster lids

Easily accommodates adult-child tandem rides

Features a slight taper at the front to increase dynamic performance

Designed for top speeds on all sorts of snow

Customers say it's *The Fastest Sled on the Planet*!

I stared at that snow sled for a long time doing remembering about Papa-Jo and how he used to take me sledding to Penguin Hill with our old wooden toboggan, and how I'd go up and down the hill over and over again while Papa-Jo sat on a bench and smoked his pipe, and never once did he ever say, "It's time to go, Denny." Instead, he'd wait until I told him I was ready to leave. So, I used the debit card I keep in my Velcro wallet and I bought George a rawhide chew bone and I got myself a White Lightning Xtreme Snow Sled to stock up for winter early ($29.95), then me and George left the store, and I carried my new sled all the way home so it wouldn't get scratched bouncing against the sidewalk in the rain.

The next day I was at Angus's house when he and his buddy Trey went on the internet and booked a vacation (first one of Angus's freaking life). They had been planning the trip for a long time and they wanted to "lock it in," so they were excited when they finally picked a resort in Mexico, typed in a credit card number, and pressed Buy. Angus did a whoop and Trey high-fived him and they told me they'd be *leaving on a jet plane* January 3. But then two weeks later Trey told Angus he couldn't go to Mexico because his girlfriend got herself pregnant, and they were getting married in December, and he needed to pay for the wedding.

Elaine came by 8B a few days later and Angus was there with us, and Nana-Jo told Elaine how Angus's friend had canceled on their Mexico vacation. "That's too bad," Elaine said. "Where were you going?"

Angus said, "Akumal."

"Oh, it's gorgeous there!" Elaine told him the beach there was *breathtaking*, that she'd snorkeled there years ago, then Angus asked her a bunch of questions about the area, and he said, "Elaine, why don't you go with me?"

She rolled her eyes. "I've already been there. Why would I go again?"

He grinned. "Because you'd be with me."

"Exactly, and if I went with you, you'd get weird about it."

"Why would I get weird about it?"

"You know how you are."

"Aw, come on!" Angus gave her arm a nudge. "Wouldn't it be nice to go somewhere hot for a week in January?"

Elaine frowned. "Well . . . if I did go on vacation with you, we'd have to agree to go as friends, nothing more. I'd sleep in my bed, you'd sleep in yours."

Angus's eyes lit up. "So you'll go with me?"

Elaine did thinking about it, then she shrugged. "Sure, why not? By the time January gets here, I'll be ready for a week on a beach."

So yeah, that's how Angus ended up going to Mexico on vacation with Elaine-the-stalker the morning after Mr. Tesky got himself killed.

And me and George kept walking every night for the next two months, and it was late when we got home and I was usually tired and that made it easier to fall asleep, which was good because I was having trouble sleeping. Some nights when I couldn't sleep, I'd put my jacket on and walk up Penguin Hill by myself and there was never anyone there in the middle of the night, so I'd sit down on a bench and do thinking. For some people it doesn't take long to do thinking, but for me it usually does; then when I finally got tired I'd head home and try extra hard not to look at the bench where Papa-Jo used to sit and watch me, because that made me sad and I was trying to get the sad to stop.

Lydia Comes Home

After I did snooping through Lydia's keepsakes and learned the truth, she came home to do a surprise visit, and at first it wasn't good, and then it became interesting, and in the end it wasn't good again, but she only stayed two nights and, like Angus said, at least we talked. So yeah, there's that. She walked in right after me and Nana-Jo finished eating dinner one night and we had lots of food left, but I didn't ask Lydia if she wanted any, I just shoved the leftovers in the fridge. Lydia looked nervous (she kept twisting her hands together) and she said, "Hi, Denny," and I nodded, then she said, "How you doing?" and I said, "That's a dumb question and I don't answer dumb questions."

Nana-Jo said, "Denny!"

And I said, "What?"

And Lydia said, "No, Mom. It's fine."

I took George for a walk and when I got back Nana-Jo seemed to have forgiven Lydia for being a liar and a jerk. Lydia told us she couldn't stay long because she was flying to a country called Norway to take pictures and she'd be gone for two weeks. Then Nana-Jo went to bed and I washed the dishes and Lydia dried them, even though I didn't ask for help. She asked if I liked my job, and if it was hard to work with Angus, and if our boss was a good guy, and I said "Yes," and "No," and "Sometimes," because I didn't want to do talking with her because she's such a dope, but Nana-Jo raised me up not to be rude, even though I figured Lydia deserved all the rude I had inside of me.

After I finished washing the dishes, I got George's brush and his Papaya Mist deodorizing spray and I flipped him over on the Elvis rug so I could brush out the knots on his belly, same as I do every Tuesday, and George let me do it because he's used to me brushing out the knots on his belly every Tuesday.

Lydia opened a bottle of wine she'd brought with her and she poured a glass; then she went into Nana-Jo's sewing room, where she sleeps on the futon when she's here, and she called Marco in New York, which was good because I didn't want her hanging around me and George. And because the sewing room door didn't close all the way I heard her say, "I'll explain more about it when I get home," and "I decided to come at the last minute, Marco."

When she came back into the living room, I was putting on my coat to take George for his nighttime walk. "Can I go with you?" Lydia asked, and I said, "It's a free country," which doesn't mean yes, but it also doesn't mean no.

Lydia put on her high-heel boots and a short jacket that looked puffy like a bubble roll and she came with us, and, like always, even though she was forty-eight years old, she looked like she was trying to be a teenager because her pants were too tight and she was wearing lots of makeup. And there were puddles everywhere and she kept jumping onto the grass to avoid them; then she slipped and fell on her butt in the wet grass, so I grabbed her arm and yanked her back onto her feet because that's how Nana-Jo raised me up.

The streetlights were on by then because it was 9:00 p.m. and I crossed the street with George and we took the walking path up to Penguin Hill Park, and Lydia followed us and she would not shut up. She kept saying things like, "Mom used to bring me here when I was little," and "I had my first kiss on that bench right there," and "I forgot how peaceful it is up here," and she kept talking and me and George kept walking, and I kept thinking how lucky George was to be deaf because he didn't have to listen to Lydia's dumb voice.

A few minutes later she stopped and said, "Oh, my God! My friends and I used to sled here every winter, on that hill right there."

And I said, "I sled here all the time in the winter."

Lydia looked surprised. "You do?"

"Sometimes Angus comes too."

"Angus sleds?"

"Only when he's drinking."

There wasn't any snow on the hill yet but there would be pretty soon and when it came it would look like a ski hill with a wide-open area all the way down the middle and trees that went down one side, and more trees that went down the other side, and the whole thing would be lit up at night from two streetlights at the top that were next to some benches and a wooden sign that said **PENGUIN HILL**.

Lydia finally stopped talking. She hugged herself and stared at the hill for a long time, then she turned to me and said, real quiet-like, "I'm sorry, Denny. I was young and scared. I honestly didn't know which end was up. I wasn't ready to be a mother."

And I said, "You would've been a shitty mom."

"You're probably right."

"I am right."

Lydia looked at her boots. "My therapist says it's completely normal for you to be angry. He also said it'll take time for you to process this, so no matter what you're feeling inside"—she slapped her chest—"you need to honor those feelings and allow them space. You also need to talk about them, though, because if you don't let them out, you'll get backed up emotionally and that's not healthy . . ." And she kept talking and talking, and she would *not* shut up, so me and George started walking home and she had to run to catch up to us.

Halfway down the hill, George wandered off the path to do his business and I asked Lydia to hold his leash while I picked up his poo, and while I did that, she said, "It's important that you talk about this, Denny. Tell me what you're thinking." George's poo smelled REALLY BAD so I tied a knot in the bag and handed it to Lydia, and I said, "I'm thinking, 'George's poo stinks and I don't want to carry it, so maybe Lydia should because she stinks too.'"

Lydia smiled. "See?! That's a good start. You're being honest with me and I respect that even if the anger is making you say unkind things."

And I said, "I'm saying the truth."

"Okay, then."

Me and George walked away and I was thinking how good it would feel to hip check Lydia into a mud puddle, but I also knew Nana-Jo would get mad if I did, because we'd talked about stuff like this before and I knew it was something I could IMAGINE in my head, but I shouldn't DO in real life.

On our way back down the walking path, Lydia got herself going too fast and her ankle twisted in her boot and she fell down again, but she was behind me so I pretended not to see her. I kept walking with George while she crawled around on her hands and knees with his poop bag, then she finally pulled herself up against a signpost and hurried to catch up to us. "Denny, I know I shouldn't push, but did you want to talk about . . . well, any of it?"

And I said, "No way, José."

"You must have some questions."

"I have no questions."

Lydia nodded, then she wrapped her arms around her middle. "All right, then. That's fine. I just want you to know that I'm here for you, now and in the future. Please know that, okay? Because you can ask me *anything*. This might be too soon, but the time will probably come when you'll have questions and—"

"Lydia?" I said.

"What?"

"Please stop talking."

"Of course. I'm sorry."

And the rest of the way home, she didn't talk, she just walked beside me carrying George's poo bag, then she tossed it in our garbage can before we went inside. I checked on Nana-Jo and she was asleep, doing snoring, so I put a glass of water on her bedside table in case she woke up and got thirsty. Lydia turned on the TV and flipped through the channels and she found an episode of *Schitt's Creek* on one.

"Have you seen this show, Denny? It's so good!"

And I said, "Yup."

"Do you like it?"

"Yup."

Then she poured herself more wine and I don't like Lydia, but I love *Schitt's Creek*, so I decided to watch one episode. She poured more wine during the commercial break. She told me how much she loved photography, and even though I didn't say anything back, she kept talking like nothing was different between us, even though everything was different now.

"Life isn't easy, Denny." Her voice was slurry. "Especially when you're young because you're so damned naive. You fall in love and you trust people you shouldn't trust and in the end you get screwed. Do you get what I'm saying?" and I said, "No," because I didn't. Lydia kept talking and she said stuff I didn't understand about *emotional trauma* and *growth*, then she said, ". . . and sure, you *think* you're in love, but then you spend time with that person and you find out that their heart is black." Her voice got all wobbly and she seemed sad. "I guess I'm just a shitty judge of character. I attract assholes."

And I said, "It takes one to know one."

Lydia put her wineglass down. "I deserved that."

She was a traitor and the biggest liar of all, and I didn't want to do visiting with her anymore, so I poked George with my foot and said, "Time for bed, George."

Lydia said, "Already? Don't you want to stay up a little longer?"

"Nope."

"Please, Denny? Just a few more minutes? I'm leaving tomorrow and I know you don't want to talk about it, but I'd like to tell you how I got pregnant and how I ended up in Duluth. I think it's important because at some point you will have questions, so why not let me fill in the blanks for you now?"

I could feel myself getting angry, because Lydia was being VERY pushy and she wouldn't leave me alone, so I said, "*You* want to talk to *me*, but *I* don't want to talk to *you*!" And I got up and George followed me to my room, and he climbed up on the bed and I turned off the light and got under the covers, but I left my door partway open so I could hear Nana-Jo if she called out for me.

—

Dr. Harland had his elbows on the table while he listened to me.

"So yeah," I said. "The next morning we had breakfast, then Lydia and Nana-Jo went outside and Nana-Jo hugged her goodbye and Lydia left in her rental car. I watched from the window and before she drove away, she waved at me, and I gave her the middle finger when Nana-Jo wasn't looking because, like I said, even though Nana-Jo raised me up not to be rude, I think Lydia deserves all the rude I have inside of me."

Dr. Harland nodded. "Denny, can we back up again? You mentioned that when Lydia slipped and fell on the wet grass you yanked her back onto her feet because *that's how Nana-Jo raised you up*?"

And I said, "Uh-huh."

He sat back in his chair. "Have you considered that maybe you helped her up because deep down inside you actually love her, even though it's a complicated kind of love?" and I said, "Please, I just ate," which is what Angus always says when I tell him something that makes him want to vomit up his lunch.

Doing Talking About Motive

Bridget came to the jail today to do lawyering. She wanted to talk about *motive* (which is the reason why people do things) and she told me that the police had two theories. They thought I'd used the Smith & Wesson .38 Special snub-nose handgun to kill Mr. Tesky because I was upset with him for hitting me with his Tesla when I was biking down Bendmore Road.

And I said, "Nope. Not true."

Bridget opened her leather bag and pulled out a folder. "How did you feel when Mr. Tesky hit you with his car?" and I said, "First I was scared, and then I got angry." She nodded, then she told me that the police's second theory was that I used the Smith & Wesson .38 Special snub-nose handgun to kill Mr. Tesky because I was angry that he'd fired Nana-Jo and *put us in the poorhouse*.

And I said, "Nope. Not true. We live in 8B, not a poorhouse."

"Yes, but things have been pretty tough for you and Nana-Jo financially since she lost her job, haven't they?"

"We've never had lots of money."

Bridget squinted at a piece of paper. "Denny, is it true that you accosted Mr. Tesky at the drugstore?" and I said, "I don't know what that means." Then she took a breath and blew it out real quick-like. "It means that you approached him *in a menacing manner*. The prosecution says you were aggressive with him that day, Denny, that you demanded that Mr. Tesky give Nana-Jo her job back."

"Nope. Not true."

Bridget tilted her head. "But you *were* at the drugstore?"

I nodded. "Yup, I went there to buy stockings for Nana-Jo's birthday present and I saw Mr. Tesky and did talking with him, and I was polite because that's how Nana-Jo raised me up. All I did was ask if he could *please* give Nana-Jo her job back."

"And what did he say?"

A bunch of quiet followed. I scratched my cheek and looked out the window at the snow piling up on the cars in the parking lot, and I wondered what kind of car Bridget drove, and if she had a snow brush to clean it off, because if she didn't have a snow brush then maybe Dr. Harland could lend her his.

"Denny?" Bridget said.

More quiet. More staring out the window.

She leaned forward. "What did Mr. Tesky say when you asked him if he could please give Nana-Jo her job back?"

"I don't remember."

Bridget shook her head. "I find that hard to believe. You remember everything. Matter of fact, I've never met anyone with your kind of recall."

My hands went into fists and I took them off the table and put them in my lap. I didn't want to talk about this, but Dr. Harland had already told me (three times) that being 100 percent honest was important so we could get this whole mess cleaned up and he also told me there might be times when he and Bridget would need to have *uncomfortable conversations* with me that couldn't be avoided.

I looked at Bridget. "When I asked Mr. Tesky if he could give Nana-Jo her job back, he said, 'That's never going to happen' and 'Irene hired Joanne full time, not me, and she employed her for a lot longer than she should've. Joanne's retirement was long overdue, so I let her go. That's just the way the ball bounces.'"

"How did that make you feel?" Bridget asked.

I scratched my arm, then I looked out the window again. "I started to feel dizzy and my heart started going *boom-boom-boom*, so to calm myself down I closed my eyes and sang the theme song for *Toy Story*—'You've Got a Friend in Me'—which is what I do whenever a situation goes sideways on me."

"What happened then?"

More quiet.

More staring out the window.

I looked at Bridget and said, real quiet-like, "People were staring at us and Mr. Tesky's face went red, and he looked mad. Then he came closer to me and he called me terrible, horrible, lousy names and he left the store."

Bridget opened her mouth.

Then she closed it.

And my heart started going BOOM-BOOM-BOOM and I looked at her, and said, "The police are wrong, though, Bridget. If I wanted to kill Mr. Tesky, it would've been because of something he did a long time ago that was way worse than hitting me with his car, or firing Nana-Jo, or calling me terrible names."

Bridget leaned forward. "What did he do?"

I scratched my ear. "I don't want to talk about Mr. Tesky anymore. Not today."

"Then when?" Bridget pushed her glasses back on her nose. "This is ridiculous, Denny. I can't put this case together and defend you without us having a conversation about Henry Tesky. When are we going to talk about him?!"

Bridget was being VERY pushy but I could also tell she wasn't happy with me and we were on the same side, so I said, "Next Wednesday," because that was seven days away and that would give me seven days to do thinking about the words I needed to say out loud that I'd never said out loud before . . . and it would also give me seven days without Bridget asking me questions about stupid Mr. Tesky, who went and got himself killed.

Soap-on-a-Rope

This morning I told Dr. Harland how I ran into Mr. Tesky at the pharmacy.

Nana-Jo's birthday was two weeks away and she was going to be seventy-four years old and I wanted to get her something special, so I decided to do a few soap-on-a-ropes. Nana-Jo showed me how to make them after Papa-Jo died because we had to be careful with our money (still do). This is how you make them: You take a knee-high nylon stocking and you fill it with slivers of soap or baby soaps like the kind you get when you stay in hotels, then you tie two knots at the top of the stocking, leaving space between them, and you hang your soap-on-a-rope in the shower and—**BAM!**—it lathers up when you add water.

I was at 8A with Angus and he was wearing a T-shirt that said **NOT HERE TO MAKE FRIENDS** and I asked if he'd drive me to the Cotton Thistle, which is a store that sells lots of different things, including fancy soaps, and because Nana-Jo loves the smell of grapefruit, I asked Alison, who owns the shop, if she could order me seventy-four baby grapefruit soaps, and Alison laughed and said, "I can, Denny, but they come in packages of ten, so that means we'd need to order eight packages."

And I said, "That's fine."

Alison looked it up on her computer, then she punched some numbers in and said, "The total would be one hundred eighty-two dollars," and I put my wallet on the counter, and I said, "Money is no object," which I heard someone say once in a movie.

After I paid for the soap, Angus drove me to the drugstore so I could buy knee-high nylon stockings and when I asked if he wanted to go in with me, he said, "Nah, I'm good here," and he took out his phone to play *Angry Birds* while he waited.

So I went inside and was looking for nylon stockings when I saw Mr. Tesky at the pharmacy counter at the back of the store. He was wearing sunglasses and dress pants and a golf shirt, and he had a much fancier watch than my waterproof Timex. I hadn't seen him in a long time, but he looked the same as he did in all the posters that were tacked up around Woodmont that said **HENRY TESKY FOR MAYOR**.

And I thought about Nana-Jo and how, after she turned sixty, she'd had trouble getting cleaning jobs because she wasn't as fast as she used to be and how she'd come home after work and I'd help her make dinner, then she'd fall asleep while we were watching TV because she was tired. She'd been working part time for Irene Tesky for five years and then one day Irene called and told Nana-Jo to quit all of her other cleaning jobs because she was going to hire her full time to take care of the Teskys' McMansion, and she'd be vacuuming and washing dishes and doing errands like dropping off dry cleaning, and Irene said she didn't care how long it took to get everything done.

But that was years ago and now Nana-Jo didn't have a job because Mr. Tesky fired her and she'd spent the whole weekend going through bills, and the day before, when Angus stopped by, she told him she couldn't afford to pay our half to get the roof reshingled and could he please wait another year to have it done?

That's when the pharmacist (lady who hands out all the drugs) said, "I'm sorry, Mr. Tesky. I have no record that your prescription was called in," and Mr. Tesky looked at his watch and said, "Please check again."

And the pharmacist said, "Of course," and she started going through baskets of prescriptions that were waiting to be picked up, and while she did, Mr. Tesky tapped his foot and said, "My wife called it in yesterday. She said I'd be here before noon to pick it up." And when he said *my wife* I knew he meant Malinda Tesky, his new wife who used to be his secretary, the same one Angus caught him doing sex on a desk with.

The pharmacist said, "I'll be right back. I need to check your file on the computer," and she left the counter to go look something up.

Seeing Mr. Tesky made my stomach hurt, mostly because when I was twelve, after Nana-Jo pulled me out of school to do the rest of my training at home, he wasn't nice to me when Nana-Jo brought me to work with her, even though I was super quiet and I sat in the Teskys' kitchen and worked on my numbers (math) or my coloring (art) and sometimes I fell asleep with my face on their kitchen table, but I never got in the way.

One day Mr. Tesky came home early from work, and I was sitting in the kitchen and he told his wife, Irene, that it was inappropriate for Nana-Jo to bring me to work with her, and Irene said it was fine, but Mr. Tesky got mad and said, "It sure as hell isn't!" That's when Nana-Jo walked in with her dustrag and she told Irene not to worry, that we'd make it work some other way—and we did. After that, I did my lessons at home and Nana-Jo called to check on me every hour, and by then I was thirteen, and after that I became fourteen, and then I became fifteen, and everything worked out fine.

But now I was looking at Mr. Tesky in the drugstore and I wasn't a little kid anymore, but I also wasn't dressed like he was, and I didn't have fancy sunglasses, or a cell phone, or an expensive watch. I was wearing cargo shorts (lots of pockets) and a Toronto Raptors T-shirt, and a baseball cap Nana-Jo got me that said **BLESSING IN DISGUISE** and all I could think about was how worried Nana-Jo was about paying our bills. That's when I decided to talk to Mr. Tesky *man to man*, but I decided to do visiting first, because that's what you do when you talk to people you haven't seen in a long time.

He was looking at his phone when I walked up to him. I did a wave and said, "Hello, do you remember me? I'm Denny Voss. Are you playing *Angry Birds*?"

He stepped back. "I'm sorry?"

"Are you playing *Angry Birds*?"

"No, I'm not."

And I said, "Huh," and I scratched my ear. "Are you doing a sports bet, or are you looking at dirty pictures?" Mr. Tesky's eyebrows jumped. "Neither!" Then he looked around to see if anyone was listening to us, and he said, "Did you follow me in here?" and I said, "Nope, I came to buy nylon stockings for soap-on-a-rope," and his eyebrows scrunched up and he looked confused, then I thought about how Angus was always saying, "For the love of God, Denny, stop beating around the bush," or "Get to the fucking point!" when I was explaining something, and I wanted to help Nana-Jo fix her money problems and I didn't want to waste Mr. Tesky's time, so I decided to just *spit it out.*

"Nana-Jo worked for you for twenty-four years—"

Mr. Tesky frowned. "Joanne Voss?"

"—and then you fired her for being too old."

Mr. Tesky looked over both of his shoulders real quick-like. "I didn't fire Joanne for being too old; I let her go because she was no longer capable of completing the job she'd been hired to do at the level the job requires." Mr. Tesky put his phone in his pocket. "Seriously, what do you want from me?"

"Could you give Nana-Jo her job back?"

"That's never going to happen."

I blinked at him. "But she needs her job because she's worried about money, and she gets money from doing her job, and she spent the whole weekend going through bills. You don't have to hire her back *now* but maybe when her broken-down knee heals up again?"

Mr. Tesky folded his arms. "You really are a full-on idiot, aren't you? Did you not hear what I said? No means no; it doesn't mean *try harder*. This isn't rocket science. It's actually quite simple, even for someone with your limited capacity. I don't owe you people anything and I'm not responsible for Joanne because she didn't plan for the future. Irene hired her, not me, and she employed her for a lot longer than she should've. Unfortunately, she also paid her more than she was worth, but there's nothing I can do about that. Joanne's retirement was long overdue. That's just the way the ball bounces."

I stared at him. "So, you won't give Nana-Jo her job back?"

"Absolutely not."

If Angus was there, he'd probably say, "You're a pompous ass," because that's what Angus always says about Mr. Tesky, but I'm not Angus.

Instead, I started to shake and my heart started going **BOOM-BOOM-BOOM**, so to calm myself down I closed my eyes and sang the theme song for *Toy Story*—"You've Got a Friend in Me"—and when I finished, I opened my eyes and lots of people were staring at us, and Mr. Tesky's face was red like a tomato.

"Stop acting like an idiot," he said.

And I said, "I'm not an idiot. My number is 72."

Mr. Tesky looked at the floor for a second. Then he turned and smiled at all the people who were watching us and he stepped closer to me, and he leaned in by my ear and said some terrible, horrible, lousy things. And the pharmacist lady was looking at us from her counter and I think she heard what he said, because she gasped (inhaled air quickly) and she glared at him and said, "Here's your prescription." Then she stuck her arm out and Mr. Tesky took the bag and he left the store without paying for it, which is called stealing.

And a whole bunch of people were staring at me and my heart wouldn't stop going **BOOM-BOOM-BOOM**, so I picked up a bottle of cough syrup and I pretended to read the directions on the back because doing visiting with Mr. Tesky hadn't gone well and now I knew for sure that Nana-Jo was never EVER going to get her job back.

One week later, the doorbell rang when I was wrapping up Nana-Jo's soap-on-a-ropes in tissue paper for her birthday and I opened the door and there was a man wearing sunglasses, and he said, "Are you Denny

Voss?" and I said, "Yes," and he gave me an envelope and said, "You've been served," and I said, "Did you want me to sign for it because that's what I did with Nana-Jo's UPS Express envelope?" but he just walked away, got in his car, and left, and I thought to myself, *I guess not.*

Nana-Jo wasn't home and my name was on the envelope, so I opened it and inside was an official-looking paper that said *HRO* at the top and below that it said, *Minnesota Statutes Section 609.749, which prohibits harassing another person by engaging in conduct that causes the victim to feel frightened, threatened, oppressed, persecuted, and intimidated,* and my name was there, and Mr. Tesky's name was there, and a judge had signed his name at the bottom.

And I thought to myself, *Wow, someone must have told the judge what Mr. Tesky said to me in the pharmacy and now he's in trouble because he made me feel frightened, threatened, oppressed, persecuted, and intimidated.* So yeah, I did a smile, then I slid that paper back into the envelope and I put it in the basement freezer with our other official papers, and I finished packing up Nana-Jo's soap-on-a-ropes for her birthday.

Doing Lawyering

The law is confusing for someone who doesn't do lawyering. Today after breakfast (oatmeal with four packets of brown sugar), Grant-the-corrections-officer took me to our special meeting room and Bridget was there waiting for me, but she wasn't smiling. She was wearing a purple blouse with white splashes on it and she smelled like lemons (same as always) and she said, "Good morning, Denny. Please take a seat."

So I did.

Then she said, "I have good news and bad news. Your trial date has been set. Jury selection begins in two weeks. The bad news is, during discovery, I found out that Mr. Tesky was given an HRO against you."

"I don't know what that is."

Bridget frowned. "It's a harassment restraining order. It means when you talked to Mr. Tesky at the pharmacy that day, he felt threatened and harassed by you, and because of that he was given an HRO signed by a judicial officer." She took her glasses off. "It's a problem for us, Denny." And I felt my face get hot because Bridget looked unhappy with me, so I sat back and tried to do thinking, then I said, "I have an idea! Why don't we ask the judge to give *me* an HRO against Mr. Tesky and that'll make things even because he also made me feel *frightened, threatened, oppressed, persecuted, and intimidated.*"

Bridget squeezed her eyes shut. "Mr. Tesky's dead, Denny. It's too late to file an HRO against him," and I said, "Oh."

Also, because he's my *temporary legal guardian*, Angus has been doing talking with Bridget and he came by the jail this morning and joined us in our meeting room. And when he got there he was wearing a T-shirt that said **I'M A LOVER, NOT A FIGHTER** and he kept pacing back and forth while Bridget sat at the table with papers in front of her.

Bridget said, "Denny, we're here to talk about your defense strategy. I know we've talked about it briefly before but now that I've been through discovery, it's imperative that we agree on how to move forward. I've talked to Angus, but his temporary guardianship is limited in scope and that means he can make financial and medical decisions for you as his ward, but he can't make legal decisions without your consent."

And I said, "That's good."

Bridget looked at Angus, then she quickly looked back at me. "We're here because we need your help, Denny."

"Okay, I'll help."

Bridget leaned forward. "You know those papers you keep in your freezer that say you're *developmentally challenged* and *neurodiverse*?"

I nodded. "My number is 72."

Bridget pointed at me. "Yes, and here's an interesting dichotomy that may help us in this case. You see, technically if someone scores below 70 on an IQ test, they're defined as having *mental retardation*, as offensive as those words are to me and everyone else in modern society. However, you have an IQ of 72, and according to the laws of this state that means you have a *developmental disability*, which opens an avenue of defense we need to explore."

"I'm not disabled, Bridget."

Angus put his hands on his head. "Here we go!"

Bridget tidied her papers. "I know, Denny. However, according to the laws of this state, you *do* have a developmental disability."

I crossed my arms. "I'm not disabled. I'm fine just the way I am."

Bridget lifted her hands. "Of course you are—but just listen to me for a second—what I'm trying to say is that we *could* change your plea to 'guilty based on limited capacity' and argue for treatment."

Angus snort-laughed.

I frowned. "What's *treatment*?"

Bridget sighed. "It's when someone like you pleads guilty to the crime you're accused of and instead of being sent to jail you're placed in the care of a mental health treatment facility, where they're better able to handle your needs."

"I don't have needs."

Another snort-laugh from Angus. "This just keeps getting better," he said, then he rubbed his face with his hands, and he turned to Bridget. "Can't we have Dr. Harland say he's not mentally fit to stand trial?"

Bridget shook her head. "We won't win that battle, Angus. Denny's been assessed and he's been deemed competent. He understands that shooting someone is wrong, no matter the level of intent, and that will make him criminally responsible if he's found guilty. Unfortunately, it's becoming far more common in this country for people with cognitive disabilities to end up behind bars. That's my concern here."

Angus crossed his arms. "But you said their case isn't solid."

"It's not a slam dunk," Bridget said, "but there's enough incriminating evidence that it certainly has me worried."

Angus did thinking about that, then he sat down beside me and said, "Denny, I want you to look at me and pay attention," so I did. "Here are your options." He held up one finger. "Bridget can take your case to trial and argue that you're innocent, just like she would if I were on trial for murdering Henry Tesky, or"—he held up another finger—"she can plead guilty for you and argue that you're developmentally disabled, and that way you wouldn't have to go to prison. They'd send you to a treatment facility instead. What do *you* want to do?"

And I said, "It's my decision?"

"Yup, it's your decision."

Bridget jumped in. "To be clear, Denny, we don't know how long you'd be at a treatment facility. It could be anywhere from five to fifteen years."

I squinted my eyes and looked out the window and did thinking because until then I hadn't thought about *not* going home after the trial was done or what it would be like to STAY IN JAIL or what it would be like to get myself sent to a TREATMENT FACILITY. I thought about Nana-Jo and how she was going to need my help now that she'd had a stroke, and then I thought about Nori and Theo, and how Theo had said me and George were his *lucky charms* and I knew if the jury said I was GUILTY, then Nori probably wouldn't want me to be Theo's friend anymore. Then I thought about George and who would take care of him if I wasn't at 8B and I knew I had to be strong so I could get myself home, and this was MY DECISION and I also knew I wasn't MORE than other people but I wasn't LESS either.

Then I said to Bridget, "I want you to do my defense just like you would if Angus was on trial for Mr. Tesky's murder."

Angus put his forehead on the table.

"All right, then," Bridget said, and a bunch of quiet followed. "I guess now it's time to look at the bright side, gentlemen."

"There's a bright side?" Angus said.

Bridget put her papers back into her leather bag. "There is," she said. "Minnesota abolished capital punishment in 1911, so if Denny is found guilty, he won't have to face the death penalty." And that sounded like good news to me, so I said, "Hallelujah," because like Nana-Jo always says, it's important to end every conversation on a positive note. Then I said, "Thank you for believing in me, Bridget," and we shook hands, and she told me and Angus it was time to *move forward*.

Video Visit #2

This morning, Grant-the-corrections-officer took me to the same room I used last time to do another visit with Irene Tesky's sister, Toni Hale, and, same as before, he did some clickety-clicking with the mouse to bring the computer to life. Me and Grant were a bit early for the call, though, so instead of looking at my nose hairs on the computer screen, we did talking. He told me lots of people work from home now instead of at an actual office and they do meetings using something called Zoom or Teams, which works just like my last video visit worked with Mrs. Hale, only sometimes groups of people do meetings and when that happens, they show up in boxes on the computer screen, stacked one on top the other.

And I said, "Then they all do talking?"

Grant nodded. "They do."

I frowned. "Who gets to talk first?" and, "Are there any rules?"

Grant laughed. "The moderator probably speaks first—that's the person who sets the call up—but I think the number one rule should be *don't forget to wear pants*!"

And I guess my face looked confused because Grant took his phone out and showed me videos of people messing up on Zoom calls, and in those videos people were doing talking on their computer screens and they *looked* normal sitting down, but then they stood up and they had no pants on—just underwear. And my face got hot because I was embarrassed watching people in their underwear.

Then Grant showed me another video where a woman was doing a meeting with her boss and her husband walked into the room behind her, and he was naked, and he didn't know her boss could see him. And even though Grant had already seen that video, he laughed and laughed, then my computer screen flish-flashed, and my face shrank down into a tiny box, and the rest of the screen got itself filled up with a room that had a fancy fireplace and a coatrack in one corner, and there was Toni Hale.

She lifted one hand. "Hi, Denny."

And I said, "Uh . . . hi, Mrs. Hale," and I smoothed down my orange jumpsuit and thought, *Whew, I'm sure glad I have pants on.*

"I have good news." Mrs. Hale did a smile. "I'm hiring you a new lawyer. He's one of the best criminal defense attorneys in the state. His assistant emailed a release form to the jail. All you have to do is sign it and then Ms. Klein will be asked to hand over her case files. Of course, the first thing we plan to do is ask for a continuance—"

And I said, "I don't understand."

Toni shook her head. "Oh, right—I'm sorry, Denny! This must be confusing for you. A continuance is when your lawyer asks for extra time to prepare for trial," and I said, "But I want a speedy trial so I can go home and see George and Nana-Jo."

Toni nodded. "Yes, well, I imagine you do, but—"

"And Mrs. Hale? I don't want a new lawyer. I like Bridget Klein because she's on my side and she's been working VERY HARD doing lawyering to win my case, and she's kind and thoughtful, and she makes me feel warm inside."

Toni Hale did a sigh. "I'm sure she does, Denny, but she also has no experience."

"I know, but that's okay. Like Nana-Jo always says, practice makes perfect, and I think it would hurt Bridget's feelings if I got myself a new lawyer and I don't want to hurt her feelings . . . So yeah, I don't want a new lawyer. Thank you, though."

Mrs. Hale's mouth opened, then it closed again. "Denny, please let me do this for you," but I shook my head and said, "No, thank you." That's when tears came up in her eyes and she said, "Denny, I'm *trying* to fix a wrong here. I want to help you." She reached past the computer screen, got herself a Kleenex, and dabbed at her eyes. "You shouldn't be in jail and I have the financial means to help, so let me. Your new lawyer will push for an acquittal; he may even get the case thrown out altogether. At least let him try."

"No way, José."

"Denny, I think if you just—"

And I said, "I'm keeping Bridget Klein, Mrs. Hale. Thank you for the video visit, though. You're a kind lady." And I did a wave and said, "Best wishes, warmest regards," just like David and Stevie do on *Schitt's Creek*, then I used the mouse to click on the red phone button on the screen and—**POOF!**—Toni Hale was gone.

—

Grant didn't take me back to my cell right away. Instead, he took me to see Dr. Harland, and when I got to our regular meeting room, there he was, waiting for me with his pencil and his notebook, same as always. He was also drinking tea and he had my vanilla sprinkle doughnut on a napkin on the table.

"Morning, Denny."

I did a wave. "Morning."

He looked at his watch, then reached into his bag and pulled out a laptop. "Why don't you go ahead and eat your doughnut while I give Bridget a call? We keep missing each other and we have a few things to go over."

"Are you doing a Zoom call?"

He frowned. "Uh . . . yes. Just a short one, though."

He turned on his laptop and I took a bite of my doughnut while he fiddled with the built-in mouse, then I froze (went very still) and I slowly put my doughnut down. I scooched forward on my chair and ducked my head down under the table. I heard Bridget say, "Morning, John," and Dr. Harland said, "Hi, Bridget. Denny and I are just getting started—" and that's when I smacked my head on the table, trying to get it out from under the table.

—CLUNK!

"Denny?" Dr. Harland said. "What are you doing?!"

I sat up and smoothed down my hair, then I straightened the front of my jumpsuit and said, real quiet-like, "I was just making sure you have pants on," and Bridget said, "Excuse me? John, did I hear that right?" and she sounded a bit freaked out, and then Dr. Harland wasn't doing talking anymore, he was just staring at me with his mouth open.

After that, our meeting went sideways for a bit while Bridget and Dr. Harland asked me a bunch of questions, then Dr. Harland went to get Grant and he explained about the videos. He apologized and begged Dr. Harland not to tell his boss because he didn't want to get *canned* (fired) and that's when I told everyone to "chill out" and "calm down" because being in jail was a stressful place to be and Grant was only trying to make me laugh.

So yeah, no big deal.

It was a busy morning and when Grant finally took me back to my cell, there was an envelope on my pillow and inside was a note from Theo, and this is what it said:

Denny, me n mom saw George lying in the street and cars were honking at him and peeple were shouting at the lady who was tryen to walk him, so I went over and said, "I think he wants a long john from the Doughnut Hole" and she went across the street to get one, and George ate it, then he got up and started walking again.

Problem fixt!

P.S. When r you coming home? George misses you.

I'm Not Eating If George Isn't Eating

Angus came to visit me today and he said Nana-Jo is still having trouble speaking. She also has something called *paralysis* (can't move the left side of her face or her body) and she's going to need speech therapy and physical therapy and a wheelchair when she gets home, so we have to build a ramp for the front steps. Hearing that made me sad, and then Angus said, "Denny, I also need to talk to you about George."

"Why? What's wrong?"

Angus tugged on his goatee. "He's not eating. He was fine at first—you know how much he loves Elaine—but he stopped eating days ago. He goes outside to do his business and he drinks water, but he won't touch his food."

"Try giving him bacon."

"We did. We also tried peanut butter toast and roast beef and homemade cinnamon buns. Elaine barbecued him a steak last night. Nothing."

And I said, "He loves ice cream."

"Not right now, he doesn't." Angus did a sigh, then he looked at his watch and told me he had to go, but he'd be back tomorrow.

That night I couldn't stop thinking about George because he LOVES almost any kind of food. I fed him three times a day—7:00 a.m., noon, and 5:00 p.m.—and he couldn't tell time, but he knew when it was 7:00 a.m. and noon and 5:00 p.m., and if I didn't feed him on time, he'd hunt me down and nudge me with his nose; then when I filled his bowl he'd do a little happy dance, probably because that backyard breeder lady starved him for years. But now George wasn't eating at all, so maybe he was sick?

Just so you know, if you're incarcerated and you can't sleep because your dog stopped eating and you ask if you can go home to feed him, the night guard laughs and says, *Fat fucking chance!* I also asked if someone could call Bridget Klein and have her come to the jail to do talking and he said, "Sure thing. How about I order pizza for you too?" and I said, "No, thank you. I'm not eating if George isn't eating."

That was four days ago.

Today, Dr. Harland came at lunchtime to do talking and he brought me a cheeseburger, and I shook my head and said, "No, thank you," then Bridget came and she brought me lasagna, and I said, "Is George eating again?" and she said, "No," so I pushed the lasagna away. Angus came to see me a few hours later, and he said, "Hey, Einstein, I'm your legal guardian so if I told you to change your fucking underwear, you'd change it, right?" and I said, "Yes." Then he said, "All right, stop screwing around and eat your meals. I've got enough on my plate right now—I don't need anything else!"

And I said, "I'm not eating if George isn't eating."

Angus closed his eyes. "I'm not kidding, Denny."

"Me either."

Just so you know, if you don't eat for four days, your stomach hurts and you get diarrhea and you feel dizzy and all you want to do is sleep. And the more I didn't eat, the more I worried about George, and the more I worried about George, the less I worked on writing words down in my notebook for Dr. Harland.

That night, the guard on duty—her name was Nevis—came to my cell and there was an older man with her, and he had a crew cut (hair that stands straight up). He told her to open my cell, then he handed me a jacket and said, "Put this on."

So I did.

Nevis put my handcuffs on in the front, the way I like them, then the crew cut man took me down the hallway and out the front door, and there was a car waiting there and Bridget was standing beside it. She opened the back door and helped me get in, then she got in next to me. The man with the crew cut got in the driver's seat and he said, "Denny, I'm Sheriff Becker. I know your Nana-Jo. She cleaned house for me and my wife for twelve years."

And I said, "Nana-Jo's an excellent house cleaner."

"She's the best. I'm sorry to hear she's in the hospital, by the way." He put the car in drive and pulled onto the road. "You have a lot of people rooting for you, Denny. Ms. Klein told me what's been happening at home and although this is highly unusual, I agreed to sign you out on a domestic visit so you can go see your dog."

And I said, "You're taking me to see George?"

"I am."

"He stopped eating."

"That's what I heard."

"I'm not eating either."

And he said, "I heard that too."

When we pulled up to 8B, Elaine and Angus were waiting on the front steps. Sheriff Becker turned to Bridget and said, "The handcuffs need to stay on, but you've got an hour," and she said, "Thank you." Then Bridget got out of the car and she helped me out, and Sheriff Becker drove away.

And my heart started going BOOM-BOOM-BOOM because I couldn't wait to see George. Angus said, "Hi, buddy," then Elaine gave me a hug and said, "He's in your room." So, I went to my bedroom and there was George, asleep on my bed.

I knelt on the floor and blew on his face real gentle-like, and his tail started THUMP-THUMP-THUMPING because that's how I always wake him up. Then I touched my nose to his nose, and I whispered, "I love you, George," and even though he's old, George jumped off the bed like a puppy, and he did barking at me like he was giving me heck. He looked skinny to me, so I led him to the kitchen and Elaine gave me a bowl of dry dog food with roast beef and gravy on top and I sat on the floor and George lay next to me with his paws around the bowl, and he ate the whole thing.

Elaine also made me a plate of roast beef and green beans and mashed potatoes with gravy, and it was 100 percent better than any of the food I'd had at the jail. When George was done eating, he drank some water and I wiped his mouth so he wouldn't drool on the floor; then he put his head in my lap and I leaned against the wall and closed my eyes and pretended I didn't have to go back to jail. I also pretended Nana-Jo was there with us instead of by herself in the hospital and we'd just had dinner and now we'd watch *Schitt's Creek*, and then it would be time for me to take George for a walk, and when I got back, Nana-Jo would turn down the thermostat and say, "Make sure the door is locked, Denny," and I would. After that, it would be time for bed, and I'd say, "I love you, Nana-Jo," and she'd say, "You have no idea, kiddo," because that's what she always said.

Bridget was talking to Angus and Elaine, and I heard her say, "We're definitely making progress"; then she told them that some important test results were coming back tomorrow, and my heart was doing pounding and I felt sick to my stomach, because I hated Mr. Tesky and I didn't care that he was dead, but a tiny part of me wished he was still alive because then I wouldn't have to be in jail for doing his murder.

An hour goes by very fast. I sat on the floor with George the whole time and he kept his head in my lap, and he fell asleep and did snoring. Then Sheriff Becker's police car pulled up out front and Bridget looked out the window and said, "I'm sorry, Denny. It's time to go."

Elaine said, "Don't worry. I'll take care of George."

Angus helped me up and I said to him, "I'm almost done with my story for Dr. Harland about how *this whole mess got started* so I should be home pretty soon." But he just looked past me and chewed on his thumbnail, and I didn't want him to worry about me, so I leaned closer and I said, real quiet-like, "Everything will be okay."

"Denny?" Bridget said. "We have to go."

George woke up and followed us to the door, and he leaned against me and whined, which he never does. Angus had to hold on to his collar so I could leave, and George started barking when I walked down the sidewalk and got into Sheriff Becker's car, and I'm pretty sure I could still hear him barking when we drove down Deyton Avenue.

"How'd it go?" asked Sheriff Becker. "Did your dog eat something?"

And I said, "Yeah, he did. Thanks for taking me to see him."

"You're welcome."

I looked out the window and did thinking about George, then a few minutes later we stopped and Sheriff Becker turned to Bridget and he said, "They're expecting you. Again, the handcuffs need to stay on, but you've got an hour." Bridget touched my arm. "Denny, I talked to Dr. Harland and Angus, and we all agreed it was important that you see Nana-Jo tonight too. Would you like to see her?"

"Yes, please."

She got out and opened my door, then she took my arm and she led me through sliding glass doors that swished open when we got close, and we stopped at a check-in desk and Bridget showed the lady a piece of paper. The lady read it, then she stood up and said, "Follow me, please," so we did.

The Woodmont Hospital and Care Center has four floors and when Bridget told me Nana-Jo was in Room 418 on the fourth floor, I said I couldn't go up to the fourth floor because if there was a fire and the elevators shut down, I'd have to jump out the window, and if I jumped out a fourth-floor window I MIGHT die but I would DEFINITELY break my legs, so could they please bring Nana-Jo down to the main floor?

Bridget rested her forehead against the wall next to the elevator. "I'm sorry, Denny. That's not possible." So, I walked in circles with my handcuffs on, and I thought about that, then I said, "Could they prop her up at the window and I'll go outside and yell up to say hello?" and Bridget sighed. "No, Denny, they can't do that either."

She led me back to the check-in desk and explained the situation to the lady who works there, and the lady looked at my handcuffs, and she said, "Give me a minute," then she went down the hallway. Five minutes later, she came back with an emergency fire escape rope ladder and she asked us to return it before we left the hospital.

Bridget turned to me. "Will that work, Denny?" and I said, "Yes, it will," because now if there was a fire and the elevators shut down, I could use the emergency fire escape rope ladder to climb down to the ground and I wouldn't die or break my legs, and I could probably carry Nana-Jo down the ladder and save her life too.

On our way up in the elevator, Bridget told me that the fourth floor was a good place to be because that's where all the doctors were who knew how to take care of someone who'd had a serious stroke. She also told me all about strokes and paralysis so I wouldn't get myself scared when I saw Nana-Jo. She said every year over 795,000 people in the US have strokes and most of those people are over sixty-five but anyone can have one, including children. "Essentially," Bridget said, "strokes happen when the blood supply to your brain is cut off or reduced, and because blood carries important nutrients and oxygen to your brain, without it, your brain cells can die or become damaged."

And I said, "Did Nana-Jo's brain cells die?"

Bridget sighed. "Well, some of them were damaged, that much we do know. And because our brains control everything we do, think, and feel, like walking or speaking or remembering, if the part of your brain that controls any of those is damaged, your ability to do those things will also be affected."

"Angus said Nana-Jo can't walk anymore."

"That's right. For now, anyhow. Hopefully, in time, she'll learn to walk again."

"He said she can't talk either."

"She's been trying, but she's virtually unintelligible."

"What's that mean?"

And Bridget said, "It means no one can understand what she's saying. Angus visits every day and sometimes she tries to talk to him, but he can't understand her. He gave her a pencil and paper, but her left side is paralyzed and because she's left handed, everything she scribbles is unintelligible too."

Then we were at Room 418 and my heart was going **BOOM-BOOM-BOOM**, and Bridget opened the door and we went inside. There were two beds and one was empty, but Nana-Jo was in the other one, only she didn't look like Nana-Jo because she usually sleeps with foam curlers in her hair (pink) but there were no curlers. Her hair was flat and gray, and there were hairpins holding it back from her face and it didn't look as nice as it usually does.

And she was sleeping, so I put the emergency fire escape rope ladder on the floor by the window and I sat in a chair next to her bed, and Bridget said she'd wait outside to give me some privacy, then she left.

Nana-Jo's mouth was open and there was drool sliding down from the corner of her mouth, so I got a Kleenex from the bedside table, and I wiped her mouth, then I took her hand and I said, "I'm sorry I got myself arrested again, Nana-Jo."

She didn't answer, but I kept talking anyhow. I told her all about being incarcerated and how the food was awful, but how the guard who worked night duty liked to watch *Schitt's Creek* on her iPad and if I was really quiet I could hear it from my cell. I also told her that George had stopped eating and how Sheriff Becker got me out of jail so I could go visit him, and how he drove me to the hospital so I could visit her too.

And I said, "Do you remember working for him and his wife?"

Nana-Jo didn't answer, but I kept talking anyhow. I told her all about Bridget, how lawyering was new to her and how I was her first real case, and how she smelled like lemons. I also told her I'd done two video visits with Mrs. Hale and that she was very upset I was in jail and wanted to hire me a new lawyer, but I said no because that didn't seem fair to Bridget. I also told her how Dr. Harland was helping me and how a judge signed official papers so Angus could be my *temporary legal guardian* until she got herself out of the hospital.

Nana-Jo's eyes flickered, then she licked her lips like she was thirsty, so I got a glass of water that was on her bedside table and it had a bendy straw in it, and I put the straw in her mouth and she took a sip.

She blinked a few times, then she looked at me and her eyes got big. And the right side of her face was the same as always, but the left side was folded down like she was making a face at me, but Bridget had already told me about that, so I knew she wasn't making a face at me; it was just the *paralysis* that the stroke had done to her. To me, she looked smaller than before and older, but I didn't care. I told her I loved her and Nana-Jo made a sound at the back of her throat, then I said, "Everything'll be okay," even though I wasn't sure it would, because that's what she always says when I'm scared.

Nana-Jo squeezed my hand and I squeezed back. "When I get out of jail, I'm going to take care of you, Nana-Jo. I'll make breakfast and lunch and dinner, and I'll do laundry and sweep and buy groceries." A tear slid down Nana-Jo's cheek and I got another Kleenex and wiped it away for her. "Did you want me to have Angus bring you your pink foam curlers?" I asked and she shook her head YES, and she kept squeezing my hand, then more tears came and I wiped them away too.

I looked away and said, real quiet-like, "I miss you, Nana-Jo. This is the longest I've ever been away from you." When I looked back, the right side of her face was doing a sad smile, but the left side was still folded down. And me and Nana-Jo used to laugh about the silliest things sometimes and I didn't want her to be sad, so I made the same face she was making to try to make her laugh—right side up, left side down—but she just blinked at me.

Bridget stuck her head inside the room. "It's time to go, Denny."

When I stood up, my handcuffs made a clanking noise and Nana-Jo's eyes got big and she made more sounds in her throat, so I pressed my forehead against her forehead, and I said, "Everything'll be okay." I looked out the window and said, "I'm sorry I smashed your favorite vase when I found out the truth about Lydia and I'm sorry I said those lousy things to you, Nana-Jo." And she squeezed my hand and started to do moaning, then I left with Bridget and I didn't look back because my heart was breaking into a million pieces.

Me and Bridget went down the elevator and I returned the emergency fire escape rope ladder to the lady at the front desk.

Sheriff Becker was parked outside, waiting, and he drove us back to the jail. When we got there, he escorted me into the building and back to my cell, and I said, "Thank you for taking me to see George and Nana-Jo," and he nodded and said, "I hope everything works out for you, Denny." After he left, I heard Nevis-the-corrections-officer watching *Schitt's Creek* on her iPad, so I closed my eyes and listened, and I pretended I was at the Rosebud Motel with David and Alexis and Stevie instead of sleeping in a cell at the Woodmont County Jail, where they keep drunks and murderers and people who steal cars.

Robbing a Bank

After we ate our doughnuts this morning, Dr. Harland threw his tea bag in the garbage and said, "Tell me about the bank robbery, Denny."

So I did.

And I told him everything.

Like how robbing a bank in real life is nothing like how they do it in fast-moving TV shows and how the day it happened was payday, which automatically made it a good day. That morning, I was waiting at Angus's truck at 7:40 a.m. when he came outside wearing a T-shirt that said **There's a 99% Chance I Don't Care** and when we got to DOT, Lonny gave us a work order to replace two broken road signs, then we drove over to Fletcher Road and replaced a stop sign someone had hit, and after that we went to Meadow Drive and replaced a yield sign someone had spray-painted boobs on.

After that, me and Angus stopped for lunch at Bertie's Bistro, then we did a roadkill loop around Woodmont County and found a dead racoon, then we listened to music while we drove to the dump to drop off the dead racoon, and then it was four o'clock so we *hightailed it* back to the shop (drove very fast) so we could get our paychecks. And DOT was changing our paychecks so in the future they'd be *electronically deposited* (I don't know how that works) so this was our last time getting paper paychecks and, same as always, we had to take them to our bank and deposit them ourselves.

On the drive to the bank, Angus told me I was getting on his nerves, so he tossed me his phone and told me to play *Angry Birds*. A few minutes later, he parked, and I put his phone in my pocket, and we jaywalked across the street (crossed illegally instead of using a crosswalk). And I took my knapsack with me because that's where I keep my wallet and my bank card, and the bank was closing soon so we were in a hurry, but then Angus saw Malinda Tesky coming out of the bookstore and he stopped to do visiting with her.

Angus said, "Hey, Malinda. You're looking good."

She smiled. "Thanks, I make it a priority. Yoga every morning, running on weekends," and Angus said, "Well, I'm sure Henry appreciates all the work you do, especially since he's such a stud himself." Malinda squinted at him. "Don't start, Angus. I already have half the town judging me; I don't need you joining in," and he laughed and said, "Hey, I heard you signed an ironclad prenup, huh? But then again, Henry is twenty-five years older than you, so I guess it makes sense from his perspective."

She stepped closer, ran a finger down Angus's nose. "Oh, don't you worry about me. Prenup or not, I've got it all worked out. Trust me, there's no way I'm coming out the other side of this anything but flush," and Angus said, "Careful, Malinda. You don't want people thinking you married Henry for the money."

She smiled. "At least he has money. What're you up to these days? Oh, right! You're driving a ten-year-old F-150, you work for DOT, and you have a side hustle selling weed." She laughed. "Like I said when I picked you up a few weeks ago, that ship has sailed, Angus. I don't need to buy from you anymore. Weed's legal now and your stuff isn't bad, but it's not as good as what I can buy right here in town."

Angus looked past her, nodded. "You know what I just realized, Malinda? You and Henry Tesky were made for each other."

"Fuck you, Angus."

"It'd be my pleasure. You have my number. Call anytime."

And to me their visiting sounded mean AND stupid, so I went into the bank to get us a spot in line, and there were *Happy 25th Anniversary!* balloons hanging everywhere (blue) and a table to the left with comfy-cozy armchairs around it (brown) and a HUGE chocolate cake with paper plates and napkins and all kinds of sodas. A lady with curly hair smiled at me and said, "Welcome to our branch. Help yourself to some cake and a soda. We're celebrating twenty-five years of service in Woodmont this week!"

And I said, "That's a lot of years."

She touched her hair. "Longer than all three of my marriages put together, honey."

So I cut myself a piece of cake and I opened a can of Mello Yello and I sat in one of those comfy-cozy chairs and waited for Angus to finish doing visiting with Malinda Tesky. And there were bank tellers behind the counter and customers waiting in line (four women, two men) and when I took a bite of cake a chunk broke off and bounced down the front of my shirt and landed on the floor under the table. I grabbed a napkin, got down on my hands and knees, and reached under the table to get that chunk of cake, then I tried wiping the icing off the floor, but it's hard to wipe up icing because it smears everywhere.

That's when a man came into the bank in a long-sleeved shirt with a black vest over top and he was wearing a Halloween mask with fake blood on it, and the mask looked like it was screaming, and the guy was moving *really fast*. He locked the top part of the door so no one could get in or out, then he flipped the **OPEN** sign over so it said **CLOSED**, and he spun around with a gun and shouted, "Hands up where I can see them!"

And everyone put their hands up.

I didn't, though, because I was on my knees, trying to figure out what was happening, because the bank robber in the weird mask was wearing a vest and people who wear vests are good—that's just how vest-people are. That's when I decided something terrible/horrible/awful must have happened to make him *go off the deep end* (act reckless or insane).

The man waved his gun at one of the tellers. "Open your cash drawer, then step out front here . . . *now*!" He said the same thing to the lady with curly hair and a man who came out of an office on the right. He kept pointing his gun and shouting, then he'd point it at someone else, and everyone looked scared, especially the customers. They lay on the floor and the robber said, "Don't do anything stupid!" and "Do exactly as I say," then he said, "This is my world, people, you are *not* in Kansas anymore!"

And I said, "*Wizard of Oz*," because me and Papa-Jo used to watch that movie all the time when I was growing up.

The robber turned and saw me on my knees by the cake table. "What do you think you're doing?" he asked, and I said, "Eating cake," then I carefully set my napkin down on the table and I put my hands up, and I slid into a comfy-cozy chair. And I said, "Did something terrible/horrible/awful happen to you?"

"What?" said the robber.

My hands were still up. "Because when people rob a bank, or do violence to a neighbor, or do road rage, it usually means something terrible/horrible/awful happened to them and *stress* made them lose their minds."

"What are you, a fucking doctor?!"

And I said, "No, but I do watch *Dr. Phil* on TV."

The robber stepped closer. "Shut your mouth. Do you understand?" and I nodded, then he waved his gun at me. "Get up and close all the blinds, now!"

And I got up and I moved *extra slow* so he wouldn't think I was trying to *make a break for it* (run away) but then he yelled, "Move your ass!" so I went faster and I lowered all the blinds on the windows and when I got to the last one Angus was there looking at me, and I couldn't hear him, but I could read his lips, and he said, "What are you *doing*?!"

"Close that blind *now*!" yelled the robber.

So I tried, but it was stuck at the top and I couldn't get it to come down, then I tugged harder on the cord and it snapped off and the blind dropped on one side but it stayed stuck at the top on the other side, and now only half the window was covered up and there was nothing I could do about that.

Angus was outside, trying to open the door. I could hear him yelling, "This isn't funny, Einstein! You're in deep shit." Then he came back to the window with the broken blind and there was another guy with him, and they cupped their hands against the glass, then their eyes got big when they saw the bank robber and they backed away real fast.

The bank robber yelled at me, "Get over here!"

So, I turned and walked over to him, and that's when he said, "I want you to tie everyone's hands behind their backs," and I looked at the people on the floor, then the robber reached into his pocket and he said, "Shit, I forgot the zip ties!" and he took a breath and blew it up at the ceiling, and I could tell he was having a bad day. "You'll have to use the cords from the blinds," he said.

And I put my hand up and said, "I have duct tape."

"Are you serious?" he said.

"Yeah, it's in my knapsack."

"Well, get your fucking duct tape, then!"

I walked over to the cake table and got my duct tape, then I went to where everyone was lying on the floor and I taped their hands behind their backs one by one while the teller behind the counter emptied her cash drawer into a pillowcase for the bank robber. He made her empty a second cash drawer into the pillowcase, then he pointed his gun at her and yelled, "Move! Move! Move! I haven't got all day here," and that's when she started crying, and I started to feel dizzy, because everything was happening *very quickly* and I could tell this was a REAL bank robbery and not a fast-moving TV show.

Someone's phone rang and the robber spun around and pointed his gun at me. "Find a garbage can!" he said, so I did. Then he said, "Throw everyone's phones in it!" so I did. Then an alarm went off inside the bank and it was SUPER LOUD and it would NOT stop ringing, and the lady with the curly hair who'd been married three times started to cry, and a few other people on the floor started to cry too.

I was doing pretty good until the robber handed me the pillowcase full of money and he pointed his gun at a teller who was crying and told her to *lie down*, then he pulled out a knife with his other hand and held it against my neck. "Get behind the counter and empty the last two cash drawers," he said, and my stomach started to slosh back and forth like it does when someone makes me ride in the back seat of a car.

And I said, "I—d-don't—want—"

"You don't want what?!" he said.

"I—f-feel—feel . . ."

The bank robber yelled, "I don't give a damn how you feel. You're going to do exactly what I tell you to do."

And my mind was jumping around, and everything started to spin and wobble, so I rocked back and forth and did moaning. The robber said, "Holy shit, what is *wrong* with you, dude?" Then Angus's cell phone rang in my pocket, and the robber said, "I thought I told you to throw everyone's phones out. That means you too, idiot!" and I said, "I—I'm not an idiot. My n-number is 72," then he asked me to give him my phone, so I did, and he dropped it on the floor and smashed it with the heel of his boot, and I stared at it and thought, *Angus is gonna be so mad.* And that's when I started to feel dizzy because the lady with the curly hair was still crying and the alarm would NOT STOP RINGING.

"Empty the cash drawers!" yelled the robber.

And I hugged the pillowcase against my chest and I felt like I couldn't breathe, and my heart was going **BOOM-BOOM-BOOM**, so to calm myself down I closed my eyes and sang the theme song for *Toy Story*—"You've Got a Friend in Me."

And the robber said, "Are you fucking kidding me?"

And I kept singing.

"Seriously, is this some kind of joke?" he asked, and I wanted to say, *Please be a good guy and put your gun down,* but I couldn't talk, so I kept singing.

And the bank robber guy said, "Shut. The. Fuck. Up!"

Then . . .

—*Thwack!*

My forehead suddenly felt warm and wet, and I reached up and touched it and thought, *Uh-oh, blood.* When I opened my eyes, the robber was in front of me and my stomach was sloshing back and forth, so I bent over for a second and then I stood up again and I projectile vomited and some of the vomit hit the robber's black vest and some dripped down my chin onto the pillowcase full of money.

"What the fuck!" The robber dropped his knife on the counter, ripped off his vest, and threw it on the floor. And a gray-haired cop was sneaking up behind him on the other side of the counter and there were two more cops with him and they were crouched down and all three of them had their guns drawn, just like they do in those fast-moving TV shows.

"Drop your weapon!" shouted the gray-haired cop.

The robber spun around and for a second he seemed to be doing thinking, but then he finally set his gun on the counter and put his hands up. One of the cops ran over and yanked his arms down, snapped handcuffs on him, and shoved him up against a wall. "Spread your legs," he yelled, and the robber did; then the cop did what's called a *pat down*, which is when they search you for weapons you might be hiding on your body.

And I thought, *Whew!* and I wiped the vomit off my mouth with the back of my hand. That's when one of the tellers lifted her chin at me, and she said, "He has all the money," and the gray-haired cop pointed his gun at me and said, "Drop the bag."

So I did.

Then he said, "Put your hands up."

So I did.

But the alarm inside the bank wouldn't STOP RINGING and my heart was going **BOOM-BOOM-BOOM** and the gray-haired cop came over and he yanked my arms down and snapped the handcuffs on behind me where I couldn't see them. They were tight and they hurt, so I asked him to *please* take the handcuffs off—but he didn't—so I rocked back and forth and did moaning, which is what I do when I don't feel safe.

One cop said, "This guy's having a meltdown."

Another one said, "He's probably on something."

And before I could say, *I'm not a threat . . .*

—*Thwack!*

I was lying on the floor face down and when I turned my head sideways, blood dribbled down my forehead onto my nose. That's when I saw Angus banging on the window and he was yelling and he looked VERY MAD but I don't think he was mad at me; I think he was mad at the cops. I stared at him and thought about the actor Matt Damon in those Jason Bourne movies we watch all the time and I thought about how Angus thinks he looks like Matt Damon (he doesn't) and how he thinks Matt Damon is good at everything (he is) and how when Matt Damon gets himself beat up in those movies (he gets beat up a lot) he's always brave, and he bounces back, and he keeps going. I don't have lots of brave inside me, though, so when I was lying there I told myself I needed to be more like Matt Damon. I needed to bounce back and keep going, even though that's hard to do when you're face down on the floor in handcuffs and you feel like you can't breathe and the alarm *won't stop ringing* and your throat feels like it's closing up.

And it was all just **TOO MUCH**.

So, yeah, that's when my mind shrank down to a tiny ball and—**BAM!**—that was it, I didn't come back for a while.

Newspaper Story #2

Bank Robbery Averted in Woodmont
by Brenda Kuzyk

Claydon Wheeler, 48, of Bemidji was arrested on Friday for the attempted robbery of First Commercial Bank in Woodmont. Armed with a knife and a gun, Wheeler entered the bank wearing a skeleton-style mask, approached a teller, and demanded money. An automatic holdup alarm was triggered, and Woodmont police were dispatched.

Employees and customers inside the bank at the time were not physically injured, although Denny Voss, a resident of Woodmont, suffered a series of cuts and bruises. Mr. Voss was initially arrested, but then later cleared of any wrongdoing after police learned that Wheeler had coerced him with a knife to help him rob the bank.

Woodmont police have officially apologized to Mr. Voss for the misunderstanding but cited the need for extreme caution during situations like these. Denny

Voss is now being lauded for thwarting Wheeler's plans to rob the First Commercial Bank.

Wheeler has been charged with one count of attempted robbery and one count of assault. He faces up to 15 years in prison.

Happy Birthday × 2

The next time I heard about people dying from *fatal gunshot wounds* was on Nana-Jo's birthday, which was also Papa-Jo's birthday, only he got himself born two years before she did. And every year on Nana-Jo's birthday we go visit Papa-Jo at the cemetery but this year her birthday was the day after the bank robbery and she was tired, so she asked Angus to drive us. Angus was wearing a T-shirt that said **I May Be Wrong, But It's Highly Unlikely**, and Nana-Jo asked him to stop at the grocery store so we could buy flowers.

Angus doesn't like cemeteries.

On the drive across town, he told us how, hundreds of years ago, people couldn't always tell if someone was actually dead or if they were just in a coma, so they started making coffins with bells on top. They'd tie a rope to the bell and run it through a hole into the inside part of the coffin so the dead person could ring the bell if they weren't dead and they woke up and needed to get out, and that's where the expression "Saved by the bell" came from.

And I said, "What's a coma, Angus?"

He said, "It's when someone slips into a deep state of unconsciousness, usually after they've had a bad accident."

"How long do comas last?"

"Depends. It could be days or weeks, but I've heard of people who were in comas for years." And I thought about that, and I started to rock back and forth, then Nana-Jo said, "What's wrong, Denny?" and

I said, "When I die, I want a bell on my coffin in case I'm in a coma." Angus laughed. "Hey, why don't we buy a coffin from Costco and I'll drill a hole in it and we can test-drive how the bell works."

And I said, "Costco has *coffins*?!"

"Damn straight!"

"Enough!" Nana-Jo added, "Angus, why do you encourage him like this?!" Then Angus pulled into the grocery store parking lot and me and Nana-Jo went inside and bought flowers—carnations for Papa-Jo and daisies for Irene Tesky.

Like I said before, Irene Tesky hired Nana-Jo years ago to clean her house and they became friends, and Nana-Jo was always there when Irene needed her, which was good because Irene was *a closet drinker*, which means she hid her drinking from everyone. Then one day Nana-Jo went to work and Irene was so drunk she couldn't stand up, so Nana-Jo dumped every liquor bottle she could find down the drain. Then she yelled at Irene and she told her to *shape up* (get her act together) so Irene did. She joined Alcoholics Anonymous (a club people go to when they have a drinking problem) and for years Nana-Jo drove her to her weekly AA meetings, then they'd go for coffee on their way home.

I asked Nana-Jo once, "Why does Mrs. Tesky drink so much?"

And Nana-Jo said, "I think she's grieving because she knows she can't have children," and I said, "What's *grieving*?" and Nana-Jo said, "It's a deep sadness you feel after you lose someone, or something, you love. You learn to live with it, but it never goes away." But I didn't know what that really meant until Papa-Jo died, then I learned about grieving, which is like a bruise someone keeps punching over and over again so it never heals up and stops hurting. And I'm older now and it still hurts to visit Papa-Jo's grave but I never started drinking like Irene Tesky did because I didn't want to join a club and have to go to meetings every week.

On our way out of the grocery store with our flowers, we ran into Elaine-the-stalker, and when we got back in the truck Angus said to

Nana-Jo, "Did she get her hair cut?" and Nana-Jo said, "She did. Looks good, doesn't it?"

Nana-Jo brought rags from home and a bottle of soapy water and she cleaned Irene Tesky's gravestone and did talking with her even though Irene wasn't alive anymore to hear the words. She told Irene that Mr. Tesky got himself married again and he was running for mayor, and that she was worried about Irene's sister, Toni Hale, because Toni hated Henry Tesky and could not let go of the past.

"That woman is out for blood," Nana-Jo said, shaking her head.

After that I took Nana-Jo's arm and helped her walk to Papa-Jo's grave and she cleaned his headstone and told him all about her broken-down knee operation, and how Lydia was having marriage trouble, and how our basement got flooded. And while she talked to Papa-Jo, I could feel myself going **DOWN, DOWN, DOWN**; then Nana-Jo stopped talking and it was my turn, but I didn't know what to say, then Nana-Jo squeezed my hand and she said, "It's okay, Denny. He knows you love him. He's always known."

So yeah, that morning sucked.

But the rest of the day was better because we had a potluck birthday party for Nana-Jo and I got balloons from the Dollar Tree, and Elaine-the-stalker baked a cake, and Sharon and Bill brought Caesar salad, and Jean and Ted brought sour cabbage rolls. The Timkos also brought a Hungarian stew called gulyás and I waved and said hello but then Angus pulled me to the side and told me to steer clear of the Timkos (avoid them) because they still weren't over the whole "kidnapping Tom Hanks" thing.

And I said, "Should I apologize?"

Angus said, "Hell no! One apology was fine, five was excessive. More than that and you're going to get punched out."

Angus's new cell phone rang and he gave it to Nana-Jo so Lydia could wish her a happy birthday, and people were hugging George and sneaking him food, and when I gave Nana-Jo her soap-on-a-ropes with the seventy-four baby grapefruit soaps stuffed inside, tears came up in her eyes and she said, "Denny, you always give me the best gifts." Then the party was over, and Angus helped Elaine-the-stalker clean up, and he kept staring at her, and when she went inside he said to Nana-Jo, "Has Elaine lost weight?"

Nana-Jo smiled. "She sure has."

That night, Nana-Jo went to bed early and I turned on the TV and flipped through the channels. A few minutes later, I was watching a not-very-good show when the news cut in and the screen said *Live in Orlando* and a lady reporter was talking, and she said: "There was a mass shooting tonight at an LGBTQ nightclub in Orlando called Q-Pride. Shortly after eleven p.m. a twenty-year-old man opened fire inside the club with a semiautomatic weapon, killing twelve people and injuring six before shooting himself. Survivors have confirmed that the gunman was hurling insults and anti-LGBTQ slurs at patrons before the shooting . . ."

My heart was going **BOOM-BOOM-BOOM.**

Behind the reporter were broken windows and there was blood on the sidewalk and yellow tape that said **CRIME SCENE DO NOT CROSS**. There were also bouquets of flowers on the sidewalk and a big rainbow-colored heart that said **CHOOSE LOVE, NOT HATE**. Lots of people were standing behind the crime scene tape, and some were young and some were old, and there were two men with a rainbow flag wrapped around their shoulders and they were crying.

And I felt sick inside.

And everything started to spin.

So, I turned the TV off and I sat down at the kitchen table and I rocked back and forth and did moaning for a bit, and when that didn't help, I put my head between my knees and counted the tiles on the floor.

Getting Hit by a Tesla

Dr. Harland opened his notebook. "Denny, I think it's time we talked about the day Mr. Tesky tried to kill you with his Tesla. That's a very serious accusation, by the way." I was looking out the window at the parking lot and there was a truck outside with a long metal arm that went up in the air and at the end of that arm was a bucket and a man was in the bucket and he was changing a light bulb on a streetlight and my stomach was getting itself all twisty because he was very high up and I didn't want him to fall out of the bucket.

Dr. Harland snapped his fingers—once, twice. "Denny? I said that's a very serious accusation."

"I know, Dr. Harland, but I'm not lying. I'm telling you the truth so I can get myself out of jail and go home. Mr. Tesky tried to kill me *twice*." I held up two fingers. "The day he hit me with his Tesla and one other time I've never told anyone about."

"All right, tell about that time too."

But then I thought about Bridget and how I'd promised her that we'd talk about Mr. Tesky on Wednesday, so I said to Dr. Harland, "Why don't I tell you about him hitting me with his Tesla today and then you can sit with me and Bridget on Wednesday, when I tell her about the first time he tried to kill me?"

Dr. Harland pinched the hump on his nose. "Fine. Let's do that."

Then I said, "I didn't feel safe when Mr. Tesky hit me with his Tesla. And just so you know, Teslas are *high-performance electric vehicles* that run on batteries and a guy called Elon Musk runs the company and he says safety is NUMBER ONE when it comes to his cars, which is good because it is important for people to feel safe."

I told Dr. Harland it happened six months after Mr. Tesky fired Nana-Jo, when I was riding my bike home after doing consequences at the library and then volunteering at the Cross Fellowship Church. And I liked doing my consequences at the library better than any of my other consequences because I got to work with a girl named Regan and she was kind and beautiful, and she always said, "Denny, you're doing an excellent job." When I finished my consequences at the library that day, I biked over to the Cross Fellowship Church to do volunteering. I was polishing the pews with lemon oil when a guy named Howard hobbled in with a cane and asked if I wanted to play cards, so I said, "Sure," then we sat in a pew for two hours and Howard taught me how to play Texas Hold'em, which was fun, even though I kept losing.

Howard used to be in the army until he got himself hurt by an IED (homemade bomb) in a country called Afghanistan (very dry, lots of sand) and part of his leg had to be amputated (cut off) from the knee down. After that, the army sent him home and they gave him what's called a *prosthetic leg* (fake leg made from titanium), then Howard got himself addicted to painkillers and he got himself fired and couldn't pay his rent, so he became a homeless person, which is someone who sleeps on park benches or under bridges.

Howard said he used to take his fake leg off when he went to sleep at night because it made the stumpy part of his leg itchy if he left it on too long, then one morning he woke up on a bench and some fuckwad (person he didn't know) had stolen it. So yeah, he lost his fake leg and he didn't have a home, but he had a pillow and a backpack with a sleeping bag tied to the top and he liked playing Texas Hold'em and each time he won, he'd throw his head back and yell, "In your face, motherfucker!" then he'd take a drink from a flat metal thermos and I'd have to pay him ten dollars, which is part of the rules.

And I always keep cash money in my wallet, but I had none left when Pastor Palmer walked into the church and Howard waved some bills at him, and said, "In your face, motherfucker!" and that's when we both got kicked out.

Later that day, Pastor Palmer called Nana-Jo to tell her *my services were no longer required* but he also said he *appreciated my giving nature* (which means he thinks I'm a kind person). So, yeah, that's when I stopped doing volunteering at the church.

Anyhow, after I said goodbye to my new friend Howard, I got on my bike and pedaled down Bendmore Road, being careful to stay on the shoulder, which is a strip of pavement to the right of where cars drive, and then—**BAM!**—Mr. Tesky hit me with his Tesla, and I flew through the air on my bike and landed in a mud puddle in the ditch.

At first, there was no sound—just silence—then I lifted my head and I heard someone yelling and there was Mr. Tesky, high-stepping through the muddy water. And he slipped and fell twice while he tried to drag me up onto the grass, and he said, "Jesus, I did *not* need this shit today!" and I said, "Me either." I wiped my muddy hands on my shirt and that's when I noticed that my right arm was bleeding. My forehead also felt warm and sticky, so I took my helmet off and I reached up and touched it, and thought, *Uh-oh, blood.*

Mr. Tesky said, "Are you all right?"

And I said, "I don't know."

He stepped away and he made a phone call on his phone and he was pacing back and forth, and I heard him say, "Of course I called 911! There's an ambulance on the way," then I looked at his car, which has *falcon-wing doors* (Angus told me the name later) and they aren't like regular car doors because they have hinges on the roof of the car so they lift UP instead of having hinges on the side of the car so they swing OUT.

I said to Mr. Tesky, "Nice car."

And he turned to me and said, "I'll get you a new bike." Then he went back to chatting on the phone, and my bike was all twisted, and one wheel had broken off, and the orange flag Nana-Jo had put on the back for safety had snapped off its long bendy pole, and the metal basket Papa-Jo had welded on years ago had broken off and was sticking out of the mud puddle. That's when I went very still inside because I'd had that bike for a long time and when I saw it wrecked like that, I felt myself going **DOWN, DOWN, DOWN** to a very sad place. Mr. Tesky squatted in front of me, and he asked me to look at him so he could see my pupils, but I just kept staring at my wrecked bike, even when he snapped his fingers in front of my face. Then he stood up again and he walked away, and he said into his phone, "I have no idea. I'm not a fucking doctor! He's not talking, so maybe he's in shock."

I heard a siren and a few seconds later an ambulance pulled up and the lights were flashing and two people jumped out, and a police car pulled in behind it and the lights were flashing and a gray-haired cop got out.

And two EMT people (emergency medical technicians, who are experts at all kinds of medical stuff) helped me over to the ambulance, and one of them was a guy with a name badge that said **ALEX** and the other was a lady with a name badge that said **JENNIFER**, and she said, "We're going to take care of you."

And I said, "Thank you."

Jennifer asked if I was having trouble breathing and I said, "No," and she asked me to breathe in and out while she checked my chest; then she explained that she was going to do a quick *head-to-toe exam* and she had me bend my arms this way and that way, and she did the same thing with my legs and my knees and my feet. Alex checked my pupils with a flashlight that looked like a pen, then Jennifer used a *stethoscope* (metal disc with two long tubes connected to earpieces) to listen to my lungs.

Alex asked me a bunch of questions like "What's your name?" and "What day of the week is it?" and "Do you feel dizzy?" and I said, "Denny Voss," and "Wednesday," and "No," and Jennifer asked me to squeeze her fingers with both of my hands at the same time and then she had me push against her hands with both of my hands as hard as I could.

Alex asked if I hurt anywhere and I said, "Everywhere."

"Can you be more specific?"

So I said, "My right arm hurts and my thumb on my left hand hurts, and my left ankle hurts too. I also bit my tongue so it's swollen on one side, and the insides of my ears feel itchy, but that might be from all the mud. Oh, and I have a headache," then he asked if I had any allergies and I wasn't sure what that meant so I looked away and said, "I don't like birds," and Alex said, "You're allergic to birds?" and I shrugged and said, "I don't know. I just know I don't like when they flap their wings and attack me the way Tom Hanks attacked me."

Alex looked at Jennifer. "Tom Hanks attacked you?"

"Yeah, he did. Seven or eight times."

Alex checked my pupils again and he explained what allergies are, then I said, "I don't think I have any of those but Nana-Jo would know for sure," and he asked who Nana-Jo was, and I said, "She's my mom," and then I gave him the number for our green wall phone in the kitchen, which I'd memorized. I also told him my number was 72 and that I had official papers at home in our basement freezer if he wanted to see them.

Alex blinked at me, but he didn't say anything.

Jennifer asked if I was taking any medication and I said, "Does Compound W count?" and she said, "No, it doesn't," then she put a clip on my finger to *check my vital signs* (which is more medical stuff EMT people need to know when you get hit by a Tesla). After that, Alex and Jennifer told me to *stay put* (don't move) and they stepped away and did a chat while I drank water to *stay hydrated*. Then they called Nana-Jo to tell her what happened.

Jennifer cleaned my forehead and she put something called a Steri-Strip on a cut up there (she said it didn't need stitches) and she did the same thing with a cut on my arm but she covered that one with what's called a *dressing* (big bandage) to help keep the dirt out, and when she was finished, she stepped back and looked me over.

"Looks like you're going to have a nasty black eye," she said, and I said, "I have a black eye?" and she nodded. "You certainly do."

I thought about how Angus got himself a black eye in a bar fight one time and how much he didn't like Mr. Tesky, and how, if he was there with me, he'd probably be wearing his new T-shirt that said **Born to Lie on a Beach, Forced to Work.** He'd also be filming my mangled-up bike and Mr. Tesky's Tesla, and he'd be talking to Mr. Tesky about lawyers and lawsuits because Angus is smart like that.

By then, the gray-haired cop had finished doing talking with Mr. Tesky, who was checking out a scratch on the front fender of his Tesla. The gray-haired cop came over to ask me some questions for his report, and he told me that Mr. Tesky said I was biking on the road instead of on the shoulder, and I said, "Mr. Tesky's lying."

"Pardon me?"

"He's a liar. I was NOT on the road."

"Well, uh—maybe you weren't paying attention and you wandered onto the road?"

"No way, José. I was on the shoulder."

The gray-haired cop nodded. "Right. Well, situations like this can be confusing after the fact, but I think we can all agree this was an unfortunate accident."

And I said, "This wasn't an accident."

"Pardon me?"

"Mr. Tesky is a liar, and he did sex on a desk with someone who wasn't his wife, and he likes to fire people, and I think he hit me with his Tesla on purpose because he doesn't like me. I'm not stupid—I know what's what."

The gray-haired cop's eyebrows jumped. I looked at Mr. Tesky, who was still doing chatting on his phone, and I thought about all the fast-moving TV shows I'd watched with Angus and how some cops in those shows were *dirty* (not honest) and how dirty cops sometimes take bribes, which is when they take money from people who are doing illegal stuff who don't want to get themselves arrested for doing that illegal stuff.

And I said, "You're not going to arrest Mr. Tesky, are you?"

The gray-haired cop said, "No one's getting arrested, Mr. Voss."

"Did he bribe you?"

"Pardon me?"

And I said, "Did Mr. Tesky offer you money to make this problem *go away*? I know how stuff like that works. I watch fast-moving TV shows."

The gray-haired cop crossed his arms. "This was an accident, Mr. Voss. No one offered me a bribe."

And I had a terrible headache and I wanted to go home, but my mind kept jumping around. I was thinking about Nana-Jo and how Mr. Tesky fired her for being too old, and how she came home that day and went to her bedroom, and she didn't come out for a long time. I also thought about how, after Angus got fired by Mr. Tesky, he couldn't find a job for a year because Mr. Tesky told everyone in town not to hire him, and how I'd probably never get to ride my old bike again, and how much I was going to miss it after riding it around Woodmont for years and years. And the whole time I was thinking those things, Mr. Tesky was on his phone, doing chatting with someone.

Then suddenly I wasn't going **DOWN, DOWN, DOWN** anymore—I was getting **ANGRY**. If Nana-Jo was there she'd probably say, "Count to ten, Denny. Calm down," but instead I thought about my homeless friend, Howard-the-army-guy, and how when we played Texas Hold'em at the church he told me he couldn't find a job because he had PTSD (which is a mental disorder you get after you see a war happen in person) and how he felt *rejected by society* (which is when people act like you're invisible, even though you're not) and I nodded and said, "Sometimes I feel like that too."

And that's how Mr. Tesky was making me feel now—invisible and rejected and ignored—even though *he* hit *me* with his Tesla.

That's when Nana-Jo pulled up in her Subaru and she got out with her cane, and she looked tired because her new knee wasn't 100 percent healed yet. By then I was so mad at Mr. Tesky for being Mr. Tesky that I was shaking. He wasn't a good guy, and I was not invisible, and he shouldn't treat me like I was, so I stood up, and said, "Hey, you!" and I waited for Mr. Tesky to turn and look at me, and when he did, I leaned forward and shouted at him SUPER LOUD, "In your face, motherfucker!"

I heard Nana-Jo gasp.

And Jennifer-the-EMT snort-laughed.

And the gray-haired cop wrote that part down in his report.

One week later, Mr. Tesky's lawyer sent me a letter that was delivered by a guy with a FedEx badge on his pocket and he said, "I have a delivery for Denny Voss," and I said, "That's me," and he had me sign for it on his mini-computer and this is what it said:

> Please be advised that our office represents Henry Tesky of Woodmont, Minnesota, and although Mr. Tesky doesn't admit fault in the accident noted below, he has agreed to pay any medical bills related to said accident and asks that these be forwarded to this office. In addition, he's agreed to pay for a replacement bicycle up to a maximum of $5,000 US. We ask that you sign the attached release of liability. By signing this the Releasor acknowledges that he/she understands the risks and claims involved and agrees not to sue the Releasee for any past or future injuries or damages. We also ask that you sign the attached financial release form, which ensures you won't ask for additional compensation in the future. Lastly, given

> the public nature of Mr. Tesky's position in the community, we ask that you sign the attached confidentiality agreement, which prohibits you from sharing any information about said accident and its outcome. Once we've received these signed forms, your medical bills, and a quote for the replacement bicycle, funds will be released accordingly.

I showed the letter to Nana-Jo, and she said, "That's fair, Denny. Your old bike didn't cost anywhere near five thousand dollars, and they want you to sign these forms because Mr. Tesky doesn't want you, or this problem, to bite him in the ass when he's running for mayor."

"I'd never bite Mr. Tesky in the ass."

Nana-Jo laughed. "I know, Denny. What this means, though, is that you can't tell anyone about the accident or that Mr. Tesky bought you a new bike. Do you understand?" and I said, "Yeah, I understand."

And that's how me and Angus ended up driving to Duluth to pick out a new bike for me. We went to three bike shops, then we went back to the first one because they did custom orders and they sold something called e-bikes. Angus gave the owner a picture of my old bike and some measurements he'd written down, then he pointed to me and said, "He wants an e-trike with a cargo hold. Can you build it?"

The man said, "Absolutely, it'll take two to three weeks."

"How much?" Angus asked the bike shop owner. The man wiggled his hand back and forth and said, "Between $4,000 to $4,300." Angus nodded. "Tell you what, throw in a helmet, bike gloves, and a spare set of winter tires, then write up a quote for $5,000 and we'll have a check couriered to you next week."

So, the man wrote up the quote and when I got home, Nana-Jo drove it over to Mr. Tesky's lawyer's office and she asked them to courier a check to the bike shop in Duluth. Twenty-eight days later a delivery truck came to our house and the driver had me sign for my bike, and it was in a crate and he used an electric lift to get it out and then Angus used a crowbar to open the crate and—**BAM!**—there was my new bike. And it was blue and when I rode it down Deyton Avenue, I pressed the button for the e-motor and it made pedaling SUPER EASY.

So yeah, that was a good day.

And then it wasn't.

Later, after I parked my new bike, Angus went home and Nana-Jo went to bed early. Then I turned on the TV and there was a story about another shooting, and it said **Breaking News** at the bottom, and this is what the reporter said:

"Nine children and two teachers were killed today in a shooting at the Learning Academy in Lyster, Texas. The gunman, Brian Fopal, twenty-three, allegedly texted his mother about his intentions moments before the shooting. He then entered the school through an unlocked door and began shooting. We've also learned that a teacher at the school who'd been harassed by Fopal in the past had filed a harassment restraining order against him a month ago . . ."

And I was shaking real bad so I leaned against the wall and slid down to the floor and my heart was going **BOOM-BOOM-BOOM**. Then I turned the TV off and I crawled into my bedroom and climbed into bed, and a few seconds later George got up there with me and he put his head on my chest, same as always.

Winner Winner Chicken Dinner

Tomorrow is Wednesday and me and Bridget will be doing talking about Mr. Tesky, and Dr. Harland will be there too, and each time I think about it I feel sick inside, but a promise is a promise—so yeah, tomorrow is going to suck.

Today it's just me and Dr. Harland, though. He wants me to tell him what happened at the DOT awards dinner and Lonny's bachelor party, and I'm not sure Angus wants me to talk about that stuff but I don't even care anymore because I need to get myself out of jail and to do that I need to be 100 percent honest about everything that happened last year, so that's what I'm going to do. Also, I can't ask Angus about it anyhow, because Bridget came by this morning to tell me that he can't visit me anymore because he's been *subpoenaed as a witness for the prosecution*, and I said, "What's that mean?" and she said, "It means he's being called to testify for the prosecution."

And I said, "Angus is working for the other side!?"

Bridget closed her eyes. "No, Denny, he's not working for them, but he does have to take the stand and answer their questions."

"What if he doesn't want to?"

Bridget explained that if Angus decides not to show up they'll throw him in jail, and I said, "He'll show up then, because I know he doesn't want to go to jail." So yeah, now I can't even ask Angus if it's okay for me to tell Dr. Harland what happened at the DOT awards dinner and at Lonny's bachelor party.

This is what happened: Angus clocked out at DOT for the day and he was wearing a new T-shirt that said **Running Late Is My Cardio**, then Lonny stuck his head into the hallway and asked if he could talk to me for a few minutes. Angus tipped his head back and said, "Son-of-a-beeech!" because he wanted to go home but now he had to wait until I was done.

Lonny is tall and skinny, and he has a small potbelly and a Fu Manchu mustache, and when I went into his office, he shut the door and put his hand on my shoulder. "How's the job going, Denny?"

"It doesn't always suck."

Lonny laughed. "You're a funny guy."

"No, I'm not. Some days it sucks, but not every day."

"Right." Lonny frowned. "Denny, how long have you worked here?"

"Two years, three hundred forty-eight days."

Lonny went around his desk, handed me an envelope, and told me to open it, so I did. Inside was a letter from Mr. Pyle congratulating me on getting an award I'd never heard of called the Extra Mile Award. Lonny explained that Mr. Pyle was his boss and that this award was given out each year to one DOT employee who is celebrated for going *above and beyond* when it comes to doing their job.

"And that's me?" I asked.

"Yes, that's you."

"People at DOT celebrate me?"

Lonny nodded. "That's what the letter says, right?"

The letter also said: *Mr. Voss, it is our honor to cordially invite you and a guest to DOT's Annual Awards Dinner at the Up/Down Bistro on Peeler Street from 6:00 to 11:00 p.m. on November 8th. Please RSVP to Maria at reception with a meal choice for each guest: Teriyaki Chicken or Elk Short Loin.*

"What's elk short loin?" I asked.

Lonny was busy tapping something into his phone. He looked up and said, "Just choose the chicken, Denny."

"Should I bring Nana-Jo with me?"

He shrugged. "Bring whoever you want."

"Does Angus get to bring someone too?"

Lonny put his phone down. "Uh . . . well, Denny, not every employee gets invited to the annual awards dinner. Just employees who've gone above and beyond in the last year, employees we feel deserve an award for their effort."

"So, Angus isn't getting an award?"

"No, he's not."

Before I put the letter back in the envelope, I read this at the bottom: *We're excited to welcome Henry Tesky, CEO of Norida and Woodmont mayoral candidate, as our guest speaker. A believer in honesty, integrity, and hard work, Henry will share time-tested, proven methods on how to create productive, thriving work environments where employees excel, no matter what business you're in.*

And I said, "Mr. Tesky's going to be there?"

"Yeah. Do you know him?" he asked, and I nodded, but Lonny wasn't looking at me; he was squinting at his computer screen. "We were lucky to get him," he said. "He's got a ton of grip-and-grin events coming up with his campaign for mayor." Lonny looked up at me. "You'd better get going, Denny. You're gonna miss your weekend."

Angus was waiting in the parking lot. I jumped in his truck and he started driving away before I could even close my door. "What was that about?" he asked. I showed him the envelope and told him I was getting the Extra Mile Award, that I'd been invited to DOT's annual awards dinner at the Up/Down Bistro on Peeler Street, and I was allowed to bring a guest so I was going to bring Nana-Jo, but we had to let them know what we wanted to eat for dinner in advance: teriyaki chicken or elk short loin.

Angus hit the brakes and pulled over. "Let me see that." He took the envelope from me, pulled out the letter, and read it; then he shook his head and he laughed and laughed. And I said, "What's wrong?"

He gave me the letter. "Nothing. It's just affirmative action at its best, buddy. You see, government departments like DOT have quotas and policies that give minorities preference when they hire for certain jobs, and you're a minority, and you've been doing this job for a while, so this kind of thing"—he waved at the letter—"is an event that celebrates DOT's commitment to diversity, that's all. And Henry Tesky's going to be there too? That's rich. The whole thing's like putting lipstick on a pig. Not that I'm minimizing the fact that you're getting an award, because I think that part's great."

And all of that was confusing and I didn't know what *putting lipstick on a pig* meant, so I said, "What's a minority?"

Angus frowned. "Uh . . . it's someone who's different from the larger part of the population. It's like when you go to bingo with Nana-Jo on Sunday night and there's a roomful of old people with white hair. In that situation, you'd be a minority because everyone else is old and you're young."

And I said, "Lots of young people work at DOT, Angus."

"Sure, but there aren't many disabled people, are there?"

"I'm not disabled."

"Technically you are."

"But I'm not blind or deaf and I don't need a wheelchair."

Angus nodded. "You're not *physically* disabled, but when it comes to the rules, you're considered *developmentally disabled.* We've talked about this before, remember?"

And I said, "My number is 72."

"Unfortunately, that's not good enough. Like it or not, there are people at DOT who consider you developmentally disabled and please do *not* freak out when I say that. I personally think you're a unique and cool human being and I also think it's great that you're getting this award. I'm just laying out the facts about affirmative action, that's all, because I refuse to lie to you, buddy."

I looked at Angus for a long time and I thought about what he'd said. "You're trying to ruin it for me."

He started driving again. "No, I'm not."

"You're jealous I'm getting an award. I know what's what, Angus."

Angus laughed. "I don't give two shits about your award."

"You're lying. I think you give three shits about my award." He shook his head and kept driving, and I felt myself getting angry. "I'm *not* disabled, Angus."

"Well, you don't *feel* like you're disabled, buddy, and that's good. I wish I could float through life wrapped up in a happy cloud of delusion too. But remember when we googled it a few years ago? Remember how it said that a person is considered disabled 'when it comes to any physical or mental condition that limits you.'"

I crossed my arms. "I don't know what that means and I don't remember googling it with you." Then Angus said, "Oh, I think you do. It took an hour to explain it to you, then you had a meltdown when I finally got you to understand what it means. Remember?"

And I said, "Nope," but I did remember because I have an excellent memory. Google said that being *limited* was the same as being *inadequate,* which means *not enough,* and I remember being mad about that, because I am enough.

Angus did a sigh. "Look, I don't make the rules about minorities or what does and doesn't make a person limited. Unfortunately, though—yet again—I have the great fucking pleasure of explaining the technicalities to you. I have ADHD, but you don't hear me whining about it, do you? No, you do not because I embrace who I am, and that's what you need to do too."

I stared out the window and thought about that for a bit, and my heart started going BOOM-BOOM-BOOM, and I was mad at Lonny, and Lonny's boss, and DOT, and Angus too, because even though Google thinks I'm *not enough* and the government thinks I'm *mentally disabled*, they're all wrong.

I said to Angus, "Pull over and let me out."

"What the—? Why?!"

"I'm enough, Angus. I am *enough*!"

"Whoa, Denny! Calm down." But I was breathing fast and I scrunched up the envelope Lonny gave me, because this day was not a good day anymore. I turned to Angus and said, "You're an asshole," and he said, "I can be, I'll give you that, but—"

"Pull over, Angus!"

"Denny, you're taking this too personally. Don't shoot the messenger, okay?" Which I know means you aren't supposed to blame someone who's telling you bad news because they're *just a messenger*, like last week when a guy delivered a letter to Nana-Jo that said the taxes on 8B must be paid *as soon as possible*, but she didn't get mad at the messenger guy because he was just doing his job—he didn't *write* the letter.

I closed my eyes and yelled at Angus, "Don't tell me not to shoot the messenger. I'll shoot any messenger I want!"

Angus hit the brakes and the truck skidded sideways.

I got out and said, "You're a big fat asshole." Then I kicked his truck tire and Angus *flipped me the bird* (gave me the middle finger) before he drove away. I shoved my scrunched-up DOT envelope into my knapsack, pulled out Papa-Jo's old Walkman, and put his headphones on with the orange foam earpads and I pressed play on his old George Strait tape, and I listened to "Amarillo by Morning" over and over again while I walked home.

It took me an hour to get home because on the way I saw my homeless friend, Howard-the-army-guy, sitting under a bridge, so I went and bought him butter chicken from Nana-Jo's friend Smita, who has a restaurant called Curry in a Hurry, then I took it to Howard under that bridge and we did visiting. He told me he'd been clean for eighteen days and I said, "That's great. It must be hard to find a shower when you're homeless."

I saw Angus twice while I was walking home: once when he was driving slow down a side street and a second time when I walked past Walgreens and his truck was in the parking lot and he was slumped down like he didn't want me to see him.

I yelled, "Get lost, Angus!"

And he flipped me the bird again.

When I got home, Angus's truck was parked under his carport, and Nana-Jo and George were waiting for me on the front steps.

I hugged George and his tail wagged and I said, real quiet-like, "I love you, George. You're enough for me and I'm enough for you." Nana-Jo asked what happened between me and Angus, and I said, "Nothing," because she was already worried about other stuff and I didn't want her doing worrying about me, and I didn't want to talk about how Google thought I was *limited* or how the government thought I was *mentally disabled.*

Extra Mile Award

Nana-Jo took me to a thrift shop (a store that sells secondhand clothes) and I used my DOT money to buy dress pants and a jacket, then we dropped them off at the dry cleaners and we drove over to Mr. G's Fine Fashions and I bought a dress shirt from Mr. G. "Congratulations, Denny," he said. "I hear you're getting an award." And I said, "Thanks. It's called the Extra Mile Award, which is hard to get because you have to do extra things for a whole year to win it." (That's how Nana-Jo explained it to me.) Mr. G asked if I needed a tie, and I said no, I was wearing Papa-Jo's tie, then I used my bank card to pay for my shirt, and me and Nana-Jo left for home. She stopped to put ten dollars' worth of gas in the Subaru, and when she got back in the car, she said, "Papa-Jo would be proud of you, Denny."

And I said, "He was proud of me before."

"Yes, he was. He thought you walked on water."

"I'm pretty sure he knew I couldn't walk on water, Nana-Jo."

And she laughed and laughed.

A few days later, she picked up my pants and my jacket from the dry cleaners and they were covered in plastic wrap, and I hung them in my closet. DOT's awards night was one day away and I was excited but my stomach was also twisty inside. I was helping Nana-Jo make dinner when the phone rang, and I answered it and it was Lydia.

"Hi, Denny. Can I talk to Mom?"

I gave the phone to Nana-Jo and she listened to Lydia for a bit, then she said, "Where are you now?" and "What did the doctor say?" She opened the junk drawer, pulled out a pen and paper, and wrote down a phone number and North Memorial Health Hospital. And when she hung up, she said, "Lydia flew to Minneapolis this morning for a photo shoot and she wasn't feeling well. Her appendix ruptured after she landed. They rushed her to the hospital and operated this afternoon."

"What's an appendix?"

Nana-Jo folded the paper in half. "It's part of the body attached to our intestine."

"Did they fix it?"

"You can't fix an appendix, Denny. They removed it."

"Does she get to keep it?"

"I'm not sure she'd want to."

And I thought about that and how hard it would be to be alone in a hospital when you're sick and had to be cut open to have a piece of your insides yanked out. Nana-Jo said, "Lydia told me it'll take two to four weeks to recover. They had to insert a drain and she's on pain meds. They'll release her in a day or so, then she'll fly home to New York."

"Are you going to see her?"

"I can't, Denny. We have your awards dinner tomorrow night."

And I thought about how I'd given Maria at DOT our meal choices, and how Nana-Jo was planning to wear her favorite dress with blue swirls on it. And I knew how much she loved me, but I knew how much she loved Lydia too, and it seemed like maybe Lydia needed her more than I did right now, so I said, "Nana-Jo, I think you should go see Lydia."

She looked at me for a long time, then she shook her head. "Where in the world did you come from, Denny Voss?"

"Duluth. I was born in Duluth."

She smiled. "Yes, you were. I was there. I'll never forget that day." Then she said, "Okay, I'll drive to Minneapolis tomorrow and I'll ask

Elaine if she can go to the awards dinner with you." Nana-Jo got herself busy doing things for her trip and she dragged her suitcase out from under her bed.

The next morning, she got in her Subaru and she said, "Elaine will be here at five to pick you up. Make sure you're ready," and I gave her a thumbs-up, which means, *No problem*, and she drove away and I knew it would take her five hours and eighteen minutes to get to Minneapolis because I asked Google about it and Google knows everything.

The kitchen wall phone rang at 2:48 p.m. and it was Nana-Jo. She said she was at the hospital in Minneapolis and they were releasing Lydia in a few hours. They were staying in a hotel for the night before Lydia flew back to New York the next day.

After I said goodbye, I took George for a walk and he likes to lead the way even though he's blind, so I let him decide where to go and he took us up Penguin Hill, where he did some happy trotting. We ran into Mrs. Trout and she gave George a kiss on the nose (people do that all the time because he's so kissable). Then I went home and I had a shower and got dressed in my new clothes. I was combing my hair when I heard Angus call out, "Anybody home?" and I yelled, "I am, but Nana-Jo's in Minneapolis."

"I know. She called me."

He was all dressed up and he had his hair slicked back and we were kind of talking to each other again, but not 100 percent because I was still mad at him. Nana-Jo had been driving me to work and I'd been taking Papa-Jo's Walkman with me so when me and Angus were in the DOT truck together, I'd listen to Papa-Jo's George Strait tape over and over.

I said to Angus, "Do you have a date tonight?"

"No, I'm going to the awards dinner with you."

"Elaine-the-stalker is going with me."

Angus looked at his watch. "Something came up and she can't go now. You're stuck with me. By the way, you need to stop calling her 'Elaine-the-stalker.'"

"Why? That's what you always call her."

Angus straightened his jacket. "I haven't called her that in a long time—you just haven't noticed. It's not polite to say things like that anyhow, so let's be polite from now on, okay?" and I shrugged and said, "Okay."

"Ready to go?" Angus asked.

I told him I needed help with my tie, so he followed me to the bathroom and I stood in front of the mirror and he stood behind me. He said, "Here, I'll show you how to do it so you can do it yourself next time." Then he did a lot of things that are hard to describe and he pulled the knot snug (tight) against my neck, folded my collar back down, and said, "Voilà!" which means, *There you go!* And I said, "Thank you, sir," which I heard David say one time on *Schitt's Creek*.

Angus's hair was all slicked back and I knew if Nana-Jo were here she'd say he looked spiffy (handsome) and I wanted to look spiffy too, so I told Angus I needed to fix my hair and I closed the bathroom door. "What are you doing in there?" he said. "You look fine, Denny. We're not trying to boil the ocean here; we're just going to a DOT awards dinner!"

I opened the cabinet under the sink, found some hair gel, and squeezed a blob out, then I rubbed both hands together and spread it on my hair. I combed it straight back and it stayed in place, and I thought it looked good with road maps from the comb, and that's when I knew I was ready for my Extra Mile Award. Angus was waiting outside in his truck, so I said goodbye to George, stepped outside, and locked the door, and when Angus saw me, he said, "Are you fucking kidding me?!"

And I said, "What?"

He closed his eyes. "Just get in before I change my mind."

On the drive across town Angus said we *looked like idiots* and *I owed him for this big time*. We got to the Up/Down Bistro early and I had my letter with me to prove I was supposed to be there. Angus said I wouldn't need it but I showed it to the guy at the door anyhow, and he hooked his thumb over his shoulder and said, "Seating cards are on the tables.

There's an open bar at the back." Angus said, "There's an open bar?!" He turned to me. "Listen, buddy, I'm drinking so we'll take an Uber home later, okay?" An Uber is a driver who uses his own car like a taxicab and there were only two of them in Woodmont. One was a grumpy old guy we hardly ever used, and the other one was a young guy named Mason who drives a white Honda Civic with a cracked windshield.

I found my name on a card at one table and next to it was a card with Nana-Jo's name, and that's how I knew where to sit. But when I turned to tell Angus, he was over at the bar and the bartender was mixing him a drink, so I went over there. "Want a drink?" Angus asked, and I said, "Can I have a Mello Yello?" The bartender said, "On the rocks?" and I asked what that meant, and he said, "It's when you add ice to your drink?" and I said, "Yes, I'd love that journey for me," because Alexis always says that on *Schitt's Creek* and it sounded cool.

Angus walked away and when I caught up to him, he said, "This is your night, Denny, just don't act like Rain Man. It's bad enough you look like him with your hair like that." And I said, "Who's Rain Man?" and he walked away again.

Other people started to show up and I saw Lonny and his new fiancée, and our receptionist, Maria, and Mr. Tesky and his new wife, Malinda. They sat at a table at the front and Angus kept staring at them. I could tell he liked Malinda's slinky dress, but he hated Mr. Tesky because he'd *blacklisted* him after he fired him (which is when someone tells other businesses not to hire you) and because of that it took Angus a year to find a job and for that whole year he had to use money from his savings account to pay his bills.

One of the guys at our table knew Angus, and his wife was with him and they were lots of fun. By the time me and Angus got our dinner—elk short loin because chicken is boring—Angus had had five drinks and I'd had two Mello Yellos.

During dessert, Lonny's boss got up to the microphone and he introduced Mr. Tesky and thanked him for agreeing to speak to the regional DOT team. "We're fortunate to have Henry Tesky here tonight.

As you know, he's running for mayor of Woodmont"—he stopped to do clapping, which made others clap too—"and he has a history of success in this community. Henry was a town councilor for years while also building a thriving nationwide business. He's spent years supporting Woodmont's Canine Rescue Shelter as well as volunteering with youth sport in Woodmont. He's a vocal proponent when it comes to the physical and mental health of our younger generation. To sum things up, Henry is a good man, a man of integrity, and we're honored to have him join us tonight."

Mr. Tesky got up and he took the microphone and he talked and talked. He said a bunch of stuff I didn't understand about *creating positive work environments*, and that it *was a privilege to spend time with men and women who strive for excellence*. He also talked about how it was a source of personal pride for him to live and work in this community, and how he cared deeply about serving the people of Woodmont.

Angus said, "What a bunch of bullshit," and when Mr. Tesky finally finished talking, everyone clapped but me and Angus; then Lonny slow-walked himself up to the front of the room and he started calling out people's names to come up and get their awards, and my heart started going **BOOM-BOOM-BOOM.**

And Maria from reception got an award for being *consistently cheerful* (which is when you act happy even if you're not) and Lonny also gave her a gift-wrapped box. Then he called Fred up to the front, a janitor at DOT, and he got an award for his *dedication to excellence* and a gift-wrapped box. And my heart kept going **BOOM-BOOM-BOOM** while Lonny called out more people's names, but I don't remember who they were because I was rocking back and forth in my chair. Then Lonny called out my name and I did a bit of moaning, and Angus said, "You okay, buddy?" and I said, "Nope."

"What's up?"

"No one told me I had to go up there to get my award."

Angus smoothed his hair back. "No worries. I'll get it for you."

He stood up and walked to the front of the room in a zigzaggy way because he was having trouble walking straight, and when he got there, he lifted Lonny off his feet and gave him a hug (Angus is a happy drunk), then he took the microphone. "Hello, everyone. I'm accepting this award on behalf of Denny Voss. DOT hired him three years ago, thinking, I'm sure, that they were doing him a favor, but in reality it was Denny who did them a favor. Me too, for that matter, because if it weren't for him, I'm not sure I'd have gotten out of bed each morning to do my job."

Angus lifted my award up. It was made from glass and had **EXTRA MILE AWARD** scratched into it. "There isn't one person in this room"—Angus squinted at Mr. Tesky—"not *one*, who measures up to Denny because he has true integrity, not the manufactured kind some men claim to have when it's convenient for them to look good publicly, and I think we all know men like that, don't we?" Everyone clapped and then Lonny took the microphone. He thanked Angus, then Angus took the microphone back, and he shouted, "Denny Voss is a class act and I'm honored to accept this award on his behalf."

Angus grabbed Lonny and danced with him, then he looked at Mr. Tesky and did a smirk (smart-ass smile) and Mr. Tesky stared back (no smirk) and they did what Nana-Jo calls a stare-down until Malinda tugged on Mr. Tesky's arm and he looked away.

Lonny gave Angus my gift box and Angus did a cha-cha-cha dance all the way back to our table (which is when you do lots of small steps while you sway your hips) and people kept high-fiving him. He gave me my award and my gift box, and I opened it and inside was a new iPhone with a *prepaid plan* for one year with T-Mobile (Angus said that means it's 100 percent free for me). So yeah, that's how I got my first ever cell phone at the Up/Down Bistro on Peeler Street after Angus won a stare-down with Mr. Tesky.

Lonny's Bachelor Party

Two weeks after I got the Extra Mile Award, Lonny invited me and Angus to his fourth bachelor party. He got himself married three times before and he had three other bachelor parties, but then those ladies did a divorce with him and now he was trying again with a new lady. When I told Nana-Jo, she said, "Lonny must be an optimist" (which is a person who looks at the bright side of things) and Angus said, "Nah, he's just stupid."

Lonny's party happened at the Cat House, which is a jiggle joint (strip club) where ladies dance and take their clothes off. On the way home from work the day of the party, Angus stopped at the bank to get a bunch of one-dollar bills and he gave me some and I asked what they were for, and he said, "When a girl does a pole dance, wave a few bucks and she'll come over and you can tuck them in her G-string," and I said, "What's a G-string?"

Angus showed me some pictures on his phone and my face got hot. "Why would I put money there?" and he shrugged and said, "It's just your way of saying you appreciate the way she dances."

"What if she's a bad dancer?"

Angus laughed. "Give her a few bucks anyway. It takes guts to get up there and do what they do, especially in Woodmont. They need all the encouragement they can get."

The Cat House had a guy at the door with a list of names and if your name wasn't on the list he wouldn't let you in because it was

Lonny's bachelor party, so friends only. But our names were on the list, so we got in. And I was wearing a white button-up shirt with a red bow tie and Angus was wearing a T-shirt that said **Drink Till You Want Me**. On our way inside Angus told me my bow tie looked stupid, but I just ignored him. Then we found a table with some guys we knew from DOT and we pulled up two chairs and a waitress came over and I asked her for a Mello Yello on the rocks.

"Is this guy serious?" she said to Angus.

And he said, "Did you not see the bow tie?" He gave her twenty bucks. "Mello Yello him all night long, please!"

A man got onstage and congratulated Lonny on his fourth wedding, then he introduced a dancer named Shy Shayna and she was pretty but she wasn't that shy and her underwear didn't cover her up very good. And the music was loud and Shy Shayna danced and swung around a pole and a guy at our table whooped and said, "Look at her gyrate!" and Angus was busy talking to someone else, so I took out my new phone and I asked Google what *gyrate* meant, and it said, *To dance in a wild or suggestive manner.*

After that they played a song called "You Shook Me All Night Long" and two pretty girls danced with a guy named Evan the Beast and Evan didn't have a shirt on and he was wearing tear-away pants (pants held together by snap buttons) and the girls ripped them off and all Evan had on underneath was a shiny gold pouch covering his genitals. One guy at our table laughed and said, "Isn't he the manager of Walmart?" and his buddy rolled his eyes and said, "Yeah, he does this as a side hustle!"

Then they played a song called "Wild Thing," which was bumpy and bouncy and everyone loved it, then another one called "Girls, Girls, Girls" and after that they played "It Wasn't Me" by Shaggy and I sang along because I knew all the words.

One hour went by, then another one went by, and a new waitress came over and Angus did flirting with her, then all the dancers took a break for *intermission* (rest time for dancers) and a guy from Woodmont got onstage with a guitar and he played a song called "Fire and Rain" and the new waitress said, "Wow, he's *really* good!"

Angus sighed. "I wish I'd brought my guitar."

"Oooh," the waitress said, and she touched Angus's arm to do flirting with him. "What kind of music do you play?" And I said, "Angus doesn't have a guitar. He's just messing with you," and the waitress gave Angus a dirty look and she walked away. Angus swatted me on the arm. "What the fuck, Denny?!" and I straightened my collar and said, "Maybe next time don't make fun of my bow tie."

"Keep it up, Einstein, and you'll be walking home!"

By the time I finished my third Mello Yello, more girl dancers had come out from behind the curtain and I tried not to stare at their boobs or their bums or their legs because they were half-naked. And I wasn't STARING but I did some LOOKING, then my penis got hard and my face got hot, and some of the guys from DOT asked if I wanted a beer, and Angus said, "Denny doesn't drink, guys. Leave him alone!"

Angus and his friends ordered a tray of *shots* (tiny glasses filled with booze) and they drank all of them. Lonny was at the table next to us and Angus and his buddies lifted him onto the stage with two of the dancers, and he looked different up there than he does at work because he was wearing blue jeans and a hat called a *fedora* and he was dancing with his small potbelly and his Fu Manchu mustache, but Lonny looked happy, so that was good, because before you get married you should be happy.

Lots of Lonny's friends were smoking cigars and my eyes hurt from all the smoke, and the lights onstage were blinking *on and off, on and off,* which made me dizzy, so I went to the bathroom, then I went outside through the back Exit door so I could breathe in fresh air. And I stood in the parking lot and stared at the stars, but it was November so pretty soon I got cold and I decided to go back inside and get Angus's keys so I could wait for him in the truck, but the Exit door was locked so I couldn't get back inside.

I knocked and knocked but nobody heard me, so I tried to solve the problem by myself. I walked around to the front door but it was locked too and there was a sign on the door that said **Private Event**; then I went over to Angus's truck and I took out my new phone and sent Angus a text that said: **I AM STUCK OUTSIDE THE JIGGLE JOINT. CAN U OPEN THE DOOR?** Then I rocked back and forth to try to stay warm.

I'm a texter now because Angus and Elaine showed me how, so now I text them and Sharon and Bill, and Nori, and sometimes Jean and Ted, but not my new homeless friend, Howard-the-army-guy, because he doesn't have a phone. I also have the Timkos' number but Angus said I'm ONLY allowed to text them if our house is burning down and so far that hasn't happened. So yeah, no texting with the Timkos.

Next to the Cat House was a bar called the Last Call Tavern and two guys came out laughing, and they saw me standing by Angus's truck. The fat guy said, "Hey, dude, what's up?" and I said, "Nothing." Him and his friend came over and I looked at my feet because I didn't know them and they were drinking beer and I was pretty sure you aren't allowed to drink beer in a parking lot. When I told them that, the fat guy lifted his chin at the Cat House and said, "Do you work at the bar in there?"

"No, I pick up roadkill for DOT."

He chugged the rest of his beer, then he grabbed the neck of the empty bottle, smashed it against Angus's truck, and pointed the broken end at me. "Are you fucking with me?" he said and that's when I started to stutter, which happens whenever someone points a gun at me, or a knife, and now a broken beer bottle.

"I . . . I'm not—not—eff-effing with you." I smacked the side of my head to make the stuttering stop. "I . . . I pick—pick up road . . . roadkill for DOT."

The fat guy looked me up and down. "Ahhh, you pick up roadkill for DOT. I get it. You're one of those *special hires*, aren't you?" He smiled at his friend, then he looked at me and said, "You got a wallet?" and I nodded.

He wiped his mouth with the back of his hand. "Let me see it."

"No, it's private."

The fat guy looked at his friend. "You hear that? His wallet's *private*," and his friend laughed. The fat guy came closer. "Give me your wallet, idiot." And I was cold and I'd had enough fresh air, but I couldn't get back inside the Cat House and there was nobody outside to help me, and that's when my heart started going **BOOM-BOOM-BOOM** so I rocked back and forth and did moaning, then I closed my eyes and sang the theme song for *Toy Story*—"You've Got a Friend in Me."

"What the fuck—" said the fat guy.

His friend laughed. "What is *happening*?"

The fat guy said, "No clue. He's got some screws loose, though." And I kept singing, then the smaller guy said, "He's messing with you," and he shoved me and I stumbled sideways and fell down. The ground was cold and I tried to crawl away, then one of them kicked me in the stomach so I curled up and covered my head with my arms. And they had work boots on and they were kicking me over and over and over again, and calling me lousy names.

"Get off him—NOW!"

The punching and kicking stopped. I looked up and saw Angus and one of his friends running across the parking lot. The fat guy and his friend took off the other way, but before the smaller guy could get in their truck, Angus grabbed his jacket and yanked him back, and while the fat guy got the hell out of Dodge, Angus pinned the smaller guy up against a car and punched him over and over again.

Angus's friend helped me up and I said, "Stop hitting him, Angus. Please stop!" I'd never seen him that angry before and it scared me, because when he was hitting that guy Angus looked like one of those assassins in the Jason Bourne movies we watch all the time. Then suddenly he stopped and he was breathing hard and the smaller guy's face was bleeding. Angus leaned over and said, real quiet-like, "You come near him again and I'll kill you, understand?" and the guy nodded, then he stood up and limped off into the dark.

So yeah, that's what happened at Lonny's bachelor party at the jiggle joint—Angus started the night by making fun of my bow tie, I saw lots of half-naked women gyrating onstage, then I got myself locked outside in the parking lot by accident and Angus came out there and beat some guy to a pulp to protect me.

That's just how Angus is.

No matter what kind of trouble I get myself into—it doesn't matter what it is—he always has my back.

Another Big Secret

Bridget and Dr. Harland were waiting for me when I got to our special meeting room this morning and Bridget smelled like lemons, same as always, and her fingernails were painted a color called *mauve* (I asked her) and she had on a purple sweater. She smiled and said, "Good morning, Denny," and I smiled back. Then Dr. Harland pushed a vanilla sprinkle doughnut across the table on a napkin and he had a nick (cut) on his head, maybe from when he did shaving to stay bald, but I didn't ask if that's what happened because that would've been rude. Instead, I just stared at him and did wondering.

Bridget folded her hands together. "Thank you for joining us, Denny. Are you ready to talk about Mr. Tesky?" And I said, "No, but it's Wednesday so I will do talking about him and I'll tell you everything like I promised, but I need to start at the beginning because the beginning is the best place to start."

"That's fine," Bridget said. "Take your time."

So I did.

And I started with Christmas.

I told her how George got rawhide bones from each of us and Nana-Jo got me headphones to plug into my phone so I could listen to "It Wasn't Me" by Shaggy whenever I wanted. Angus gave me a T-shirt that said **Pizza Fixes Everything** and he gave Nana-Jo a new used vacuum because her old one quit, and I gave Nana-Jo SOREL winter boots and Angus a *Sports Illustrated* calendar of girls in bathing suits. So yeah, Christmas was nice.

Then me and Nana-Jo got invited to Sharon and Bill's for a New Year's Eve party and they also invited the Timkos, and Jean and Ted, and Angus and Elaine, and some other people I didn't know. There was a table set up with lots of food and we all wore **Happy New Year** hats, and they gave us horns to blow for when the clock went to midnight, and when the clock went to midnight, we all blew our horns.

Everyone was laughing and shouting, "Happy New Year!" and Nana-Jo looked happy, and I saw Angus kiss Elaine quick-like, then Ted gave his wife Jean a swat on the bum, and Mr. Timko smiled when Mrs. Timko rested her head on his shoulder. And I watched everyone and I thought about how people are always doing flirting—old people and young people, people who know each other, and people who don't know each other—and how sad our planet would be if people stopped doing flirting.

Sharon and Bill lifted their wineglasses, and Bill said, "Here's to a brand-new year. Happiness and health to each of you!" and then we all toasted but because I don't drink alcohol, I had apple juice instead of champagne.

A few minutes later, I went home because I didn't want George to be lonely. He was asleep on my bed when I got there and he didn't wake up when I climbed into bed, he just kept sleeping. Nana-Jo said that's because he's getting old and he sleeps deeper than he used to, but I think it's because he's happy and he feels safe at 8B.

That night we got twenty-six inches of snow and the next morning, the first day of the new year, Woodmont's snowplows were extra busy, so to help out Angus hooked a snowplow blade to the front of his truck and we threw shovels in the back and we cleared the snow off most of Deyton Avenue. When we were done, we also cleared snow off our neighbors' driveways, including 9A, where Mr. and Mrs. Chen live (they own a Greek restaurant), and 9B, where the Chumak family lives—they moved here six months ago after their country got itself invaded by another country and their lives were in danger.

And it was mostly fun because me and Angus like clearing snow in Woodmont after snowstorms, even though sometimes Angus complains about it. This time when he grumbled about it, though, I did a *turn the tables* on him (which is when you say something to someone that they usually say to you) and I said, "Buck up" and "Don't be a pussy" and "Life is hard all over" and then I laughed and laughed.

The next day was January 2 and Angus and Elaine spent the day packing for their Mexico vacation because they were leaving early the next morning to drive to Minneapolis to catch their flight. And while they got packed, Nana-Jo worked on a puzzle, then she washed her hair and put her pink foam curlers in. The doorbell rang at 7:00 p.m. and it was Mrs. Timko, and she asked Nana-Jo if she'd like to go play bingo and Nana-Jo said, "Absolutely," and she tied a kerchief over her curlers and off they went.

And because it was a new year, I decided to clean my room, so I got Nana-Jo's new used vacuum out and I vacuumed my bedroom and tidied up my closet, and that took an hour and the whole time George was asleep on the Elvis rug in the living room. Then I got thirsty so I went to the fridge and I got a Mello Yello and even though Nana-Jo told me to stop doing snooping, I decided to do a bit more because I was bored.

So I went down to the basement, which was still a mess, and I put some of Lydia's keepsakes from the folding tables back into her trunk, which I'd wiped out with Mr. Clean a few weeks earlier. I held up Lydia's **Woodmont High** sweater and thought about trying it on, but it looked too small, and so was the sweatshirt that said **Regional Champs**. Then I opened her shoebox of old Polaroid photos and there were a bunch of Lydia with her basketball team and of her playing basketball.

I also put two of Lydia's photo albums back in the trunk, but I flipped through them first and they were boring because most of the pictures were of Lydia and I was sick of looking at her. She had a cloth bag with strings that pulled it closed at the top and it was full, so I dumped it on the table and there was Papa-Jo's watch (which made me sad) and a bracelet with dangly charms, and a rabbit foot key chain with keys on it, and some handwritten notes that said, *You're amazing!* and, *I think about you all the time!* and, *You drive me crazy!*

I put everything back in the cloth bag, then I found Lydia's diary and it was green with yellow butterflies, but I couldn't open it because it had a teeny-tiny lock holding it shut, so I did thinking and I went back to the keepsake trunk and got Lydia's rabbit foot key chain out of her cloth bag. It had two regular keys on it and one teeny-tiny one, and the teeny-tiny one opened the lock on Lydia's diary so I could do more snooping.

And that's what I did.

I sat on the basement steps and read Lydia's diary. She said lots of mean stuff like how her science teacher, Mr. Lipton, was an asshole and how the boys she went to school with were stupid. She also said she wanted to live in New York or Paris. There were pages and pages about everything Lydia *wanted* (lots of money, big house, to travel the world, blah, blah, blah) and what she *needed* (lots of money, jewelry, expensive cameras, blah, blah, blah) and that her biggest fear in the world was being poor.

Lydia also wrote about her basketball team and how she liked out-of-town tournaments because she got to stay in hotel rooms with her friends and sometimes they'd drink and party with guys they met at those games. At one of those tournaments, Lydia said she made out with a guy named Mikkel and that Hank saw them and got jealous, which made her feel special, because until then she wasn't 100 percent sure how Hank felt about her.

Lydia wrote a lot about Hank and how nobody else had ever made her feel the way he did, and she said sometimes she'd use a pay phone in Woodmont to call him at work so Nana-Jo wouldn't know what she was up to, and they'd talk and talk, and how one time he picked her up from that pay phone and they drove thirty miles away to the next town so they could eat dinner together at a fancy Italian restaurant.

She wrote about Hank's *boyish smile.*

And how he was *so confident.*

And *sophisticated.*

She said Hank was always leaving notes in her basketball bag that said things like, *You're beautiful*, and, *I can't stop thinking about you*, and one day he left a note that said, *This is crazy. I'm married to someone who doesn't even come close to you!* but then after basketball practice that day Lydia said Hank asked her to rip that note up, because he didn't want anyone to see it and ruin things for them.

So, Lydia did.

And I sat there with Lydia's diary on my knees and thought about that, and it bothered me because this Hank guy said he was married and him doing flirting with Lydia like that wasn't good. On one page in her diary she'd drawn hearts around Hank's name and her name and she wrote about how she'd used her own money to buy *thong panties* and a matching *lace camisole* (which is an undergarment for the upper body held up by shoulder straps), then a week later, they went to another out-of-town tournament and Hank told her to sneak out of her room when everyone was asleep and come to his room.

So, Lydia did.

On the next page, she'd taped a Polaroid picture of her sitting in Hank's lap in her uniform and the picture was kind of blurry but Lydia was smiling and she looked young and pretty. Hank was wearing jeans and a golf shirt, and his head was turned sideways but he looked older than Lydia. There was also a newspaper story with a picture of the team and all the girls' names were typed at the bottom from LEFT TO RIGHT and there were also two coaches in that picture, and the coach on the left was Ian Scott and the coach on the right had dark hair and a mustache and his name was Henry Tesky.

I stared and stared, and my heart started going **BOOM-BOOM-BOOM.** Then I held the picture close and I squinted at it, and the newspaper story said, *Woodmont's girls' 17U basketball team wins regional tournament. Coached by Ian Scott and Henry (Hank) Tesky, this team shows incredible promise.*

I think maybe I stopped breathing.

Because Mr. Tesky was Lydia's basketball coach.

And Mr. Tesky was Hank.

I felt sick inside, and dizzy. But I turned the page and read what Lydia wrote next, and here's what she said: *Hank's been acting distant. When I called him today he said he couldn't talk. I told him I'm pregnant, that I didn't notice I'd missed a few periods, and he said, "A few?! Holy shit! Have you told anyone else?" and I said no, then he told me not to panic, that he'd help me take care of it and he hung up.*

What does he mean, though?! He'll help me take care of the baby? What am I going to do? I can't tell Mom and Dad, they'll kill me . . . unless Hank leaves his wife like he keeps saying he's going to. They'd still be mad, but they'd get used to it. Hank says he doesn't want to stay in Woodmont, so maybe we could move to New York and raise the baby there. Maybe we could live near Central Park. That'd be nice! P.S., I checked my calendar. I'm pretty sure I'm 12 weeks pregnant. Hank said he'll pay for an abortion, he can set it up at a clinic in Minneapolis next week. We met at Penguin Hill Park last night. He wouldn't even look at me. He said he's not ready to leave his wife and if I have this baby, it'll ruin his life—HIS LIFE, not mine. Holy shit, I'm scared!

I set Lydia's diary down on the stairs, then I put my hands between my knees, and I rocked back and forth and did moaning for a bit because it felt like someone was running around inside my head with spiky shoes on.

Mr. Tesky was Hank and Hank was Lydia's basketball coach.

And he made Lydia pregnant.

With me.

When I finished telling Bridget and Dr. Harland that part of the story, I felt myself going **DOWN-DOWN-DOWN**. "So yeah," I said. "Mr. Tesky is my *biological* father but he didn't raise me up like Papa-Jo did so he's not my *actual* father." Bridget's hands were folded together and she didn't look shocked or surprised, and that's when I decided that Angus or Lydia must've already told her about Mr. Tesky being my biological father.

I'm not stupid.

I know what's what.

But I didn't even care anymore. I just wanted to get myself out of jail so I could see George and Nana-Jo, and Nori and Theo, and my new homeless friend, Howard-the-army-guy, and telling the whole truth and nothing but the truth was the only way I could think of to help Bridget win her first ever case in a courtroom.

"How did you feel about that, Denny?" Bridget asked.

And I said, "It made me want to throw up, then it made me VERY ANGRY because I used my new phone to ask Google what *abortion* meant and it said: *the deliberate termination of a human pregnancy*, then I asked Google what *termination* meant, and it said: *the act of bringing something to an end*, and that's when I figured out that Mr. Tesky wanted to kill me before I even got myself born."

Bridget nodded. "That must have been upsetting. I'm sorry that's how you found out." She leaned forward. "But Denny, now I need you to walk me through everything you did *after* you learned that Mr. Tesky was your biological father until you got arrested two days later at the bottom of Penguin Hill. Can you do that?"

I said, "Yes, I can."

So yeah, that's what I did.

Liars and Traitors AGAIN

After I read Lydia's diary I remembered doing moaning in our basement, but I didn't remember my throat closing up, or feeling like I couldn't breathe, or my mind shrinking down to a tiny ball, but that must've happened too, because I went away for a while and when I came back I was curled up on the cold basement floor, shaking, and I heard Nana-Jo THUMP-THUMP-THUMPING down the stairs with her cane.

"Denny! Oh my God. Are you all right?"

I slowly sat up.

Nana-Jo crossed herself, then she helped me up. "What happened?! Is this about Papa-Jo?" she asked, and I shook my head and I said, "No," then we went upstairs, and I sat down in the kitchen with Lydia's diary.

"What's that?" Nana-Jo asked.

I said, "It's Lydia's diary. I did more snooping and I read everything she wrote in there, and now I know the whole wide truth, and that makes YOU and LYDIA and ANGUS even bigger liars and traitors than you were before!"

Nana-Jo rubbed her forehead. "Denny, what are you talking about?" she said, and she looked tired. The day before, when we were shoveling driveways, Angus told me he was worried about Nana-Jo because she'd lost weight since her broken-down knee operation and she seemed *frail* lately (which means weak and delicate) and he told me to take care of her while he was away in Mexico on vacation.

But I was **ANGRY** and it felt like there wasn't enough air in the room, and my heart was going **BOOM-BOOM-BOOM** so hard I could feel it inside my head. I didn't want to say the words out loud—I didn't want to say HIS name out loud—so I found the page in Lydia's diary with the newspaper story and the picture of Lydia's whole team, and I shoved it across the table and said, "I'm talking about the guy who made Lydia pregnant when she was young and stupid. I'm talking about HIM!"

Nana-Jo's eyes got big.

I shouted at her, "Why didn't you tell me the truth?!"

Nana-Jo's shoulders jumped a little. She pulled the diary closer, put her glasses on, and squinted as she read Lydia's words. She flipped back one page to read what was there, then she flipped forward to read those pages too. And by then, her hands were shaking, and I kicked the table leg—hard—and she jumped again. "You didn't tell me the truth for my whole wide life, Nana-Jo, and that means you're a liar. A liar and a traitor!"

She stared at Lydia's diary. Then tears came up in her eyes, and she put one hand over her mouth, and said "Oh my God" over and over again.

And I felt like I couldn't breathe again and I couldn't sit still, so I got up and I rocked back and forth a bit, and Nana-Jo was very pale (no color in her face) and it seemed like she was upset that I'd found out the truth about Mr. Tesky and that made me **EVEN ANGRIER** because she's always saying, "Tell the truth, Denny. Don't hide stuff from me," but that's exactly what she'd done to me. Her and Lydia and Angus.

I said, "Did Papa-Jo know?"

Nana-Jo reached for my hand, but I stepped back so she couldn't touch me. "Denny, neither of us knew," she said. "I swear to God. When Lydia told us she was pregnant, we asked her who the father was and she said it was a young guy she'd met at an out-of-town basketball tournament. She told us she only knew his first name, that she'd made a stupid mistake, and she was humiliated about it."

And I said, "I'm not a stupid mistake. My number is 72."

Nana-Jo sat up straighter. "No, no! That's not what I meant, Denny. Of course you're not a mistake. But Papa-Jo and I didn't know any of this." She picked up Lydia's diary and shook it, then dropped it back on the table like she hated it. "I would never lie to you about something like this—never."

"I don't believe you. You lied to me before about Lydia."

Nana-Jo slumped a little. "That was a mistake. We let her talk us into not telling you the truth and we shouldn't have. We should've been one hundred percent open with you, but Lydia was so young then—she was only seventeen when she got pregnant; she gave birth to you two months after she turned eighteen—and she was upset and adamant that it'd be better for you, and her, if no one in Woodmont knew the truth. So, yes, our family knew—Uncle Maynard and Aunt Ruby, Papa-Jo, Angus, and my sister, Mary, who lived in Duluth. She took Lydia in and cared for her until you were born. I'm sorry, Denny. I'll be sorry about that for the rest of my life. Papa-Jo and I were trying to deal with a difficult situation, but I can see now that we handled it wrong."

But I was still shaking and I was still **ANGRY**, and I wasn't sure if Nana-Jo was doing more lying or if she was telling *the honest-to-God truth* (which is a kind of truth that can never be a lie) but I didn't want to be doing this kind of talking with her anymore, and I didn't want to be in 8B anymore either. So I grabbed Lydia's diary off the table and I pulled on my jacket and my boots and I opened the front door.

Nana-Jo got up with her cane. "Denny, wait—" She sounded scared.

And I said, "I don't want to be here anymore."

"Where are you going?"

I was so **ANGRY** that I kicked the wall by the door. "I'm going over to 8A to yell at Angus." Because that was the honest-to-God truth, and I was pretty sure Angus was being a liar and a traitor again too.

—

It was 10:48 p.m. when I knocked on the door at 8A and Angus opened it. He was wearing boxer shorts and a winter hat with ear flaps, and a T-shirt that said **I'm Not Responsible for What My Face Does When You Talk.** "Hey, buddy, what's up?" He stepped back. "Come on in. I'm getting ready to go to Elaine's. She's worried I'll miss my alarm in the morning, so I'm sleeping there tonight."

I made my hands into fists. "You aren't my cousin anymore, Angus!"

He lifted one eyebrow. "Having a good day, are we?"

"No, I'm having a VERY bad day!"

Angus waved at me to come inside. "Well, get your ass in here anyway. I'm freezing." So, I went inside and said, "I did more snooping tonight." Then I waved Lydia's diary at him. "This is Lydia's diary from when she was young and stupid, and I read everything she wrote in it and now I know the WHOLE WIDE TRUTH."

"The truth about *what*?" Angus frowned. "I swear, Denny, half the time when I talk to you I feel like I'm having an out-of-body experience."

"I know you lied to me AGAIN and so did Lydia and Nana-Jo."

Angus put his hands up. "Whoa! Slow down and start over. You lost me." And I was **ANGRY** and my heart was going **BOOM-BOOM-BOOM** and I didn't want to say the words out loud, so just like I did with Nana-Jo, I found the page in Lydia's diary with the newspaper story and the picture of Lydia's team, and I gave it to him, and I said, "I know who made Lydia pregnant."

Angus's eyes got big. "Seriously?!"

"Seriously."

"Holy shit, that's big news."

I crossed my arms. "It is, and I'm UPSET because just like Lydia and Nana-Jo, you didn't tell me the truth again and that means we can't be friends or cousins anymore. I also don't think we should work together either, so you'll need to quit your job at DOT."

Angus picked at a tooth with his fingernail. "Right. Well, yet again, I have no idea what you're talking about, buddy. Can you give me a little more?"

I pointed to Lydia's diary. "Read what she wrote."

I stayed standing while Angus sat down and read the page I'd opened it to, then just like Nana-Jo, he frowned and flipped back a few pages to read what was there and his eyes got big, and he said, "What the *fuck*?!" Then he flipped forward again and he said, "Fuck me." And I rocked back and forth and watched his face (very pale) and I waited for him to tell me he was sorry, that he should've told me about Lydia and Mr. Tesky a long time ago, but how it really didn't matter in the *grand scheme of things* because Tesky was an asshole, and I wasn't and *blah, blah, blah*.

But that's not what Angus said.

He held his head in his hands. "Have you talked to Lydia about this?" and I said, "Not yet," then he said, "What about Nana-Jo?" and I said, "Yeah, I just talked to her," and he asked me what she said. I told him Nana-Jo said she didn't know it was HIM and neither did Papa-Jo, because when Lydia got herself pregnant, she told them it was a guy she'd met at an out-of-town basketball tournament, and she only knew his first name.

"Jesus." Angus stood up, bent over, and put his hands on his knees. "Denny, I need you to believe me. I did not know about Henry Tesky and I honestly don't think Nana-Jo did either." He closed Lydia's diary and pushed it across the table. "I've always known that Lydia had you when she was eighteen, and that Nana-Jo and Papa-Jo raised you, but not the rest of this stuff. Lydia kept it from everyone."

And I said, "Are you telling me the *honest-to-God truth*?"

Angus said, "Scout's honor," and he put his right hand in the air with three fingers pointed up, then I felt myself going **DOWN, DOWN, DOWN**, because I was pretty sure Angus was telling the *honest-to-God truth*, which was good, but it also looked like everything in Lydia's diary was 100 percent true and that wasn't good.

I said, "I want to punch Mr. Tesky!"

Angus pulled off his winter hat. "Trust me, I want to do worse than that." He took a breath, blew it up at the ceiling. "Henry Tesky got Lydia pregnant. Un-fucking-believable!" Angus made his hands into fists. "Denny, listen to me. When I get back from vacation, we'll talk, just you and me. Tesky's going to pay for this, I promise. Until then, though, think about it as much as you want but do *not* talk to anyone about it and don't do anything, okay?"

I stared at him for a long time.

Then I nodded.

"I'm not kidding, Denny. I know this is a lot to process, but don't do *anything* until I get back, okay?" and I said, "Okay," because I was tired, and I didn't want to do talking with Angus anymore. I also didn't want to go home yet, though, so I asked if I could stay and watch a fast-moving TV show, and Angus said sure. So, I took my jacket off and I sat down in his La-Z-Boy chair and loaded one of the Jason Bourne movies from his black box.

Angus got himself dressed, then he pulled his suitcase over to the door, got a big roll of clingy plastic wrap, and went round and round his suitcase, wrapping it until it looked like a shiny plastic pod. And I guess I was staring because he looked up and said, "It protects your suitcase from getting damaged *and* it stops people from slipping illegal shit into your bag."

He put his jacket on and his winter hat, then he did a sigh. "I'm sorry, Denny, this news really sucks. I don't know what else to say." And I was sort of listening to him, but my mind was also thinking about how Mr. Tesky wanted Lydia to have an *abortion* so he could kill me before I could get myself born.

"You going to be all right?" Angus asked.

I nodded. "Yup."

Angus looked like he didn't believe me, though, so I gave him a thumbs-up and said, "Have a nice vacation," then he left for Elaine's house so they could drive to Minneapolis in the morning. After he left, I felt myself going **DOWN-DOWN-DOWN** and my mind kept jumping around, doing thinking, and I was kind of watching the Jason Bourne movie and I remember Jason beating up a bad guy and I think maybe someone got shot and I'm pretty sure there was lots of blood, but I don't remember anything else.

Then suddenly it was 1:04 a.m.

And I was blinking at Angus's living room clock.

And I guess I must've gotten cold watching the Bourne movie, because I was still sitting in Angus's La-Z-Boy chair but I had my jacket on again. Also, I was very tired and the inside of my brain felt bruised (sore) so I locked up 8A and went home. Nana-Jo's bedroom door was closed and George was asleep on my bed, so I took my jacket off and crawled under the covers, and George woke up and he put his head on my chest, same as always, and that was the only good thing about my day.

Dead as a Doornail

When I woke up in the morning, I heard water running in the bathroom.

I got dressed, clipped the leash to George's collar, and took him for a walk so he could do his business. It was cold out (minus twenty-two degrees) and Elaine's car was gone from her driveway, and that meant she and Angus were on their way to Minneapolis to catch a jet plane to Mexico. Angus's truck was parked under his carport at a funny angle, though, and he'd forgotten to plug it in, which was weird because that's something Angus never forgets to do when it's cold. So I went over and plugged it in so it'd start when he got back.

Then I went home to 8B and Nana-Jo was in the kitchen. I hung up my jacket and took my boots off, and she said, "Denny?" I looked up and she was holding her right arm, and there was a red mark on her neck and one on her face too. She said, "I fell getting out of the bathtub," and she looked tired, and smaller than usual. That's when I remembered what Angus said about her being frail lately and how I needed to take care of her while he was away, and I hurried over to her and forgot all about our fight the night before.

"You need to see a doctor, Nana-Jo."

"I'll be fine," she said. "I'm just a bit bruised. Sharon's bringing over an ice pack. I couldn't find any in the fridge freezer." She pulled her sleeve down and showed me her shoulder and there was a red mark there too. And seeing that made me feel sick inside because Nana-Jo always took such good care of me, and now I needed to take good care of her. She reached out and squeezed my hand. "Denny, listen," she said. "I didn't know about Henry Tesky. I was as shocked as you were."

I nodded. "Yeah, Angus said he didn't know about it either. I believe you guys, Nana-Jo, and I don't think you're liars and traitors anymore. I'm sorry for yelling at you and saying all those lousy things."

Nana-Jo looked sad. "You have every right to be upset. I'm still trying to process it myself. I can't imagine how hard this is for you. I also can't tell you how much it hurts that Lydia didn't tell us what was really going on." She stared out the window. "When she told us she was pregnant, she begged us not to tell anyone. She was scared. She wanted to give you up for adoption but we said no. Letting someone else raise our grandson? Never." She turned back to me. "I have no regrets. I'd do it all over again. Every minute of it."

The doorbell rang. It was Sharon, bringing an ice pack for Nana-Jo. I let her in and she hugged George, then took off her boots and went into the kitchen. "I tried to call you back—" Sharon stopped and stared. "Oh, Joanne! That must have been a nasty fall."

Nana-Jo said, "I'll be fine."

"Did you take ibuprofen?"

Nana-Jo nodded. Before Sharon went home, she told Nana-Jo that she'd tried to call earlier, but she kept getting a message saying the phone had been disconnected. "I tried three times, same message each time." So, I walked over and picked up the green wall phone but there was no dial tone, just a beep-beep-beeping sound. "Yup," I said. "It's not working, Nana-Jo."

Her face went red. "I must have forgot to pay the bill."

I said, "That's okay. We have my cell phone," and I gave the number to Sharon and then Nana-Jo asked her to please give it to Jean and Ted and the Timkos too until we could get our phone hooked up again.

Later that day, my cell phone rang and rang, and each time it was Lydia and she left a bunch of messages that said, "Denny, call me back when you get this," and "Why's the landline disconnected?!" and "Why aren't you calling me back?" And when I was done listening to them, I'd pressed Delete and she'd start leaving new ones, and when me and George went to bed, she was still phoning, so I pressed a button that said **Do Not Disturb**, which was good because it SHUT LYDIA UP.

So yeah, I *was* talking to Nana-Jo, but I wasn't talking to Lydia, and the phone company cut us off so our green wall phone wasn't working, and that meant nobody else was talking to Nana-Jo either unless they came by the house or they called my cell phone and asked for her. For most of that day I felt quiet inside (and sad) and some of that day I felt quiet inside (and mad) but I was busy taking care of Nana-Jo, giving her ice packs for her arm and her neck, and the red mark on her face, which was already turning into a purple bruise. I also took George for two long walks and that made him happy, which was good because, like I said before, at least someone was happy.

Sharon came by the next day with a copy of the local paper and she dropped it on the kitchen table. "Joanne, did you hear about this?! Henry Tesky is dead as a doornail."

On the front page was a picture of the Teskys' house on Penguin Hill with five police cars out front (that's every police car we have in Woodmont) and yellow tape across the front door that said **Crime Scene Do Not Cross**, and below that was a smaller picture of Mr. Tesky sitting at his desk at Norida wearing a suit and tie.

Unknown Assailant Shoots and Kills Local Businessman

by Sheila Bahry

> Henry Tesky, 62, mayoral candidate for Woodmont and co-owner of Norida, Inc., one of North America's top yogurt manufacturers, was shot and killed in the foyer of his home in the early-morning hours of January 3rd. His wife, Malinda Tesky, discovered his body after returning home from an out-of-town trip.
>
> A neighbor came forward to say he heard a gunshot shortly after midnight, but he didn't call the police because he thought it was someone shooting at the coyotes that have been frequenting the area lately.
>
> Chief of Police Eric Raymond has confirmed there was evidence of a scuffle. He also made this statement: "We'll learn the caliber of the bullet as soon as we get the ballistics report back. There are currently no suspects, but we're continuing to investigate and we won't give up until Henry Tesky's killer is arrested and brought to justice."

Nana-Jo picked up the paper and clamped a hand over her mouth, then she set it down again and listened to Sharon do talking.

I walked over and read the story, and I know you're supposed to be sad when someone dies, but I wasn't sad about Henry Tesky being dead, not one bit. And I stood there and thought about it. The newspaper said he was shot and killed on January third, *shortly after midnight*, which was the same night I did more snooping at 8B, and the same night I read Lydia's diary and found out the truth about her and Mr. Tesky. I also yelled at Nana-Jo and I went over to Angus's house and yelled at him, and now Mr. Tesky was *dead as a doornail* (I asked Google and that means NOT ALIVE and UNEQUIVOCALLY DEAD).

So yeah, you just never know what might happen.

Life is strange like that.

—

Before they left for Mexico, Elaine put something on my phone called WhatsApp (which is a free *instant messaging app* that lets you send messages, pictures, and videos to other people). She showed me how to use it and we did practicing, then one afternoon her and Angus sent me a *selfie* (picture of them together) all the way from Mexico. They were wearing bathing suits and holding fancy drinks with tiny umbrellas in them, and they were on a beach with palm trees in the background.

And I said, "Look, Nana-Jo, palm trees," and she put her glasses on and looked at the picture. "Should I tell them you fell in the bathtub?" I asked.

"No. I don't want them to worry about me."

"Should I tell them Mr. Tesky is dead?"

"No, Denny, they can get caught up on everything that's happened in Woodmont when they get back. Leave them be."

An hour later Sharon came by and even though Nana-Jo argued with her, Sharon made her put on her coat and her new SOREL winter boots and she took Nana-Jo to a doctor to make sure she didn't break anything when she fell in the bathtub.

While they were gone, I took George for a walk and when we finally got to the top of Penguin Hill—he'd been walking a lot slower lately—I had him sit down and I squatted beside him and took my first ever selfie picture. It took me twelve tries to get it right, though, so now I have twelve selfie pictures on my phone, and in some of them my head is cut off and in two of them you can only see half of George's face, and in one George knocked me over so all you see is my boots, but the rest were good.

The selfie I liked best was one where George is giving me a slurpy kiss and I'm laughing, so I sent that one to Angus and Elaine on WhatsApp just like how we practiced, and I typed a message with it that said: **me and george**

Two minutes later, my phone went DING and I checked, and Elaine sent a message back and it said: **heaven**

I typed back: **no, penguin hill**

Then there were three dancing dots and she sent me a smiley face. And after that, more dancing dots happened, and then Elaine said: **angus wants to know what you've been up to since we left**.

I typed back: **nothing**

Then she said: **good, he says keep doing nothing until we get home**.

George was asleep on Nana-Jo's Elvis rug, so I went over to 8A and I sat in Angus's La-Z-Boy chair and did surfing with his remote control (which is when you go through a lot of TV channels *very fast*) but I couldn't find anything good to watch. Then I stopped on a news channel where a reporter said, "A woman is dead in Louisiana after her three-year-old son accidentally shot her with a loaded handgun he found in her purse . . ."

My heart started going BOOM-BOOM-BOOM.

And I made my hands into fists.

And I could hear Nana-Jo in my head saying, *Turn off the TV, Denny.*

So that's what I did. I turned it off and I sat there in Angus's living room all by myself doing thinking about how Papa-Jo died after a stranger shot him in the back and how I missed him every day and how much it hurt to lose him. Then I rocked back and forth, and did moaning, and I could feel myself going DOWN, DOWN, DOWN and I stayed like that for the rest of the day.

—

The doctor said Nana-Jo didn't break any bones, but she'd have to be more careful in the bathtub and the shower in the future because it's harder to *maintain your balance* (stand up straight without falling down) when you get older.

And she is.

Getting older, I mean.

Nana-Jo looked tired that morning but she said she was feeling better, so she went to the Take It or Leave It with Mrs. Timko to sort through all the stuff people had dropped off after Christmas to give away. As soon as she left, I decided to do a surprise for her. I put on my jacket and my boots and I walked to Walmart to buy *nonslip safety bathtub strips*, then I walked home and I stuck them to the bottom of our bathtub so she wouldn't ever slip and fall again. These strips are sticky on the side that faces down and scratchy like sandpaper on the side that faces up, and they come in white or black or pink, so I got the pink ones because she has pink foam curlers and a pink Elvis rug and I thought she'd like that color best.

Then I had lunch (leftover pizza) and I went next door to 8A to check on Angus's secret plants, and when I finished watering them, I sat in his La-Z-Boy chair and turned on his TV and did surfing with his remote control. I saw a show with people playing poker and a cooking show, then I stopped on a channel with these words at the bottom, which Angus told me is called a logo: *National Organization for Unwanted Firearms.*

A man was doing talking about gun violence and he was wearing a brown vest, and behind him was a map of the country with red dots on it, and next to each dot were words like, "School shooting, nine dead," and "Ten people killed at a concert," and "Seven shot and killed in a grocery store" and I started to feel sick inside. The man in the vest kept talking and he said there were 14,400 gun-related homicides in 2019 and that killings involving a gun accounted for nearly three-quarters of all homicides in our country annually.

He said it was "time for change" and that people needed to "do the right thing" and that "every little bit helps," then he showed two videos: one of a man in Kentucky who sawed his AR-15 gun in half to show that *one less gun in our country will hopefully result in fewer shooting deaths*, and a second one that showed a town in Washington where they dug a hole in a field and people came and threw their guns in that hole, then a cement truck filled it with cement and they had a party after to celebrate.

That's when the man in the vest looked into the camera and said, "Do you have guns in your home that haven't been used in years?"

I nodded. "Yes."

And he said, "Do you want to get rid of them?"

And I said, "Yes!"

The camera zoomed in closer to the man's face and he pointed at me. "Let me ask you an important question. Do you want to be part of the problem or part of the solution when it comes to gun control?"

I got out of Angus's La-Z-Boy chair, and I said, "I want to be part of the solution."

The man pointed at me again. "Do you want to help end gun violence?"

And I said, "I do!"

"How many of you have inherited guns you want to get rid of?" he asked.

I paused the TV and used my phone to ask Google what *inherited* means and Google said that's when *the previous owner of something leaves it behind for you after he/she dies*, which was exactly what happened to me and Nana-Jo with Papa-Jo's guns. Then I pressed play and the man kept talking and some of what he said was confusing, but some of it I understood, like when he said, "There are more law enforcement departments accepting firearms for destruction all the time," and, "More than two hundred unwanted civilian-owned guns were destroyed in Flandell County alone last year."

I thought, *Wow, that's a lot of guns!*

I listened to him for a while and I found out that his organization would send you an empty box if you were donating unwanted firearms and they'd include a shipping label for you and instructions about how to ship your firearms, but there were a lot of steps and it sounded confusing, and I wanted to *do the right thing* without asking anyone for help. That's when the man in the vest said there were, of course, other options and they were also good options, and he held up one finger for each option. He said:

1. "You can donate your guns to a museum."

And I thought, *Woodmont doesn't have a museum.*

2. "You can sell your guns to a licensed dealer."

And I thought, *Nope, because Bob's Gun Emporium would just sell them to other people and those people could use them and someone could get hurt, and I think the world needs LESS guns, not MORE guns.*

3. "You can also take your guns to your local police station."

And I thought, *That's a great idea!*

I wasn't really listening after that. Instead, I rocked back and forth and did thinking while the man talked about "responsibly disposing of or repurposing unwanted firearms" and my heart was going **BOOM-BOOM-BOOM** and my mind started jumping all over the place. Then he talked about the proper way to take guns to your local police station and the steps involved, but I knew I could figure that part out by myself.

That's when I decided to *make a plan* and *be a good guy* and *do the right thing*, because if Papa-Jo's guns and bullets were gone from 8B, I'd feel much better and I could show Nana-Jo and Lydia and Angus that I could solve important problems by myself so they wouldn't have to worry about me anymore.

I looked at my watch and it was 1:38 p.m. If I hurried I could probably take Papa-Jo's guns and bullets to the police station and be home by 4:00 p.m. to watch *The Price Is Right* with Nana-Jo when she got home. Then I locked up 8A and I hurried over to 8B, doing thinking to make a plan. I wondered how heavy the guns would be and if I should maybe use my e-bike to take them to the police station, but I decided the basket on the back wasn't big enough and they'd probably fall out, so my e-bike wouldn't work.

That's when I saw my sled called White Lightning leaning against 8B outside and I made a better plan. Instead of using my e-bike, I would put all Papa-Jo's guns and bullets in my sled and I'd pull it to the police station. But then I did a frown because Woodmont's police station was far away on the other side of Penguin Hill. So I closed my eyes and I went inside my brain and did a pretend walk from 8B all the way down Deyton Avenue, then up Bendmore Road and down the other side to Wheeler Drive, and then all the way to the end of Wheeler Drive to the police station. And I thought, *Too much walking!*

Then a brand-new idea jumped into my brain and I thought, *It'd be MUCH faster if I put the guns and bullets in my sled, pulled it to the top of Penguin Hill, and then rode it down the other side to the police station.*

And I did a smile for myself.

Because that sounded like an excellent plan.

Getting Arrested at Penguin Hill

The kitchen clock said it was 1:54 p.m. when I went downstairs to the root cellar.

I opened Papa-Jo's metal gun box and carried all his rifles and bullets upstairs and I had to make three trips because there was lots to carry. I also found a gun that was not a rifle—it was a handgun—and I took it too, then I went outside and piled everything up in my sled. I was excited about doing this without anyone's help because I was *being a good guy* and *doing the right thing*, but pulling a sled full of guns and bullets wasn't easy because the sled was hard plastic and the guns were metal, and they kept slip-sliding around the bottom of my sled and two of them fell out when I stepped off the sidewalk onto the road.

And I thought, *This won't work!*

Then another idea jumped into my brain and I turned around and went back to 8A, and I used my key to get inside and I grabbed the big roll of clingy plastic wrap Angus had used to wrap his suitcase before he left for Mexico. I hurried outside and knelt down next to my sled and stood all the guns up so they were leaning against each other, then I went round and round and round them with that clingy plastic wrap until they were stuck together in a shiny bundle. After that, I laid the bundle down and took the bullets and the handgun and set them on top in a neat row, then I went round and round the whole thing again with Angus's clingy plastic wrap until they were part of the bundle too. After that, I found a bungee cord in the back of Angus's truck and I clipped it to one side of my sled, stretched it up over the bundle, then clipped it to the other side to hold it all in place.

And I thought about leaving a note on the kitchen table for Nana-Jo that said, *I took Papa-Jo's guns and bullets to the police station*, but it was getting late, so I decided to just tell her about it later when I got home.

Then off I went.

I pulled my sled up the walking path to the top of Penguin Hill and when I finally got there, I had to pee real bad, but there aren't any bathrooms on Penguin Hill, so I looked to the left and then I looked to the right, and I saw Mrs. Trout's garage, which backed up onto the park, and there were a bunch of spruce trees over there, and I thought I could probably pee there without anyone seeing me.

So that's where I went.

I kind of walked and kind of ran while I pulled my sled to the back of Mrs. Trout's garage and when I got there, I snuck around the side to make sure nobody could see me, and I went pee. I was almost finished when I heard someone shout, "What are you *doing* in my yard?! And what have you got in that sled, Denny Voss?" And I zipped up my pants extra fast, looked up, and there was Mrs. Trout at her kitchen window, doing glaring at me, and my heart started to go **BOOM-BOOM-BOOM**, and I thought, *Uh-oh!*

Mrs. Trout looked very upset. "I'm not asking you again, Denny. What have you got in that sled? Is that a dead body?!"

—BOOM-BOOM-BOOM.

"No, it's a bunch of guns and bullets wrapped in plastic."

Her eyes got very big. She had a fork in her hand and she pointed it at me. "Stay right there. I'm calling the police!"

Mrs. Trout held up her phone, punched in some numbers, and did talking. She walked to the right a bit, then to the left, and she looked out the window again to make sure I was still there. Then she hung up and shouted, "They're on their way! Don't you move an inch. Not one inch, Denny Voss!"

So, I looked down at my feet to make sure they weren't moving an inch, and my heart was still going **BOOM-BOOM-BOOM**, then Mrs. Trout shouted, "By the way, why were your pants unzipped? Are you a pervert? Were you trying to flash me?!"

I felt sick inside, and dizzy, because I knew a pervert was a *sicko with a dirty mind* and I was NOT a pervert, and when Mrs. Trout asked if I was trying to *flash her*, I knew what that meant too, and I was NOT trying to show her my genitals. I just had to pee real bad and it was an emergency and the side of her garage seemed like a private spot to do it without anyone seeing me. But yeah, I guess not.

That's when I heard police sirens—they use them in Woodmont for everything—and my heart went from **BOOM-BOOM-BOOM** to **WHAM-WHAM-WHAM!** and I got even more scared. I looked down at my feet (still not moving an inch) and then I looked at my sled with my plastic wrapped bundle of guns and bullets and . . .

. . . I put my gloves back on and I grabbed my sled's pull cord and I ran away from Mrs. Trout's garage as fast as I could run. And while I was running, I zigged and zagged (ran to the left, then to the right) to make myself harder to hit in case Mrs. Trout decided to shoot at me because I'd moved more than an inch.

She didn't shoot at me, but I could hear her shouting, "I told you not to move!" and "Come back here, Denny Voss!" but I was running VERY FAST and pretty soon I couldn't hear her anymore. I tripped and fell twice but both times I got up again and I kept running toward the sledding hill, and it was a school day but school wasn't out yet so nobody was there, which was good. I could hear police sirens somewhere behind me and they were getting louder—**WHOOP! WHOOP!**—so I pulled my sled to the edge of the hill at the top, then I pushed the bundle of guns forward as far as it would go so I could fit my bum in behind it. Then I got in the sled with one leg on the right side of the bundle and one leg on the left side, and I held on to the sled's pull cord with one hand while I used the other one to push the sled forward on the packed snow, and it moved a little bit.

Then it moved a bit more.

And then . . .

P-U-S-H

. . . it tipped over the edge and slid down the hill very fast.

It had snowed last week, then it warmed up and the snow melted, and then it got cold again and everything froze, and now the hill had lots of icy spots and my sled called White Lightning hit them and it went faster and faster. And me and all those guns and bullets and my sled went sailing up into the air and landed back on the snow, then we went up again and we landed again, and we were going *crazy fast.*

I couldn't keep the sled straight.

And there were a bunch of oak trees at the bottom of the hill to the right and my sled was heading straight for them, so I put my hand on the ground to try to slow myself down, but that didn't work, then I yanked on the pull cord to steer away from them but that didn't work either. I wasn't far from those trees when I leaned to the left and the sled flipped over and—**SNAP!**—the bungee cord broke and my shiny bundle of guns and bullets went flying through the air and when it finally hit the ground, the clingy plastic wrap ripped open and . . . suddenly there were guns and bullets everywhere.

I skidded past them and crashed into an oak tree.

T-H-U-M-P!

And that was it. There I was, staring up at the sky with my ears ringing, and for a few seconds that's all I could hear. Nothing else. When I rolled over, I saw all the guns and bullets spread out on the snow and ice, and I heard a police siren getting closer—**WHOOP! WHOOP!**—so I crawled over to a tree and used it to pull myself up.

Then my face suddenly felt warm and wet, and I reached up and touched my forehead and thought, *Uh-oh, blood.*

And I felt dizzy and sick inside, and I wanted to run away.

But my legs were too wobbly to run.

Going to Trial

Just so you know, it's Monday and if you're incarcerated at Woodmont County Jail on a Monday you get beef stew for dinner and JELL-O for dessert. Also, I've been incarcerated for two months and twenty-eight days now and I had my last meeting with Dr. Harland today. He brought me a vanilla sprinkle doughnut and we did chatting, then he said, "I'm confident everything will get sorted out at the trial, Denny," and I said, "How?" and he said, "Just tell the truth. Tell the truth and there should be enough reasonable doubt for jurors to believe you didn't do this."

"So, no lying?"

Dr. Harland did a sigh. "No lying, Denny. Stick to the truth."

And I said, "What about the parts I can't remember?"

"Tell them you can't remember."

He closed his notebook and rubbed his face with his hands (up/down, up/down), then he said, "You won't see me again until I'm called to the stand to give my professional assessment," which is when he said he'd tell Bridget and everyone else what he thought about me and my brain. And I looked out the window and it was raining, then Dr. Harland put his jacket on and he held his hand up and we did a high five even though I didn't feel like doing a high five.

And that was it.

No more meetings with Dr. Harland.

From now on, it would be just me and Bridget.

Bridget vs. Mr. Easterville

This morning, Bridget sent a girl named Michaela to the jail and she had a purple streak in her hair and she was very pretty and I asked her not to cut my hair too short, so she didn't, then she shaved the back of my neck and I told her I didn't have any money to pay her, and she laughed and said, "Bridget already took care of it."

Then Bridget came by the jail and she brought me dress pants and a button-up shirt, and now we're sitting at our table in the courtroom and Bridget has asked me (three times) to stop staring at Mr. Easterville, who is the prosecutor (a man who thinks I killed Mr. Tesky), but Mr. Easterville only has one good eye and the other one is a glass eyeball, and it never moves, and Bridget said he's had it for years and, no, she doesn't know if it gets itchy, or if he takes it out when he goes to bed at night, or if he has another one for backup in case this one falls down a sewer drain, then she said none of that matters anyhow because he's the best prosecutor in Woodmont County and he hasn't lost a case in years.

Bridget tugged on my arm. "Denny?"

"Yeah?"

"Stop it."

"Stop what?"

She closed her eyes. "Fidgeting. And stop staring at Mr. Easterville and stop asking questions about his glass eyeball. Pay attention to what's happening in the courtroom, please." And I like Bridget a lot and she works hard for me, and I want her to win her first real case, so I sat up straight and I stopped staring at Mr. Easterville.

Bridget was wearing a navy jacket and a navy skirt, and a white blouse and hoopy silver earrings, and, like always, she smelled like lemons. The courtroom was full of spectators (people who like to watch court cases) and journalists (people who write stories for newspapers and magazines and websites) and they were staring at me and doing whispering, but Angus had already warned me weeks ago that the trial would be like this because unfortunately "it doesn't get any better than having someone with a low IQ on trial for murder."

And I said, "I'm not disabled, Angus."

He was playing with his goatee and he turned and pointed at me, and said, "I know that, buddy, and you know that, but now you're going to have to show everyone else in Woodmont that you're not."

And I said, "How do I do that?"

"Listen to Bridget. She's your lawyer and she knows best. And no matter what anyone says in the courtroom, don't rock back and forth, or moan, or sing to yourself. Just sit up straight and stay focused."

"No singing?"

"Ab-so-fucking-lutely not!"

And that was the last time I talked to Angus because the next day Mr. Easterville gave him that subpoena (official piece of paper) telling him he had to testify in court as a witness for the prosecution and he wasn't allowed to talk to me anymore. Bridget also told me that Lydia got a subpoena to testify in court too and so did Mrs. Timko and Mrs. Trout and Lonny at DOT, but not Elaine, and not Nana-Jo, because she's still in the hospital recuperating (getting better from her stroke).

Yesterday, Bridget showed me pictures of the courtroom we'd be in, which is much bigger than the one I got myself arraigned in, and she explained what a bailiff does and what the court reporter does and what the judge does, then she showed me where we'd be sitting, and where the jury box was, and she explained how the jury would be picked by the defense (our side) and the prosecution (their side), and I gave her a thumbs-up and I told her again how I'd seen *Judge Judy* on TV so I knew all about courtrooms, then Bridget kissed her cross necklace and I said, "Hallelujah," because like Nana-Jo always says, it's important to end every conversation on a positive note.

Bridget told me that Mr. Easterville got to go first, which didn't seem fair to me so I asked if we could do a coin toss to make it more fair, and she told me it doesn't work like that in a court of law. Woodmont's courthouse is two blocks from the jail and the judge's bench sits up high and it's made of dark wood. His bench looks down on the courtroom and there was a swirly smudge on the front where maybe someone had cleaned it with a rag but didn't dry it properly? And that smudge looked like an angry tornado and I hoped it wasn't bad luck because me and Bridget needed all the good luck we could get.

The bailiff walked to the front of the courtroom and said, "All rise. This court is now in session. Honorable Judge Milton Saginaw presiding." And it got very quiet and a door at the back of the courtroom opened and Judge Saginaw came in and he sat down at the bench and he didn't smile, even when I waved at him.

Bridget grabbed my arm. "Denny, please."

Judge Saginaw looked at Bridget and nodded, then he looked at me and he said pretty much the same thing he'd said when I got myself arraigned two months and a bunch of days ago. "Dennis Joseph Voss of Woodmont, Minnesota, you've been charged with murder in the second degree of one Henry David Tesky, formerly of Woodmont, Minnesota, which carries a maximum penalty of forty years in prison. If found guilty of this crime, the prosecution will be seeking the maximum penalty without parole."

Then he said, "Ms. Klein, how does your client plead?"

Bridget said, "Not guilty, Your Honor."

And everyone behind us started doing whispering and chatting, same as last time, and Judge Saginaw banged his gavel and he said, "Order in the court," and then they stopped doing whispering and chatting.

Judge Saginaw nodded. "We will now begin jury selection," and Bridget had already told me about this part, so I knew what was happening when Judge Saginaw turned to two rows of people sitting on the right called *potential jurors* (jurors are picked to be part of the jury and a jury is a group of people who will decide if I'm innocent or guilty of killing Mr. Tesky). He read out a bunch of rules the jurors would have to follow and one was that they couldn't discuss the trial with anyone, including other jurors, until they were *seated on the jury*, and they wouldn't be *allowed access to any media or social media* about the case, and they weren't allowed to *investigate details of the case online*.

So yeah, no talking to anybody, or reading anything, or sneaking onto the internet (World Wide Web) to ask Google questions.

Just sit still and listen.

Judge Saginaw said, "Please raise your hand if you feel you have a legitimate reason to be excused from this jury," and one woman raised her hand and said she'd worked for Papa-Jo years ago as a receptionist and that she'd met me many times and she didn't believe I could kill anyone, so Judge Saginaw excused her from the jury. Then he looked at the rest of the group, and he said, "Please raise your hand if you feel you cannot listen to the testimony and decide whether Mr. Voss is guilty or innocent based solely on the evidence presented in this courtroom."

Nobody else raised their hand.

Then Bridget and Mr. Easterville each did talking with *potential jurors* one by one and they asked them questions like, "State your name for the record," and "How are you employed?" and, "How much schooling have you had?" and, "Have you formed an opinion as to Mr. Voss's guilt or innocence in this case?" and Bridget decided she didn't want two of them on the jury (one man, one woman) and she talked to Judge Saginaw, and he said, "The following prospective jurors are excused," and then there were also three people Mr. Easterville didn't want on the jury (all women) so he talked to Judge Saginaw and they were asked to leave too, then a bunch of new people were brought into the courtroom as *potential jurors*, and the whole thing started all over again. And that went on and on and on until four o'clock, when Judge Saginaw closed things down for the day.

And the second day was filled with lots of the same boring stuff over and over again and the third day was the same until 1:02 p.m., when there were finally eight women and four men sitting in the jury box, and Bridget leaned over and told me they were our official jury, and to me they looked like nice people other than one man with a handlebar mustache who kept staring at me. And I told Bridget he was "freaking me out" but she said there was nothing she could do about it, that I needed to "grow thicker skin," and I told her I didn't know how to do that.

After that, Judge Saginaw did something called *swearing the jury in*, and he said, "Please raise your right hand," and they did, then he said, "Do each of you solemnly swear that you will try this case before you and render a true verdict according to the evidence and the law, so help you God?" All those people agreed to do that, then Judge Saginaw banged his gavel and he called for a lunch recess until 2:00 p.m., and Bridget explained to me that that meant he was giving everyone a break to eat lunch.

While me and Bridget ate our lunch (BLT sandwiches, orange juice) in our meeting room, she said that Mr. Easterville would begin calling witnesses after lunch and then she'd do talking with them when he was done to try to show the jury a different side of each witness than what Mr. Easterville had shown them.

And I said, "What do you mean?"

"Well . . . for example," Bridget said, "let's say that Easterville calls a witness and that witness testifies that he saw you knocking on Mr. Tesky's door the night of the murder, then I'd get up and try to *discredit* that witness, which means I'd try to get him to admit that he has bad eyesight and he didn't have his glasses on, and because of that how could he possibly recognize you in the dark, from so far away?"

And I said, "Did he forget his glasses at home?"

Bridget blinked at me. "I'm just giving you an example, Denny. There is no man with bad eyesight who said he saw you knocking on Mr. Tesky's door."

And I said, "Oh, that's good."

Bridget tilted her head. "Denny, that's just an example of how cross-examination works and how I'll try to minimize the damage any of Easterville's witnesses have on the stand in relation to what the jury hears. Do you understand?" and I said, "Yes," even though I only half-way understood.

So yeah, it seems like Bridget knows what she's doing.

At 2:00 p.m. we walked back into the courtroom and the trial was about to start and now there were more people sitting on the benches behind me and Bridget, and I knew some of them. Nori was there and so was Irene Tesky's sister, Toni Hale (she looked worried), and so was my new homeless friend, Howard-the-army-guy, and my library friend, Regan, who I shelved books for when I did my consequences, and Mason, the Uber guy me and Angus always call when we need a ride, and our neighbors, Sharon and Bill, and Jean and Ted, and some people from DOT but I couldn't remember their names.

There were also lots of people I didn't know.

Judge Saginaw asked Mr. Easterville if he was ready to call his first witness.

"I am, Your Honor."

Mr. Easterville called the coroner, Eden White (a lady who investigates violent or suspicious deaths), and he asked her some questions and she said Mr. Tesky's time of death was between 12:15 and 12:45 a.m. on the date in question and that the murder weapon was a Smith & Wesson .38 Special snub nose.

And Mr. Easterville had a laptop computer on the table next to him and he pressed a key and a photograph of the Teskys' foyer came up on a big screen in the courtroom and in the photo Mr. Tesky was lying on the floor and a pool of blood was coming out from underneath him, and a large plant was tipped over on its side next to a bag of golf clubs, and a bunch of dirt from the plant was on the floor next to Mr. Tesky.

"Ms. White, how many times was the victim shot?" asked Mr. Easterville.

She talked into the microphone. "Once, in the neck."

"And how long did it take for him to die?"

And she said, "The bullet penetrated the ICA, or the internal carotid artery. The victim would've bled out and died within fifteen to twenty seconds."

Mr. Easterville nodded. "No further questions. Your witness."

Judge Saginaw looked at Bridget. "You may cross-examine, Counsel."

Bridget stood. "Ms. White, were there any bruises on Mr. Tesky's chest or arms that would indicate he'd been pushed or shoved?"

"No, the only bruising found was on his back, which coincides with the victim falling backward onto the stone floor after getting shot."

"I see," said Bridget, frowning. "And was there any alcohol or other substances found in the victim's blood?"

"Objection," said Mr. Easterville. "Irrelevant."

Bridget said, "Your Honor, I'm laying a foundation."

Judge Saginaw said, "I'll allow it. Overruled," then he looked at Ms. White and he said, "You may answer the question."

Ms. White leaned toward the microphone. "The victim had a blood alcohol concentration of point one eight percent at the time of his death."

Bridget nodded, then she wrote something down on her notepad. "For the record, Ms. White, under state law, motorists can be charged with driving under the influence with a blood alcohol concentration of point oh eight, isn't that correct?"

And she said, "Yes, that's correct."

"So Mr. Tesky's blood alcohol concentration was twice the legal limit?" Bridget asked.

"Yes, it was."

"Thank you. I have no further questions."

"You may step down," Judge Saginaw said to the lady witness, and she did.

The next witness Mr. Easterville called to the stand was a man named Jason Leon, who was a *ballistics expert* (which is someone who is an expert on guns and someone who is trained to catch people who've used guns in a crime) and Mr. Easterville asked Mr. Leon lots of boring questions about his schooling, and how long he'd worked here, and I didn't understand all of it, but I did understand the part where Mr. Easterville walked over to the witness box and held up a handgun in a plastic bag marked **People's Exhibit One**.

"Mr. Leon, can you confirm that this was the murder weapon used to kill Mr. Tesky?" and Mr. Leon said yes, the bullet that killed Mr. Tesky was fired from that gun, which is a Smith & Wesson .38 Special snub-nose gun. Then Mr. Easterville asked Mr. Leon if the gun had been tested for fingerprints or for DNA and Mr. Leon said yes, one fingerprint was found on the gun and it matched the defendant, Denny Voss, and when the gun was swabbed, Denny Voss's DNA was also found on the gun.

"Thank you. I have no further questions," said Mr. Easterville, then he turned to look at the jury and I could see that his good eye was looking straight ahead but his glass eyeball was looking a bit to the left.

Judge Saginaw turned to Bridget. "You may cross-examine, Counsel," and Bridget stood up and walked to the witness box, and she pointed to the gun in the plastic bag marked **People's Exhibit One**. "Mr. Leon, can you tell me who owns this gun?"

"Irene Tesky owned it."

Bridget nodded. "So, to clarify, this gun, the murder weapon, belonged to Irene Tesky, the victim's first wife, not his second wife, Malinda, whom he married a month after Irene Tesky died?" and Mr. Easterville said, "Objection! Relevance," and Bridget folded her hands together and she said, "Your Honor, I'm simply clarifying that the gun belongs to Mr. Tesky's first wife, not his second wife."

Judge Saginaw said, "Sustained. Rephrase the question."

Then Bridget said, "Mr. Leon, you said Irene Tesky owned the gun, so does that mean it was legally registered to her?"

Mr. Leon frowned. "Um . . . yes. Irene Tesky filled out a permit and bought this gun from a licensed dealer in Minneapolis eighteen years ago." Then Bridget turned to the jury the same way Mr. Easterville did, and she gave them a lawyerly look, but both of her eyes were looking straight ahead instead of in different directions.

"Thank you," she said. "I have no further questions."

And when Bridget sat down at our table, I told her she was doing an excellent job, just like a lawyer in one of those fast-moving TV shows, because Nana-Jo always says it's important to encourage people we care about, and I care about Bridget and I think she needs someone to encourage her because this is her first case and her hands keep shaking, and her blouse has sweat stains under her armpits and that's not a good sign, no matter how you look at it.

Witnesses for the Prosecution

Before the trial, Bridget gave me a list of witnesses for the prosecution (people Mr. Easterville wants to call up to the witness box so he can ask them questions) and she talked to me about the people I knew so she'd be ready for *anything that might get said on the stand*, and these were some of the names on that list:

Etta Trout (Mrs. Trout)
Londell Williams (Lonny from DOT)
Tom Feller (gray-haired cop)
Louella Johnson (Louella-the-lady-cop)
Olga Timko (Mrs. Timko)
Angus Voss
Lydia Voss

And after I read the list, I rocked back and forth and I told Bridget that Mrs. Timko doesn't like me because I kidnapped Tom Hanks and didn't bring him back, and I know Mrs. Trout doesn't like me either, because last fall, months before she caught me peeing against the side of her garage, I had Papa-Jo's old kneepads on and I was throwing mothballs under our front porch to keep skunks from moving in (same as I do every fall) and Mrs. Trout was out for a walk and she stopped to do visiting with Elaine, and she kept looking over at me and I heard her say I was *an odd duck*.

Bridget patted me on the arm. "Relax, Denny. Even if someone doesn't like you, they still have to tell the truth when they're on the stand," and I said, "Whew, that's good, because not everyone likes me."

The next five days were kind of boring while Bridget and Mr. Easterville did talking with a bunch of witnesses, including Mrs. Trout (who said I *scared the bejesus* out of her when she saw me peeing against the side of her garage with all those guns and bullets in my sled) and Mrs. Timko (who said I kidnapped her pet goose, Tom Hanks, and now she isn't sure if he's dead or alive). One good thing, though, was that Mrs. Timko got herself dressed up for the witness stand and I could tell she was wearing a bra, which was good, because she usually doesn't and when she doesn't her boobs look like sock puppets, which isn't good.

After that, Mr. Easterville called the gray-haired cop named Tom Feller to the witness stand and he said that I had shown "a burst of *verbal aggression*" toward Mr. Tesky the day Mr. Tesky hit me with his Tesla.

"Can you tell me what Mr. Voss said?" asked Mr. Easterville.

And Tom Feller leaned in close to the microphone, and he said, "'In your face, motherfucker.'"

After that, Mr. Easterville called Lonny to the witness box and his Fu Manchu mustache was trimmed all neat and tidy, and he was wearing a shiny green button-up shirt and the same fedora hat he wore to his bachelor party, and I wanted to give him a wave or a thumbs-up, but Bridget had already warned me (three times) that I'm not allowed to do stuff like that in the courtroom, so I didn't.

Mr. Easterville did talking with Lonny first, and after a few minutes of doing talking Lonny said that, yes, there was a rifle in the DOT truck that was to be used, if required, to *shoot and kill critically wounded animals found on our roadways*.

Then Bridget got up and she asked Lonny if he knew if the defendant—she turned and pointed to me—had ever shot and killed a critically wounded animal or if, in fact, my work partner, Angus

Voss, typically did that for me? And Lonny said he didn't know for sure, but he suspected that was probably the case.

"Hearsay!" said Mr. Easterville.

"Sustained," said Judge Saginaw. "I direct the jury to disregard that statement."

"No further questions, Your Honor," said Bridget.

Judge Saginaw looked at Lonny. "You may step down."

So yeah, that was it for Lonny. He got up and he straightened his fedora hat, and then he slow-walked himself out of the courtroom.

It was a long week and sometimes I got sleepy because there were lots of things that got said over and over again, like, "Please raise your right hand," and "Do you swear to tell the truth, the whole truth, and nothing but the truth, so help you God?" and "Let the record reflect that the witness has identified the defendant."

And Judge Saginaw gave us recess breaks each day, just like they do when you're a little kid in school, only we didn't go outside and run around. Instead, me and Bridget were escorted to a special room where we ate our lunch (club sandwiches) or a snack (tea for her, mixed nuts for me), then we'd go back to the courtroom. One day, though, I got the hiccups after lunch and they wouldn't go away, so Bridget asked if we could take another five-minute recess break and Judge Saginaw let us.

He's a good guy like that.

But yeah, nothing exciting happened that first week.

On another day in court, while everyone else was doing talking, I did some staring at an empty chair at Mr. Easterville's table and I saw that one of the legs was cracked, and it looked like someone had broken it and glued it back together. I wondered if somebody in another trial got upset and threw it across the room, and if they did I wondered if Judge Saginaw gave that person a fine because chairs are expensive. And if someone did glue that chair back together, I hoped they used wood glue, because that's the only kind of glue that'll hold properly (Papa-Jo taught me that years ago).

Bridget nudged me. "Denny, pay attention."

So I did.

There were also lots of witnesses I didn't know and they were kind of boring too. Mr. Easterville would ask them questions like, "What is your profession?" and "How much schooling have you had?" and "What was the trajectory of the bullet?" and Judge Saginaw kept saying things like, "Counsel, please lay a foundation," or "Please rephrase the question," or "You've exhausted that subject, move on," and then he'd look at Bridget and say, "You may cross-examine, Counsel."

So yeah, lots of stuff to make you sleepy.

Here's some more.

One of the people Mr. Easterville did talking with was an accountant lady who worked for the Tesky family and she said yes, Nana-Jo had worked for the Teskys for twenty-four years (which I already knew—yawn) and yes, she had seen me at their house now and then when she stopped by with paperwork. Then Mr. Easterville called a man to the witness stand who was the neighbor who'd heard a gunshot the night Mr. Tesky was killed (which was already in the newspaper story—yawn). And when Mr. Easterville was done asking that man questions, Bridget got up and pointed to me, and she asked that man if he'd seen me, the defendant, going into the Teskys' home that night, or if he'd seen me leaving the Teskys' home that night after he heard the gunshot.

And the man said, "No, ma'am, I did not."

The next person Mr. Easterville called to the witness stand was Louella-the-lady-cop and her hair was in a ponytail, and she didn't smile or even try to be friendly. She told Mr. Easterville that when I was arrested at the bottom of Penguin Hill, she *felt threatened* and, in her opinion, I came off *aggressive and unpredictable* and she felt that it was necessary *to take defensive measures*.

Bridget got up from our table and smoothed down her blouse. "Is it not true, Ms. Johnson, that on the day you arrested Denny Voss, after he sang the theme song for the movie *Toy Story*, you kicked him in the genitals and used excessive force to manage a situation that was unusual but in no way threatening?"

"Objection!" said Mr. Easterville.

"Sustained," said the judge.

Bridget did a smile. "I'll rephrase the question. Ms. Johnson, how long have you been a police officer?"

"Seven years," said Louella-the-lady-cop.

"Have you been employed in Woodmont for all of that time?"

"No," said Louella-the-lady-cop. "I spent three years in Chicago and three in Detroit. After that I moved to Woodmont."

Bridget raised her eyebrows. "I see. And in the history of your employment as a police officer, have you ever arrested anyone who rocked back and forth while singing the theme song for the movie *Toy Story*?"

Louella-the-lady-cop frowned. "No, that's never happened to me before."

"That must have been terrifying for you," said Bridget.

"Objection!" said Mr. Easterville.

"Sustained," said the judge.

"I have nothing further for this witness, Your Honor," said Bridget.

And when Judge Saginaw decided he'd had enough each day, he would bang his gavel on a coaster on his high-up desk and say, "Court is adjourned [which means *done for the day*] and we will reconvene [*hang out again*] tomorrow." Bridget explained that part to me.

Angus in the Witness Box

Mr. Easterville called a few other witnesses up to the witness box to ask them questions too, but they were all boring, and then it was Angus's turn and here is the *trial transcript* (printout of the words the court reporter lady typed into her machine that day) from his time in the witness box. Bridget gave me a copy so I could put it in my notebook. Angus had a new haircut and he looked spiffy and I think Elaine must have told him what to wear because instead of his T-shirt that says **Sarcasm Is Just One of the Services I Offer**, he was wearing a dress shirt, and I was proud of him and I think Nana-Jo would've been proud too, because Angus was honest and he answered every question, and he didn't lose his temper like I thought he would.

First Circuit Court of Woodmont County

State of Minnesota

v.

Dennis Joseph Voss

Indictment—Murder

Proceedings at Trial
in Woodmont, Minnesota
DIRECT EXAMINATION BY DISTRICT ATTORNEY EASTERVILLE:

Q: Will you please state your name to the jury?

A: Angus Voss.

Q: Mr. Voss, where do you live?

A: 8A Deyton Avenue, Woodmont, Minnesota.

Q: We don't need your full address. Town and state will do.

A: Whatever.

Q: Does the defendant live near you?

A: Yes, Denny lives next door in 8B. We share a duplex.

Q: And are you related to the defendant?

A: I'm his cousin.

Q: All right. For the sake of clarity then, and to ensure no confusion for the jurors, would you mind if I called you Angus for the balance of this direct examination, given that you and the defendant share the same last name?

A: Go for it.

Q: I'm sorry?

A: You can call me Angus.

Q: Angus, last year in November, did you and the defendant, Denny Voss, attend a party for Londell Williams at an establishment in Woodmont called the Cat House?

A: Yeah, we did. Lonny's our boss. It was his bachelor party.

Q: Did you and the defendant drive to the Cat House together?

A: We did. We took my truck.

Q: And how close is your home to the Cat House?

A: I'd say four or five miles.

Q: Angus, would it be correct to say that you and the defendant often attended events like that together?
A: What do you mean?
Q: For example, I'm referring to events like the DOT annual awards dinner, which was also held last year in November.
A: Yes, I went with Denny to the DOT awards dinner.
Q: And how did you get there?
A: I drove my truck.
Q: You also drove him to Londell Williams's bachelor party in November?
A: I did.
Q: Did you also drive the defendant home from both events?
A: Uh . . . well, we were going to take an Uber.
Q: Is that what happened?
A: No.
Q: Angus, did you drive the defendant home from those events?
A: No, I didn't.
Q: Did an Uber driver pick you up and drive you home from those events?
A: No, we tried to arrange one but both Uber drivers in Woodmont were booked solid those nights and couldn't take us home.
Q: All right. So how did you and the defendant get home?
A: We figured it out.
Q: How did you figure it out?
A: (Inaudible . . . 00:03) Denny drove my truck.
Q: You mean the defendant, Denny Voss?
A: Yes.

Q: Angus, do you know if the defendant has a driver's license?

A: No, he doesn't.

Q: Have you ever let him drive you home on any other occasion?

A: (Inaudible)

Q: Can you please answer the question?

A: Uh . . . yeah, I have.

Q: And why would you do that?

A: Because now and then when I've had too much to drink, I figure it's safer to let Denny drive than for me to drive drunk.

Q: I see. And in your opinion, is Denny Voss a good driver?

A: Yes.

Q: Is he as good as you are? When you aren't drunk, that is?

A: Pretty damned close.

Q: A yes or no will suffice.

A: Okay, then. Yes.

Q: Did you teach Denny how to drive?

A: No.

Q: Who did?

A: Papa-Jo taught him how to drive when he was a kid. They had 360 acres. They called it a farm, but Papa-Jo had his own welding business, so mostly he just grew hay to sell to local farmers. I remember Denny driving the hay truck when he was twelve or thirteen.

Q: And who is Papa-Jo?

A: Denny's grandpa. He died when Denny was fourteen.

Q: I see. To the best of your knowledge, Angus, do you know if Denny has ever driven Joanne Voss's car?

A: (The witness nodded)

Q: Can you please respond to the question?
A: Yes, he's driven Nana-Jo's car a few times that I know of, usually when she gets it stuck in the snow or mud and she can't get it out.
Q: So, in your opinion, on the night Henry Tesky was murdered, which was too cold to logically use a bicycle—for the court record, it was twenty-eight below—would it have been possible for the defendant—who doesn't have a driver's license, but who knows how to drive, and whom you yourself have said is a good driver—to have driven your truck or Joanne Voss's car to Henry Tesky's home on Penguin Hill?
A: No, I don't think that's something Denny would do. I mean, he's driven my truck when I'm in it, and he drove Nana-Jo's Subaru a few times when she got it stuck, but I don't think he'd drive a vehicle by himself.
Q: I didn't ask you if he did, Angus. I asked, in your opinion, if it would've been *possible* for Denny Voss to have driven your truck or Joanne Voss's car to Henry Tesky's home on Penguin Hill on that cold winter night?
A: (The witness asked for a glass of water, took a drink)
Q: Can you please respond to the question?
A: (Inaudible . . . 00:04) Yeah, I guess he could have.

The Scarf Expert

Mr. Easterville called a woman up to the witness box and her dark hair was in a braid that hung down her back, and she was pretty, and she had very white teeth. Mr. Easterville nodded at her and said, "Please state your name and occupation."

"My name is Charlene McNeil. I'm a fiber analysis expert."

"Thank you, Ms. McNeil. According to your official report, you found blue wool fibers in the Teskys' foyer, is that true?"

"That's correct."

"Can you tell me where they were found?"

Ms. McNeil talked into the microphone. "They were found inside the stowaway bench as well as on the stone tile in the foyer."

Mr. Easterville picked up a piece of paper from his desk. "Your report also states that those fibers were tested and it was found that they didn't come from any of the clothing Mr. Tesky was wearing, correct?"

"That's correct."

Mr. Easterville lifted a clear plastic bag from his desk with a blue wool scarf inside and he handed it to Ms. McNeil. "Is it true that the wool fibers found in the Teskys' foyer match the fibers from this scarf?"

Ms. McNeil nodded. "Yes. The fibers found at the crime scene match exactly with the fibers taken from this scarf."

"And where was the scarf found?"

Ms. McNeil handed the bag back to Mr. Easterville. "It was found in the defendant's home, hanging on a hook behind the front door."

Then the spectators in the courtroom started doing whispering and chatting, and Judge Saginaw had to bang his gavel on his desk and say "Order in the court!" to make them stop.

Mr. Easterville turned back to his witness. "Ms. McNeil, was there any evidence found that would prove the defendant has ever worn this scarf?" and Ms. McNeil said, "Yes, four strands of the defendant's hair were found on the scarf." And I was upset that Mr. Easterville had my scarf and I wanted Bridget to get it back for me when the trial was over, but when I tugged on Bridget's arm to ask her to do that for me, she said, "Not now, Denny."

Mr. Easterville said, "Thank you, Ms. McNeil. I have no further questions."

Judge Saginaw said, "You may cross-examine, Counsel."

Bridget stood and walked toward the witness box. "Ms. McNeil, I'd like to talk about the blue fibers that were found in the victim's foyer. First, is there any way to scientifically determine how long they were in the Teskys' home?"

Ms. McNeil talked into the microphone. "No. I can tell you where they were found but not how long they've been there."

Bridget nodded. "So, in theory, those blue fibers, which you say definitively came from the scarf shown here today, could have been in the Teskys' home for years?"

Ms. McNeil frowned. "I suppose they could've."

"In addition," Bridget continued, "if someone—the killer or maybe even Mr. Tesky—reached inside the stowaway bench in the Teskys' foyer, where I understand scarves and gloves were typically kept, could he or she have transferred fibers that were *inside* the bench onto his or her own clothing, and then they fell onto the tiled floor in the foyer?"

Ms. McNeil thought about it. "I guess that could have happened."

Bridget nodded. "Ms. McNeil, in your opinion, does the presence of these fibers in any way prove that Denny Voss was in the Teskys' foyer when Mr. Tesky was killed?"

Ms. McNeil blinked. "No, they do not."

Bridget nodded. "Ms. McNeil, beyond the blue fibers in question from that specific scarf, was any other evidence found that would prove Denny Voss was in the Teskys' home that night? For example, were there any fingerprints or DNA evidence left on Mr. Tesky's body or on his clothing, including strands of hair?"

"No," Ms. McNeil said. "There was no additional evidence found that would indicate Mr. Voss had been in the foyer the night Mr. Tesky was killed."

Mr. Easterville scribbled something on his notepad.

Bridget straightened her blouse. "To recap, earlier testimony has confirmed that Joanne Voss worked as a house cleaner for the Tesky family for twenty-four years—part time for five, then full time for nineteen—until her employment was abruptly terminated without cause—"

"Objection!" Mr. Easterville said.

"Sustained," said the judge.

Bridget looked at some papers on our table. "Ms. McNeil, one of Mr. Tesky's neighbors confirmed in previous testimony that it wasn't uncommon to see Denny Voss biking to the Tesky home to deliver a bagged lunch to his Nana-Jo, especially during her final months on the job, and it also wasn't uncommon to see him wearing a blue scarf, even during summer months. Given this, and that Denny Voss had been in the Teskys' foyer on many occasions in the past, would it be fair to say that those blue fibers, which you say came from the scarf shown here today, could have been in the Teskys' stowaway bench for months, or possibly longer?"

Ms. McNeil thought about that. "Yes, they could have."

"I have one final question."

Bridget approached the bench, lifted the clear plastic bag with the blue scarf inside, flipped it over, and said, "When you examined this scarf in your lab, did you notice this label sewn onto one end of it?" Bridget pointed to a small white label on the scarf and Ms. McNeil frowned at it, and said, "Yes, but it didn't seem relevant because we were comparing the blue strands on the scarf to those found at the crime scene."

Bridget nodded, then she squinted at the label, and she asked Ms. McNeil if she could make out what was written on it.

"Objection!" Mr. Easterville said.

"Overruled," said the judge. "I'll allow it."

Ms. McNeil lifted the bag up to take a closer look. "It appears this label has four letters embroidered on it—MBIT."

Bridget smiled. "Thank you. Were you aware that MBIT stands for 'made by Irene Tesky' and that one of Irene's favorite pastimes was knitting? Apparently, she knitted four of these blue scarves—one for her neighbor, one for her sister, Toni Hale, one for Denny Voss, and one for her husband, Henry."

"Objection!" said Mr. Easterville.

"Sustained," said the judge, then he turned to Bridget. "Counselor, let me warn you, if you wish to explore this line of questioning any further in my courtroom, with any witness, you *must* provide evidence to confirm the validity of your claim." That's when Toni Hale stood up in the courtroom and said, "I can verify her statement," and she pulled a blue scarf out of her bag and waved it at the judge, saying she was Irene Tesky's sister, then she pointed to a white label on one end of her scarf with the same initials my scarf had: MBIT.

Mr. Easterville jumped to his feet. "Objection!"

"Sustained," said the judge.

And it got very loud in the courtroom then because the spectators were suddenly doing lots of loud whispering and chatting, so Judge Saginaw banged his gavel and said, "Order in the court!" to make them stop, but they wouldn't stop, so he banged it again and again, and he shouted, "Order. In. The. Court," and everyone got very quiet.

Mr. Easterville said, "Your Honor, I move to strike these comments."

Judge Saginaw said, "Granted," then he turned to the jury and said, "I direct you to disregard any statements made about scarf fibers or labels unless they came from Ms. McNeil." Then he turned to Bridget. "As for you, Counselor—"

Bridget lifted her hands. "I'm sorry, Your Honor. I have never met Mrs. Hale and in no way did I sanction that outburst."

Judge Saginaw shook his head, then he told Mrs. Hale that she was banned from any future proceedings during the trial and he asked the bailiff to remove her from the courtroom. Toni Hale stood and gathered her things, then she slow-slow-slowly looped her scarf around her neck before walking out with the bailiff.

Judge Saginaw cleared his throat, then he said to Bridget, "Counselor, are you finished with this witness?" and Bridget said, "Yes, Your Honor, I am. I have no further questions." And I guess that's when Judge Saginaw decided he'd had enough because he told Charlene McNeil that she could step down, then he banged his gavel and said, "Court is adjourned until nine a.m. tomorrow morning."

And that was that.

We were done for the day.

And I know Angus probably won't believe me, but after Judge Saginaw left the courtroom, Mr. Easterville got up and left too, then me and Bridget stood up and she put some papers in her leather bag, and she looked at me and winked, and I'm not stupid—I know what's what—I'm 99 percent sure she was doing flirting with me, but even if she wasn't, I still think that was a good sign, no matter how you look at it.

Lydia in the Witness Box

Mr. Easterville was almost finished doing talking with his witnesses when Bridget told me I wasn't getting a turn, and I kicked the table leg and she grabbed my arm and said, extra quiet-like, "We went over this, Denny. I'm not putting you on the stand because Easterville will cross-examine you and I'd like to win this case, not light a match to it." Then she opened my notebook to an empty page and she told me to do doodling to calm myself down, because I'm not allowed to sing, or rock back and forth, or do moaning.

Mr. Easterville called Lydia to the witness stand next and I stopped doodling when she came into the courtroom.

I looked up and I stared and stared because I'd never seen Lydia wear reading glasses before (she always wears contact lenses) and she had on a dark-green button-up sweater over a white blouse and a string of pearls around her neck, and she was wearing dress slacks and shoes with heels, but not the extra-spiky kind that make her look like she's trying to be younger than her forty-eight-year-old self.

DIRECT EXAMINATION BY DISTRICT ATTORNEY EASTERVILLE:

Q: Please state your full name for the record.

A: Lydia Voss.

Q: Where do you live, Ms. Voss?

A: New York.

Q: How long have you lived there?

A: Thirty years.

Q: And how old are you?

A: Forty-eight.

Q: Ms. Voss, are you related to the defendant?

A: I am.

Q: How are you related?

A: (Inaudible . . . 00:03) I'm Denny's biological mother.

Q: I see. And did you raise Denny?

A: No. I had him when I was eighteen and my parents raised him, specifically my mother. My dad died when Denny was fourteen.

Q: Can you state your mother's name for the record?

A: Joanne Voss.

Q: Did your mother know Henry Tesky?

A: Yes. She was the Teskys' house cleaner.

Q: How much was she paid?

MS. KLEIN: Objection.

JUDGE SAGINAW: Overruled.

A: I have no idea.

Q: How long did she work for Henry Tesky?

A: She didn't work for Henry Tesky, she worked for his first wife, Irene, who hired her after a friend recommended her.

Q: All right. How long did she work for the Tesky family?

A: Twenty-four years.

Q: Did Denny grow up knowing you were his biological mother?

A: No.

Q: May I ask why?

A: No, you may not.

Q: I'll rephrase the question. As an eighteen-year-old woman who'd given birth to a child, was it difficult to imagine raising that child on your own?

A: It was something I didn't want to do.

Q: Why not?

A: I don't know (inaudible . . . 00:03), I guess it was just never on my vision board?

MS. KLEIN: Objection. This line of questioning isn't relevant.

JUDGE SAGINAW: Overruled.

Q: Was Denny born healthy, Ms. Voss?

A: No.

Q: Can you explain for the court?

A: (Inaudible . . . 00:02) He was born six weeks early. I went into labor and was rushed to a hospital that wasn't equipped to deal with the problems that came up. During the birth, he suffered from oxygen deprivation and it caused a brain bleed. They moved him to another hospital with a neonatal intensive care unit and my mom stayed with him. She refused to leave Denny's bedside.

Q: How long was he in the NICU?

A: Five weeks.

Q: Did his premature birth, and the subsequent problems you've described, have any long-lasting mental or physical implications?

A: Yes.

Q: Can you explain for the court?

A: I was told Denny would have diminished mental capacity.

Q: And how did that make you feel?

A: (Inaudible . . . 00:03) How do you think it made me feel?

Q: I move to strike that comment, Your Honor.

JUDGE SAGINAW: Granted. I direct the jury to disregard that statement.

Q: Ms. Voss, does Denny have diminished mental capacity?

A: Yes.

Q: Did you ever consider putting him up for adoption?

MS. KLEIN: Objection.

JUDGE SAGINAW: Sustained.

Q: I'll ask another question. You said Denny grew up not knowing you were his biological mother. Was there a time when he learned that you were?

A: Yes.

Q: When did that happen?

A: In September last year.

Q: When in September?

A: At the end of the month.

Q: Was it you or your mother who told the defendant that you are his biological mother?

A: He found out by accident.

Q: How did he react?

A: (Inaudible . . . 00:05)

Q: Ms. Voss?

A: He was upset.

Q: And who is Denny's biological father?

MS. KLEIN: Objection.

JUDGE SAGINAW: Overruled.

Q: I'll repeat the question. Who is Denny's biological father?

A: (Inaudible . . . 00:03)

Q: Can you please repeat your answer, Ms. Voss?

A: Henry Tesky.

(Outburst from the gallery)

JUDGE SAGINAW: Quiet in the courtroom.

Q: Did the defendant grow up knowing Henry Tesky was his biological father?

A: No.

Q: Did he ever learn the truth about Henry Tesky being his biological father?

A: Yes.

Q: When did that happen?

A: In January this year.

Q: What day in January?

A: January second.

Q: For the court record, the coroner has previously confirmed that Mr. Tesky was killed shortly after midnight on January third. I'll ask another question, Ms. Voss. Was it you or your mother who told the defendant that Mr. Tesky was his biological father?

A: He found out by accident.

Q: How did he react?

A: (Inaudible . . . 00:04)

Q: Ms. Voss?

A: He was upset.

Q: I see, and does the defendant have a temper, Ms. Voss?

A: No more than I do.

Q: Your Honor, I move to strike the answer as nonresponsive.

JUDGE SAGINAW: I direct the jury to disregard that statement.

Q: Ms. Voss, as you've confirmed for us today, the defendant, who has diminished mental capacity, learned, at twenty-nine years of age, that you're his biological mother and Mr. Tesky was his biological father, and he

learned those two specific pieces of information by accident and within months of each other, correct?
MS. KLEIN: Objection. Asked and answered.
JUDGE SAGINAW: Sustained.
Q: I'll ask another question. Ms. Voss, did either of your parents know that Henry Tesky was Denny's biological father?
A: No.
Q: Did Henry Tesky take responsibility for his son?
A: (Inaudible . . . 00:04) No.
Q: Ms. Voss, did he give you any financial assistance?
A: He paid my tuition and my residence fees for four years.
Q: Did he pay for anything else?
A: He gave me a monthly stipend while I was in college.
Q: How much was that?
A: Seven hundred dollars a month.
Q: For how long?
A: Four years.
Q: Did he give you any child support for Denny?
A: (Inaudible . . . 00:03)
Q: Let me remind you that you're still under oath, Ms. Voss. I'll ask the question again. Did Henry Tesky give you any financial assistance to help support Denny?
A: Yes, he gave me a thousand dollars a month.
Q: For how long?
A: Eighteen years.
Q: Did you have a legal agreement that outlined Henry Tesky's commitment to you?
A: He made me sign a nondisclosure agreement.
Q: That's not what I meant. Did you and Henry Tesky sign a legal agreement that outlined his financial commitment to you in relation to child support?

A: Yes.

Q: Thank you, Ms. Voss. To recap then, for eighteen years, Henry Tesky gave you one thousand dollars a month in child support. What were those funds used for?

A: None of your business.

JUDGE SAGINAW: Ms. Voss, I'm going to caution you at this point. Any more of that and I'll find you in contempt.

Q: Ms. Voss, did you give those funds to your mother to help her raise Denny?

A: No.

Q: Does your mother know you received a thousand dollars a month from Henry Tesky for eighteen years?

A: No.

Q: Why didn't you tell her?

A: None of your business.

JUDGE SAGINAW: Again, Ms. Voss, I'm cautioning you. This is your last warning. Continue in this manner and I'll find you in contempt.

Q: Can you explain for the court the nature of your relationship with Mr. Tesky when you became pregnant?

A: No.

Q: When was the last time you spoke with Henry Tesky?

A: (Inaudible . . . 00:04)

Q: Let me remind you that you're still under oath, Ms. Voss. Can you please answer the question?

A: I called him last year in June.

Q: And why did you do that?

A: None of your business.

JUDGE SAGINAW: I direct the jury to disregard that statement. Ms. Voss, I find you in contempt. You're being fined three hundred dollars.

Q: What prompted you to call Henry Tesky?

A: (Inaudible . . . 00:04)

Q: Please answer the question.

A: I asked him to pay for my mom's knee replacement surgery.

Q: And why would you do that?

A: (Inaudible . . . 00:05)

Q: Can you please answer the question?

JUDGE SAGINAW: The witness will answer the question.

A: Because she couldn't afford to pay for it herself and I felt it was the least Henry could do after she'd scrubbed his fucking toilets for twenty-four years and spent twenty-nine years raising Denny.

Q: Ms. Voss, how much was your mom's knee replacement surgery?

A: $22,748.

Q: You said it was the least he could do, but didn't Henry Tesky, over a period of eighteen years, provide you with $216,000 in child support?

MS. KLEIN: Argumentative. Badgering the witness.

JUDGE SAGINAW: Sustained.

Q: I'll withdraw the question. Ms. Voss, did Henry Tesky give your mother $22,748 to pay for her knee replacement surgery?

A: He paid the bill anonymously.

Q: Was he happy to do that?

A: No.

Q: Then why did he pay the bill?

A: (Inaudible . . . 00:05)

Q: Please answer the question.

A: Because I told him if he didn't pay it, I'd tell everyone he was Denny's father.

Q: So, you blackmailed him?

A: I encouraged him to do the right thing.

Q: You blackmailed him, even though you had a binding nondisclosure agreement that stated his identity as Denny's father would forever remain anonymous?
MS. KLEIN: Asked and answered.
JUDGE SAGINAW: Sustained.
A: I blackmailed him because Henry Tesky was a fucking predator and I felt like it was time he paid for what he did to me and my family.
Q: Your Honor, I move to strike the answer from the record.
JUDGE SAGINAW: I direct the jury to disregard that statement. Ms. Voss, I'm sentencing you to six days in county jail and I'm giving you another three-hundred-dollar fine.

JUDGE SAGINAW: Counsel (directed to MS. KLEIN), before I have the bailiff remove Ms. Voss from the courtroom, would you like to cross-examine?
MS. KLEIN: I would, Your Honor.

CROSS-EXAMINATION BY DEFENSE ATTORNEY BRIDGET KLEIN:
MS. KLEIN: Ms. Voss, in your opinion, is Denny mentally disabled?
A: (Inaudible . . . 00:03) Yes, he is.
MS. KLEIN: And do you think Denny has any serious anger issues beyond what would be considered normal?
A: No, he doesn't.

MS. KLEIN: Do you love him?

MR. EASTERVILLE: Objection. Irrelevant.

JUDGE SAGINAW: I'll allow it.

A: Of course.

MS. KLEIN: And how would you describe Denny?

A: Thoughtful, funny, kind. He has a huge heart.

MS. KLEIN: Are you proud of him?

A: Yes.

MS. KLEIN: Do you think Denny killed Mr. Tesky?

A: Absolutely not.

MS. KLEIN: Ms. Voss, how old were you when you met Henry Tesky?

A: I was seventeen.

MS. KLEIN: And how did you meet?

A: He was my basketball coach.

MS. KLEIN: I see, and as a seventeen-year-old girl spending time with a thirty-one-year-old married basketball coach at practices, games, and out-of-town tournaments, do you feel like Henry Tesky groomed you so he could have sex with you?

MR. EASTERVILLE: Objection. Leading the witness.

JUDGE SAGINAW: Sustained.

MS. KLEIN: I'll rephrase. Ms. Voss, how would you describe your relationship with your basketball coach, Mr. Tesky?

A: As a seventeen-year-old girl spending time with a thirty-one-year-old married basketball coach at practices, games, and out-of-town tournaments, I felt like Henry Tesky groomed me so he could have sex with me.

MR. EASTERVILLE: Objection.

JUDGE SAGINAW: Overruled. I'll allow it.

MS. KLEIN: Ms. Voss, were you a virgin the first time you had sex with Henry Tesky?

A: (Inaudible . . . 00:04) Yes.

MR. EASTERVILLE: Objection, Your Honor.

JUDGE SAGINAW: Overruled.

MS. KLEIN: Did he use protection?

A: No, he did not.

MS. KLEIN: And how did he react when you told him you were pregnant?

A: He told me to get an abortion.

MS. KLEIN: What did you say?

A: I told him I was having the baby because I was too far along to get an abortion.

MS. KLEIN: And how did he react?

A: He put his fist through a wall.

MS. KLEIN: Thank you, Ms. Voss. I have no further questions.

Then, just like that, Judge Saginaw banged his gavel and said the day was done. The bailiff took Lydia out of the courtroom and Bridget explained that the judge was making her spend six days in Woodmont County Jail because she broke the rules, but Woodmont County Jail is my jail and there aren't many people in there right now, so I asked Bridget if they were putting her in the cell across from me now that Dirty Doyle got himself moved for threatening to kill me, and she said, "I have no idea, Denny."

And I said, "I hope not, because Lydia snores."

What Did Mr. Tesky Say?

Two hours later, I was back in my cell at Woodmont County Jail when Grant-the-corrections-officer (he was working a night shift) came down the walkway to put Lydia in the empty cell across from me, and she was wearing an orange jumpsuit with **County Inmate** printed on the back and orange rubber shoes, and she wasn't wearing any makeup.

I jumped up and moved closer to the bars. "Grant, can you please put her in one of the other cells?" I asked, and he looked at his clipboard and said, "Nope, she was assigned to this one." Then he squinted at his clipboard again and did a frown. "Huh . . . Lydia Voss." He tapped his pen against the paper. "Are you guys related?"

"Whether we like it or not," Lydia said.

And I raised my hand. "I don't like it, not one bit."

More frowning from Grant. "Wow, okay. I know why you're in here"—he nodded at me, then he looked at Lydia—"Can I ask why you're here, though?"

I raised my hand again. "It's because she has a bad attitude."

Lydia crossed her arms. "Zip it, Denny, he wasn't talking to you." Then she looked at Grant and said, "I'm in here for contempt, and I'm guessing if you look at the fine print on my intake form—you *can* read, right?—it's probably all there in black and white. Now, if you don't mind, I'd like to end this wildly inappropriate and invasive conversation because I don't feel like chitchatting, with you or anyone else."

Grant's eyes got big.

And I said, "See? Bad attitude."

Then he quickly locked Lydia's cell door and he left with his clipboard. And I sat down on my bed to write in the blue notebook Dr. Harland had given me, same as I do every day, only this time I wrote down everything that had happened in the courtroom so I wouldn't forget, and then my mind started jumping all over, and I said, "Hey, Lydia, did you meet Chaunce and Tahni when you did processing?"

She was sitting on her bed. "What?—who?!"

"Chaunce and Tahni. They work in the intake center and they do processing? Tahni has a flowery plant on her desk with a 'Save the Bees' sticker on the pot—she takes all the booking photos—and Chaunce is the guy who asks people to take their clothes off before he gives them their orange jumpsuit."

Lydia rested her head in her hands. "You know what, Denny? It's been a long day and I don't know—nor do I care—who processed me, but I do know I can't do *this* if we're going to be across from each other for six days. I'm not your new best friend."

And I did thinking about that, then I said, "You could never be my best friend, Lydia. You're too selfish." And she laughed and said, "Look, I know things haven't been good between us lately, Denny—"

"—ever. They haven't been good between us *ever*."

Lydia did a sigh. "Fair enough. But I do want you to know that no matter what happens, I plan to be here for you in any capacity that I can."

And I said, "I don't need your capacity."

Then Grant came back to deliver our dinner and he gave me a plate with a snap-down lid on it and he gave one to Lydia too, and when he left, Lydia lifted the lid and said, "What fresh hell is this?" scrunching up her face. And I said, "It's Thursday and if you're incarcerated at Woodmont County Jail on a Thursday you get liver and onions for dinner."

She covered her mouth. "You can't be serious."

"Serious as cement."

Lydia put the lid back on and set her plate on the floor, then she lay down and pulled the blanket over her. And a little while later I thought I heard her doing sniffling and even though I don't like Lydia, I felt a bit bad for her because I don't like liver and onions either, and the first night I was in jail I did sniffling too. So, after doing thinking about it, I said, "Lydia, if you ask Grant for a fruit cup, he'd probably get you one."

She didn't say anything.

And I said, "You'd have to be nice to him, though."

Nothing.

"Try being polite."

Not one word.

An hour later, Lydia was doing snoring (loud) when Grant came down the walkway to make sure Dirty Doyle wasn't trying to escape or commit suicide in Cell #10. When he was done checking on him, I called him over and we did chatting, real quiet-like, then Grant left and when he came back a few minutes later he had another blanket with him, and a tray with peppermint tea and a fruit cup on it. He unlocked Lydia's door—**CLANG! CLANG!**—and when it slid open, she quickly sat up and rubbed her face.

Grant set everything down beside her, then he left.

And it was 9:30 p.m., and if you're incarcerated in Woodmont County Jail on any day of the week at 9:30 p.m., the lights go dim, then they shut off completely at 9:45 with only the pot lights in the walkway left on. Also, the floor in the front office creaks and groans when people walk around on it, and the furnace is REALLY LOUD when it first kicks in, but none of that bothers me like it did when I first got here, because I've gotten used to it and now I think those things help me sleep *better*.

Because I can count on them.

And when you can count on something, you feel safe.

So yeah, all the lights went dim at 9:30 p.m. and then they went dark at 9:45, same as always, and that's when I heard Lydia say, real quiet-like, "Thank you, Denny," and I went very still inside, and I pretended to be asleep so I didn't have to say anything back because, like I already said, I don't need Lydia's capacity.

The next morning it was Bridget's turn to call witnesses to the witness box and the first person she did talking with was the pretty woman with dark hair who I saw at the pharmacy the day I bought nylon stockings to make Nana-Jo's soap-on-a-ropes.

Bridget said, "Can you please state your name and occupation?"

"My name is Brenna Talmage. I'm a pharmacist."

"Thank you, Ms. Talmage."

Bridget walked closer to the witness box. "Ms. Talmage, can you confirm for the court that you were the pharmacist on duty at Value Drug Mart in Woodmont, Minnesota, on October tenth of last year?"

"Yes, I was."

Bridget smiled. "Do you recall seeing the defendant"—she turned and pointed to me—"in Value Drug Mart that day?"

"I do," Ms. Talmage said.

"Was he there to fill a prescription?"

Ms. Talmage shook her head. "No, he came to the back of the store, where Henry Tesky was waiting to pick up a prescription."

"Did you hear the defendant speak with Mr. Tesky?"

"I did, though at first it was hard to hear what they were talking about because I stepped away from the counter to use the computer."

"I see." Bridget tilted her head to one side. "And was there a point when you could hear what was being said?"

Ms. Talmage lifted her chin. "Yes, I heard Mr. Tesky say, 'This isn't rocket science. It's actually quite simple, even for someone with your limited capacity.' Mr. Voss was very polite. He said, 'So, you won't give Nana-Jo her job back?' and Mr. Tesky said, 'You really are a full-on idiot, aren't you? Did you not hear what I said? No means no; it doesn't mean try harder.' After that, Mr. Tesky seemed to realize he was talking quite loud, so he stepped closer to Mr. Voss and he lowered his voice."

"Did you hear what he said next?" Bridget asked.

Ms. Talmage nodded. "I did."

"Can you share that with us?"

It got very quiet in the courtroom and it felt like everyone was staring at me, and I started to feel hot inside. Ms. Talmage looked at me, then she quickly looked away again. "Mr. Tesky said, 'You are a fucking retard, a dim, slow-witted embarrassment to the human race who never should've been born. Stay away from me!'"

Bridget nodded, then she straightened her jacket and slowly walked back to our table. "And during this exchange did the defendant, Mr. Voss, get upset or angry or in any way aggressive with Mr. Tesky?"

Ms. Talmage spoke into the microphone. "No. He was meek and polite. It was Mr. Tesky who was a complete asshole."

"Objection!" Mr. Easterville said.

"Sustained," said the judge.

"Thank you," Bridget said. "I have no further questions."

It got extra quiet again, and my heart was going **BOOM-BOOM-BOOM**, so I did doodling in my notebook so I wouldn't have to look at anyone. Then Judge Saginaw told Mr. Easterville he could cross-examine the witness, but Mr. Easterville said he didn't have any questions for her, so Judge Saginaw told Ms. Talmage she could step down, and she did. After that, we got a one-hour break for lunch and they brought egg salad sandwiches for me and Bridget but I wasn't hungry, so I didn't eat.

—

I don't remember much about the other witnesses Bridget called to the stand that afternoon. There was lots of talking, but I wasn't really listening. All I know is that Judge Saginaw finally banged his gavel at 4:00 p.m. to end the day and then a deputy took me back to my cell at the Woodmont County Jail.

When Lydia saw me, she said, "How'd it go today?" and "Catch me up, Denny," but I didn't answer, I just lay on my bed and stared at the cement wall, doing thinking.

Later, Grant came to my cell, and he said, "Denny, you have a visitor," but I didn't say anything back. "It's someone named Nori," he said, and I rolled over to tell him I didn't feel like talking to anyone, but he was gone.

And there was Nori.

"Hi, Denny."

She gave me a little wave.

Nori had been sitting behind me and Bridget in the courtroom every day, watching the trial, and now here she was visiting me in jail again. Lydia stood up in her cell all smiley and said, "Who's this, Denny? Introduce me," but I think because Nori had been in the courtroom and now she knew who Lydia was, she whispered to me, "I've got this." Then she turned to Lydia, smiled back, and said, "I'm a friend of Denny's and today was kind of rough, so could you maybe give us some privacy?"

Lydia lifted her hands. "Of course."

Nori turned back to me. "Sorry I didn't bring any baking." And I said, "That's okay," then she told me Theo was at a friend's house, that he'd been invited over for pizza and she'd encouraged him to go. "He asked me if we can go to your house and visit George when you get home," Nori said. "Would that be okay?"

And I said, "Sure."

"He wants to bring him a bag of Cheetos."

"George would like that."

Nori handed me an envelope through the bars. "Grant said it was okay for me to give you this. Theo wanted to give it to you himself, but I told him I didn't know when you'd be home and he didn't want to wait."

"What is it?"

"Open it and see."

So I opened it and inside was a square white badge with red trim around the outside and a red fish in the middle, and above that fish it said **Guppy** embroidered in blue. Nori looked at her feet. "He passed his Guppy test yesterday."

"He took the lessons again?"

She shook her head. "No, they let him take the test again, though. He called his swim instructor all by himself and asked him if he could do it again because his tics get bad when he's stressed and maybe they wouldn't be so bad if no one was watching him. I have to say, he was pretty persuasive."

"He didn't want me to watch him?"

"No, Denny. He wanted to surprise you."

It'd been a terrible day, but this made it better. "Wow, Theo's a Dolphin now," I said, and Nori smiled. "He certainly is." Then she tucked a piece of wild kinky hair behind her ear, and she said, "You've been so good for him, Denny. I haven't seen him this happy or confident in a long time. Thank you."

I looked up at her. "For what?"

Nori reached through the bars and squeezed my arm. "For being you."

Who Killed Mr. Tesky?

It was early and I was in my jail cell, waiting for another day to start in the courtroom. Grant came to get me and he took me to the special meeting room where I usually meet Bridget, but when he opened the door, Bridget and Dr. Harland were both there waiting for me. I saw Dr. Harland bump Bridget's arm with his elbow and Bridget set her laptop on the table. "Good morning, Denny," she said. "Have a seat."

So, I sat down.

She opened her laptop and turned it sideways so we could all see the screen, then she looked at me, and she said, "I asked Dr. Harland to be here with me because we need to talk about the night Mr. Tesky was killed."

And I said, "I don't want to talk about that."

Bridget nodded. "I know, Denny, but we have to. There's been a new development. We know who shot Mr. Tesky."

I stared at her, but I didn't say anything.

Bridget looked at Dr. Harland and he nodded, then she turned back to me. "After Malinda Tesky found her husband's body, investigators went through the house looking for evidence, but because Malinda had only recently moved in, she wasn't a hundred percent familiar with the house, so when investigators asked if they had a security camera, she said no. She was wrong, though. We now know that Henry Tesky installed a security camera years ago. There was a tiny camera hidden in the chandelier in the foyer."

And I said, "What does that mean?"

Bridget folded her hands together. "It means we have a security video from the night Mr. Tesky was killed," and I said, "Oh," because that's how the Timkos found out I'd kidnapped Tom Hanks, so now I understood what she meant.

"Listen, Denny," Bridget said. "I spoke to Judge Saginaw and he's going to ban spectators from the courtroom tomorrow so this video can be played. Because of that, Dr. Harland and I talked about it, and we think it'd be better if we played it for you now instead. Is that all right?"

And I stared at her and I thought about it, and I wanted to say, *No, I don't want to see the video*, because my heart was going **BOOM-BOOM-BOOM**, and I wished Nana-Jo was there to help me, but she wasn't, and I knew I had to do things like this on my own from now on because Nana-Jo had had a stroke and she wasn't going to be with me forever, and also Bridget Klein had worked very hard on my case.

So I said, "Okay."

Bridget pressed a key on her laptop and the screen lit up with a video of the Teskys' foyer, and I knew it was their foyer because I'd been in their house lots of times, and on one side of the foyer were glass closet doors that rolled open, and on the other side was a built-in bench where you could sit down to put your shoes on. And not everyone knew this, but the lid of that bench lifted up and it had a secret hiding spot underneath where Irene Tesky used to keep her purse and her gloves and a container of coins for when little kids came to the door selling cookies. She also kept a metal box in there.

And there was a bag of golf clubs by the sliding closet doors and a plant in a ceramic pot, and the plant was quite tall and bushy. But there were no people in the video—the Teskys' foyer was empty. At the top of the screen it said the date (January 3) and there was also a clock, and I could tell the clock was keeping track of the time, because it said, 12:17 . . . then 12:18 . . . and then 12:19. The doorbell rang and a few seconds later Mr. Tesky came around the corner with a glass in his hand and he was wearing dress pants and a golf shirt.

He opened the door and I felt scared inside.

I wanted to look away, but I didn't.

And there was Nana-Jo.

I felt dizzy, and there was fluttering inside my chest like a bird was trapped in there, flapping around, trying to get out. In the video Nana-Jo had foam curlers in her hair (pink) just like she did when she went to bingo with Mrs. Timko earlier that night, and she was wearing her puffy winter coat that went down past her knees, the new SOREL winter boots I got her for Christmas, and my blue scarf, wrapped around her neck.

Mr. Tesky said, "What are *you* doing here?" and his voice sounded a bit slurry, like how Angus sounds when he's had too much to drink.

"We need to talk," said Nana-Jo, and I could tell by her voice that she was angry. She pushed past Mr. Tesky into the foyer, and she said, "Where's that new wife of yours? She should hear this too."

Mr. Tesky finished his drink, then he shut the door and shivered like he was cold. "Malinda's not here. She's in Minneapolis." He looked at his watch like he was confused. "What makes you think you can show up like this, uninvited? For Chrissake, it's after midnight, Joanne. We have nothing to talk about. I don't owe you people anything."

"You *people*?"

Mr. Tesky was a big man and Nana-Jo was small and bent over and she had a bad back, but she walked up to him and poked him in the chest with her finger. "Don't talk to me like that, Henry, like me and my family are a bunch of insects. What makes you think you're so much better than anyone else?"

He looked at his empty glass. "Jesus, I need another drink."

Nana-Jo yelled at him. "We trusted you, Henry! You were her coach and we trusted you. She went to out-of-town tournaments with you and that team, and you preyed on her. All those years, all that time, Joe and I believed some teenage kid got her pregnant, but it was you. You groomed our daughter, got her pregnant, and then left her twisting in the wind. For the love of God, Henry, she was just a child."

Mr. Tesky held his hands up. "Listen, I don't know what Lydia told you, but that's not what happened."

Nana-Jo said, "Really?! Tell me, then, how is it that my daughter—my *underage* daughter—got pregnant with your child? She was seventeen and you were thirty-one and a married man. I read her diary. You had sex with her many times; then, when she got pregnant, you told her to get an abortion. You offered to pay for it and when Lydia refused, thinking she was too far along and that maybe one day you'd leave Irene for her, you paid her to keep her mouth shut, didn't you? She told us she got a scholarship and that her residence fees were included, but you paid those too, didn't you? That and a monthly food allowance. I read the nondisclosure agreement you made her sign, Henry. It was tucked away at the back of her diary and it lays everything out nice and clear—"

"I never forced her to sign anything."

Nana-Jo glared at him. "She was seventeen!"

He shrugged. "She was eighteen when she signed the agreement."

Nana-Jo stared at him for a long time. "You're a sexual predator, Henry, a pervert. You make my skin crawl."

"Joanne, calm down—"

"Calm down?" Nana-Jo laughed. "You got my teenage daughter pregnant, I raised *your* son, and you want *me* to calm down? Henry, you haven't seen anything yet. I'm just getting started." Nana-Jo's voice scared me and my heart was going BOOM-BOOM-BOOM and I grabbed the arms of my chair and squeezed them extra hard because I'd never seen her that mad in my whole wide life.

Her voice wasn't shaky anymore. "You put us through hell, Henry. Lydia didn't want anyone to know she was pregnant. She wouldn't tell us who the father was. All she said was that he was young and stupid. And the whole time, it was *you*." Nana-Jo shook her head. "If Joe was alive today, he'd put a bullet in your head."

Mr. Tesky ran a hand through his hair. "Listen to me, Joanne. I did right by Lydia when she got pregnant. I gave her a future. Yes, I paid her tuition and residence fees, and I gave her a monthly food allowance.

Lydia was whip smart, way beyond her years. She was always focused on taking care of number one. She used to say how much she hated living in Woodmont and, in the end, getting pregnant was her ticket out of here, wasn't it?" He shook his head. "For all I know, she probably even planned it."

Nana-Jo laughed. "For the love of God, don't flatter yourself, Henry. You're not the catch you seem to think you are. If Irene had known about this, she would've divorced you and left you without a penny."

Mr. Tesky held up both hands. "It was a lapse of judgment."

"No, Henry, it wasn't. You're a sick man."

He tilted his head back and talked to the ceiling. "Holy shit, why now? After all these years, why is this happening *now*?"

"Because I found out the truth," said Nana-Jo. "And the only good thing about that is you can't shut me up or pay me off. I'm going to ruin you, Henry. Everyone in town is going to know what kind of man you are. You know what? I might even call a press conference. Wouldn't that be interesting?"

Mr. Tesky went very still.

Nana-Jo kept talking. "You crossed a line thirty years ago and now you're going to pay the price. I won't stop until you're a registered sex offender wearing an ankle bracelet for the rest of your life. I'll make sure it's in all the papers. You'll be the laughingstock of Woodmont, a pervert running for mayor."

"No, Joanne." Mr. Tesky set his empty glass down on the bench. "That's not going to happen. I'll never let that happen."

He yanked a golf club out of the bag that was leaning against the wall and swung it like a baseball bat. Nana-Jo lifted her arm to protect herself but she wasn't fast enough. Mr. Tesky hit her once and she stumbled back and fell down, then he hit her again and again—harder each time—and he dropped the golf club and stumbled out of the foyer.

And I was rocking back and forth, doing moaning, because I was scared and I wanted to help Nana-Jo, but I couldn't because this was a videotape and it had already happened, and it was awful to watch. Nana-Jo was on her knees in the Teskys' foyer and she was trying to get up, but the snow from her new SOREL boots had melted all over the tiled floor and made it slippery, so she was having trouble.

Nana-Jo crawled over to the bench and lifted the heavy lid, and Mr. Tesky's empty glass slid back against the wall. I could see that her hand was shaking when she reached inside, but I couldn't see what she was doing. Then she dropped the lid and the end of my blue scarf got itself stuck underneath the lid, and she had to yank on it twice to get it unstuck. And she was on her knees again, trying to get up, when Mr. Tesky came stumbling back into the foyer and he had a knife and his shirt was untucked.

"You stupid old bitch," he said. "Why couldn't you just leave it alone?! I won't let you derail my career. I won't."

He rushed at her with the knife.

Nana-Jo was on her knees on the floor.

And she had a gun.

She pointed it at Mr. Tesky, but the gun was moving all over the place because her arm was shaking so badly.

He was only a few feet away when Nana-Jo closed her eyes and pulled the trigger—**BOOM!** Then he stopped and the knife fell to the floor. He put his hand on his neck and said, "What did . . . you . . . do?" He dropped to his knees on the wet tile and sagged sideways onto the floor, then onto his back, and there was blood spreading out underneath him like someone had spilled a bucket of it.

Nana-Jo was still holding the gun.

And she was crying.

She crawled over to Mr. Tesky, reached out, and touched his neck. "Oh God, no! No!" Nana-Jo stood up and she was still crying when she put the gun in her pocket and she stumbled over to Irene Tesky's built-in bench and sat down, holding her arm. She was rocking back and forth like I do sometimes, and she kept wiping her nose with the back of her hand, then she got up and wiped down the bench with the sleeve of her jacket and she picked up the golf club. After that, she walked over to the closet, slid one of the doors open, and stood on tiptoe to reach up inside to grab something—

And the screen went black.

That's when Bridget pressed the STOP button on her computer and my heart was going BOOM-BOOM-BOOM and I felt sick inside, so I put my head between my knees and did moaning while I counted the tiles on the floor.

Dr. Harland came over beside me and he rubbed my back, and said, "It's all right, Denny. We're here to help you."

And I said, "I don't need your help."

I took one deep breath and another deep breath, and then I rocked back and forth, and I tried to remember what had happened after I read Lydia's diary that night, but it was all jumbled up in my mind. I know I yelled at Nana-Jo and I called her a liar and a traitor, then I went over to 8A to yell at Angus, and when I got home later that night Nana-Jo's bedroom door was closed, and the next morning her arm and her neck and her face were red and bruised, and she told me she'd fallen in the bathtub, and I believed her.

But Nana-Jo lied.

"Denny, are you all right?" Bridget asked.

And I said, "No," because I wasn't all right. Nana-Jo lied to me. She didn't slip and fall in the bathtub. After I left for Angus's house that night, she got herself into her Subaru and she drove to Penguin Hill to see Mr. Tesky, and even though Nana-Jo hates guns, she shot Mr. Tesky with a gun.

In the neck.

And he died on the floor.

I rocked back and forth and did moaning, then I said, "Uh-oh! Uh-oh! Uh-oh . . . Bridget, I think Nana-Jo came home to 8B that night and she put Irene Tesky's gun in the root cellar with Papa-Jo's guns and now she's a murderer, and the police are going to arrest her and there'll be a trial, and Judge Saginaw will send her to jail, and she'll have to live with dangerous people like Dirty Doyle, and this is just like one of those fast-moving TV shows, only it's not a fast-moving TV show, it's real life."

Bridget hurried around the table to squat beside me, and she smelled like lemons (same as always) and she put her hand on my arm, and said, "No, Denny. Nana-Jo shot Mr. Tesky in self-defense. When you shoot someone in self-defense, they don't arrest you and send you to jail. They had an argument and Nana-Jo was protecting herself; she didn't mean to kill Mr. Tesky. It was an accident. Do you understand?"

I looked at Bridget and I thought about that for a bit, then Dr. Harland said, "Take a deep breath, Denny. Everything's going to be fine."

And it was.

Bridget explained that while we were doing the trial, the doctors had moved Nana-Jo to a *rehabilitation ward* (where they teach people who've had strokes to walk and talk and eat with a spoon so they don't get yogurt all over their face) and Elaine went there every day to help Nana-Jo with her exercises. Then one day Nana-Jo had Elaine get her a pen and paper and she wrote words down telling Elaine to check her sock drawer at 8B. So Elaine did that and inside Nana-Jo's sock drawer was a CD (round silver disc) and Elaine took it to Bridget, and Bridget found the video of Nana-Jo shooting Mr. Tesky on that CD. The next day, Bridget showed it to Judge Saginaw, then she showed it to me today, and then Judge Saginaw played it in the courtroom, and after that I guess he must have said, *Enough is enough,* because that's when they dropped all the charges against me.

And just like that . . . no more trial.

Getting Out of Jail

I got out of jail three days before Lydia did.

Grant-the-corrections-officer opened my cell door—CLANG! CLANG!—and he said, "Up and at 'em, Denny. Your lawyer's here. You're getting out," and I rolled off my bed and grabbed my notebook and stepped out of my cell. And I said, "Did you hear that, Lydia? Bridget's here. I'm a free man." She'd pulled her mattress off her bed onto the floor (I don't think you're allowed to do that, but Lydia's always breaking the rules) and now there she was, sitting on her mattress with her legs criss-crossy, doing yoga, and her eyes were closed and she was breathing real slow because she was in a place called THE ZONE (where I've never been), which is where you go when you don't want to be where you are.

"Lydia, did you hear me? I'm leaving."

She breathed in real slow, then she breathed out. "I'm not deaf, Denny. I heard you."

"Do you want me and Angus to come visit tomorrow so you don't get lonely?"

"Please don't."

And I said, "It's okay to be scared. I know how hard jail can be."

And she said, "Denny?"

"What?"

"Fuck off."

In some ways Lydia's a lot like Dirty Doyle. She only has one tattoo, though (a tiny camera on her wrist) but her hair is long and she keeps it tied back with an elastic band, and yesterday she told me she didn't want to hear another word about George, or Penguin Hill, or my smashed-up sled called White Lightning. She said I talk too much and if I don't shut up, she's going to smack me when we get home.

Grant said, "It's time to go, Denny." And I said, "All right," and I turned away from Lydia, but then I looked back and said, "When they bring your dinner, can you put some breadcrumbs on the floor so Pinky doesn't starve?"

"Who the hell's Pinky?"

"The mouse that lives in the wall under your bed. He doesn't come out every night, but when he does I share my dinner with him."

Lydia opened her eyes. "There's *a mouse* in here!" And I'd never seen her move that fast. She undid her criss-crossy legs, threw her mattress on the bed, jumped up on it, and then—**BOOM!**—just like that Lydia wasn't in THE ZONE anymore. "Why doesn't someone put a trap in here to catch it?" she yelled.

Grant laughed. "We've tried that. It never works. They just keep coming back."

Lydia's face was red and splotchy. "There's more than *one*?!"

Grant didn't answer. Instead he rolled his eyes and took me to an empty room with a bathroom attached where he had me take off my orange jumpsuit with **County Inmate** printed on the back and then he gave me my clothes and my waterproof Timex watch and my key to 8B and the comb with two missing teeth I had in my pocket when I got myself arrested. After that, he took me out front, where Bridget was waiting for me.

Grant gave me a high five. "Take care, dude. I hope I never see you again."

And I said, "Same," because that's how we talk now.

Grant's a good guy.

Then Bridget drove me over to the Doughnut Hole and she went through the drive-through and got doughnuts (vanilla sprinkle for me, chocolate dip for her) and she turned to me, and her voice went funny, and she said, "I'm going to miss you, Denny."

I said, "Same."

And just like that . . . no more jail.

Newspaper Story #3

Murder Charges Dropped
by Carol Nazaruk

Murder charges have been dropped against Denny Voss, a 30-year-old man from Woodmont accused of murdering Henry Tesky, 62, also of Woodmont, after new evidence was presented that exonerated the accused. In a ruling issued on Monday, Judge Milton Saginaw dismissed all charges with prejudice against Mr. Voss.

Voss, who wore a dark-gray suit and a white button-up shirt, clutched a blue notebook but said nothing during his brief appearance in court Monday morning, which was expected to be the start of his fourth week at trial for second-degree murder.

Prosecutor Reginald Easterville offered this comment on the judge's decision, saying, "All I can tell you is that new evidence came to light that fully exonerated Mr. Voss from these charges."

Details of the case are currently under a publication ban.

Terrible, Horrible, Awful Day

Lydia gets out of jail tomorrow and Angus is going to pick her up. He thinks it's funny that Judge Saginaw threw her in jail because he said, "Lydia needs a lesson in humility," and I didn't know what *humility* meant so I looked it up on Google and it said: *Humility is the state of being humble.*

So yeah, whatever that means.

I rolled over and looked at my phone, and it was 7:12 a.m., and it was Sunday, and it was nice to be back home at 8B. I'd missed watching *Schitt's Creek* and my pillow and the quilt Nana-Jo made me years ago. Most of all, though, I'd missed George.

Last night, we walked up Penguin Hill and when we got to the top, George sat down for a rest and I squatted next to him and told him about the guns and the bullets and how I got myself arrested. I also told him about Bridget and Dr. Harland and how Nana-Jo shot Mr. Tesky in self-defense. Then George got up again and I rubbed his hips (they get stiff when he sits too long) and we walked home.

Now he was asleep on the floor next to my bed, so I tried to be quiet as I stepped over him. I went to the kitchen and got my Cheerios out of the cupboard, dumped some in a bowl, then got milk out of the fridge and poured some on them. I carried the bowl to the table and ate them, and while I ate, I looked out the window at the yellow birdhouse I'd made for Mrs. Timko that was hanging in her yard . . . then Sharon and Bill drove by with a wheelbarrow in the back of their truck . . . and Elaine ran past on the sidewalk wearing running shoes.

When I finished eating, George still wasn't awake so I went back to my room and knelt on the floor and I blew on his face so he'd know it was me.

Nothing.

"Time to get up, George."

But his tail didn't thump, not even once.

George's favorite treat in the world is Cheetos (he does a happy dance whenever I give them to him) and he still had Cheeto dust on his mouth from the night before, so I got up and ran to the kitchen. I grabbed his Cheeto bag out of the cupboard, then ran back to my room and dumped some on the floor in front of him.

Nothing.

George's eyes stayed closed.

And I started to feel funny inside and my heart started going **BOOM-BOOM-BOOM.** I touched the dog collar Nana-Jo had bought him with pineapples on it and his silver dog tags that said **GEORGE** and **ADOPTED AND ADORED** and they had scratches on them from where they had rubbed together during all our walks, and it felt like someone was running around inside my head with spiky shoes on, and I didn't know what to do.

So, I blew on George's face again.

Nothing.

Then I touched his face and it was cold and I could tell he wasn't breathing and that's when I knew he was gone. I rocked back and forth on my knees, and I said, "Don't go, George. *Please don't go!*" even though I knew he was already gone.

I curled up beside him on the floor and I touched his face gentle-like and my insides tipped over and I whispered, "I love you, George," in case he wasn't 100 percent gone yet because I've always talked to George even though he's deaf. I told him he was a good boy, that he was special and heaven was a beautiful place and when he got there, he'd be able to run and jump because he wouldn't be blind or deaf anymore, and there'd be lots of other dogs to play with and he could eat as many Cheetos as he wanted. I also told him Papa-Jo would be there to take care of him and all of that was a big fat lie because I don't know what's going to happen to George now that he's stopped breathing, but I hope it's like how I said because I don't want him to be scared because there's nothing worse than being scared.

I was crying.

And my nose was running.

And I wrapped my arms around George and hugged him, and I said, *Sorry, sorry, sorry,* because I was sorry he couldn't live forever, and my heart hurt. Then I said, "Don't worry about me, George, I'll be fine," which was another big fat lie.

RIP at Turtle Creek

When I'm at DOT, I usually do the heavy lifting (hard work) and Angus supervises, which is what supervisors are supposed to do. They also train employees (something Angus hasn't had time to do with me yet) and they watch over their employees' *day-to-day performance*, but right now it's Sunday afternoon and me and Angus aren't at work at DOT, we're at Turtle Creek, behind 8B, and Angus is doing the heavy lifting while I sit on the wet grass next to George, who's wrapped in a soft gray blanket.

Angus is digging a grave.

In George's favorite spot next to a weeping willow tree.

And it's cold and it's raining, so before Angus started to dig, we set up Elaine's pop-up gazebo to keep us dry, and Elaine helped. She started crying when we carried George from the house to the creek and then she went back inside to make coffee and Angus put gloves on and he got a spade out of the shed and he started digging.

I sat next to George so he wouldn't be alone.

And I was doing remembering about the first time I ever saw him at the Canine Rescue Center, and the first night I brought him home, and the first time we walked up Penguin Hill and the very first time I brought him to Turtle Creek. It was a hot summer day and I led him down to the creek and there were two painted turtles sitting on a rock, and George put his toes in the water but then he backed up all scared-like. A few minutes later, he found himself a spot under a weeping willow tree and that's where he lay down and it became George's special spot and I used to sit there with him all the time.

George didn't bark very much and he couldn't talk, but when he was here with me at Turtle Creek he was all kinds of happy. I could tell. There's lots I don't know about the world, but I do know that much.

Angus was throwing dirt on a pile next to George's grave, but then he hit a rock with his spade and he had to use the spade to dig the rock up, and it was huge and he grunted when he lifted it out of the hole with his gloves. Then he rolled it down the creek bank and it landed in the water—SPLASH! Angus wiped his forehead with the back of his glove and some mud came off on his forehead, then he stared up at the sky for a bit and it was cloudy and gray, and I said, "Do you want me to help?" and Angus's voice got wobbly and he said, real quiet-like, "Nope. This one's on me, buddy."

Elaine came across the grass in her raincoat and her rain boots, and she was carrying coffee mugs and two thermoses (one with coffee for her and Angus, the other one with hot chocolate for me). And we stood side by side and sipped them, and nobody was doing talking, then Angus got back in the hole to dig some more.

He dug and dug.

Then he finally stopped.

He got out of the hole and nodded at me, and that's how I knew it was time to say goodbye. So I put my mug down on the grass and me and Angus each took one end of the blanket and we carried George over to the hole and we gently put him down inside, and he was still wearing his pineapple collar and his dog tags.

I knelt down and carefully covered his face with the blanket so dirt wouldn't get on him, then I put a big bag of Cheetos in there with him.

Elaine burst out crying and she threw her arms around me, then Angus started covering George up with dirt and I looked up at the sky so I didn't have to watch. It was a horrible day and I felt EMPTY EMPTY EMPTY inside because without George I knew my whole wide life would never be the same again.

Nana-Jo Comes Home

I'm pretty sure George made me a better person when he was here because ever since he died, Angus has said I've been mildly unpleasant to everyone and I'm trying not to be mildly unpleasant; I just don't feel like doing visiting with people. After he helped me bury George, I went home and crawled into bed and slept for two days until Angus used his key to get into 8B and he came into my room and said, "Time to get up!"

I showed him my middle finger. "Go away!"

"Not gonna happen, buddy."

Angus leaned against the wall. "Nana-Jo comes home tomorrow and we have lots to do. I finished building the ramp out front for her wheelchair, but I need you to find Papa-Jo's staple gun and staple some indoor/outdoor carpet onto it. I got a roll from Home Hardware and left it on the grass for you. Can you do that today, Denny? Do it, then call me on my cell phone when you're done."

And I said, "Okay, Angus."

So yeah, I got out of bed and that's what I did.

The next day, me and Angus brought Nana-Jo home from the Woodmont Hospital and Care Center, and while Angus and a nurse went upstairs to get her, I did some rocking back and forth. Then the elevator door slid open and there she was! And as soon as she saw me, half of Nana-Jo's face smiled and half didn't, and she had a plastic bag in her lap with her pink foam curlers inside, but I guess the nurses hadn't used them because Nana-Jo's hair was flat and pinned back with two clips, and she didn't look regular.

But I didn't care.

Because Nana-Jo was coming home.

I hugged her and we both did a bit of sniffling, then I wiped my eyes with the sleeve of my sweatshirt and it was time to go home. And I was excited because I had two helium balloons waiting for Nana-Jo outside in Angus's truck—one said *Welcome Home* and the other one said *You're Simply the Best.* We also stopped at the Take It or Leave It on our way home and found a used baby monitor to put in Nana-Jo's bedroom.

That was four days ago, and now we're back home at the firepit and Nana-Jo's inside, resting, and I have a receiver in my pocket (looks like a walkie-talkie) and if she needs me all she has to do is ring the bell on her bedside table.

Angus nudged me. "Look who's back."

I turned and watched Lydia park her SUV under the carport. After Angus brought her home from Woodmont County Jail, she flew back to New York and now here she was again, yanking two suitcases out onto the ground and they looked heavy, and if Nana-Jo had been sitting there, I knew she would have told me to go help her, but Nana-Jo was inside resting, and I didn't want to help Lydia, so I didn't.

After I got out of jail, Dr. Harland offered to meet me once a week free of charge to make sure I was *acclimating to the new reality of my life* (which means getting used to the truth instead of worrying about my old life, which was full of lies). So far, we've only met once, and he brought me a vanilla sprinkle doughnut, same as before, which was nice.

I turned to Angus and said, "Dr. Harland thinks Lydia's a tormented soul."

Angus shrugged. "He's right. On a positive note, though, tormented souls are usually more interesting than people who haven't gone through a lot of crap in their lives. I don't think now's the best time to get into that, though." He lifted his chin at Lydia, who yanked two duffel bags out and set them on the ground next to her suitcases.

Lydia's forty-eight but sometimes she reminds me of Alexis in *Schitt's Creek* (not as pretty, though) because whenever she comes to visit her bags are always bulging with clothes and she has lots of shoes with high heels, and most of them have shiny red bottoms, which looks dumb to me. One time, she pointed a shoe at me and said, "Are you listening, Denny? Don't touch my shoes, *ever*," so I took off one of my Crocs and I pointed it at her and said, "Same." Also, when she stays here, her makeup bag takes up too much space in the bathroom and she uses a special shampoo because the Pert shampoo we use isn't good enough. She also smears mud on her face each night before bed and when she gets up in the morning it's dry and cracked and she looks like a lizard.

Lydia came walking across the grass in a pair of high heels and she was wearing a floppy sweater and tight jeans and she looked nervous (playing with her hair). "Hi, guys. How are things going with Mom?"

Angus gave her a thumbs-up. "Good. She's talking again, but it's hard to understand her. Elaine gave her an iPad so she can type messages to us. She's glad to be home but she was pretty sad when she found out George died. Have you heard from Marco?"

Lydia scratched her arm. "Yeah. He wants a divorce." Angus told me Marco is thirty-eight years old, which is ten years younger than Lydia, and he's a Broadway singer/actor/dancer, which is someone who works in a fancy theater in New York City.

"Sorry to hear that," said Angus.

"Don't be. Things haven't been good for a while." Lydia wrapped her arms around herself. "I'm going inside." And she left.

Mrs. Timko walked by and waved at us. I think she missed Tom Hanks because she'd adopted a wiener dog and called him Tom Cruise, but she had to carry him everywhere because his belly dragged on the ground and he was always trying to bite people's ankles. Yesterday, when Mr. Timko got home, Tom Cruise ran toward him, barking, and Mr.

Timko said, "Come closer, you little shit, and I'll give you something to bark about!" and "You're about as useful as a screen door on a submarine, aren't you?"

So yeah, some things change but some things stay a lot the same.

I had to give Bridget Klein back to the government so she could be somebody else's lawyer, but after I got home, she called and offered to help me iron out a few wrinkles *pro bono* (free of charge). She came by and rubbed a cotton swab inside my mouth, then she mailed it to a laboratory where they have microscopes and sciency stuff so they could do a DNA test. And when the results came back, she called to tell me and Angus that Mr. Tesky was my biological father, which was good news "from a legal standpoint."

After that, Bridget did more lawyering and she talked to Mrs. Hale (Irene Tesky's sister who lives in Canada) and more official papers got signed (they're in the basement freezer) and those papers say I now own 18 percent of Norida, which is nice because every year they're going to mail me a check for my share of the company's profit, which is confusing, but Bridget explained it'll be more money than I've ever made at DOT.

I also get all the yogurt I can eat.

So yeah, there's that too.

Lydia's Useless

By the time Lydia gets up each morning, I've already helped Nana-Jo wash her face and brush her teeth, and I've made breakfast for her. After she's done eating, I make her tea and she does her puzzles but she can only use her right hand because her left hand shakes a lot and it makes the puzzle pieces go flying, and then I have to pick them up. And when Nana-Jo gets tired of doing puzzling, she uses her walker with the yellow tennis balls on the legs to go up and down our hallway for exercise. That's Nana-Jo's morning *routine* (which is when you get up in the morning and do things the same way over and over again each day).

Here's Lydia's morning routine.

She sleeps on the futon in Nana-Jo's sewing room and sets the alarm on her phone for 7:45 a.m. and when it goes off (sounds like a train) she swears at it and presses a button, which gives her ten more minutes of sleep before the buzzer goes off again, and she keeps pressing that button until 8:45 a.m., then she gets up and she goes to the bathroom and she has an extra-long shower until there's no hot water left. And when Lydia gets out of the shower, she fixes her hair and puts on makeup, then she asks Nana-Jo what she'd like for breakfast, and Nana-Jo says, "Denny already made me breakfast," in her slurry voice, and by then I'm doing the dishes, so there's nothing left for Lydia to do.

Me and Lydia have also been taking turns making dinner, but on the nights she's supposed to cook, she does DoorDash (a place you call that delivers all kinds of take-out food to your house) and I don't think it's fair because she's not actually cooking but Nana-Jo typed me a note on her iPad that said LEAVE IT ALONE DENNY, so I don't complain anymore, I just eat the food. On the nights I cook, I buy vegetables and hamburger or chicken and rice, then I open Nana-Jo's recipe book and I follow the steps, and I make tacos, or spaghetti with sauce, or pork chops and broccoli. Last night I made Nana-Jo's favorite soup with chicken and rice and carrots and celery and dill, and Lydia liked it so much she had two bowls, and I watched her eat and thought, *Suck it, DoorDash.*

—

I like it better when Lydia's not here.

She can't cook (burns everything) and she can't do laundry (shrinks everything). Nana-Jo likes to put foam curlers in her hair at night so it's not flat against her head all the time and Lydia tried to put them in for her a few times, but they kept falling out and the next morning Nana-Jo's hair would look like a bird's nest. Then one day I got the foam curlers out and I used Nana-Jo's comb and dipped it in water like I'd seen her do, and I put them in one by one just like she used to and none of them fell out when she was sleeping, and the next morning Nana-Jo looked in the mirror and smiled.

So yeah, now I do her curlers instead of Lydia.

Lydia helps Nana-Jo shower, though, so that's one good thing. But other than that, she's useless. She carries her camera everywhere and she makes the lens zoom out, then she makes it zoom back in, and she's always snapping pictures (snap, snap, snap) when she should be helping me with Nana-Jo.

Dr. Harland told me I have anger issues to work on which is *perfectly natural after everything I've been through.* He also said that before I talk to Lydia, I need to ask myself if what I'm going to say will *add to the relationship* or *take away from the relationship*, and if it's going to take away from the relationship, I shouldn't say it. I told him I don't have a relationship with Lydia, and he said, "Sure you do. It might not be good, but it exists, and for your own sake, you need to work on it because if you can carve out a healthy relationship with her, it's going to help you psychologically and you'll be happier."

Today I was napping in my hammock at Turtle Creek when something heavy dropped onto my stomach. I pushed it off and swung my legs onto the ground, and it was a baby brown bear only it wasn't a baby brown bear because he was wearing a collar, and he ran down to the water and stuck his face in. Lydia was standing next to my hammock, and she said, "So . . . what do you think of him? I took a detour through North Dakota on my way home to see a friend and while I was there, I took some pictures for her dog breeder website—"

"And you bought a puppy from her?"

Lydia laughed. "I did. His name's Wilson."

Wilson-the-puppy was playing in the water and he was the biggest and fluffiest puppy I'd ever seen. He dragged a stick out of the creek, then he dropped it, and he shook from side to side and water went flying everywhere. After that, he lay on the grass and he got the hiccups, and they wouldn't go away, so he rolled onto his back and hiccuped at the sky.

"George didn't like the water," I said.

Lydia shrugged. "This guy seems to." Wilson-the-puppy flipped sideways on the grass and then he started chewing on his stick with both paws wrapped around it to keep it steady. "What kind of dog is he?" I asked.

Lydia chewed on her fingernail. "He's a Newfoundland. Some guy bought him but then sent him back to the breeder two weeks later because his kid slammed a car door on Wilson's tail and now it has a kink in it and he didn't like that."

"So . . . he's broken?"

Lydia shrugged again. "I guess that's one way to look at it."

"I learned all about puppies doing volunteering at Woodmont's Canine Rescue Shelter, Lydia. You have to spend time with them and train them or else all the little problems that pop up when they're small become big problems when they grow up." I sat down on the grass and called Wilson-the-puppy and he ran over and plunked down next to me. Then he yawned and he put his head on my knee, and I said, "Why'd your friend sell him to you? Doesn't she know you've never had a dog before?"

Lydia laughed. "I didn't get him for me, Denny. I got him for you."

And I went very still inside and my heart started going **BOOM-BOOM-BOOM**. I looked at Wilson-the-puppy and said, "Take him back, Lydia. I don't want him."

"Wait, Denny. Can we talk about this?"

"No way, José!"

I jumped up and opened the gate, and I walked across the yard very fast into 8B, then I got six potatoes from the root cellar and I peeled them for dinner, and Nana-Jo looked up from doing puzzling and she said in her slurry voice, "Waz rong?" and I said, "Nothing."

Four days later, Wilson-the-puppy was still sleeping in his crate in the sewing room next to Lydia's futon, and Nana-Jo thought he was adorable and so did Angus and Elaine, but George was gone and Mr. Tesky's murder trial was over, and I was a free man and I didn't want a puppy, especially not one that Lydia had picked for me.

"You need to take Wilson back, Lydia."

I was washing dishes and Lydia dumped her cutlery in the sink, and said, "I heard you the first six times, Denny, but like I said, I can't take him back until I get my car fixed." Her SUV was in the repair shop because it was leaking oil.

That night, I turned on Nana-Jo's computer and asked Google about Newfoundland dogs and I found out you can get black ones, brown ones, gray ones, and black-and-white ones (which are called Landseers) and they're big (females are 110–120 pounds, males are

140–160 pounds) and they're called *gentle giants* because they're *sensitive* and they have *sweet temperaments* and *calm dispositions* and they also have *webbed feet*, which make them great swimmers and excellent water rescue dogs.

Two more days went by, then Angus took Lydia to pick up her SUV from the repair shop, and when they got back her phone was ringing and she hurried into the sewing room to answer it. When she came out, she said she had to leave for work but she'd be back by the end of the week, then she packed a bag and two cameras and off she went, and she didn't even ask if I'd take care of Wilson for her because that's Lydia—useless *and* selfish.

I woke up the next morning and Wilson was crying in his crate so I went into the sewing room and I opened it and he ran out and I had to say "Down!" three times before he stopped jumping on me. I clipped a leash on his collar and took him outside and he peed twice (one short, one long) but both times he squatted because he's not big enough yet to lift one leg and balance himself without falling over.

After we got back inside, I went into the sewing room to get his water bowl and I saw one of Lydia's cameras on the dresser and it was the camera she always uses when she's at 8B, so I picked it up and turned it on.

And I knew if she was there, she'd say, "Don't touch my gear, Denny!"

So I sat on the futon and I touched her gear.

I made the camera lens zoom way out, then I made it zoom back in, and I looked through the lens and pressed a button to take a picture of Wilson-the-puppy, who was chewing on one of Lydia's high-heel shoes with the shiny red bottoms. Then I found a Menu button and I pressed Display and saw a hinged door, so I swung it open and there was a screen, and on that screen was the picture I'd just taken of Wilson, and it was terrible.

There was an arrow pointing like this: ➡

And an arrow pointing like this: ⬅

I pressed the right arrow and Wilson's picture went away, and then I was looking at a new one of Elaine and Angus talking at the firepit. There was also a picture of me putting foam curlers in Nana-Jo's hair (pink) and one of me showing her how to put on her new Velcro shoes and one of us watching an episode of *Schitt's Creek* with our heads bent a bit to the right and that one made my throat hurt, then I saw one of me and George walking up Penguin Hill and that made my throat hurt too.

I snooped through all of Lydia's pictures, then I went back to the one of me and George walking up Penguin Hill. And in it, I was wearing my favorite red-and-black plaid hat with ear flaps and there was snow on the ground and the trees had hoarfrost on them. I was pulling my sled and George was on a leash, but my hand was also on his back to help steer him up the hill because of him being blind. And I stared at that picture for a long time, and it made my throat hurt because I couldn't remember how many times me and George had walked up Penguin Hill to do thinking after he came to live with us at 8B, but I know it was a lot. And I was pretty sure that anyone else who looked at that picture would be able to see how much I loved George, and that's when tears came into my eyes, and I thought to myself, *Lydia's useless, but maybe she doesn't suck at everything. Maybe she's good at this one thing.*

I'll Be Your George

Today is our annual neighborhood party and we're doing a tradition (which is when you do something every year on the same day with the same people) and our tradition is a party at 8B and the people who always come are Angus and Elaine, Sharon and Bill, Ted and Jean, and the Timkos, but this year we also invited my homeless friend Howard-the-army-guy, and Nori and Theo too because like Nana-Jo always says, *The more the merrier*, which means the fun you're having is funner when you share it with more people.

And there'll be lots to eat at our party because everyone is bringing food and instead of cooking this year, Nana-Jo gets to sit at the firepit in her *luxury folding camp chair* (Walmart, $149.95) all comfy-cozy.

When everyone's done eating, Angus will lean a piece of plywood against the shed and he'll cover it with a sheet, then Elaine will hook her laptop up to a projector unit (machine with cables) and press play and a movie will show up on the plywood pretend TV so everyone can watch it. And this year Angus picked the movie *Cast Away*, which is cool because Tom Hanks is in it and I've seen it twice already.

Lydia came back for three days but then she left to fly somewhere else and Wilson-the-puppy is still here, and he keeps following me around.

When Nori and Theo showed up for our party, Theo stayed real close to his mom—blink/twitch/blink—but then I introduced him to Wilson-the-puppy and a few minutes later all the blinking and twitching stopped. Nori helped me and Elaine put all the food out on a table while Theo played with Wilson. He'd throw a ball and Wilson would run and get it but he wouldn't bring it back, he'd just stand there, wagging his tail, and Theo would have to chase him to get the ball back so he could throw it again.

They did that over and over again.

Then me and Angus left to go pick up my friend Howard, because he doesn't have a car. And Howard got a new fake leg from the VA (which is a group that helps people who served their country and now need new legs) and he's doing much better because he joined Alcoholics Anonymous (same club Irene Tesky joined) and he got himself a job as a janitor, and he also got himself a room to rent over someone's garage.

Elaine made a bowl of punch for the party and some people added vodka to theirs, but not me or Howard or Elaine. And after everyone finished eating, I helped Elaine clean up and I said, "It's sure been a crazy year, hasn't it, Elaine?" and she quickly looked across the yard at Angus, then she put one hand on her belly and she said, "Oh, Denny, if you think this year was crazy, just wait until next year." Then she winked at me, and I thought, *Uh-oh! I wonder who else is going to get themselves killed.*

Nori and Theo left an hour later because it was getting late. Then it was time for the movie and I've seen *Cast Away* before and I know I can't watch the first part where the plane crashes (too upsetting) so before Angus pressed play he hooked his thumb at me to go inside and I did, and when that part was over, he yelled for me to come back out and Wilson was sitting beside my chair, waiting for me.

In the movie, Tom Hanks is stuck on an island by himself and he gets lonely so he makes friends with a volleyball and he calls his new friend Wilson and he paints a face on the ball to make it seem less like a ball. And twice Tom Hanks accidentally loses his new friend and he throws his head back and shouts, "W-I-L-S-O-N!" and both times he did that, Wilson-the-puppy jumped up and ran around the yard, trying to figure out who was calling him—and we all laughed and laughed.

Later, after everyone else went home and Nana-Jo was asleep, I sat down in the living room to do thinking and I figured out that all the craziness started when Nana-Jo said it was time for me to *start thinking for myself*, and then I got myself arrested three times and Nana-Jo shot Mr. Tesky *in self-defense* (which nobody knew about) and I met Bridget and Dr. Harland, and there was the trial, and a whole bunch of other stuff happened that made it a tangled-up mess, and sometimes I freaked everyone out, including me.

But I also learned a lot about life.

And here's what I know.

It's hard.

Also, love can be confusing because when someone loves you, they don't always say the words out loud. Instead, they might say something like, "What are you, Denny Voss?" and I'd say, "One of the best things that ever happened to you," then that person would say, "You got it, cowboy!" Or someone else might say, "You're worth ten of those other kids, Denny, and don't you ever forget it!" and another person might say, "Buck up" and "Don't be a pussy" and "Life is hard all over" and it might not *sound* like any of them are saying they love you, but that's what they're doing—you know it all the way inside your bones.

I also know it hurts when someone you love dies, but I think it's supposed to because if it didn't they'd be easy to forget and who wants to forget all the louds and quiets about someone you love after they're gone?

Not me.

My phone went DING so I pulled it out of my pocket and read a text from Lydia that said: **I should be back Wednesday if my shoot wraps up on time, but Friday the latest. Have Wilson ready so I can take him back to the breeder.**

I put my phone in my pocket.

Wilson was asleep with his head on my foot and I decided I didn't want to listen to him crying all night in his crate in the sewing room (he hates his crate) so I picked him up like a sack of potatoes (I weighed him yesterday, he's already fifty-eight pounds) and I carried him to my bedroom and carefully set him down on the floor. Then I turned out the light and I climbed into bed and pulled the covers over me. A few minutes later, Wilson did a whimper and he tried to get up on the bed with me.

He jumped up and slid back down onto the floor.

Then he jumped up and he slid down again.

Up . . . slide down . . . thump.

Up . . . slide down . . . thump.

And it seemed like maybe he'd keep doing that forever, so I grabbed his collar and gave him a tug to help him up on the bed, and I could tell he was happy because he went around and around on the blanket like he was making himself a nest to sleep in, and he seemed pretty serious about making that nest, and when he was finally done, he flopped down and put his head on my chest just like George used to.

And I went very still (like a statue).

And I tried to make my heart go hard inside.

But it stayed soft.

I stared into the dark, doing thinking for a bit, then I said, real quiet-like, "I miss you, George, and I love you, and Wilson-the-puppy isn't blind or deaf, but I hope it's okay if I love him too, because I think he needs me, and I think maybe I need him." Wilson-the-puppy's head was still on my chest, and he did a yawn, and I rubbed his forehead with my thumb and said, "I don't know when Lydia's coming back, but don't worry. I won't let her take you anywhere. You're family now."

So yeah.

I guess that's just how life works.

Some days it's like a fast-moving TV show and some days it's not, and when things go sideways—like they usually do for me—you might find yourself going in a whole new direction, and when you're doing life, going in that whole new direction, some things will change, but some things will stay a lot the same.

AUTHOR'S NOTE

One of the biggest joys of my life has been writing this novel. I wrote the first thirty pages at a writers' retreat in 2010 and immediately fell in love with Denny. He was stubborn and funny, and he had an undefinable charm. I couldn't stop thinking about him; I even dreamed about him. I understood that he was mentally challenged, that he'd been arrested for murder, and that this novel was somehow meant to be his coming-of-age tale, but beyond that I knew nothing else about his story. It didn't matter, though, because I also innately knew I didn't have the chops to write it. Not then, anyhow.

I was intimidated by Denny.

He wasn't a cardboard character, and I knew I'd have to nail the authenticity of his voice before I could even begin to tackle his story. He had to feel believable on the page. He had to feel real. Could I do that, though? Could I write an entire novel from a mentally challenged man's point of view? I worried that I'd get it wrong, but Denny wouldn't leave me alone. I thought about him all the time, and eventually I convinced myself that if author Mark Haddon could write *The Curious Incident of the Dog in the Night-Time* narrated by a boy with all the characteristics of someone with Asperger's syndrome—he'd worked with children on the autism spectrum but wasn't autistic himself—then I could be Denny on the page.

The development of his voice was influenced by a few factors:

One of my relatives is cognitively challenged, and many of her traits became Denny's (her purity and innocence, her trusting outlook on life, how she's sometimes unaware of the seriousness of situations and can't always properly communicate using her own words, so instead she mimics other people's responses). As a teenager, she was sexually groomed by an older man. I got involved and he was eventually arrested, convicted, forced to wear an ankle bracelet, and placed under house arrest. He's now also registered as a sexual predator in whatever registry these things are listed in. Beyond that (side note), his indefensible behavior and sick, narcissistic persona inspired me to create the character of Mr. Tesky in this novel.

It bothers me that society often perceives those with mental disabilities as people who need constant support, as resource-draining members of society who have little to contribute and don't have the ability to influence or enrich other people's lives. I wanted Denny, as the protagonist of this novel, to challenge those stereotypes.

There's a stigma that surrounds both diversity and mental health, even though many of us are broken in some way; for example, one in four adults suffer from a diagnosable mental disorder, me included. I don't talk about it publicly because I'm intensely private, but I suffer from severe anxiety. On some days, I need hours of preparatory mental time just to do one Zoom call. I was asked to speak at my high school graduation, and before the event, I broke out in a rash of painful, blistery welts that covered my arms, torso, and neck. I later learned it was shingles, which is unusual for someone so young, but under extreme stress your immune system can activate the virus, and that's what happened to me.

I also have ADHD and I struggle with depression. Like Denny, sometimes my mind jumps all over the place, or else I'll get fixated on something and my mind will start to loop, covering the same ground over and over again. Beyond that, my social battery runs out very quickly, and when that happens, I use humor as a way of getting through social situations I find overwhelming. I adopt a big personality and I try to make people laugh. I've gotten good at it, but as a coping mechanism it's exhausting.

Like Denny, I grew up poor in a small town, and reading quickly became my escape. Also like Denny, I had (still have) a nurturing mom like Nana-Jo, who cleaned houses for twenty-five-plus years and always put her children's needs first.

So . . . in one way or another, the development of Denny's voice, and his personality, was influenced by all these factors, though as I came to know him better, I wanted him to have an almost untouchable quality too. I didn't want his story to be dark and depressing. I wanted readers to get the feeling that he was going to be okay, no matter what.

It was important to me that I portray him sympathetically—as different rather than handicapped. I didn't want to stigmatize him with a label. Denny is a sensitive, lovable man with diminished mental capacity, full stop. Beyond that, I wanted his character to touch people and make them feel (and, perhaps, act) differently when dealing with someone like him. I hoped that getting to know him would encourage people to look at the world from a different perspective. I also hoped Denny's story would spark conversation.

For a long time, I'd load the manuscript on my laptop and let Denny take me wherever he wanted to go; then I'd spend days cleaning up behind him, akin to using a broom and a dustbin. And in doing that, it quickly became clear to me that his story was going to be as unique and unconventional as he was.

I asked myself a lot of questions: Who murdered Mr. Tesky, and why? Could I make the gun violence that crops up in the novel a human issue versus a political one? Most important, through Denny's eyes, could I have readers see the potential our world has to be a better place, while at the same time showing them how horrible it can sometimes be?

I wrote and deleted, edited, and rewrote until eventually, finally, the plot and subplots began to reveal themselves. To round out Denny's world, I then happily filled it with elements from my own life, from the firepit in his backyard (I've never lived in a home that *didn't* have a firepit), to the soap-on-a-rope I grew up with, to George's very real love for Cheetos, to my mom wearing pink foam curlers and having her knee replaced after cleaning houses for twenty-five-plus years, to a strange man wandering into her living room to sell her an Elvis rug when she was drugged up on the couch, recuperating.

And then there's this little nugget . . . Like Theo in the novel, my youngest son has Tourette's syndrome, and as a kid he was sometimes bullied because of his twitching and stimming. What he went through broke my heart, and then it became a priority to help him navigate what I already knew would be a hard road ahead. Today, he's twenty-five and thriving after graduating from university with a business degree.

My family has also had Newfoundland dogs for thirty-plus years, including one named Wilson, just like the puppy in this novel. After Wilson died, we made the life-altering decision to adopt a blind and deaf Saint Bernard named George. Taking care of him was a unique challenge, but it quickly became clear to me that we needed George as much as he needed us. At the time, I wasn't in a good place. I was sad and disillusioned about my writing career, which I'd had to temporarily set aside while we faced some personal challenges as a family. One night, I was at my desk in tears when George appeared, put his head in my lap, and stayed there until I stopped crying. That's just how he was.

When I created Mrs. Timko in the novel, I gave her a pet goose named Tom Hanks because the juxtaposition of naming an angry, combative goose Tom Hanks, which is the absolute antithesis of Tom Hanks's beloved persona in real life, felt thematically correct. (Nothing in this story is as it seems: Mr. Tesky is the murder victim, and we're supposed to have sympathy for him, but when readers learn how he died, and why, they have zero sympathy for him.)

I'm Canadian, but I chose to set the novel in Minnesota because of the gun violence that plagues the US, which is the underlying issue that drives Denny's story forward in the novel. I don't live in the US, but I watch the same news channels Americans do, and each time I hear about another senseless shooting, I feel like Denny does.

In some ways, I think we should all be more like Denny because, for him, there are no class issues, only people issues. He lives in the same world we live in, where he experiences, and is affected by, the same things that affect us all. On top of that, he's been dealt a shitty hand, but still he powers through each day he's given, doing the best he can with what he's got.

As I wrote his story, I wanted Denny to misunderstand and then, at times, understand what was happening in his life so readers could witness his growth in that way. I also wanted him to have family and friends who loved him for exactly who he was, people who'd step in when he needed help, doing their best to guide and support him.

I wanted this novel—not unlike the heartwarming sense of community in shows like *Ted Lasso* or *Schitt's Creek*—to sneak up on readers, with a surprisingly relatable protagonist and a cast of imperfect and improbable characters they couldn't help but root for.

In many ways, this is a novel about community, about the families we inherit and those we create. At its heart, though, it's about individual limitations and human potential, and while it does grapple with some messy issues—mental disability, gun violence, ageism, health insecurity, sexual grooming, teenage pregnancy—with Denny as the narrator, it also evolves into a unique and uplifting story (both poignant and funny) about a mentally challenged man who sets out to make the world a better place and discovers unexpected truths about himself, his family, and the world along the way.

I have always gravitated toward stories that explore the very hard work of being human, and at its core I wanted Denny's novel to be that kind of story, but I also wanted it to explore humor as a source of connection, because the fine line between humor and an emotional gut punch is often incredibly close.

I think *The Sideways Life of Denny Voss* offers readers what we all long for: human connection. And although I'm not sure that it will answer any big questions, I do believe Denny's story will prompt a barrage of smaller ones that are equally important, like *How are you? What are you doing to bring joy to your life in small ways, every day?* And, more importantly, *How can I help?*

ACKNOWLEDGMENTS

I loved writing this novel, even though it challenged me more than any other that I've written, from mastering Denny's voice to attempting the most complicated structure and premise I've tackled yet. It was a labor of love, but all that aside, you absolutely wouldn't have it in your hands, or on your e-reader, without the encouragement and support of so many people I'm grateful for. They include:

My agent, Liza Dawson, who loves Denny as much as I do and somehow managed to coax my best work from me as I revised the manuscript for submission. Thank you, Liza.

Alicia Clancy, my savvy editor. I'm so glad you chose to champion this novel. Jodi Warshaw, who has been a delight to work with, as well as Danielle Marshall, who came up with a new title for the novel when the old one wasn't working. Also, Carissa Bluestone, Jen Bentham, Bill Siever, Katherine Kirk, and the rest of the team at Lake Union, including publicity, marketing, production, the sales force, and the foreign rights team. Thank you for helping me get this book into readers' hands. You're all rock stars!

A special thanks to early readers Meg Blackstone, Margaret South, Peg Burington, and Regan Holt, who offered such thoughtful input, as well as Karen Joy Fowler, who read the first chapter years ago and encouraged me to keep going. Also, Lynn Wu, who offered many insightful and important suggestions as I worked on revisions.

The Sideways Life of Denny Voss is a work of fiction. It's Denny's story, although many of my own personal experiences are scattered throughout the pages, and for that, I thank my family, especially my mom, Ann Holt, who cleaned houses for a living, had her own broken-down knee operation, and chose *not* to buy a rug from the traveling salesman who walked into her living room one day when she was drugged up on the couch, recuperating. Also, my mom's partner, Al Finlayson, my dad, Hans Holt, and his partner, Ruby, all the Kennedys, as well as my siblings—Ian, Eric, Marilyn, and Randy—and their families. A special shout-out to my brother-in-law, Ron, my adviser in all things gun related. Any errors are mine.

And I can't forget George, the blind and deaf Saint Bernard we adopted during the pandemic and spent an unforgettable year with before he passed away. In my heart I believe you were always meant to be ours, George, and when it comes to this novel, I believe you were meant to be Denny's too.

I also want to mention my Newfoundland dogs—Montana, Sully, Wilson, and Wallace—three of them long gone and one who was caught counter surfing just minutes ago, because, like Denny, I'm a dog person, and they, too, each played a part in the fabric of this story.

Thank you to friends Nancy Knowlton and Dave Martin, because two chapters of this novel were written in a creative flurry in Honfleur,

France, in 2019 during one of my favorite vacations. Also, Jennifer Evans for answering all my EMT questions (again, any errors are mine).

For their unwavering support and encouragement, I'd like to thank Jacquelyn Mitchard, Lesley Kagen, Chandler Crawford, Linda Holeman, Jeannie Thiessen, Larry Thiessen, Andy Scontras, Lisa Scontras, John Fetto, Glenn Finockio, Michaela Chronik, Lanette Andreas, Julie Block, Karen Veloso, Pat Evans, Evan Raugust, Shayna Evans, Smita Patel, Meegan Read, Vivian Felix (Luoma), Darreld Shepel, and Mary Lou Talmage.

Thanks to Patricia Wood, who fell in love with Denny years ago, when I wrote the first chapter, and never stopped pestering me to finish his story. Thanks, Pat, for believing in this book and for reading and rereading countless drafts of the manuscript (I truly did lose count). Also, a special thank-you to Gordon Wood, who laughed (and cried) in all the right places.

Thank you as well to the Canada Council for the Arts for their support during the writing of this novel. Also the 2021 Kauai Writers Conference that never happened (thanks to COVID) and the magical writing that did.

Last of all, and most importantly, my family . . . Andrea, Russell, Thomas, and Marcus. I could not be prouder of each of you. Individually, and as a whole, you've improved my whole life and made me a better person. A special hug also goes out to Trey Talmage, who I consider one of my own and always will.

As for my husband, Rick, who's been there from the beginning (when I published my first novel) and has watched this one evolve through its many iterations, thank you for believing in me, even when I didn't believe in myself, and for giving me the time and space to write. I've come to realize that I'm at my best, in every way, when I'm writing, which is, of course, something you've known all along . . . xo.

ABOUT THE AUTHOR

Born and raised in Canada, Holly Kennedy currently lives near the Rocky Mountains in Alberta with her family and their Newfoundland dog, Wallace. She is the author of four novels, and her books have been translated into multiple languages. When she's not writing, you'll typically find her reading, spending time with family, or (her not-so-secret obsession) watching true-crime shows like *Dateline*. To find out more, visit www.hollykennedy.com, or follow her on Facebook and Instagram.